Awesome Reviews for

Evidence

"Thanks for writing an amazing book! I enjoyed every part of it. Changed my perspective on everything especially my marriage! Bless you!" – Lisa B.

"This book is AMAZING! Very compelling, very emotional... the characters have realistic problems that every day couples and marriages face all of the time. Excellent writing!!!!" – Jessica G.

"I loved Evidence, actually read it twice. I liked the inclusion of God in every aspect, from marriage, friendship, and forgiveness. Hope to learn more about Silvia's past in the next one. Told the hubby about it and he can't wait for the movie!" – Ammie B.

"This book is a great masterpiece. This book covers so many issues that we as people and more importantly as Christians need to deal with; everything from forgiveness of family, friends, and spouses/lovers. This book was divinely inspired to reach a generation of people who need to know there is a God and He loves you, and He wants to have a relationship with you. He also wants to heal you of every hurt, whether it be emotional, physical or mental. This book covers that and deals with those issues. I could not stop reading this book. I finished it in two days and was asking for more. I'm excited about the next installments of this series of books. Terri T. Thrash is a brilliant author and definitely reflects the heart of God for this generation through her writing. I look forward to seeing more from this young rising star." – Minister James C.

"AWESOME!! FAITH IS MANDATORY IN THIS WORLD TODAY!! I'm sure that this book is going to lead someone to salvation and reassure/increase somebody else's faith, as well as teach a lot of people on the importance of forgiveness!! I've laughed, cried, and praised while reading this book!!! It really touched my heart!! Job well done!! You definitely let God use you!!!" – LaQuana O.

"I really enjoyed "Evidence"! It was really a good book to read!! I enjoyed every page of it! It portrayed things that happen in everyday life! It's true what they say, "you reap what you sow" and "what's done in the dark will come to light"! I also enjoyed the strong message about "Faith"! We all face different circumstances day to day and our Faith in God is always tested! It's up to us to always put our trust in Him, for we may not always see His works right away, but it is evident that He is forever working! It really made me think when I read the phrase, "God has proven to be God all my life, why would He stop now?" Hmmmmm, something to ponder on! I was blessed by this book!! Thanks Terri for sharing this gift God has given you!!! (Hebrews 11:1) Now faith is the substance of things hoped for, the evidence of things not seen." – Michelle S.

"I read the entire novel today and loved it. I can't wait till your next one. Every emotion possible was channeled while I was reading it. Awesome job, Terri!" - Nikeya C.

Ulterior Motives

Also by Terri T. Thrash

Evidence

(In order to really understand the journey, it's best to start at the beginning. "Evidence"… "Ulterior Motives")

Ulterior Motives

Terri T. Thrash

Creative Hearts
Publishing

Creative Hearts Publishing, L.L.C.

Ulterior Motives

For more information about special discounts for bulk purchases, please contact Creative Hearts Publishing, L.L.C. at www.creativeheartspublishing.com

Cover Designed by: Jazmin Jernigan with Aesthetic Innovations

Cover Models are simply models portraying the characters in the book.

Editing by: Deloris Lynch

ISBN (soft cover) 978-0-9888002-5-0

ISBN (ebook) 978-0-9888002-1-2

Printed in the United States of America

First Edition December/2012

Dedication

This book is dedicated to all of those who have been bruised and broken, mistreated, abused and misused. To those who are brokenhearted, this is for you. There is hope. "We are hard pressed on every side, yet not crushed; we are perplexed, but not in despair; persecuted, but not forsaken; struck down, but not destroyed-- always carrying about in the body the dying of the Lord Jesus, that the life of Jesus also may be manifested in our body." II Corinthians 4: 8-10

Acknowledgments

I cannot go any further without first acknowledging the One who made this all possible. To my Heavenly Father, you did it again. Thank you for your continuous grace and mercy and for all of your many blessings. Thank you for giving me the gift of creativity and for allowing me to share it with the world. Thank you for giving me vision because without that, I couldn't have given birth to this amazing story. You are my awesome God who has kept me covered, and I will continue to trust you as you lead and guide me on this journey. Words cannot express how grateful I am. Thank you for loving me beyond measure and for your unmerited favor. I love you very much.

To my father and mother, James and Marilyn Thrash, thank you for continuing to encourage me and push me to give my all every day. You have been amazing parents thus far, and I thank you for always being there. Thank you for your love, prayers, and support. I love you both very much.

To my beautiful daughter, Tierra Thrash, thank you for inspiring me to be better daily. You always keep me focused, and you push me to keep going past any limits! I thank God that he allowed me to be a mother to someone so brilliant! Thank you for praying with me and standing with me. I love you so much. You are truly amazing.

To my sister, Shereka Thrash-Stephens, thank you for believing in me in everything that I do. You have been a great support. Thank you for being my sister, best friend, legal counsel, and publisher of my literary works. You are awesome and I love you very much.

To my brother, Derrell Thrash, thank you for encouraging and pushing me. You and your prayers are greatly appreciated. I could not have asked God for better big brother. Thank you for your love, prayers and support. You are awesome and I love you very much.

To all of my family and friends, thank you for every prayer, for every word of encouragement, and for all of your love and support. You all are awesome and I thank God for each and every one of you. I appreciate and love each of you very much.

To Ms. Deloris Lynch, thank you so much for assisting me in the editing process. You and your words of encouragement are very much appreciated. I thank you so much for your feedback. You, your prayers, and your support are greatly appreciated. You are amazing and I love you.

To the book cover models, Summer S. Bluford, Yuri Varela, and Patrick Adams, you all did an awesome job on set, and you made the characters look amazing on this cover. Thank you so much for being a part of this Evidence Journey. It means a lot to me and you are greatly appreciated. You all are awesome and I love each of you.

To the book cover designer and photographer, Jazmin Jernigan with Aesthetic Innovations, your work is always amazing. Thank you so much for your assistance with making the book cover vision, come to life. I love and appreciate you.

To all of my readers and supporters, you are one of the reasons why I love to do what I do. I am so thankful for every one of you. Thank you for every Facebook wall post, inbox, email, letter, text message, and/or phone call with words of encouragement. You all help to make this journey worthwhile, and it is my heart's desire that you will continue to be with me on this journey as I continue on with this vision. You all are awesome. Thank you for your love, prayers, and support. Each of you means so much to me and I love you.

To my nay sayers, thank you. You know that I love you too.

To those of you who eagerly awaited *Ulterior Motives*, thank you so much for your patience. Believe me when I say, this storyline is well-worth the wait! Enjoy!

Grace and peace be unto you all,

"God loathes the sacrifice of an evil person, especially when it is brought with ULTERIOR MOTIVES." Proverbs 21:27 (NLT)

"Beloved, do not avenge yourselves, but rather give place to wrath; for it is written, "Vengeance is Mine; I will repay,'' says the Lord." Romans 12:19 (NKJV)

"There is no greater agony than bearing an untold story inside you.'' – Maya Angelou

"What breaks in a moment may take years to mend.'' – Swedish Proverb

Evil Intentions...

ULTERIOR MOTIVES

The Evidence Journey

What happens when you take revenge into your own hands and find out that it isn't as sweet as you thought it would be?

Chapter One

Silvia was headed for the checkout line with a bottle of grape juice in her hand. She turned the corner and as she looked up, she looked right into the eyes of the man who has haunted her memories for the past twelve years. She instantly released the grape juice from her hand and it crashed to the floor, shattering to pieces. Grape juice and glass covered the entire floor around her. Her mind went back in time as her eyes burned with tears and the hate grew stronger in her heart . . .

"Hey! You are not supposed to touch, remember?'' she whispered in a seductive tone, her lips brushing against his ear.

Silvia was used to men trying to grope her as she danced for them. She was one of the most beautiful exotic dancers that Boss Gentlemen's Club had to offer. Her breast were full, thighs were thick, small waist, voluptuous bottom and a beautiful face to go with all of that. She was the one who all the men came in and requested for their sexy entertainment.

Jazzy was her stage name, the Latin Mamacita. She was one of what they called the, "top notch,'' exotic dancers. She was also one of those who refused to go beyond dancing. She allowed them only to watch her in her little uniforms and her sexy lingerie as she danced for them. They desired to have her, but knew that they never could. She was a little different from most of the other girls there. While many of them took off all of their clothes and had sex with their clients, she never did.

She was never interested in any of her clients, but there was something about this man that intrigued her. He was mysterious and beautiful with his light-skin, beautiful wavy hair and gorgeous green eyes that seemed to stare into her very soul as he looked back into her eyes. But she kept her clients, clients… nothing more nothing less. She has never gotten her feelings involved and she wasn't about to start now. This was about business, not pleasure, at least not for her.

She was just doing what she thought she had to do in order to pay her way through college. This brought in fast money, and she was hooked once she was hipped to the game. At the tender age of seventeen she began her journey as an exotic dancer. Now, at the age eighteen, she was one of the very best at what she did after being there for only a year. She could do all the pole tricks, floor dances, chair dances, table dances and lap dances as if she was a pro. The other girls said that she had an advantage because she had that Latin blood flowing through her veins. She was blessed with the "sexy gene" is what they always told her.

She continued to give this man a lap dance as she looked into his green eyes which were fire red at the moment, but still gorgeous. She began to redirect her focus not wanting to get drawn in by this man who had her amazed by how attractive he was. She began to look around the VIP room at the other five men who drank their liquor and watched as she gave this man what he wanted. Each one of the men reeked of liquor, especially the one she was on top of now. She felt his manhood rise to attention as she continued his lap dance.

"Hey!" she exclaimed as this attractive man touched her again.

"What? I'm buying," he said, grabbing her arm as he looked into her eyes.

Little did she know, he found her just as attractive with her beautiful flawless skin, dark-brown eyes and gorgeous long hair. She was one of the most beautiful women that he'd ever seen. She tantalized him as she circled her hips around while on top him. Lust had taken full control of him as she danced for him. There was something hypnotic about her and his desire was to have her and he wasn't willing to tame it. Oh, yes. He wanted her and whatever he wanted . . . he got.

"Let go! You are hurting me!" she screamed as his grip tightened and immediately bruised her arm. He slapped her and she fell onto the floor, crying hysterically.

He got up and grabbed her by her throat. He then squatted down next to her to look her in her eyes to let her know just how serious he was. "Look! Me and my boys are here to have a good time and I chose you to show us a good time. So, you *are* going to show us a good time." He paused. "Aren't you?" He spoke calmly as his grip tightened around her throat. He nodded as if coaxing her on what to say.

Frightened by the look in his eyes, she nodded slowly. Her heart seemed to skip beats, scared of what he may do to her next. She knew that she was in a bad situation. She could feel it. Her heart began to get heavy as the man continued to look her dead in her eyes. His deafening silence warned her that she'd better not do anything that he didn't tell her to do, like run to that door, which is what she desperately wanted to do.

He saw the fear in her eyes, then he whispered, "Good girl." He loosened his grip a little and gently kissed her lips as he now reached down below and fondled her with his other hand. No man's hands had ever touched her in that place before! His lips brushed her ear as he whispered exactly what he wanted her to do. He then released her throat from his grip.

"I'm sorry, but I can't . . . I . . . don't . . . do that." Her voice now trembled with fear.

He grabbed her by her hair. "Well, tonight you are. It's your lucky night. There's a first time for everything. Right?" He chuckled, and then let her go. He unzipped his pants, then sat back in his seat.

Even though this was one of the most attractive men that she had ever laid eyes on, she was not willing to do what he asked of her in front of the other five men who were in the room. She wouldn't be willing to do it even if they were alone. Of course, men looked at her as if she were nothing but a stripper. But she still possessed some innocence in that she had never performed any sex acts of any kind. She was a virgin, never touched. She carried a gift.

After taking a minute to look around the room, tears filled her eyes. She watched as the other men talked among themselves and continued to drink.

The green-eyed man-turned-maniac grabbed Silvia again by her throat. "What are you waiting for?" he growled.

Tears now fell from her eyes as she got on her knees, looked around the room one final time as her heart told her to get prepared. She finally began to do what the man commanded her to do. After six minutes into it, without stopping she looked up at him and stared into his eyes as her own eyes begged him to tell her to stop and leave so that she could turn and never look back at this shameful moment. He stared back into hers, his eyes empty and cold. He leaned his head back and continued to moan while grabbing the sides of the chair as Silvia continued to please him.

He grabbed Silvia by her hair as his pleasure neared its peak. She stopped and his eyes turned into slits as he looked at her. His eyes told her that she just made the biggest mistake of her life because he had not given her permission to stop. Now she would pay for that mistake. He slapped her and she fell back onto the floor. He got up, grabbed her and began dragging her behind the couch.

She tried to grab hold of something so that she could pull herself away from him . . . anything in order to keep him from doing what she feared was coming next. Her hands grabbed nothing but the air as he continued to drag her. She kicked and cried out, "Me ayuda . . . Por favor . . . Help me!'' as the other men now watched in total shock. Fear had taken full control of her.

"Don't worry about it. I'll finish it,'' he told her as he spread her legs and pulled her underwear to the side. He got on top of her and forced himself into her body without her consent. She kicked, she pulled and she scratched and tried to scream as he covered her mouth. She was in excruciating pain as he moved in and out of her body. She felt as though she was going to die with each one of his strokes.

She was trying to fight but he was far too strong and she started to feel much too weak. She ripped his shirt and saw the tattoo of a scorpion on his chest. Two other guys came and held her down as they waited for him to finally finish. He slid himself out of her and looked down at all the blood that now covered him. He knew that it came from her. As he took his hand from over her mouth she wailed loudly from the pain she was in. Her mind, body and spirit cried out from all the pain, and every bit of her ached.

He stared at her, then quickly got up and zipped his pants. His eyes were fixed on hers and were now apologetic as if he realized that he had just taken something precious away from her and that was not his intention. She lay on the floor crying uncontrollably as she looked up into his green eyes with eyes that pled the question "Why?" She looked at the man who now towered over her, the man who left her empty and broken . . . the man who took a part of her. He touched her in a place no man has ever touched her before and bruised her in a way that no man had ever bruised her.

Lost for words, he left the room ashamed of what he had just done. The other five men each took their turn with Silvia without hesitation. That night, she was severally beaten by one of the men and was left for dead after she blacked out on the floor. She could not clearly remember the faces of any of the men except for one and she had good reason to remember his.

That night she was rushed to the hospital where she spent the next three weeks. She was devastated. The hospital offered her counseling but she refused. A part of Silvia died the night she was raped and beaten. She was left with nothing but a broken spirit and a cold hard heart. The men never paid for what they did to her that night; but she promised herself that if she ever came across the one who she felt killed a part of her on that dreadful night, he would pay, even if he had to pay with his own life.

She snapped back to her present moment as the world around her seemed to go in slow motion. She watched the woman pushing the buggy and the man who stood beside her with a bouncing baby girl in his arms. There he stood tall, handsome, slender yet muscular, light-skinned, wavy hair and with green eyes that now stared back into hers. She stood still and glared at the man who had left her bruised and broken.

"Ma'am, are you okay?" the clerk asked her. She was concerned by how distraught Silvia appeared.

Silvia stood frozen in place, still as a statue. She wanted to run. She wanted to walk away. She wanted her feet to move, but they were stuck in one place. Her brain couldn't register how to move them.

"Be careful ma'am! There's glass everywhere and I don't want you to cut yourself! Just be still so that you don't get hurt," another worker said, as he swept the glass from around her feet. At this point Silvia's feet wouldn't stay still. She backed away with her eyes locked on the man's green eyes. She did an about face and ran from the building and to her car. Once she got there, she broke down into tears. She sat there for a while, beating the steering wheel as if it were to blame for her pain.

She sped off, rubber burning. It was as if running away was going to leave behind the thoughts of this man from her past. She tried to bury her thoughts . . . her hurt . . . her hate . . . all at once, but it grew uncontrollably and somebody was going to have to pay for her pain. Now, she was ready for sweet revenge . . .

Chapter Two

Silvia walked into her office at Bradberry and Co. Michael Bradberry, the CEO, had put her as Lead Designer in the division of floor plans. All her life, she had wanted to work in the architecture arena and now, here she was working for one of the largest architecture companies in Baton Rouge, Louisiana. She sat down at her desk and tried to shake away her memories from the past. She kept seeing those green eyes in her mind as tears formed in her eyes. Then she heard the voice of one of the workers in the store, *Just be still, so that you don't get hurt.* She wondered why she kept hearing those words and what they truly meant. She rubbed her temples as she tried to clear her mind.

Michael knocked on the door. She pulled away from her thoughts as she watched him walk in. "Hey, Silvia. Were you able to pick that grape juice up for me on your lunch break?'' he asked. He walked closer to her when he noticed the look of sadness in her eyes. "Is everything okay?''

She stood up and closed in the space between them. "Kiss me,'' she said. She threw her arms around his neck and gently kissed his lips.

"Silvia, no,'' he told her, looking confused as he pulled her arms from around his neck. "What are you doing?''

"I want you.'' She kissed him again, disregarding his question. "I know you want me, Michael. Come on. This will be our little secret.'' She rubbed his biceps.

"I said no, Silvia.'' He gently pushed her away from him. "You work for me and we will *not* do this. Simple as that.'' He looked at the tears formed in her eyes. After all the years of her working for him, he had never seen her show any kind of emotion except anger. "What's wrong, Silvia? Talk to me, tell me what's going on with you.''

"I'm fine.'' She waved her hand in the air as if brushing him out of her way. "Just forget about it.''

She left out of her office, leaving a confused Michael behind.

She walked into the break room and saw Lionel, her co-worker of three years standing at the microwave. Lionel was a very attractive man in his early thirties. He was clean cut, blonde hair, blue eyes, tanned and handsome, and has been married for ten years. Yet, Silvia disregarded the ring he wore, as she did with many of the men she encountered. He and Silvia flirted throughout their years of working together, but never came close to having a sexual relationship.

She locked the door behind her, seeing that he was the only one in there. She walked up behind him and whispered into his ear, "Hi handsome,'' her lips brushing his ear. "You want to have some fun?'' she asked, now kissing the nape of his neck as she ran her fingers through his blonde hair.

He turned around and studied her for a minute to see just how serious she was. He picked her up without preamble and sat her on the counter. He kissed her passionately. He raised her skirt and reached for her panties only to realize she didn't have any on.

He looked into her eyes as she leaned in closer and whispered in his ear, "I don't wear them," as if she read his thoughts.

She licked his lips and he began kissing her once again. Their bodies connected. As he looked in her eyes, she looked away as he satisfied her for the moment.

One of their co-workers, Donna, turned the doorknob to the break room and realized it was locked. She knocked on the door.

No response . . .

Lionel continued to please Silvia as she moaned loudly. Then the microwave began beeping just as loudly. Donna heard all the noise and she knew that someone had to be in there. Hearing the moaning, she felt as though she knew exactly who one of them was. She rushed to get maintenance.

"Silvia . . ." Lionel called out to her as he kept his strokes steady.

She put her finger over his lips. "Shhh . . . Don't stop, Lionel," she whispered.

Donna decided to make a quick detour before getting maintenance. She stormed into Michael's office with her arms folded across her chest. "I believe someone is having sex in the break room!'' She rolled her neck before adding, "Again!" She walked over to his desk. "When are you going to stop this kind of behavior?''

Michael studied Donna hard before saying, "Did you catch someone having sex in the break room?''

"No, but I heard them and they are still in there."

"Well, we can't say for sure that someone is doing what you are claiming.'' He stood up. "Where's Bill?'' he asked her. Bill is one of the guys who work with maintenance.

"Probably in the maintenance room.''

"Okay, well, I will get him. I left my keys at home today. You can go back to your office, and I will take care of this.''

"I'm on lunch break; and I need to get in the break room to eat my food. They are wasting my time.''

Michael looked at his Kenneth Cole watch and hesitated before saying, "Okay, well, let's go get maintenance so we can see what's going on. You can have an extra thirty for lunch.''

They started walking down the hall.

"Michael,'' Donna began. "You are way too nice and you are going to have to put your foot down. Silvia is going to keep doing what she is doing because she knows that you are going to let her get away with it every time.''

Michael stopped abruptly, which made Donna stop and look at him. "Donna, you are not going to tell me how to run this business. Just like many others, you have been given chance after chance instead of me letting you go for many different things that you've done. Sometimes mercy goes a long way, and I suggest you worry about what's going on with you and not with Silvia. Let me handle my business and my staff," he said firmly, and it shocked Donna. "Thank you," he added before he continued walking towards the maintenance room to get Bill.

Maintenance walked up to the break room door with Donna and Michael.

Lionel brought the moment to an end after hearing the keys rattle at the door. Silvia continued to moan even louder as she felt him finish. He quickly helped her down from the counter and fixed his pants. Silvia fixed her skirt as she giggled at the thought of getting caught.

Maintenance finally unlocked the door. Donna was the first one in, hoping to catch them in the act. She looked at Silvia with a look of disgust, knowing what had just taken place. This was not the first time that Silvia had an office fling and Donna, along with many others, knew that.

Michael walked in and saw Silvia straightening up her skirt with a smirk on her face. He looked over at Lionel, then back at Silvia. "Silvia, I need to see you in my office in ten minutes," he told her. Then he looked at Lionel and said, "And I need to see you in my office in thirty."

Silvia looked at Lionel, rolled her eyes at Donna and walked out of the break room.

Donna looked at Lionel and asked, "How could you mess with that slut? You know how she is." She folded her arms across her chest. "And what about your wife, Lionel?" She shook her head and walked to the refrigerator to get her lunch.

Lionel sat down in his seat and rubbed his head as he realized what he had just done. From the moment he met Silvia, he had a desire to have sex with her, but he never expected to fulfill that desire. Every time Silvia flirted with him, he would flirt back, and then shake it off, but this time he followed through without even thinking twice.

Silvia walked into Michael's office and closed the door behind her. "What can I do for you, Michael?" she asked as if she hadn't done anything wrong.

He pointed to the seat in front of her. "Sit down, Silvia."

She sat down and looked Michael in his eyes. The thought of her being fired made her regret what had just taken place with Lionel. She had been sexually active with quite a few men while in the office. She knew that Michael had known about a few of her indiscretions in the workplace. She also knew that those were grounds to be terminated, and at the moment, that bothered her considering the fact that she enjoyed working for him.

"Silvia, you know that I could let you go right now," Michael began. "But I'm not going to. I will say this though. You are not going to continue to work here with those kinds of actions." He sighed and looked down at his desk. "I am trying my best to be patient with you. You are very talented when it comes to your work, but you are allowing your actions to affect your productivity. I need you to keep it strictly professional in the workplace." He looked up at her. "I am really concerned about you. Just tell me, Silvia. What is really going on with you?"

"What do you mean, Michael? There is nothing going on with me and thank you for the compliment. You know that I want to please you more than anything." She winked at him and stood up. "Oh, and yes, I will keep it strictly professional."

She was headed out the door until she heard Michael's next words, "Silvia, don't you understand? These men don't care about you. Why do you keep hurting yourself?"

She abruptly turned to face him. She tilted her head before saying, "Why do you pretend to care so much, Michael? You are a man . . . same as they are."

"I care about your well-being." He stood up and walked closer to her. "Did he even wear a condom? Do you even care about your health?" He looked at her closely. "How many men have you actually been with, Silvia?" he inquired.

Appalled by his question, "I stopped counting after six," she said coldly. "You don't know me, Michael. So don't judge me." She turned and walked out of his office.

Silvia sat at her desk and thought about Michael's question. She had had sex with a slew of men in many different places, and half of them she didn't even know their names.

She'd been with them in their homes when their wives and children weren't there, in parking lots, on out of town business trips, at their jobs, at her job and in many bathrooms of restaurants, bars, grocery stores and malls. It didn't matter with whom or where. Silvia took risks.

She began to recount the times that she had unprotected sex, and it was more times than she could ever count or remember. Sex had begun to take over her existence and she couldn't figure out how to get her life back.

Chapter Three

Silvia sat on her sofa and tried to shake the headache that she had since earlier. She tried her best to bury her thoughts as she took a sip of her Chardonnay, but her mind kept reverting to her past . . .

They called Jazzy to the stage and she began to dance for the small crowd that Boss Gentlemen's Club had for the night. They normally had great business, but to her, there was something different about tonight. It was a dark and stormy night and something was telling her to go home, but she ignored the feeling.

She walked out onto the stage and began dancing in her sexy lingerie and the men threw money at her like crazy. She did a handstand and spread eagle in front of one of the men's face and went to the floor into a split, and he placed a twenty dollar bill in her bikini.

She crawled over to another man and did a peek-a-boo in front of his face, and he made it rain dollars on the stage. She then crawled over to the pole, slinked her body up and did her sexy diva walk as she looked into the eyes of every man that surrounded the stage, fulfilling their fantasies. She started her pole dance to the Fugees, *Ready or Not*. Men watched her as she worked the pole. She slowly climbed the pole, and then did a V sit perfectly, her long legs saying "Hello boys." She then did a Gemini and went into a reverse superwoman, and they continued to throw dollars all around her. They were fascinated as they watched her perform on stage.

Silvia took advantage of knowing all the pole tricks and she gave them a show every time, never having to remove any of her clothing. As she hung upside down on the pole in a butterfly, holding the heel of her shoe, she looked into the most beautiful magnetizing green eyes and smiled as she took in his beautiful honey-colored skin and chiseled facial features from upside down.

"Man, she looking at you, dog! Look like she wanting you!" one of his boys hollered out to him. "We have got us a hot tamale up in here!"

Another one of his boys hollered out over the music, "Hey, we need us a VIP room! We got us some hot and sexy ones tonight!" He looked at Silvia. "She sexy and all, but I want that one over there!" He pointed to one of the other strippers across the room. She had on nothing but a thong as she danced topless on one of her regulars.

The handsome man with the green eyes said, "We can get that room, but this is the one and only one that will be going in there." His eyes fixed on Silvia. He then looked at his boy. "You got me?"

"Yeah, I got you." He shrugged. "That's cool."

Silvia watched as the handsome man signaled to one of the workers. The worker came over and he asked for one of the VIP rooms and for more drinks. Silvia could tell that he was a man who knew how to take charge and she found that to be very sexy.

He continued to watch her as she hung upside down on the pole doing trick after trick. She came down into a split, then crawled over to him.

"¿Cómo te llamas, papi?" she asked.

"My name?" He chuckled. "Well, I don't see how that's any of your concern, sweetheart," he said to her, his voice cold. He continued to look at her intensely.

"Okay, the shy type. I'm feeling that." She got down from the stage. "How about a lap dance?" she asked, now about to straddle him.

He grabbed her leg, stopping her before she could. "Not here," he said while looking into her eyes.

This man was gorgeous and his intensity intrigued her. "Okay. Well, did you get us a VIP room?" she asked.

"Yes . . . You ready?" he asked in a calm tone.

She looked him in his green eyes. "Ready for you? Always, papi."

He stared at her for a moment. "You sure 'bout that . . . *ma . . . mi*?" he asked, mocking her.

"I'm positive. Are *you* ready?" She then whispered into his ear, "Once you go with me, you won't want to go back."

He looked at her intensely for a moment, then grabbed her by her hand. Without saying another word, he led her into the VIP room and five of his boys followed . . .

The sound of thunder reverberated against her windows and walls, bringing her back to her present moment. She hated stormy weather. Those were the kinds of nights that she was not going to spend alone. She pulled out her cell phone and made a call.

Thirty minutes later a guy that she met last week greeted her at her front door.

"Hi, Kendrick, I know it was last minute, but I'm glad you were able to make it.'' She watched him walk in.

Kendrick was so sexy to her. He looked as though he lived in a gym morning, noon and night. She had met him at a clothing store in the mall and flirted with him like she didn't have any sense. When they were in the store that day, she spotted the ring on his finger. One thing she liked most was married men. Those were the kind who didn't want attachments, and that was fine with her because she didn't want to be attached. Attachments weren't her thing. Especially after she lost all trust in men. A relationship didn't interest her. Just sex... and, of course, maybe ruining their relationships.

She hadn't been in a relationship since college. After the night that she was raped, she immediately broke up with her college boyfriend. She left to go home for a while and when she returned, she contacted him and they had sex for the first time, even though they were broken up. She considered him to be her first since she had consensual sex with him, but that never helped her forget about her first time and who was responsible for taking away her innocence. No matter how many men she went through in order to forget, she never could.

She looked down at Kendrick's ring finger. "Where's your ring?'' she asked.

He looked down at his hand. "What ring?''

"You had a ring on when I first met you.'' She lifted his hand. "Well . . . Where is it?''

"Oh, that was for show purposes,'' he lied.

"Look, you do not have to lie to me.'' She put his ring finger into her mouth and circled the tip of it with her tongue. "I love married men.'' She looked up at him. "So, where is it?''

He put his hand in his pocket and quickly pulled it out as he slid it onto his finger.

"Now, that's what's up.'' She kissed his lips.

"Wait, I thought you called me over for dinner,'' he said. He didn't want to make it seem as though he just wanted sex from her, even though that was all that was on his mind right now.

"Uh-huh, I did,'' she lied. "But, first I will serve you dessert.'' She kissed him again. "And I serve it just right, papi. Trust me.'' She led him into her bedroom.

Silvia stood directly in front of Kendrick and slowly unbuttoned her blouse as if doing a striptease. She left it open just enough to show her Victoria's Secret black-lace bra.

His eyes traced the shape of her full breast as he licked his lips.

She started unbuttoning his shirt.

He slipped his hand into his pocket, pulling out a condom before she started unzipping his pants.

His pants fell to the floor.

Silvia took the condom from him, opened it and slipped it on for him. She looked into his eyes as she kissed his lips. "I love a man who comes prepared," she mumbled, her lips still gently pressed against his. She reached around her back, unzipping her skirt while kissing him passionately. She stepped away from him and slipped out of her skirt.

His mouth dropped as he looked down at her Brazilian waxed area.

"Ha!" She laughed when she caught his reaction.

This man was so ready for her. He's had women who have thrown themselves at him before, but he had never experienced a situation like this. Silvia was gorgeous and he captured her without even attempting to.

Silvia dropped to her knees.

He looked down at her as she began pleasing him.

She stopped, looked up at him and asked, "Do you want me?" She went back to pleasing him.

"Yes . . . ooo wee. Yes, baby. I want you," he responded to her words and everything she was doing to him at that moment.

Silvia stood up and looked him in his eyes. "Prove it!" She pushed him down on the bed and straddled him. She kissed his chest, and looked him in his eyes as she slowly unbuttoned the rest of her blouse. She removed it and threw it onto the floor. She made a gesture as if she was going to remove her bra, then stopped and smirked.

He sat up and kissed her. "Are you trying to tease me, girl?" He ran his fingers through her hair before kissing her again. "Look, I want you now, right this minute." He removed her bra, now exposing her full breast.

She then lowered herself onto him and moved around to her own tune while on top of him. He lay back on the bed and was definitely enjoying the moment as he grabbed her hips that rotated around on him. She began to moan as the thunder roared. She closed her eyes tight and moaned louder, attempting to drown out the sound of her thoughts from the past. She opened her eyes and caught him looking at her. Even though his eyes were dark-brown, they flashed green right before her eyes as she remembered the man from her past. She closed her eyes tightly, hoping to get that vision out of her mind.

"I'm almost there, baby!" Kendrick screamed, his voice pulling her away from her thoughts. His nails dug into her flank as she vigorously bounced up and down on him. "Don't stop what you doing. I am almost there. Almost . . . Ughhh, girl . . . Almost . . . " he screamed louder, and then he climaxed before he could get the rest of his words out.

Silvia quickly got up. "Here!" She handed him his shirt. "Put on your clothes."

Trying to catch his breath, he sat up. He looked confused as he looked down at the shirt she handed him. "What?" he panted.

"Get out!" She continued handing him his clothes.

He stood. "What is up with you? You married or something?"

"No, but you are and I want you to get out! "

He frowned. "Did I do something wrong?"

Almost in a panic, "No!" she yelled.

"Was I bad in bed or something?" he asked, not paying attention to the tears in her eyes.

She calmed herself, then kissed his lips. "Not at all, you were great." She ran her hand over his chest. "But you gotta go."

"Well, what is it?" He was curious to know why she was forcing him out right after a good time. He walked closer to her and touched her hair. "I would have stayed with you tonight. I really enjoyed this . . . us." He looked at her naked body and his eyes begged her to let him stay.

She threw her hair over her shoulder and sighed. "You enjoyed me on top of you, Kendrick. It was just sex, so call it like it is. There's no us . . . Go home to your wife. I'm sure she's looking for you."

"Wow." He began putting on his clothes. "Will I see you again?"

She quickly responded, "Probably not."

"Just like that, huh?"

"Yes. Just like that," she said. Still naked, she led him to the door and kissed him one final time.

She sat down on her sofa and thought about the man from her past. She was angry that she couldn't shake him from her thoughts. *He has no right to be walking this earth!* Her emotions began to overwhelm her as she cried; something she hadn't done in a long time, until she saw her past staring back at her today. It was as if seeing him triggered every one of her emotions. The night that she was raped kept playing over and over in her mind. *I gotta get out of here!*

Chapter Four

Silvia walked up to the door of her best friend of thirteen years. She knocked on the door as if she had lost her mind.

Reesie opened the door. "Silvia, it's two o'clock in the morning. What's wrong, boo?" she asked, inviting her in. She was use to Silvia coming over to stay with her whenever it was stormy weather, so it wasn't like this was new to her.

"I saw him today, Rees," Silvia said, as she began pacing the floor.

Confused, Reesie asked, "You saw who?"

Silvia stopped pacing and looked into her eyes. "The man with the green eyes." She looked at her as if she should have known who and what she was talking about.

Silvia began pacing again and she looked over at Reesie's boyfriend, Brandon, who sat at the kitchen table, smoking a cigarette. She had his full attention as he watched her pace back and forth. He stared at her and when her eyes met his, he winked at her. Vexed by his presence, she rolled her eyes.

Reesie covered her mouth and gasped. As the thought hit her, she said, "Oh, my God! The man with the green eyes?" She realized who she was talking about. "You haven't seen him since that night. Are you sure it was him?"

"I'm positive, Reesie. I would never forget his face," Silvia said in disgust. "And those eyes," her tone now filled with anger.

"Well?"

"Well, what?"

"What do you plan to do?"

"I don't know, but he has to pay for what he did to me." Silvia continued to pace the floor, focusing on holding back her tears.

Brandon got up and walked over closer to Silvia. "What y'all in here talkin' about?" he asked.

Silvia rolled her eyes and released a frustrated sigh. "Ugggh! None of your business, Brandon . . . How about you just go back under the rock you came from. This is none of your concern so go sell your dope, smoke you some weed or something."

Brandon was a big time drug dealer whom Reesie had gotten involved with four years ago. Silvia couldn't stand him because from the moment they met, he had gotten her friend caught up in a lot of drama. He cheated on her all the time, but Reesie stood beside him no matter what, and it made her wonder if Reesie was more basic than she already thought her to be.

"Brandon, just leave her alone. She going through something right now,'' Reesie said matter-of-factly.

Brandon walked over to the couch and sat down, continuing to smoke his cigarette. He cut his eyes at Silvia as he watched her continue to pace the floor. He found her very attractive and whenever she would come over, even if he had a run to make, he would stay a little while longer just to watch her. He had been asking Reesie about having a threesome with Silvia for a while now, but Reesie always took it as a joke considering that she had told him about their past together.

Reesie was the one who taught Silvia, as she called it, "the strip game" and "the tricks of the trade.'' She taught her everything she knows about getting money. Brandon knew all about their past and about how she and Silvia would do threesomes with men who paid good money. Brandon loved that idea, so he always brought it up to her from the moment she told him.

Brandon pulled a bag of cocaine from his pocket and grabbed the small mirror and a pen that sat on the end table. He set them up on the coffee table in front of him, knowing exactly what he was doing. Just last night he brought it up with Reesie about having a threesome with Silvia, and he promised to give her what she wanted most only if she could make that happen.

As Reesie saw him set up her drug of choice on the table, she knew then that he was serious about a threesome with Silvia. She walked over to the table, picked up the pen and took off the top. She squatted down and scooped the cocaine on the pen top, then put it up to her nose and sniffed it. She held her head back with her fingers now covering her nostrils. She allowed the cocaine to go through her system and got more.

Silvia walked over to her and knocked the top out of her hand. "Reesie, I can't believe you let this little *boy*," she looked at Brandon and back at Reesie, "get you hooked!" she screamed at her. "All he wants to do is keep you begging him for more. He can get you to do whatever he wants you to do just so you can get some dope and he knows it. You can't see what he's doing!"

Brandon continued watching her with a smirk on his face. He put his feet up on the coffee table, leaned his back against the sofa and took a long drag of his cigarette. He blew out the smoke and smiled even more as his eyes stayed on Silvia.

"Silvia," Reesie began. "You are overreacting as always. Relax." She stood up to face Silvia. "Look, how about we go back to the old days. Remember how much fun we use to have?" She looked at Brandon who nodded his approval, and then looked back at Silvia. "Let's show Brandon how we use to get down and it will help you forget all about green eyes." She twirled Silvia's hair around her finger. She leaned in closer, and whispered to her, "He's been asking for a threesome, Silvia. Let's just give him that experience with us. I wouldn't want to invite anyone else into our bed if it's not you . . . Please, Silvia?"

It was tempting to Silvia as she looked into Reesie's hazel-colored eyes. Her Creole friend always did have an appeal about her, and Silvia has been attracted to her for a long time. She pushed Reesie's hand away from her hair, not wanting to give in to her plea. "You are high, and you know what?" Silvia now looked over at Brandon. "I wouldn't do anything for him!" she yelled. "I'll let you two have that!"

Brandon got up and walked over to her. "You know what? I could give you what you been missing, Silvia. I promise I will make it to where you would *never* forget." He grabbed her wrist firmly and she snatched it away.

Silvia spit in his face.

He looked at her with fury as he slowly wiped her spit from his face with the back of his hand. Then he back slapped her.

She flew across the room, hit the wall and fell to the floor.

Reesie screamed, "Brandon, what are you doing!"

Brandon walked over to Silvia and she looked up at him from where she lay. The side of her face was completely red. He dropped to his knees and grabbed her by her ankle, pulling her legs a part as he got in between them. He pulled her closer to him.

"What you gon' do, big boy? You gon' rape me?" Silvia said, looking him in his eyes. "Huh?" she yelled. "Is that what you really want to do? Treat me like I'm nothing?" Tears formed in her eyes as she was reminded of the past.

Brandon wanted her, but he wasn't willing to take it. He had never raped a woman in his life. He stared at her for a minute, then got up and left.

Reesie ran over to her friend's side. "Oh, my God, Silvia! Are you okay?"

Silvia cried as Reesie hugged her.

"I'm so sorry," Reesie apologized. She had never seen Brandon act like that. Of course, he was verbally abusive to her, but he had never laid a hand on her, so it was unexpected when she saw him slap her friend.

Silvia held the side of her face that was now swollen.

Reesie ran to the freezer to get an ice pack, brought it back and held it on Silvia's face.

"I hate men! I hate them so much!" Silvia screamed out in anger as tears ran down her face.

Reesie knew exactly where Silvia's pain came from which made her hold her friend tight as she cried out to her. She kissed her lips attempting to comfort her, but that kiss did nothing for Silvia.

Chapter Five

Silvia sat at her desk, her thoughts on what had taken place the night before with Brandon. Michael knocked on the door and she invited him in.

"Hey, Silvia. How are we coming along with the business owners' meet and greet?" he asked her. He had asked her months ago to help the receptionist, Regina, get a party together for all of the Baton Rouge business owners. He got them all together at least three times a year in order to network.

She sat there silently, her focus slightly off.

"Silvia?" Michael called to her. "Are you okay?"

"Oh, yeah." Both of his questions now registering to her. "We are good to go for the meet and greet. Everything is in place and ready to go. We have our location, our caterer and our decorator. We are good," she said to him, her focus still slightly off.

He sensed that she was bothered which made him ask, "Is everything okay?"

She slowly responded, "Everything is fine."

Kimbrailee Whitmore walked up to the opened office door and tapped on it. She stood and waited to be invited in.

Michael's attention was immediately drawn away from Silvia. "Kim! What can I do for you?" He walked over to hug her.

"Well, the receptionist told me that I would find you in here. I brought you some information for your meeting tonight." She handed him the folder that she was holding. She looked over at Silvia, the woman she caught having sex with her late-husband who passed away years ago. "How do you do, Silvia?" she asked.

"I'm fine . . . I will let you two talk." Silvia stood up and prepared to leave them to her office.

Feeling the tension in the room, Kim raised her hand, stopping her. "No, I was just leaving . . . Good to see you," she said, looking at her. She then turned to face Michael. "Mike, I will see you later."

"Okay, Kim. Sure. I will see you a little later on," he said. His eyes were now focused on the side of Silvia's face. He was just noticing the big black mark that Brandon left there. He waited until Kim walked out of the door before asking, "Silvia? Who did that to your face?"

"Don't worry about it, Michael. It's nothing to be concerned with."

He waited a minute, and then said, "Look, Silvia. I'm having a meeting tonight at the Family Life Center and I think you should come. We will have a very uplifting speaker and I think you would really enjoy it." He paused after seeing the disapproval on her face. "You can bring a friend if you would like to." He thought that would help her feel a little bit more comfortable. "It will be a life-changing experience." He smiled. "I promise."

"Isn't the Family Life Center connected to your church?"

"Yes, it is."

"Well, no, thank you. I don't feel like being judged today."

"What are you talking about, Silvia? No one will judge you. These meetings are about uplifting others, not tearing them down," he informed her.

"Well, Michael. I don't do the church scene very well. I've been judged by many pastors, preachers, teachers, deacons and the list goes on. They turn up their noses, yet every one of them that has judged me, had sex with me. Many of them married and some single, but *all* of them *claimed* to be men of God." She nodded. "Yeah, you heard me right." She spoke with much attitude. "I have slept with many men of God who *claimed* that they live by the Word or whatever you want to call it, but as soon as I get them behind closed doors they be hollering for a savior all right and that savior ain't Jesus." She now waved her hand in the air with an attitude. "Sooo, I will pass on your little church meeting." She chuckled. "Those people are never real and want to judge everybody else." She crossed her arms in front of her chest. "Let me ask you something, Michael . . . If God is the judge, what makes people think that He needs a jury?"

"Well, Silvia, I don't know what people think, but it's unfortunate that you feel that way." He looked at her more closely. "I really think you should come. This will be different and I believe you would enjoy it," he said. As he looked at her, it was almost as if he could feel her emptiness. He added, "Eight o'clock tonight, Silvia . . . You know the location." He touched her hand, smiled, and walked out of her office.

Silvia sat and contemplated asking Reesie to go with her to that meeting tonight. Maybe it was going to be different from what she was use to. She pulled out her cell phone and called her friend to see what she had up for that night.

***

Silvia pulled into the parking lot of Holy Temple Ministries Family Life Center and Reesie's mouth dropped. "Oh, my God, Silvia, you didn't say we were coming to no church . . . Look at how I'm dressed," she said, pulling at her skirt as if it was going to come down further. Her scanty mini skirt showed most of her light-skinned thighs and her breast spilled over the tank top she wore.

"You look fine, girl, and they can't say anything to you anyway. Most of them ain't right," Silvia said. The cross on the top of the building caught her attention and she began to have second thoughts about coming there. "Okay, maybe you are right. Let's just go." She turned the car around to head back out of the parking lot.

"No, Silvia. I kinda wanna stay," Reesie said to her.

Silvia stopped the car and looked at her friend. "You can't be serious, Rees."

She looked at Silvia. "Yes, I am. Let's just see how it is."

Silvia saw the seriousness in her friend's eyes as she placed the gear in park. After a minute, they got out of the car and went in. There was a small group of five people. One of the group members was talking at the time they walked in.

After Michael saw Silvia and Ressie come in, he nodded and pointed to two of the seats that were left available. They took their seats and listened to the lady who was talking when they entered.

"I've tried and tried to stop drinking, but I can't. Every time when I think about that night, I have to drink. Drinking helps me to relax and not think about the pain anymore,'' the young woman said.

"What pain, Tasha? Describe how that pain makes you feel,'' Michael encouraged.

A tear ran down Tasha's face. "It makes me feel angry.'' Her tone changed and completely uncovered her hostility. "I hate him so much . . . I was six and I remember it like it was yesterday.'' This was Tasha's third meeting and she felt comfortable enough to open up a little more.

"Remember what, Tasha?'' Michael asked.

"He pointed that shot gun to her face and boom! I saw him blow her brains out. He killed my mother, and then he turned the gun on himself. She had begged for her life, but he shot her anyway. He shot her right in front of me!'' Tasha rocked back and forth in her seat. "Her blood was all over me! When he took her life, he took mine too!'' She cried. "Do you know how many times I wanted to kill myself from the thought of her blood being all over me?"

"So, you've had thoughts of suicide?" Michael asked.

"I had them a long time ago, but never have I tried to go through with it."

"When was the last time that you had a suicidal thought?"

"About two years ago." She understood that Michael was trying to make sure that she wasn't suicidal, and she wanted to make sure that she didn't confuse him. "Michael, I'm not going to kill myself. I guess what I was trying to say is that I sometimes wish that he would have killed me too, and then I wouldn't have to live with the pain of what I saw. That's why I drink so much. When I'm drunk, I forget about it. I don't feel that pain anymore," Tasha confessed.

"Don't be deceived," Michael encouraged. "It only makes you feel as though that pain is no longer there, but it is only for that moment. That pain will return and it will be even greater because you have not dealt with it, and you have not healed from it. You're just allowing it to eat away at you. As a matter of fact, you keep adding to that pain by trying to drink or smoke it away. The path that you are traveling will only lead to your destruction." He began looking at each individual as he continued, "Our situations and circumstances in life can either have a positive or negative effect on us and even though we can't always control our situations and circumstances, we can choose how we respond to them. We can choose a negative or positive response." He again focused his attention on Tasha. "Instead of drinking or smoking, try to redirect your focus to something more positive.'' He now looked around at each group member. "It is important to know your triggers and talk to someone when you are triggered by a thought or your situation and circumstances around you. It is good for you to talk about your pain and how it makes you feel. Do not hold that pain in. If any of you ever feel suicidal, please go to your nearest hospital. It takes courage to get help, and I believe each of you have courage because you are here. That's something to celebrate.''

He started clapping and everybody joined him in celebrating.

He looked at Tasha and took a sip of water. "Tasha, let's talk about this man who killed your mother. Is that okay? Do you want to explore those feelings a little more?''

Tasha nodded.

"Okay, who was this man?'' he asked.

She slowly answered, "My father.''

"How was your relationship with your father?''

"I don't remember much, but I do know that we didn't really have a relationship. He was hardly ever around. All I know is that whenever he did come around, he would beat my mother.''

Michael nodded, encouraging her to continue.

"I hate him so much, Michael. Why did he have to take my mother from me?'' She broke down in tears.

"I can't answer that question. We don't know the reason why he did what he did. Let's explore how you can move on from here? What is your plan?"

She shook her head vigorously. "I don't know."

"Do you think that journaling can help you? Maybe when you feel triggered, you can talk to a close friend or even do something that you enjoy. What is something that you like to do?"

"I love to walk around Rosewood Park. That place is so beautiful." She referred to one of the most beautiful parks in Baton Rouge. "I also love to write."

"Good! Whenever you feel triggered think about asking a friend to walk around the park with you, or you can even go by yourself; but whatever you do, try to go for that walk that you love so much. And writing can be very therapeutic as well. Try journaling your thoughts."

"But I don't know if that would work. Drinking is the only thing that helps me to forget."

"Listen to yourself, Tasha. You have allowed your father to steal a part of your life by masking your pain behind alcohol. You hurt yourself more and more as you pick up that bottle. I want you to think about trying something different, other than picking up that bottle. You can't say that nothing works until you try something different. Instead of drinking, try walking. If you want to write, write. Just see how that works for you."

She smiled. "I will try my best, Michael."

Michael nodded and looked around the room at each individual. "Let me help you all understand something. God created each of you with purpose. He has a purpose and a plan for each one of you and Satan wants to destroy your purpose. He wants you to pick up that bottle or whatever your drug of choice is, but you can choose not to pick it up. You can choose to do something different. Satan may present something to you, but you have the choice to accept or reject whatever he puts in front of you. God can and will give you strength to overcome every obstacle. All you have to do is trust Him to be your help in times of trouble."

Silvia's eyes were fixed on Michael's.

He looked directly at her and said, "God has a purpose for your life. He is calling you out of that lifestyle, but it is up to you to answer His call. Satan will try to distract you by your past hurt, your past pain and disappointments. But if you just give that pain, that hurt and disappointment to Jesus, He will lighten that load you have been trying to carry on your own for so long. I'm not saying you won't ever think about it again, but I can guarantee you that you won't dwell on it and allow it to consume you. Don't allow your past to hold you back. Don't allow it to stagnate your future."

Silvia began stirring in her seat as Michael's words touched her heart. She looked over at Reesie who was in tears along with many others. She then focused her attention back to Michael.

Michael looked into Silvia's eyes. "Does anyone else have anything that they would like to share?" he asked. "No one can or will judge you here. We stand together and uplift one another. We have no room to judge anyone. We all have done wrong, and if it had not been for the grace of God . . . where would we be?"

"I know that's real," one of the group members said as she waved her hand.

Michael continued as he looked around at each group member. "A lot of you have come a long way and now some obstacles have been placed before you. Right now, Satan is saying to you, 'just give up'. He uses people and he places obstacles in your way, and those people and obstacles are meant to discourage you and throw you off track. Satan wants you to just give up, but I want to encourage you tonight. Don't give up on yourself and don't give up on God. Keep moving forward. You have to have unshakable faith even when obstacles are placed in your path. Faith in God is going to get you through to your breakthrough. Ask God to help you and He will. He will not fail you and He will bring you evidence every single time." His eyes met Silvia's once again. "You just have to ask Him to help you and trust that He will. You don't have to beg Him for help. All you have to do is ask and He's right there waiting for you."

Silvia's eyes were locked on Michael's and by the saddened look in her eyes, he knew that she wanted help, but instead of staying in the place with people who had been hurt and were ready for healing, she stood and walked out of the door. She walked to her car and got in. She sat there and waited for Reesie to come out behind her, but she didn't. She waited for fifteen minutes and finally she saw the door to the building swing open. She exhaled as she watched everyone head to their cars.

Michael tapped on Silvia's window and she rolled it down without looking at him. "What is it, Michael? You didn't tell me that this was some kind of AA meeting," she said with her eyes straight ahead.

"It was not an AA meeting," he stated.

Reesie walked around to the passenger side of the car. She thanked Michael and got in.

Silvia then looked at him furiously and rolled her eyes. She sped off, rubber burning.

Michael waved away the smoke from her tires as he watched her speed out of the parking lot and down the street.

Silvia's actions baffled Reesie and her mouth was wide open. "Silvia, what is wrong with you? He is a nice guy."

"Yes, well, I was not expecting this. He made it seem like there was going to be some kind of speaker there and everything. I can't believe he lied. I didn't know this was an AA meeting," Silvia said, as she continued to speed down the road.

"Why are you so upset? He said it was not an AA meeting and I don't believe that it was. When you left out; he thanked me for coming and he also said that he was sorry that we missed the speaker." She touched Silvia's arm. "So, Silvia, he didn't lie to you. There really was a speaker there. We were just late. He really seems to be a very nice guy and what he was saying made so much sense . . . Where did you meet him?"

"He's my boss. Now, let's just stop talking about it!"

Reesie was silent for a moment as she stared out of the window. And then: "Silvia? I want something different out of my life . . . I mean, Mr. Michael really encouraged me in that meeting and I want to be a better person. I know that God has something greater for me. All the things that I've been through in my life, there has to be something better than this. I'm ready for change . . ."

"Just shut up, Reesie!" Silvia yelled. Tears began to run from her eyes.

"Silvia, what is wrong with you?" she asked, concerned by her friends actions.

Silvia pulled into Reesie's driveway. "I'm sorry, Rees. I didn't mean that." She nodded and looked at her. "Change is good."

"You have really been scaring me lately. I am your friend and you can talk to me about anything," she told her.

"Yeah . . . Right . . . My *friend*."

"What is that supposed to mean? We've been friends since college and you have the nerve to say something like that. That's really cold." Reesie got out of the car, slammed the door and went in the house.

Silvia turned off her engine and sat there as she began to cry from all of her past hurt. The pain she felt was almost unbearable. Her heart was heavy as her thoughts began to revert again to the past . . .

"Silvia, I've been dancing for years and it is fast money, boo. All you have to do is go in there and dance for Mr. Cato

and a few of his friends. I know he's going to hire you. He
doesn't care about your age. He just cares about what you're
able to bring to the table. Nothing's going to happen to you, I
promise,'' Reesie told her. They stood backstage behind the
curtain at Boss Gentleman's Club. "Just go out there, Silvia, and
do your thang, girl. This is going to set you up for your books,
your tuition and everything. You will have all the money you
need for school plus some, boo. It will set you up for life. I
mean, five-hundred dollars in two hours is what I make and I
know you could pull more out of these men. You gon' get paid
more than me up in here and you know my New Orleans behind
knows how to get down.'' She laughed, attempting to make her
friend laugh, but it didn't work. "Look, Silvia, don't be nervous.
You are a great dancer. I've seen you get down and you dance
better than half the girls who been here for years.'' She tried to
ease Silvia's fear.

"I've never done anything like this in my life, Rees.
This is scary for me,'' Silvia said as tears ran down her face.

"Look, you don't have to have sex. All you have to do
is dance. They can't touch you unless you allow them to. Mr.
Cato will take care of you. You don't have to worry about that
and don't no dead beats come here, only business men . . .
ballers, Silvia.'' She grabbed Silvia by her shoulders. "You need
this money, boo.'' She reached behind her and grabbed a drink
from the table. "Here, drink this. It will help you relax.'' Reesie
handed her the drink.

Silvia took it and drank it all down at once. She wasn't
used to drinking and the alcohol in it made her gag. She began
to feel funny, but she went on stage and gave them what they
were looking for. She went as far as taking off her bra that night
for Mr. Cato and a few of his friends, like he'd asked her to. She

drove them crazy as they watched her do her pole dance, lap dance, and table dance. If she was hired, her plan was to dance in her sexy lingerie and costumes and not have to take off one piece of it. Her plan was to dance only, not strip out of her clothes. After all, she was a dancer. That's what she loved to do.

When the music stopped, she kneeled down on the stage and looked down at the four men who sat and watched her audition.

Mr. Cato stared at her and said, "You are a natural, baby girl, and you worked it for me. You real jazzy and I like that. You are beautiful too, which is a definite plus." He reached up and touched her breast which made her uncomfortable. "You are hired, but I have one rule. You will not have sex in this club unless you have permission from me, and the only way you get my permission is if you do me first. Then you can have sex as much as you want, with whomever you want. So . . . you can get my permission right now if you would like to." He chuckled, took a puff of his cigar, and then blew his smoke in her face.

Mr. Cato was a handsome, Italian man who had been in the business for many years. He was well over three-hundred pounds, but he had plenty of women and he got them to do whatever he wanted them to do.

"I just want to dance," Silvia's voice trembled. She looked at the way he and his friends were staring at her as though she was a piece of meat and they were dogs, ready to tear into it.

"Okay, that's cool, but when you are ready for the sex part, you come to me first. Got it?" He looked into her eyes letting her know that there would be consequences if she broke that one rule.

She nodded. Breaking that rule was not in her plan and neither was having sex with him.

"Oh, and, Jazzy, you can start tonight," he said, now giving her a stage name.

She agreed and he watched her as she walked off stage. He knew that she was going to bring in plenty of business and the thought of her having sex with him made him smile. A lot of the girls who start always say that they are just there to dance and make their money, but it never fails. They always end up having sex with him so that they can, as he called it, "progress" in the business.

Silvia came back to her present moment when she heard Brandon slam the house door. He stood there with his eyes fixed on hers as he smoked his cigarette. He watched her as though she was his prey. She had the urge to call him to her car, pull him in and have sex with him just to get those exotic dancing days far from her mind, but the words that Michael used, *know your triggers,* stuck in her head. She started her engine, backed out of the driveway and headed home without looking back.

Chapter Six

Silvia barged into Michael's office. "How could you not tell me that you were inviting me to some AA meeting?" she yelled.

"Silvia, you need to calm down . . . I told you that it was *not* an AA meeting and even if it was, why does that bother you so much? I remember you telling my friends years ago that you use to work for Alcoholic Anonymous," he said.

"Why did you invite me there?" she asked, disregarding everything else he said.

"Because I care about you and I am concerned about the path that you have chosen," he said, with loving-kindness. "It leads to destruction. I promise you, Silvia. That was not an AA meeting. It is a group that I've been blessed to facilitate and we focus on addictions. These are people who are recovering and going through their healing process."

"Well, why did you invite me there?" she asked. "I'm not an addict. There's not anything that I'm addicted to." Her tone was defensive.

"Are you sure about that?"

"I am positive. You continue to judge me, Michael . . . Why?"

"I am not judging you, Silvia. I am simply judging your actions. Your actions prove to me that you have a problem."

"What kind of problem do you possibly think that I have and how do you plan to cure me, Michael?" she asked sarcastically.

He ignored her sarcasm. His fingers intertwined on top of his desk as he looked at her. "Do you think you have a problem with sex, Silvia?"

Her demeanor changed. "What!" Shocked by his question, she was offended and embarrassed.

"The signs are apparent and I can clearly see that there is a problem. I know that this isn't you. I can see that you are in pain and I just want the best for you. You don't have to suffer through that pain. You are not in this alone."

Tears immediately formed in her eyes and she forced them to stay at bay. "Who are you supposed to be? You are not my counselor. You are my boss." She folded her arms in front of her chest. "But since you think that I have a problem, how do you plan to cure me, counselor?" Even though she tried to hide the hurt in her tone behind sarcasm, Michael could still hear it.

"I'm not just your boss. I am your friend . . . and no, I can't cure you, but I do know someone who can."

"Well, Michael, I think being my friend would be crossing the line. Remember? I would rather you leave me alone when it comes to my personal life. I don't need your meetings,'' she said, fighting back her tears.

"I invited you to the meeting because I thought it would be something that would have interested you, and maybe could have helped you.'' He waited a minute as he watched her reaction. "Did it help you, Silvia?''

A lone tear escaped her eye and she quickly wiped it away.

"No one can help you until you realize that you have a problem and that you need help. Even then, you have to want to be helped. I can see that you have been hurt, Silvia.'' He watched her for a moment. "May I ask you something?''

"What?"

"Do you care whether you live or die?''

His question paralyzed her and it felt like she couldn't breathe as she desperately tried to choke back her tears.

At that moment, Michael saw every bit of her pain in her eyes.

After seconds of silence, she shook her head and said, "Not really.''

"I believe deep down you do.'' He placed his folded hands up to his lips and studied her for a second. "You and your friend are welcome to come to those meetings anytime. You have an open invitation.''

She took a deep breath as she tried to fight back her tears. "I thought we were supposed to keep this strictly professional, so from now on, I would like to keep my personal life out of it. So, with that being said, everything is ready for tonight's meet and greet." She turned and left his office.

***

Silvia sat at the table and looked around at all the different business owners, male and female. She was trying to figure out which married man she was going to bring home with her tonight. She paid close attention to all of the ones who didn't have their wives with them. She could smell the ones who were cheaters. She always knew how to spot them.

Someone came up behind her and whispered in her ear, "You enjoying yourself tonight, honey?"

Silvia turned to see this attractive older man in his late-forties. "I am now, handsome," she replied. "How about you get me a drink and I can help you enjoy yourself." She winked at him and smiled.

"What kind of drink would you like?"

"With the days I've been having . . . anything strong."

Silvia watched him as he walked over to the bar. She rushed to the restroom trying to hurry so that she could be back before he returned with their drinks. She walked around the corner and bumped into someone. Drinks spilled everywhere.

Silvia looked down at her red and black tight-fitting Marc Jacobs designer dress that was now soaked. "Ugggh!" she grunted. "You . . ."

Interrupting her, "I'm so sorry, ma'am," the gentleman said to her as he looked down at her dress that allowed her cleavage to peep through.

She heard the voice and slowly looked up. *Oh, my God!* Her heart began to race.

"Are you okay?" he asked.

Silvia was speechless as she stared into his green eyes.

"Ma'am, are you okay?" he repeated.

"I . . . I . . . I'm okay," she stammered aloud, but inside she was screaming *Get the hell away from me!*

The man squinted his eyes. "You look very familiar," he said as he studied her. "Wait." He held the glass in his hand as he now pointed his finger. "You were the woman in the grocery store the other day . . . You looked as though you had seen a ghost." He chuckled, and then frowned at her reaction. "Are you sure that you are okay?"

She took a deep breath before saying, "I'm sorry . . . Yes, I'm fine." She exhaled. *Just keep breathing, Silvia.* She took time to inhale and exhale. "That day I did see a ghost." She chuckled nervously and continued, "A ghost from my past." She realized that this man had no idea who she was and she planned to keep it that way . . . for now.

He became curious. "What happened that day, if you don't mind my asking?"

"Oh," her hands brushing away his words, "you wouldn't want to know." She looked him up and down in his black Versace suit that was now covered with the liquor that wasted and she thought to herself, *Mmmm . . . Still sexy*, then she asked him, "So what are you doing here?" She was surprised at how calm she now was.

"Well, I own an oil company, so I'm here to do a little networking. I just recently moved back here with my wife and my daughter Jazmin about three weeks ago," he informed her.

"Is she here with you?" Silvia asked, looking around.

"Who? My wife? Yes, she's around here somewhere... I moved her here from Chicago and she hates it here. She says she hates it because she has no family here, but I believe it's because she has no friends here to shop with. You know how you women are." He chuckled. "Maybe I can introduce you to her and y'all can, you know, talk. Maybe you can show her around a bit . . . Then, maybe she won't be tripping on me all the time because she'll have someone to shop with." He chuckled again.

"I think that would be a great idea. I'll be happy to show her around and have some girl time," Silvia told him, but in her mind she had other plans.

A tall, beautiful, young looking model type walked up behind him. "Hey, babe, what are you doing over here?" she asked, hugging him around his waist while looking at Silvia with curiosity.

Silvia looked into the young woman's eyes which looked weary and sad as though she had been crying for days and was without sleep.

He handed the young woman the cup that still had a little liquor in it. "Well, I was just talking to this young lady," he said with his eyes fixed on Silvia. "I'm sorry, I didn't catch your name." He now reached his hand out to her.

Silvia hesitated before reaching her hand out to touch his. "Excuse me," she said before her hand could even touch his. She pushed past him and ran to the restroom. She deposited everything she ate, into the toilet. She walked to the sink and rinsed her face with cold water. "Calm down, Silvia. You can do this," she whispered to herself.

She walked out of the restroom hoping that she wouldn't see the man from her past for the rest of the night. She attempted to find the man who was supposed to be getting her a drink earlier. She couldn't find him anywhere, so she hunted for her next prey.

She sat at the bar and flirted with the young bartender who seemed to be in his early-twenties with his boyish looks, reminding her of Bow Wow. "What time is your break, baby boy?" she asked him.

He looked at his watch, then answered, "In about two minutes." He smiled.

Silvia leaned over the bar and traced his ear with her tongue before whispering, "Well, meet me in the ladies room in one."

He didn't know how serious she was, but he was willing to find out.

Silvia headed to the restroom and he watched her sashay her way there. She looked back at him and winked.

He waited until it was time for his break and he told his partner that he would be back. He walked into the women's restroom as if he was supposed to be there.

Silvia grabbed him by his collar and locked the door.

Surprised, he said, "Wow! You were serious."

She pulled him into the stall. "You say that like you didn't believe me." She began kissing him passionately. Then she whispered into his ear, "When I see something I want, I make sure I get it." She started unbuttoning his shirt.

Everything was going so fast and he couldn't believe it. He dropped his pants, raised her dress up and pressed her into the wall. She wrapped her legs around his waist and he began having sex with her. Silvia just wanted every thought to leave her mind as this young man pleased her. She continued to see the green eyes in her mind and she just wanted to remove the thought of him, far away from her memory.

After minutes, she could feel that the young man was about to finish. "No, keep going," she told him as she continued to try to shake the image of those green eyes from her mind. Normally she could drown out her thoughts during sex, but this time it wasn't working. "Keep going," she whispered into his ear. "Please, just keep going," she begged as she grabbed him tighter. Her moaning got louder as someone began banging on the door to get in. "Just keep going," she kept saying, but the young man began climaxing. Once he finished, she eased herself down and they stared at each other for a moment.

The young man stood in disbelief.

Tears formed in Silvia's eyes as she thought about the man with the green eyes. "I told you to keep going!" she yelled. She opened the stall door and left out, leaving him behind.

Silvia was about to leave the party, but then someone touched her arm. She knew that touch and it made her cringe.

"Hey, you sure you okay?" the man asked.

She turned and looked into a pair of concerned green eyes. "I'm fine," she said. She turned to walk away from him.

He grabbed her arm. "Look, I'm Robert Sterling and you are?" He waited for her to respond.

She looked down at his hand around her arm. "Silvia," she replied as she pulled away from his grasp.

"Well, Silvia, my wife's name is Carla, and this is our home number." He held a piece of paper out to her. "I know my wife and I know she misses her home. So, I figured that maybe you can help her make this home. You know? Make yourself friendly," he said, but it came out as more of a demand.

Silvia took the piece of paper and stared at it. She looked up at him for a minute and walked away without a word.

Chapter Seven

$\mathscr{K}$im and Michael were finishing up with one of their community meetings at the Family Life Center when Emmanuel Matthews, son of Pastor Matthews, came in. He walked up behind Michael. "Hey, Bro, how have you been?" he asked him.

Michael turned to face him and was shocked when he saw him. "Hey!" he exclaimed. "What is going on? It has been a minute! What are you doing home?" He embraced him.

"Man, they shut down the company that I was working for in New Orleans, so I moved back here after getting hired at Harvey's Remodeling Company. I had a great job offer in Shreveport and I believe it would have been a great place to be, but something was calling me to come back home. I tell you, man, it is great being back here. I feel like God brought me back here for a reason." He paused as he looked over at Kim who was picking up the papers that some people left behind. "Wow! Who is that?" he asked, captured by her.

When Michael saw the look in his eyes, he said, "Oh, my bad." He called Kim over.

Kim walked over to them with her red two-piece Jones Wear suit on, and Emmanuel thought that she looked classy, yet sexy in it. Her long beautiful black hair accentuated her Filipino facial features and he couldn't take his eyes off of her.

"Kim,'' Michael began. "This is Pastor Matthew's son, Emmanuel Matthews. Emmanuel, this is Kimbrailee Whitmore.''

Emmanuel reached out his hand to Kim, and she hesitated before reaching hers out to meet his. "Very nice to meet you,'' he said, slipping a peek at her ring finger.

Kim was stunned at how handsome this man was. "Nice to meet you as well.'' She let go of his hand and hurried back to what she was doing.

Emmanuel looked at his hand. Then said, "Wow, that's it?'' He asked this to Michael as if expecting to hold a conversation with her. "She is beautiful,'' he said, with his eyes now back on her as she picked up the rest of the papers from the tables.

Kim was taking her meds and she was looking and feeling better than she had ever felt in her life. She missed Trey, but she had moved on with her life and she was happy in the place she was. She had found a greater love, better than any man could ever give her. It was perfect love and that love came from God.

"Yeah, man, she is beautiful,'' Michael agreed. "Inside and out,'' he added.

"So, tell me about her. Is she married, because I didn't see a ring?''

"No, she's widowed," Michael informed him.

"What happened to her husband?"

"How about you have a conversation with her and ask her as many questions as you would like," Michael said to him. "So, where are you staying?" he asked, changing the subject.

"Oh, I found me a place over on Market Street. It is nice."

"Sounds great," Michael said. He saw how Kim held Emmanuel's attention as he continued to watch her. "Look, we will have another meeting at Central Park at noon tomorrow. How about you come, and then maybe you can get to know Kim a little better."

"Man, I wish I could, but I don't go to lunch until one-thirty on most days. I will try to push for noon though because I would really like to get to know her."

After Kim came over to say her goodbyes, Emmanuel watched her walk out the door.

"So, tell me, man. What has been going on since I left?" Emmanuel asked Michael.

"Well, I am engaged to the most beautiful woman I know." His smile lit up the room. "You remember Taylor Livingston, right?"

"Yeah, I remember her, but I thought she had gotten married to oh boy," pausing to think of his name, "yeah, Keith Davenport. That's his name. What, they got a divorce?"

"No, he passed away."

"Wow, he was pretty young. What happened to him?"

"Well, to be honest, Keith had found a place of peace. He had gotten to a great place in his life and the Lord called him home. He was ready." He thought for a minute and said, "I remember one of the last conversations we had. He was saying how at peace he was and how he was thankful that he made peace with God and everyone in his life. He was happy. He and Taylor did have two beautiful children together. They are my world!" He smiled at the thought of them.

"Wow . . . I remember you use to be in love with Taylor back in the day, but you never would say anything. You know a closed mouth don't get fed, you have not because you ask not," Emmanuel said to him. "The Word tells us ask and we shall receive. He will give us the desires of our hearts according to His will."

"You are definitely right about that, but I wasn't in love with her back then. She was always my friend and yes, I did love her with all my heart, as my *friend*, Emmanuel," he replied. He stood up a little straighter. "But now, I'm in love with her as my woman." He paused for a minute. "Seriously though, you are right. I've always been in love with her, but Keith beat me to asking her out and they ended up married. I will say that Keith needed her, and God joined them together for a reason. They were meant to be together at that time and for as long as they were married. Now, my plan is to keep her happy for the rest of her life and to love our babies. She was devastated when Keith died and we both miss him greatly. We all had gotten really close before he passed away. He had grown into a great man of God. He had touched the lives of so many people and I believe God was very pleased. Pleasing Him became Keith's desire. He wanted to please God in everything he did. I can imagine hearing the voice of God saying to him, 'Servant, well done.' I strongly believe that he fulfilled his purpose here on earth. We miss him a lot and I know I can't replace him, but I did promise him that I will always be there for his family and that's a promise that I refuse to break.''

"Well, congratulations, man. I wish you the very best,'' Emmanuel said.

"Thanks, man. I believe our marriage will be blessed beyond measure. We are doing things God's way in our relationship and I know God will honor that. Waiting is hard, but I know that she is well-worth it . . . Can't wait till our wedding night though.'' He chuckled.

***

Silvia was seated at her desk working on some floor plans when someone tapped on the door. Silvia invited them in without even looking up. She figured it was none other than Michael.

"I'm sorry. I'm looking for Michael Bradberry's office. I'm guessing this isn't it. Is it?'' the familiar voice asked.

Bespectacled, Silvia looked up from her work. *Ugggh! Why in hell do you keep showing up!*

"Hey, you! So this is where you work?'' Robert asked. "I thought the receptionist pointed me to this door, but I'm guessing this is not Michael's office.'' He chuckled.

Silvia didn't know what was funny. She glared at him, her face remained serious.

"But I'm glad I ran into you here. You ran from the party the other night like something was wrong." He looked at her closely and waited for a response, but he didn't get one. He continued, "Well, was something wrong?" he asked. Then, taken by her beauty, he said, "Wow, you look just as beautiful in glasses."

Silvia quickly removed the glasses from her face. Ignoring his last comment, she answered, "Nothing was wrong, and Michael's office is down the hall all the way to the end," desperately wanting him to leave her office. *Now, get out of my office before I sharpen this pencil and stab you in your throat.*

He walked in closer. "Actually, I would like to talk to you for a minute if that's okay."

She gave him a fake smile. *Okay, I am about to make your life a living hell if you don't leave out of my office right now.* She dropped her pencil down onto her desk with an attitude. "Okay, Mr. Sterling. What can I possibly do for you?" She leaned back in her seat and folded her arms across her chest. *Besides destroy your life like you did mine.*

"Well, being that I ran into you again, I feel like it's a sign," he began. "Like I was saying last night, my wife is not familiar with this place. As a matter of fact, right now, she is not that familiar with her life period." He hesitated. "You see, my wife just went through a devastating time . . . we lost our last child about three months ago and she is still going through that. My moving her here, away from her family and friends, didn't help with the situation." He rubbed his hands together attempting to hide his emotions. "She had a stillbirth, and it was an awful experience for her; for the both of us really. Ever since we buried our baby girl, Angel, Carla has not been the same."

Silvia's stomach immediately felt queasy. "Wait." She coughed, feeling as if she were choking on her saliva. "What did you say her name was?"

"Who, my wife, Carla?"

"No, the baby's name."

"Oh, Angel. I named her that because she was so beautiful, just like an angel. She was taken away too soon." He stared off into space. "She was so beautiful," he repeated as he remembered his baby girl's face.

"I'm sorry . . . Excuse me for a minute." Silvia covered her mouth as she scurried past him.

She headed straight for the restroom. *What is wrong with me?* "Get it together, Silvia," she told herself as she hung over the toilet, continuing to deposit her breakfast into it. She went to the sink, washed out her mouth, then rinsed her face.

Regina, the receptionist busted into the restroom like she had lost her mind. She stood at the sink, fixing her lipstick. "Girrrl, I sent that *fine* man to your office because I knew you were going to want to see him. He is one of the sexiest men who has ever stepped foot in this building, and he look like he got lots of money girl, in that Armani suit. So, did you get the digits, or did you already . . ."

Silvia angrily cut off her sentence. "You should not have sent him in there."

Regina looked confused. She had sent many men to Silvia's office because that was a part of their plan. Silvia and Regina go way back to their college days. She was her roommate, and they also worked at the Gentleman's Club together. Silvia was the one who got her hired as the receptionist for Bradberry and Co.

"What is wrong with you?" Regina asked. "*You* are the one who told me to send all the sexy men to *your* office. Remember?" She now studied her friend. "What's up with you, girl?" Regina was out of town the night that Silvia was raped, so she didn't know who Robert was or the reason behind her friend's strange behavior.

"Well don't send any more men into my office unless they are here to see me," Silvia snapped.

Regina just stood with her mouth open as she watched her friend storm out of the restroom.

When Silvia came back into her office she expected for Robert to be gone, but there he sat in the chair, anxiously awaiting her return.

When he saw her walk in, he stood. "Are you okay?" he asked.

"I'm fine, but I do have a lot of work to do so . . ."

He interrupted her, "Well, I won't keep you." He was about to leave out, but then he turned back around. "Look, Silvia, my wife could really use a friend. She's been stuck in the house, depressed, and I know that her mind is on the baby we lost. I had to beg her just to come with me to the party last night... She used to love to shop. I mean, really shop." He chuckled. "Maybe y'all could hang out and go shopping one day and I will make it worth your time." He paused. "You could shop on me."

Silvia's eyebrow arched perfectly as she took his words into consideration. She twisted her hair around her finger. "How much shopping you talking?"

"I will give you a thousand per visit. But look, my wife use to spend money like crazy and all I ask is that you try to talk her out of spending so much when you see her going overboard because I know her, and she will. I just want her to get out and have fun again."

"Well, I can definitely help her do that . . . We have a deal, Robert. Oh, I can call you Robert, right?" she asked as she got back into her, *destroy him* mode.

"Of course, you can. How about you meet us tonight, seven o'clock at Raymond's Restaurant for dinner on me? I will start your payment then," he said. "Look, you don't have to mention our deal to my wife." He walked closer. "Please?"

"Your secret is safe with me." Silvia winked at him and smiled at the thought of having this man's marriage in her hands. Her first mission was to destroy his family, but she wasn't planning to stop there. She was going to have fun with dragging his name through the dirt. The thought of revenge made her feel good, and she hadn't even gotten started. She concocted her plan in her head as she gave him a big smile.

"Thank you so much. You really don't know how much this means to me," he told her.

And you don't know how much you are going to regret this. "Oh, it will be my pleasure," she said. Her plan started playing in her head and her smile grew bigger.

***

Silvia walked into Raymond's Restaurant with a beautiful, short, tight-fitting red and black Prada dress on and every eye in the building was on her. When Robert saw her come in, he stood, so that she could see where their table was located. As he watched her walk closer, he thought she was absolutely gorgeous in her dress that complimented every one of her beautiful curves. He smiled when he saw that it was red and black. He figured those must be her favorite colors to wear, considering she wore the same colors when he met her at the meet and greet. Robert could not take his eyes off of her as she came closer to him. She, too, could not take her eyes off of him.

Robert had on an Armani suit, with a blue dress shirt underneath that captured Silvia's attention. She desperately wanted to undress him. He was so appealing to her and she desired to have him right there in the restaurant. Her eyes looked him from his head to his toes. *Silvia, this is the man who raped you, not someone you could just hook up with. He's the enemy so stay focused.* She tried to shake the thought of sleeping with him as she got closer to him with each step.

As she approached him, he saw just how stunning she looked. "Wow, you look amazing," he said, pulling out her seat. "Carla had to run to the restroom, but she should be back in a minute. How was your day?"

As if you care. "It was great." Silvia watched as he took the toddler out of her booster seat. "How old is she?"

"She just turned three and she's just as active as ever. She keeps her daddy busy." He looked at his daughter. "Don't you, girl?" He tickled her belly.

Jazmin giggled as she lay back in his arms. She played with his ear with one hand while twirling her long beautiful black hair around her finger. She was light-skinned with rosy cheeks. Her eyes were green and every one of her features resembled Robert's.

Silvia continued to watch the little girl in his arms, but she was distracted when she saw his wife, Carla, come to the table. *Wow, this woman had to have been a model. She is absolutely gorgeous. Oh, my God, that Vera Wang dress doesn't even serve her justice.*

Carla had on a beautiful blue Vera Wang dress and every piece of jewelry she had on, had beautiful diamonds that lit up the room.

Robert stood and kissed her. "Baby," he pulled out her chair, then pointed to Silvia, "this is Silvia. I asked her to join us for dinner. She works for Michael Bradberry, the gentleman we met last night. He's going to be designing our new building," he said.

Carla sat down in her seat. "Nice to meet you, Silvia," she said to her.

"Nice to meet you as well. Your husband has told me so much about you."

"Wow. That's interesting, considering he hasn't mentioned anything about you," Carla said sarcastically. She gave Robert a look of disdain. "At least I know he talks about me." She now looked at Silvia.

"Well," Silvia said. "He just told me that you are new in town and I figured that maybe I can show you around."

"Really?" she said with an attitude.

"Yes, really," Silvia responded right back with an attitude. *If you keep having an attitude with me, you are going to wish that you never met me. Oh, I forgot, you are going to wish that anyway, you . . .*

Silvia was pulled away from her thoughts when the waitress came over to take their orders.

"So, Silvia, tell us a little about yourself if you don't mind." Robert tried to strike up a conversation after the waitress left the table with their orders.

Silvia replied, "Well, there's not much to tell."

"I'm sure you have a lot to tell us about yourself," he said curiously.

You want me to tell you about me. Okay, I have been looking for you for more than twelve years and now, here you are. Believe it or not, I am your worst nightmare. Don't let this pretty girl look fool you. I have plans for you, papi. A fake smile plastered on her face. "Trust me. You don't want to know about me," she said to him coldly.

Robert looked at her and clenched his jaw from her response.

Silvia saw the anger in his eyes and she knew that he didn't appreciate her statement. "So, you tell me about yourself, Robert. Or are you afraid of people knowing who you really are?" she asked, and then after she caught the look on Carla's face she thought, *What in the hell am I doing? Get back right,*

Silvia. Now is not the time to trip out on him. Let's play this thing right. He'll have his time.

Carla looked at Robert to see his reaction to the words that Silvia had spoken, but his eyes remained on Silvia.

Silvia's demeanor changed after she realized the fact that she had a problem with him became obvious to them. She chuckled lightly. "Please, forgive me. I've had a really rough day," her tone now pleasant. "I don't know what I'm thinking. I can't take my bad day out on you all, huh?" She laughed. "Seriously, Robert, there's not much to tell about me. Being around me is getting to know me." She forced a smile.

The waitress brought over their meals and they ate in silence.

Silvia looked at the food on Carla's plate, most of it untouched. She could see the sadness in her eyes and she paid close attention to her and Robert. She could see that their marriage was already suffering, and she knew then that it wasn't going to take much for her to completely demolish it. Robert paid more attention to his baby girl than he did his own wife.

"So, Carla," Silvia began. "I can call you Carla, right?"

Carla nodded. Her long beautiful hair falling in her face, she pushed it away.

Silvia continued, "What do you do for a living and what do you like to do for fun?"

"Well, I use to be an exceptional accountant, but now I'm just a house wife who, according to my husband, loves money,'' Carla said, then looked over at Robert. "I love to spend money for fun. Right, honey?'' Her eyes were fixed on his eyes.

He looked at her, leaned forward, head cocked to the side, elbows on the table, one hand balled up into a fist with the other cupping it up to his lips. It was apparent that he didn't like her comment, but he remained silent.

"Great!'' Silvia exclaimed. "Me, too, maybe we can go shopping tomorrow.'' She now fixed her eyes on Robert's eyes before saying, "I *love* to shop.''

Robert smirked at her comment.

Silvia got Carla to open up a little more as the evening went on and she learned a lot about her. Carla had graduated top of her class and she had made partner with an accounting firm before getting pregnant with their second child. After talking for another fifteen minutes, they set up a day for Silvia to come pick her up to hang out.

Silvia's plan was in action. She made eye contact with Carla and smiled. Then she looked at Robert with his baby girl sitting on his lap without a care in the world, which made her think to herself, *You are going to wish that you never walked back into my life. I promise you that.* She smiled at the thought of him paying for what he did to her.

Robert looked up and his eyes met hers. Silvia looked away and his eyes began to study her. His green eyes roamed her body as he began to wonder why is it that he came to this woman and invited her into his life. Maybe it was for personal reasons of his own. Something about her intrigued him and deep down, he wanted to find out what that something was.

Carla looked up and saw her husband's eyes on Silvia and it made her curious to know what this dinner meeting was really all about. She sat and thought about the way that Silvia reacted to his question earlier and it made her question this dinner meeting even more.

"Hey, how about we hang out after this?" Robert said, interrupting his wife's thoughts.

Carla looked at her husband with question. "It's getting late, Robert, so maybe not."

"We can take Jazmin to spend the night with Naomi. She won't mind keeping her, I'm sure."

"Actually," Silvia began. "I think hanging out would be a great idea!" She looked at Carla. "It gives us the opportunity to really get to know each other better."

Carla looked at Robert with reservation. "I don't know about that, Robert. Like I said, it's getting late and look at Jaz, she's already sleepy." She watched as Jazmin lay in her father's arms, playing with his ear while drifting asleep with her thumb in her mouth.

He looked down at his daughter and pulled her thumb out of her mouth. He then looked back up at Carla. "Naomi wouldn't mind keeping her for us." He looked at his Emporio Armani watch. The short hand laid on the 8 and the long hand hovered over the 9. "And it's not that late."

Silvia watched as his lips continued to move. She was mesmerized by the shape of them and the way they moved. Unconsciously, she licked her lips. She wanted to feel his lips against hers.

"Let's just hang out tonight," he said. "We never do that anymore."

"Okay, fine." Carla rolled her eyes at him. "We'll hang out, but you make sure you call Naomi to ask her if she minds keeping Jazmin."

"Babe, you are wonderful." He leaned over and kissed her cheek, then reached in his pocket and pulled out his cell phone to call his neighbor, Naomi. She was his neighbor when he was a young boy living with his parents. Back then, she used to keep him and he trusted her more than anyone. She practically helped to raise him. When he was a child, her home was like his safe haven whenever his home wasn't safe. When he got ready to move back home, he was thankful that she was still alive and living next door to his childhood home.

After dropping Jazmin off to Naomi, Robert, Carla and Silvia walked into Fonzo's Pool Hall a little after nine o'clock. All eyes were on Robert and Carla, and the people looked at them as if they didn't belong there.

Robert looked around the place, not really feeling the environment. Tobacco smoke filled the room and he felt as if he wanted to choke.

Carla clutched her purse tighter as she looked at all of the tatted up men. She grabbed Robert's arm tightly and whispered into his ear, "What kind of place is this? I don't like it and I want to go home."

"Just relax, Carla." He kissed her forehead. He looked at Silvia who was absolutely comfortable in the setting. "Silvia, what made you decide to come here?"

"Well," Silvia began. "You two need to stop being so uptight and enjoy life *and.*" She paused and winked at him. "This is where I like to enjoy mine . . . You'll like it." She walked towards the wall.

Robert watched her walk away. He looked at her legs in the short dress she wore.

Silvia grabbed a pool stick from the rack on the wall and walked over to one of the available pool tables. Looking back at Robert and Carla, she said, "Come on. Let's play." She racked the balls.

"I can't play," Carla stated.

"Well, let me teach you," Robert said. He took off his suit jacket and laid it on one of the chairs beside him, and then walked over to the wall and grabbed two pool sticks from the rack. He brought them back and handed one to her.

Carla took it from him with her pointer finger and her thumb, looking at it as if it were nasty. She scrunched up her nose. "Don't we need to clean it off?"

Robert chuckled. "No, just wash your hands when we are finished playing."

Silvia looked back at them after racking the balls and she did a double take of Robert in his blue dress shirt. She tried to control her thoughts. "So, you ready to play?" she asked, with her eyes on him.

"Most definitely," Robert responded. He took Carla by the hand and walked over to the table. He fixed the Cue ball on the table and looked at Carla.

Carla then leaned over the table.

Robert leaned over behind her, now touching her. "This is all you have to do, baby." He slid the pool stick through his and her fingers that intertwined with each other. He drove the stick into the ball, knocking five stripe-colored balls and two solid-colored balls into three different holes.

Carla laughed. "Wow!" she said surprised. "You are pretty good."

Robert tried to kiss her.

She gently pushed him away. "No, Robert," she whispered to him.

He wanted her to show him some kind of affection, but instead he felt her coldness.

Silvia stood and watched them with her arms folded across her chest. Her eyes filled with fury as a smirk planted on her face. She then placed her hand on her hip as she scowled. *I can't wait to repay you, you bastard.* She walked around to the opposite side of the table, now facing them. She cleared her throat and pouted her lips, "Awww . . . now that's no fair," she whined. "So I guess you are stripes and I am solids?" She positioned herself over the pool table, hiking up her already short dress. She leaned over a little more. Her cleavage was now fully exposed, capturing Robert's full attention. She glided the stick between her fingers and focused her attention on the ball, but her eyes then fell upon Robert's manhood. She hit the ball just enough to make it hike up off the table, missing his manhood by a mere inch. It fell to the floor, almost hitting his shoe. She slowly looked up, her eyes meeting his. "Oops! My bad." She laughed.

Robert glared at her, trying to figure out if she purposely hit the ball towards him.

She stood up with her eyes still on his. Her smile disappeared. "Maybe you should teach *me* before I hurt somebody."

Robert continued looking at her. "Well, I'll let you try that again." He spoke calmly, trying not to show his anger. He picked up the ball from the floor and placed it perfectly on the table.

Carla said, "I really need to go to the restroom." She looked at Silvia. "Where is it?"

Without a word, Silvia pointed towards the sign that read *Restrooms*, and Carla followed in the direction she pointed.

Once Carla disappeared from her sight, she slowly walked over to Robert and grabbed his hand. "I really want you to show me how to hit all the balls into the holes." She let go of his hand, leaned over the table and positioned her pool stick in between her fingers, sliding it slowly.

Robert looked at her ample behind and inhaled deeply.

"Well." She stayed in position as she turned her head slightly to look back at him. "Are you going to show me how to play, papi?"

He slowly walked up behind her, his manhood now touching her butt.

She turned her head, now focusing her eyes on the ball in front of her. She smiled as she felt his manhood come to life on her behind.

He leaned over her, now placing his hand over hers, but to his surprise she pushed her butt up against him even more, making him feel uncomfortable. He stood up straight and backed away.

"What is it, Robert? I just want to learn how to play the game," she said innocently, but her face showed no innocence at all as she stayed in her same position, staring back at him.

He tried it once again. He gently placed his hand on top of hers as he leaned over her.

She turned her head to the side now catching his eyes closely. His green eyes pierced hers, and she had a desire to kiss him. *Silvia, do not kiss this man,* she thought as she tried to control herself.

He leaned in closer to Silvia, and that's when they heard Carla clear her throat.

Silvia was thankful for this interruption that caused them to put a halt to what was about to happen between them.

Carla stood with her shoulders back and her arms folded across her chest. She cocked her head to the side. "Am I interrupting something?"

"No," Robert quickly said. "I was just showing her how she needs to hit the ball." He realized that he was still leaning over Silvia and he quickly stood up straight.

"It looked to be a little bit more than that," Carla replied.

Well, it sure felt like more than that. Silvia looked down at the bulge in his pants and remembered how it felt up against her. She chuckled lightly and looked at Carla. "Don't be silly. He was just teaching me the game."

"Really?" Carla replied.

"Yes," Silvia said, grabbing Carla's hand. "Now come on. Let's play," her tone jovial.

They played until one o'clock in the morning. Carla caught her husband's eyes on Silvia a few more times, which really made her uncomfortable about him interacting with her, but when they got ready to end their night, she still agreed to go shopping with Silvia the next day.

Robert and Carla walked into their dark and quiet home. She ascended up the stairs without a word spoken to him.

He walked into their bedroom and watched her for a minute as she undressed. He walked up behind her and wrapped his arms around her waist. "Hey, you." He kissed her neck softly. "You looked so beautiful tonight," he said, then attempted to kiss her lips.

Carla turned her head and his lips fell on her cheek instead.

He sighed. "What's wrong, Carla?"

"Why did you invite her to dinner?" she asked with an attitude. "And then we go out with her to that ridiculous place."

"I invited her because you don't have any friends here and I figured that it would be nice for you two to meet," he said. "And the place wasn't that bad. We had fun, Carla."

"Who is she, Robert? I saw the way you looked at her and the way she interacted with you." She abruptly turned to face him. "Are you two having an affair? Is that why she looked at you like that when she saw you in the grocery store that day?"

"Whoa, whoa, whoa! I just really met her at the meet and greet. I am not having an affair. I have never cheated on you, Carla. So, where is this coming from?"

"Something just isn't right about her. The way she said some things and the way she looked at you," she paused and looked at him closely, "as if she knows you." She shook her head as if shaking away her thoughts. "Maybe it's just me."

"I promise you that she didn't know me before tonight. We never knew each other and there's no affair. You are the only woman that I want, babe." He now kissed her lips. "You know that." He slipped her under garment strap away from her shoulder, then kissed her collar bone.

She sighed deeply and rolled her eyes. "Not tonight, Robert." Knowing where his mind was, she walked away.

"If not tonight, when? Carla, we haven't had sex since..."

"Don't you dare say it," she scolded. She knew he was about to refer to her stillbirth.

"I'm sorry, Carla, but I need you."

In silence, she went to the bathroom and grabbed the glass that sat on the sink. She rinsed it out, filled it with cold water from the faucet and came back into the room.

Robert watched her in silence as she put her glass down on the nightstand.

She opened the drawer and pulled her prescription bottle from it. She sat the bottle down next to her glass and slipped on her night gown that Robert laid out for her on the bed. She sat down on the bed and opened her bottle of Zoloft, poured two pills into her hand, grabbing her glass of water. She threw the pills to the back of her throat and chased them with the water. She put the glass of water back on the nightstand and looked at Robert. "I probably need to double up because I have been forgetting to take them." She was about to empty more pills into the palm of her hand.

Robert quickly grabbed the bottle from her hand. "No, just start taking them properly in the morning." He placed her pills in his nightstand drawer, and then softly kissed her lips. "I want to make love to you tonight."

Carla stood up, pulled back the satin sheets, got in the bed and covered up. "Maybe tomorrow night, Robert. I'm just so tired tonight."

He released a long drawn out sigh, showing that he was just as tired, not physically, but mentally. "I'm your husband, yet you always turn me away. Just tell me, why?"

"You know how I feel about that, so therefore you know why, Robert. Now I said, not tonight."

"Okay, that's fine. Not tonight," he said, without any further protest.

He went to the bathroom and turned on the shower. He removed his clothes and hopped in after waiting for the water to warm up. He soaped up his towel and began washing himself and that's when Silvia invaded his mind . . .

Silvia stood in front of him and allowed the water to run over her body as he watched. He kissed her deeply as his hands began to explore every inch of her body. He then ran his fingers through her wet hair. As they continued to kiss, the taste of her tongue was familiar to him.

"I know you want me, Robert. You can't deny that," she whispered, and then licked his lips. She gently kissed them.

His eyes stared into hers and she stopped kissing him for the moment. Staring back into his eyes, she ran her leg up his until it reached his waistline. He ran his hand up her leg to her thigh, then picked her up as she now wrapped her other leg around him. He kissed her once again.

"What are you waiting for, Robert? You've done this before," she whispered in a seductive tone, kissing his lips again.

He kissed her deeply and stopped. He felt something touching his foot and he looked down. That's when he saw the snake on the shower floor . . .

He shook away his thoughts after feeling the water turn ice cold on his body. He quickly rinsed away the soap and got out of the shower. He grabbed his towel and dried off as he tried to shake Silvia from his imagination. *What the hell? I cannot be having these kinds of thoughts about this woman . . . And that snake. What the hell was that about?* He leaned up against the wall and sighed. He thought about his image of Silvia in the shower with him once again and shook his head. *That felt so real.*

Carla turned and looked at him when she heard the bathroom door creak open. "Seems as though that was the longest shower you've ever taken," she said to him.

"Yeah . . . I got lost in there." He put on his pajama pants and got in bed.

"Yes, but how long have you been lost?"

He looked at her, taken aback by her question. "What?"

"I feel as though, I'm losing you, Robert. Or have I already lost you to someone else?"

"No, baby, you haven't lost me. I love you."

"I love you, too, but I feel like something is missing here." She grabbed his hand. "I want to be intimate with you, Robert. I just don't know how to be."

"I understand. You've been through a lot." He gently pulled his hand away from her grasp, then reached and turned off the lamp. He kissed her cheek and rolled over to his side, his back to her.

Carla could feel his coldness. She buried herself underneath the sheets and her mind began to wonder. *Will this marriage ever get better?* Her tears ran down her face.

Robert tried his best to understand his wife, but he didn't. He needed that intimacy from her and their marriage had been suffering because of that. He closed his eyes, hoping to get some rest. He lay there and Silvia began to invade his mind once again. He wondered how it would feel to be with her intimately. After tossing and turning and trying to push away his thoughts, he fell asleep, but that didn't stop Silvia's presence from surrounding him in his dreams.

Chapter Eight

$\mathcal{K}$im had just finished speaking at her meeting at the Community Center and she and Michael had begun cleaning up. Emmanuel walked in with flowers in his hand. "I'm sorry. Did I miss the whole meeting? I guess I shouldn't have stopped to get flowers." He chuckled. He walked over and handed the flowers to Kim.

"Wow! Why am I getting flowers?" she asked, then smelled them. "They are beautiful!"

"Well, I believe you are a beautiful woman and you deserve beautiful flowers. I know that I don't know you, but let me take you to dinner tonight so that I can get to know you," he said to her.

Michael looked at the both of them and smiled. He was happy that Emmanuel was interested in Kim. He knew that Emmanuel was a great guy without all the foolishness that Kim was use to.

"I don't know what to say," she began. "Nobody has ever come to me like this, so excuse me. This is a little different and I must say, unexpected.'' Her smile quickly faded. "I have so much going on right now, and I don't know about dinner.''

"Well, dinner just one time, and you can kick me to the curb after that. Give me a chance to get to know you. I see how beautiful you are on the outside. Let me at least see how beautiful your mind and heart is,'' Emmanuel responded.

She hesitated for a minute as she gave it some thought. "Okay, tonight then.''

They exchanged information and set up a time and a place to meet. Kim found Emmanuel very attractive but she was not really willing to date at this point in her life. She had dated a few men a while after Trey died, but none of them stuck around after she told them that she had AIDS. They always said the same thing. They said that it didn't matter, but in reality, to them it did. She expected the same results from Emmanuel, but since he asked, she was willing to give him the opportunity to get to know her.

***

Silvia walked into the Sterling's home a little after five o'clock. *Wow! This man must really be banking*, she thought to herself as she looked around their three story mansion. She saw an exquisite piece of art that really caught her attention. They had so many beautiful, extravagant, and expensive sculptures and pictures that it was almost unreal. Their home was absolutely beautiful. Robert walked through the front door and she watched him head straight into the kitchen.

He shrugged his suit jacket from his shoulders and laid it on the back of the barstool, then loosened his tie. He walked over to the sink and grabbed a glass from the cabinet, then pulled out a bottle of vodka.

Silvia watched him as he looked at the bottle for a while. It was as if he was contemplating pouring a drink. He then put the bottle back into the cabinet without even opening it.

He looked into the living room and realized that Silvia had been sitting there the whole time. "Hey, you, I didn't realize you two were meeting up today," he said.

She changed her posture, attempting to make it seem as though she hadn't been watching him. She replied, "Yes, I was waiting on Carla." Her eyes couldn't believe how handsome this man was.

He stared at her for a moment. "Okay, so where are you girls going to hang out at today?"

"Daddy!" His daughter interrupted as she ran over to him. He picked her up into his arms.

His attention was immediately taken away from Silvia and was now on her. "Hey, baby girl. How was your day? Did you have a lot of fun in day care?"

"Yes, lots, daddy!" she exclaimed.

"Did you miss your daddy, because daddy sure missed you, baby girl." He hugged her tightly.

Jazmin giggled and nodded.

Silvia listened to him and watched him with his daughter. She wondered why Jazmin was in day care if Carla didn't work.

A golden retriever came in barking and ran over to Silvia. "Oh, my God! I hate dogs!'' she screamed, as she put her feet up on their couch.

"It's okay. He won't bite,'' Robert said to her in a calm voice.

"I don't care. Just get it away!''

"Okay, okay.'' He put up his hands and called to the dog, "Come here, Max.'' Max ran over to him and he kneeled down to pet him. He looked up at Silvia. "I'm sorry. He's a really good dog. He wasn't going to hurt you,'' he assured her. The frightened look on her face caught him off guard. "You look beautiful even when you are scared." He didn't mean to speak those words out loudly, but realized that he couldn't take them back.

Silvia caught herself blushing from his words, then she got angry at the fact that he made her blush.

"Come on, Max. Let's go outside,'' he said, looking at Silvia one last time.

Silvia watched Robert as he walked the dog outside with his daughter in his arms, playing with his nose. He laughed, then put her down and began chasing her around the back yard. She continued to watch him through the glass doors. *God, that man is beautiful.* After minutes passed, she shook her head, realizing that her attention was on him for too long. *What the hell is wrong with me? I am not supposed to want him!* She then saw Carla come down the stairs, and she was thankful that her presence pulled her away from her thoughts.

"I'll be ready in a moment," Carla said to her before she walked out the back door to speak with her husband.

Silvia watched her as she spoke with Robert, and she paid attention to how they interacted with one another. He barely paid her any attention as he continued to play with their daughter. He stopped and reached into his pocket and pulled out his wallet. He took out his credit card and gave it to her. She smiled and walked away, not even acknowledging their daughter.

Carla walked in the door and smiled. "Ready?" she asked, waving the credit card in the air.

"Most definitely!" Silvia said without hesitation. She stood up and they headed to the car.

The first few minutes of the car ride were silent, almost awkward.

"Well, your family seems nice," Silvia said to her, trying to start up a conversation to see where her marriage really stood.

"Well, thanks. Robert is a great father," Carla replied.

"What about husband? Is he a great husband?" Silvia pried.

"Well, we've had our ups and downs, and it has been difficult. Robert use to treat me like a queen before our daughter was born. Then it was all about the baby, which is fine. He's a great dad, but sometimes I need my husband back." Her face saddened even more. "Losing our last baby has been difficult." She shook her head. "Giving birth to a dead baby was more painful than anyone could ever imagine. He says that I have changed and that it is pushing him away, but I don't know what to do anymore. I can't get rid of the image of holding my dead baby girl in my arms and the idea of her never waking up. My psychiatrist prescribed me anti-depressants, but I don't know how much they are helping. I still feel so lost . . . and scared.'' She stared out of the window.

"I'm sorry for your loss, Carla, but your husband should understand. He should be there for you, and not being there for you isn't fair. He's selfish and you deserve better. He needs to understand your pain and not only that, I notice that it seems as if he is just trying to buy you. He acts like he can just hand you that credit card and you'll be okay.'' Silvia touched her hand but continued to look at the road. "I say that you should go buy out the store and teach him a valuable lesson. Money is not going to solve the problem between you two, and he needs to know that.''

"I don't know; me spending money only causes more problems between us. In the beginning of our marriage, money almost split us up because he said I was spending way too much. I don't understand what the big deal is because he has money for years and years to come. He owns an oil company that his dad left to him, and not only that, he's heir to millions. I come from money myself, so it's not like I needed his, but I wasn't going to marry a broke man either.'' She looked at Silvia. "You see Robert called me money hungry one time and it hurt my feelings; but to be honest, he was right. I think that's why it hurt so much. I love money. That's why I chose the field that I went into,'' she admitted. "Maybe I shouldn't shop today. I know me and I know my husband . . . Just take me back home.''

"No, you should shop. You will feel better and you deserve a real shopping spree,'' Silvia said as they pulled into the parking lot of Marriot Mall, one of the largest malls in Baton Rouge. "Come on, let's buy whatever you want. Take charge again, Carla. Robert doesn't run you and it's time for him to understand that."

Silvia and Carla got in the store, and Silvia realized that Robert was not lying. *Ole girl can shop*, she thought to herself. Carla bought so much stuff Silvia thought that when she got to the checkout line she was going to max out the card. She bought and bought and bought, and Silvia wasn't about to stop her like Robert had asked her to. She knew exactly what she was doing, and Carla was going to make it easier than she thought.

Day1. Silvia smiled, knowing that her plan was in action.

They shopped and shopped and shopped as if there was no such thing as running out of money. Silvia found herself having fun with Carla as they shopped and talked over dinner.

She pulled up into Carla's driveway. "Give me your receipts," Silvia demanded as she held out her hand.

Carla looked at her strangely. "Why?"

"Trust me. You don't want him to find the receipts. When he asks you what you spent, just say that you are not for sure. Then act like you are looking for the receipts, and then say you must have lost them or that you will give them to him later," Silvia suggested. "Remember what I told you, take charge. How old are you, Carla?"

"Twenty-nine. Why?"

"That's right. You are a grown woman. Act like it. This man doesn't run anything. Give me the receipts,'' Silvia demanded as she held out her hand. *Twenty-nine! Really? You are at least ten years younger than him. What the hell is he doing with you anyway?* Silvia thought to herself while waiting for Carla to hand her the receipts. She knew that Carla was young, but she wasn't expecting her to be that young.

Carla reluctantly handed Silvia the receipts. "Okay, what happens when he looks at the bills?''

"You check the mail every day and get it first. Then you write a check to pay them. You said for yourself that he has a lot of money.'' Silvia waved her hand in the air. "He won't even miss it.'' She put the receipts in the glove compartment.

"I am the one who writes out the checks for the bills anyway but he makes sure that he checks behind me. He's always checking his accounts or shall I say *our* accounts. He allows me to work our finances because he won't let me work in the corporate world anymore. That's his way of making me feel important, like I'm doing something.''

"What do you mean, *let* you work?''

"After the stillbirth, he thought that it would be best if I stayed at home.''

"That sounds like that control stuff again.''

They got out of the car and took all of the bags into the house.

Robert was standing at the refrigerator when he heard them walk in. He turned around and walked over to the counter, setting down his glass. "Wow, that seems like a lot of stuff," he said to Carla as he looked at Silvia. Silvia already knew why he looked at her the way he did. He walked over and grabbed some of the bags from Carla's hands.

Carla kissed his lips. "Well, honey, it was all on sale. I didn't spend much at all. Trust me." She headed upstairs with the bags she had left in her hand.

Robert watched his wife ascend up the stairs, and then he looked at Silvia. "I thought I asked you to look out for her," he whispered loudly. "Looks like she went overboard to me." He put down the bags, got out his check book and wrote Silvia a check for a thousand dollars.

"Well, I couldn't control her. I told her to take it easy, but once she started, she wouldn't stop," she lied. She reached for her check as she closed in the space between them. "I bet once you start, you won't stop." Her voice turned cold when she added, "Even if I begged you to." She thought about when she begged him to stop twelve years ago. Silvia glared at him and the fury in her eyes burned a hole right through him.

He looked confused as he backed away from her. "What?"

She walked closer to him. "Do I make you nervous, papi?" Her lips curved up into the coldest smirk he'd ever seen.

"What?" he asked again, not knowing how to respond to her.

She snatched the check from his hands. "Nothing. Nothing at all." She looked at the check. "Thanks a lot." She sashayed to the door, and his eyes couldn't help but watch her until she disappeared out of his sight.

He stood there for a minute having intimate thoughts about her and sighed. *Man, I have got to shake these thoughts.*

Carla came in, interrupting those thoughts. "Hey, babe, you were so right. Hanging out with her was so much fun! I really enjoyed myself." She smiled.

"I'm so glad that you enjoyed yourself!" He was so happy to see her smiling, but then his mind went right back to Silvia and the way her hips swayed on her way out the door.

"Silvia is such a sweetheart. I'm glad you thought to invite her to dinner the other night. Now I know what you were doing." She kissed his lips. "Thank you so much!" She gazed deeply into his eyes.

"How much do you thank me?"

"This much." She took his hand and led him upstairs to their bedroom.

She closed the door and kissed him passionately. He began undressing her, kissing her neck softly.

She stopped him. "Wait."

"Wait, what?" he asked, now frustrated because he knew where it was going.

"I can't do this."

Robert released an exasperated sigh. "Do what, Carla?"

"Have sex with you. I thought that I could, but I can't."

"Are you serious!" he yelled. "I am your husband, but you can't have sex with me?" He shook his head. "I'm really getting tired of this!"

"Getting tired of what? Me? Or being my husband?"

"No! I'm getting tired of not being able to make love to my wife!"

"Okay . . . Okay, I get it." She did not want to disappoint him. "Let's have sex. Let's just do it," she said, as the tears welled in her eyes.

"No . . . I don't want you to want to *do it* for me. I want you to do it because you want to." He walked away.

She gently grabbed his hand. "I want to . . . for me," she said, then kissed his lips, "for us."

He kissed her passionately, and he removed the rest of her clothes and his. He began making love to his wife, but in his mind he was making love to Silvia. With his tempo picking up a bit, she began backing away from him.

"Just hold still, Carla," he said as he held her down.

"Robert!" she yelled. "This hurts," she groaned.

He ignored her outcry.

"Robert," she called out to him again. "You are hurting me." She tried to push him away.

He stopped and looked at her. He got up and went to the bathroom, slamming the door behind him.

She got up and followed. She burst through the door. "I'm sorry."

"No, don't be!" he said. He was angry and it showed.

Carla walked out and went and sat on the bed as she cried. She knew it wouldn't be long before her husband would want to leave her, and she was fearful of that thought.

Robert ran the shower water and hopped in. His mind reverted to Silvia, and he tried to shake the inappropriate thoughts that he was having of a woman who didn't belong to him. After having those intimate thoughts about her, he knew then that he would not ever be able to be alone with her without giving into the strong desire that he has for her.

***

Kim walked into Raymond's, and Emmanuel met her at the door.

"Wow, you are so gorgeous!" he told her as they walked to their table.

"Thank you! You look amazing," she said, taking in his beautiful features.

They took their seats as a waitress came to take their orders.

When the waitress walked away from their table, Emmanuel looked at Kim. "I see you conduct a lot of meetings in the communities. So, what is it that you really do?" he asked.

"Well, I'm a paralegal," she said, trying to steer away from the rest of the question.

"So, you hold community meetings about legal work?"

"What is it that *you* do, Emmanuel?" she asked, changing the focus from herself to him.

"Construction work, but I'm behind the desk, not in the heat." He chuckled. "So, tell me about yourself, your dreams, your hopes and your aspirations. Do you have any children? Are you saved? And you know . . . the works. I want to know all about the person behind that beautiful face."

Kim smiled at his kind words. "Yes, I am saved and I have a son." She hesitated. "My dreams and aspirations are to build up people and to make a difference in the lives of others... It's just that simple," she said. Her smile told him that she enjoyed making a difference, but he noticed that when he looked into her eyes, she looked away. That showed him her reservation.

He heard the shyness in her voice and saw the fear in her eyes. "Look, I'm not like these other men that you may be use to, so you don't have to be afraid to talk to me." He raised her head and once again his eyes met hers. "You are truly beautiful."

She smiled.

The waitress served their food.

Emmanuel and Kim held hands and he said grace. They ate and enjoyed each other's company. He made Kim laugh a lot and he made her feel safe. He paid attention to every detail when it came to her. They talked about the grace of God and about his family. They finished the rest of their meals and sat and talked some more. Emmanuel saw that it was getting very late, and the restaurant was preparing to close.

They walked out of the restaurant and when they got to her car, she turned to face him. "Look, I know you asked about the community meetings earlier." She hesitated before adding, "Well, to be honest with you, I travel around the country and bring awareness to different communities about . . . HIV/AIDS." She now looked him in his eyes. "I have AIDS."

"Okay, so you travel the country and tell your story in order to help someone else. That takes courage. So, now, I really know that I'm dealing with an amazing woman, not just a beautiful one." He smiled and kissed her cheek. "I would love to see you again."

His reaction surprised her and his statement threw her off guard. "What?"

"I would love to see you again. I mean, if that is okay with you."

She choked on her words for a second. "Yes, I would like that. I would like that very much."

He hugged her and opened her car door for her. "Promise to call me to let me know you made it home safely." He lifted her hand and kissed the back of it. "Please," he added.

She promised and they went their separate ways.

Chapter Nine

Carla put Jazmin to bed. Then she and Silvia sat in the living room eating ice cream while watching *Love Jones*. Carla started feeling better as she began to hang out more with Silvia. She felt like she had found a friend, someone to talk to; and she talked to her about almost everything. She talked about how sex with Robert was painful and how she never really wanted children, but how she fell in love with Jazmin.

There were so many things she shared with Silvia. She began to feel close to her and got very comfortable. She didn't share *all* of her secrets; but most of them, she did. Carla had called her over to stay with her for the weekend while Robert was out of town; but she had no idea that Robert had already asked Silvia to stay with her for an extra two-thousand dollars. Silvia was planning to enjoy this.

Silvia watched as Carla laughed at certain parts of the movie, and when Larenz Tate was doing his poetic flow on stage, she laughed so hard when he said, "I'm the blues in your left thigh trying to become the funk in your right . . . Is that all right?" She thought that Carla was beautiful especially when she smiled. She looked at her beautiful flawless chocolate-colored skin. Then she looked at the pictures on the table of Carla in her wedding dress with her handsome husband standing beside her in his tux. They looked so happy on those pictures, but she was going to make sure that they would never be that way again.

Carla looked over at Silvia and caught her staring at her. "What?'' she asked.

Silvia leaned over and kissed her and she kissed her back. Then Carla pushed her away after realizing what was happening.

"What was that?'' Carla asked, now confused.

"I'm sorry. I just find you attractive,'' Silvia said.

"But I'm a woman, and I'm not into women.''

"Well, it was hard for me to tell just then. You were into that kiss just as much as I was.''

Carla now had an attitude as she folded her arms across her chest. "I'm sorry. Do you need to leave?''

"You don't want me to leave and you know it. You invited me over because you didn't want to be alone with your husband being out of town on business and all. He's probably not even out of town on business. You know how men lie.'' Silvia kissed her again, and she noticed how uncomfortable she was. "Just relax, Carla. Whatever happens will be between us. Trust me.'' She continued to kiss Carla.

Silvia had a difficult time getting her to feel comfortable at the moment, but she was finally able to introduce her to a new experience, but Carla had no idea that she had set up a camera while she was upstairs putting Jazmin to bed. She was now on video committing adultery even if it was with another woman. Her plan was for Robert to find it later and she was going to enjoy watching their marriage fall apart. Silvia spent the rest of the night with Carla, and Carla enjoyed her company.

***

Robert was back from his out of town business meeting. When he walked in his front door, he saw Silvia on the couch wrapped in a blanket. "How did it go?" he asked. He went to the kitchen to grab a bottle of water.

Silvia got up and walked over to him. Staring at him coldly, she folded her arms across her chest. "Oh, I took really good care of her just for you," she told him. She shot him the most evil look as she got closer to him.

He studied her. "Are you okay, Silvia? Sometimes the way you look at me makes me think that you are not very fond of me." He chuckled, but he was serious about his comment.

"No, you are good people, right? Unless you have something that you are hiding, a well-kept secret maybe."

"What? Silvia, what are you talking about?" he asked confused. He started to wonder if she could possibly be crazy. He lost focus when his eyes fell upon the red lingerie she wore. The split in it met her mid-thigh, and it caught his full attention as her thigh peeked through. Then his eyes traced back up to her cleavage that showed.

After seeing the hunger in his eyes as his eyes landed on her breast, she took one step back, making sure that he got a really good look at her. "You like what you see, Robert?" She scowled.

"What?" He now looked into her eyes.

"Your wife is sweet, but I don't know. She may still need to go through some counseling. You know, with the dead baby and all."

Robert took two quick steps toward her and grabbed her arm. "Don't you ever speak of my child that way!" he yelled. "What the hell is wrong with you? Are you crazy?" His tone revealed every bit of his anger.

She looked at his hand around her arm. Then she looked back up at him. "I bet you like it rough, huh, Robert? You like to take what you want?"

He frowned. "What?"

Her face showed her scorn.

Carla walked into the kitchen. "What is going on?" she asked. She looked at Silvia, then at him.

He released Silvia's arm from his grip. "Nothing. Where's Jazmin?"

"Playing in her room," Carla responded.

Robert walked past his wife without even acknowledging her.

Carla looked at Silvia. "Did you tell him?"

"Nope."

"Well, what was that about?"

"I don't know. He must have had a rough trip. Maybe the mistress didn't give him what he wanted."

"What?"

"Don't worry about it." Silvia kissed her lips.

Carla pushed her away. "Silvia, please don't do that again. I made a mistake the other night, and what happened between us won't happen again. I love my husband."

Silvia wiped the corners of her lips with her pointer finger and thumb. "Okay, but does he love you? I bet he doesn't love anyone but himself," she said, and went to the guestroom to get her things.

As soon as Silvia left the Sterling's, her phone rang. She answered and Robert's voice was on the other end. "Look, Silvia, I'm sorry for grabbing you, but I kind of snapped when you had mentioned." He paused. "Well, you know . . . I'm sorry and I don't want our deal to end. Carla has been so much better since you have been coming around and she really enjoys your company . . . Are you okay?"

"I'm fine and don't worry. We still have our deal," she said.

He could still hear the coldness in her tone. "Are *we* okay?" he asked. He wasn't sure why, but for some reason, he didn't want her to be upset with him.

"We are fine, Robert. Just don't ever touch me again, and you'll be fine," she said, and hung up the phone.

Robert looked at the phone as it went dead. He placed it down on the counter and sighed. He didn't understand why he wanted to keep her around, but he knew that it wasn't just for his wife's benefits, but for benefits of his own. She had not only spent time with Carla, but she spent time with her while being around him, and he also enjoyed her company.

**

Silvia went over to Reesie's house and Regina was there along with two of Brandon's friends, Austin and Dameon. They had been smoking marijuana and were extremely high. Silvia was happy that she had made it there after they were through smoking because marijuana wasn't her thing.

Brandon and his boys were at the table with their latex gloves on as they weighed and bagged dope. Lil Wayne, Eminem and Ludacris' voices bled through the speakers as they rapped "Breaking Down." It was so loud that Silvia had to cover her ears at one point.

Dameon threw Brandon a bag of cocaine.

Brandon tossed it around in his hand, and said, "Hey!" He threw the bag back to him. "Put that back on the scale and check that weight. I want to see something." He looked at him intensely. Brandon knew that it felt lighter than it should feel.

"What? You don't trust me, Brandon? I weighed it and it's good, man," Dameon said, throwing it back to him.

Brandon threw it back to him and looked him dead in his eyes as if warning him that he had better make it right. "Weigh it again," he said firmly. He knew something wasn't right about the weight.

He knew that this was a dirty business and he wasn't trying to have anybody cross him, but lately, he felt as though Dameon was trying to do just that. He didn't want to go with his gut feeling because he wanted to trust him. Brandon was the one who brought him up in the game, and he looked at him as though he was his son even though he was not much younger than him.

Silvia just sat there and watched them. For a moment, she thought it was about to get heated. She watched as Reesie tooted the cocaine that Brandon had given to her. Brandon got up from the table and went over and sat on the couch next to Reesie as he now watched Silvia. She looked at him and he blew her a kiss. She rolled her eyes and he licked his lips. Silvia continued to look at him and how sexy she thought his lips were. She had the urge to kiss them, but she turned away.

"Silvia, you remember them Boss days, girl? We use to have so much fun," Regina said. Every time she got high, she would bring up her stripping days and every time, it made Silvia mad.

"I don't care to talk about those days, Regina," Silvia replied with an attitude.

Regina scrunched her nose and curled up her lips. "You have been acting real stank lately. What is your problem?"

Silvia pursed her lips and crossed her arms in front of her chest. "Those days are long gone. Don't want to remember them. Now what you need to worry about is getting that weed out your system before Michael does a random drug test on your butt."

"Whatever," Regina replied. "If he did test me and it came back positive, I would just let you talk him out of firing me. You know he love him some you.'' She laughed loudly. "As many men you've sexed up in that office and didn't get fired, I know he wouldn't fire me behind no drug test, at least not for no marijuana.''

Brandon's cell phone rang and he answered it. After a minute, he told Reesie, "I have to make a run.'' He got up and as he walked past Silvia, he touched her breast.

She pushed his hand away and stood up to look him in his eyes. "Don't you ever touch me again or I will kill you!'' she threatened, as the tears welled in her eyes. She was hoping to keep them at bay because the last thing she wanted Brandon to see her do, was cry.

He grabbed her arm, pulled her, then pushed her up against the wall. He was so close to her face, she could smell the marijuana that lingered on his breath. She turned her head away. "You ain't gon' do nothing to me but give me some good head. Don't make me do something to you that you are going to regret. I will turn you out and have your nose so wide open, you'll be turning tricks. Don't mess with me *little girl*. You ain't nothing and never will be nothing but a certified stripper.'' His eyes slowly roamed her body as his fingers gently ran over her breast. He bit his bottom lip. "Yeah, I heard all about you. I heard you were pretty good too.'' He whispered into her ear, "And I'm going to find out just how good.'' He licked her lips.

"Brandon!'' Reesie yelled.

"Shut up, Rees, you ain't nothing either!'' he yelled. "You already turned out.'' His eyes fixed on Silvia's. "But I'm gon' turn this one out next. Watch what I tell you.'' He let go of Silvia's arm and went to make his run, leaving his boys behind.

"Don't pay him any mind, Silvia," Reesie said. "He just likes to act stupid. He doesn't mean anything by it."

"Rees, you are so naive. You can't see he ain't no good. He talk to you like you are nothing, and you just let him!" she yelled. "He got you running round here like his lil' crack head!"

Dameon snickered at Silvia's comment.

Silvia threw up her hands. "I'm outta here," she said. She left out the door and walked right into Brandon's friend, Ronnie.

"Hey, Silvia. Brandon in there?" he asked.

"No, he just left." She kept walking toward her car, then quickly turned around. "Ronnie. Can I buy a gun from you?"

He walked up to her to make sure he heard her correctly. "What? A gun?"

"Yes, a gun," she said with tears in her eyes.

When he looked into her eyes, he knew how serious she was. "What do you need with a gun, Silvia?"

"Don't ask me any questions. I just need a gun. I will make it worth it if you just give me one."

He knew exactly what she meant by that. "Come on. I have what you need." He led her to his car.

They got in the back seat together. Silvia began kissing him. Then she unzipped his pants and straddled him.

"Wait, let me grab a condom." He gently moved her off of him as he reached over the front seat and into the glove compartment for one, and then realized that he had already used the last one with another girl. He slammed the glove compartment, disappointed. "I forgot. I'm out."

She kissed his neck and straddled him again. "What? You don't think I'm clean, Ronnie?" She kissed him. "I'm clean. Trust me." She kissed him again passionately, expecting him to give in while in the heat of the moment.

"Silvia, I want you, but I'm not going in you bare. I don't get down like that. That's why I try to keep some protection on hand."

"And I respect that, baby. I have no problem with you wanting to use protection. It turns me on even more. But trust me, you have nothing to worry about." She licked his lips and kissed him again.

"Yes, well, me having unprotected sex with you is totally out of the question," he said firmly, gently moving her off of him. One thing about Ronnie is he didn't believe in having unprotected sex. That's something he was never down with. No matter how fine he thinks a female is; protection is always a priority.

Disappointed, Silvia pulled down her skirt. She always knew that Ronnie was a little different from his boys. Any one of them would have jumped at the chance to have sex with her, with or without protection.

He pulled up his pants and looked at her as she sat beside him. "Now talk to me, Silvia. What do you need with a gun? What is that all about?'' he asked as he pulled a revolver from under his seat and handed it to her.

Disregarding his questions, she asked, "How do I use it?''

He showed her how to use it.

She kissed him, got out of his car and left.

Chapter Ten

Silvia sat in IHOP and waited for Regina to meet her for breakfast. Her cell phone rang and she looked at her caller ID and answered. "Regina, where are you? I've been waiting for you for thirty minutes, and I'm ready to order.''

"Just go ahead and order without me cuz I'm not going to make it. I'm running extremely late,'' Regina said from the other end.

"Yeah, I'm so sure.'' Silvia pressed the End button, then continued looking over her menu.

Robert stood at the counter and was about to order something to go until he spotted Silvia sitting at one of the tables alone.

"May I take your order, sir?" the lady behind the counter asked.

He put up his hand. "No, I think I'll sit and eat, but thank you.'' He walked over to Silvia's table. "Do you mind if I join you?'' he asked her.

The sound of his voice made her cringe. She slowly looked up from her menu. *Yes, I do mind.* "What are you doing here?" she asked.

"Well, I was trying to eat breakfast. Do you mind if I sit with you?"

She pointed to the chair across from her. "Have a seat." *This may be your last meal.* The thought made her laugh inside.

Robert pulled out the chair and sat down. He stared at her for a moment as she glared at him. His green eyes seemed to pierce her very soul as she stared back into them. Considering that he has been just staring at her without a word spoken, she wondered if he'd figured out who she is. The longer she looked into his eyes, the more she realized that he was truly admiring her and it made her blush.

His voice finally broke the silence. "I really want to thank you, Silvia. You've been spending a lot of time with my family, and my wife has really grown to love you."

Silvia leaned forward in her seat and touched his hand. "Not just your wife, Robert. I believe you have grown to love me as well."

He smiled at her sarcasm, then his eyes narrowed. "Do you like me, Silvia?"

She moved her hand away from his and sat her back up against her chair. *Hell no, and I'm going to show you just how much I don't.* "What do you mean?" she asked innocently.

"I get the feeling that you don't like me much. You just tolerate me."

"Do you like me, Robert?"

"Yes, I actually do like you. I just feel as though you are not that fond of me and I've been trying to figure out why . . . Do you mind explaining it to me?"

"I do like you. I like you very much and I wish we could ahhh." She slowly licked her lips. "Well, you're a man, I think you know *exactly* what I mean."

Robert loved the way her words rolled from her tongue. He leaned forward in his seat. Curiosity took over him. "No, I don't know. So, please . . . tell me."

"Would you rather me show you?"

He stared at her and smiled. *This woman can't be serious.*

"You ever made love to someone in your mind?" she asked.

He laughed bashfully. "Wow . . . No."

She smiled and studied him for a minute. The corners of her lips turned up into a smirk. "You liar."

"How do you figure I'm telling a lie?"

Her smirk still planted on her face. "Because your green eyes tell me so." She now leaned forward in her seat. Her smirk disappeared. "You make love to me in your mind all the time."

Robert stared into her eyes and she stared back into his, her eyebrow now arched perfectly as his curiosity intrigued her.

"You might as well do me for real, papi." She bit her bottom lip before saying, "It'll be better than you've ever imagined and it will be our little secret." She ran her foot up his leg underneath the table. "I'm like venom, Robert. Once I get into your system, it's hard to get me out, papi."

Oh, my God. Is she serious? He then remembered his vision of the snake he saw when he was showering the first night they all hung out. He shook away his thoughts and looked down to where her foot rested, then he chuckled lightly. He looked up at her. "I'm married." He now used his hands to gently move her foot away from his manhood. "Happily, I might add."

"And?"

He just stared at her once again and the coldness in her eyes made him curious to know the meaning behind them. A devilish smile spread across her face, yet he thought that it was still beautiful.

"Usted està viviendo una mentira," she said, her Spanish beautifully spoken.

"I'm living a lie?" he asked. "How?"

"You tell me, Mr. Sterling."

He just stared at her, waiting for her to further explain.

"I'm done here!" She got up from her seat and he grabbed her arm, making her fall back into her chair.

He spoke, "No. You tell me!" His forceful tone now reminded her of the man he was twelve years ago.

The people sitting at the table beside them stared at them, thinking that they were having a domestic dispute.

"Forget it, Robert," she hissed. "Maybe you are not the man I thought you were . . ." She stood and leaned over the table to look into his eyes more deeply. "Or maybe you are *just* who I thought you were!" She snatched her arm away from his grasp and walked away from the table and right out the restaurant door without even ordering.

She decided not to even worry about eating breakfast considering that she lost her appetite. Plus, she was going to be having lunch with Carla in a few hours anyway, and after having this encounter with Robert, she decided that today she was going to do severe damage and she couldn't wait.

***

Kim walked into her office and saw vases of roses all over and around her desk. She smiled knowing exactly who sent them. The attached card read: *Roses for the most beautiful woman in the world.* Ever since she went to dinner with Emmanuel, she had begun to feel the possibility of finding true love with a man. She and Emmanuel began spending a lot of time together, and she really enjoyed being around him. He had been nothing but a gentleman. On their seventh date, he kissed her on her lips for the first time, and she kissed him back. He didn't treat her like he was going to get infected by hanging out with her, hugging her, touching her or kissing her. He made her feel like a woman again, instead of someone who was infected.

Kim picked up her cell phone and called to thank him for the flowers, and he let her know that he was hoping to see her soon. He had been coming to her meetings, and they had been spending time together in worship. Emmanuel was so happy that his job in New Orleans had laid him off. He felt that it was God's way of bringing him back home to meet his wife. He strongly believed that Kim had every quality that he desired in his mate. He was willing to remain in prayer and willing to spend more time with her so that he would know without any doubt.

***

Silvia was at the Sterling's home waiting for Carla to finish getting ready so they could go to lunch. She sat on the stool in the kitchen and watched Robert as he played with his daughter on the living room floor. They were playing with blocks and it looked like they were trying to build a house of some sort. Silvia caught herself smiling at how he interacted with his daughter, and she quickly brushed that smile away. She could see that he loved his daughter more than anything so now she was planning to destroy that relationship as well. She felt as though he didn't deserve a daughter after what he had done to her in that VIP room, and she was going to make sure that he wasn't going to have one.

Robert looked over at her as if he felt her staring at him. His eyes met hers and he thought about the conversation they had in the restaurant earlier. He had been trying to figure her out since he met her at the meet and greet, and today she intrigued him even more. For some reason, he wanted to understand her. He wanted to know her. He stared into her eyes for the longest, and then his attention reverted to his daughter who was now calling him.

Silvia had made well over ten thousand dollars with this man paying her to spend time with his wife. He didn't even know how much his wife had been spending on top of that. She took Silvia's advice and gave her all of the receipts every time they went shopping and she checked the mail before Robert was able to even get to it. She made sure she paid all of the credit card bills. Besides, Robert left her to manage their finances and bills anyway. Even though he would check behind her back every now and again, lately he hasn't thought to do so since his mind was on trying to open a new building to expand his company. Carla knew that her husband would eventually know about her spending, but she was planning to tell him in due time.

Carla came down the stairs and she and Silvia headed for the door. Silvia looked back before closing the door behind her and Robert's eyes were fixed on her, just as she thought. She smiled, and then winked at him before closing the door behind her. She and Carla rode to the restaurant in silence. When they got there, they were seated immediately and the waitress took their orders.

Carla broke the silence, "Me and Robert got into it last night behind sex. He told me how crazy I was acting and that I needed some help just because I won't have sex with him whenever he wants it. I don't know. I guess he thinks that because I won't have sex with him, I don't love him.'' She looked down at the table. "The truth is . . . I married Robert to get away from my family. I didn't start off loving him. I mean, I loved how handsome he was and the fact that he was wealthy, but I didn't *love* him. Robert can be very controlling at times and last night, it came out.'' She now looked up at Silvia. "I thought a lot about what you've been saying, Silvia, about how he tries to control everything including me, and you were right. He doesn't respect me and maybe he doesn't love me.''

Silvia had been filling Carla's head up with all kinds of lies ever since they met, and her plan had been working. Inside her mind, she smiled at the thought of having her brainwashed into believing something that wasn't completely true. She had been around with them for many arguments, and she knew that they were being more and more driven apart by the minute; but today, Silvia's plan was to top it off with something that she knew would destroy them.

The waitress brought out their orders and they began eating, but Silvia didn't eat much. Instead, she stared off into space, part of her plan.

"Silvia, what is wrong with you? You haven't said a word all day," Carla said, putting a fork full of shrimp pasta into her mouth.

Even though Silvia had a solemn look on her face, she laughed inside her mind. *I'm about to tear your world apart.* She saddened her face even more. "I didn't want to say anything, Carla, but . . ."

"But what, Silvia?" Carla interrupted concerned by how her friend was acting.

"I saw Robert." She paused again. *Don't do this, Silvia,* her conscience spoke to her, but she ignored it. Her vengeance spoke much louder at that moment. "I saw Robert touch Jazmin."

Tears immediately fell from Carla's eyes. "What do you mean, *touch* Jazmin?"

"I'm sorry, Carla, but he touches your daughter, and I don't believe she's safe with him."

"What do you mean? This can't be true!" Carla yelled. "I know a molester when I see one. He loves Jazmin more than his own life." Tears streamed from her eyes. "He couldn't possibly. He wouldn't. He loves her too much."

"Why do you think he ignores you for her? Why do you think he pays so much attention to her and not you? Until he wants sex, that is." She paused and touched Carla's hand. "I saw him touch her, Carla."

Carla continued to cry uncontrollably as she got up from her seat.

"No, Carla, sit down." Silvia grabbed her arm. "Don't go and say anything to him about it and please, don't tell him I told you anything. I'm your friend and I am looking out for you and your daughter. Just wait till tomorrow and take her away. Go back to live with your parents for a while, just to sort this thing through and to clear your mind." She now looked her in her eyes. "He's paying me just to hang out with you, and now I think I know why. I believe it is so he can be alone with her."

"I don't believe you," Carla shot back at her angrily.

Silvia grabbed her purse, reached in it and pulled out the last check that he gave her. She was saving it for this moment. "Why would he give me this check for a thousand dollars?"

Carla looked at the check before asking, "Why are you just now telling me this?"

"Because I'm your friend and I told him that I will not take any more of his money. Please, let's just keep this between us. Just take Jazmin tomorrow and run."

"If this is true, I gotta to leave now!" Carla yelled.

"Okay, I'll take you home, but don't leave tonight. Leave in the morning. Promise me that you won't say anything. Just leave him."

"Okay, just take me home!"

Silvia noticed that the people in the restaurant had started staring at them. She went to the front desk, paid the bill and they left.

Carla cried all the way back home. She was devastated once again. Silvia tried to comfort her, and she kept telling her not to say anything and to just leave in the morning without a word to Robert.

They walked into her house and saw Robert asleep on the couch with Jazmin in his arms. Carla walked over to the couch and grabbed Jazmin. When she grabbed her, it immediately woke Robert up. She headed upstairs without saying a word.

Confused, Robert watched her walk up the stairs. He then looked up at Silvia who was staring at him with her arms folded across her chest. "What's going on?" he asked.

"Robert, I have to tell you something," Silvia whispered. "Carla has been really disturbed lately. It's as if she is losing her mind. I don't really believe she should have stopped her counseling sessions. She's been saying some really crazy things and I'm scared for her," she lied.

"What do you mean? What kind of crazy things and how has she been acting?"

"All I can say is sleep on the couch tonight and let her have some space. Maybe she'll talk and make more sense in the morning," she said, and headed for the door, leaving them to their troubles.

Robert sat on the couch and thought about what Silvia had just told him. He and his wife had been going through a lot of things their whole marriage. Carla had been dealing with major depression long before she had the stillbirth which they ignored until it got worse. After the stillbirth she went to counseling only for a little while. Then she chose to stop. What Silvia just told him worried him because he was with Carla through many of her breakdowns and they were never pretty.

Carla was brought up in money. Her father owned many businesses and she never lacked anything when it came to money and material things, but she always felt as if something was missing. Her parents had tried to fill that void with money. Robert tried to keep her happy by giving her the finer things in life, but he knew deep down that she was still very unhappy. She was never satisfied and she never felt complete.

He knew exactly what Silvia was saying about Carla. There were many times when Robert had to give Carla some space because she was not in her right mind. He learned her good days and bad days and from the looks of it, today was a bad day. He decided to go with what Silvia told him, and he lay down on the couch hoping that Carla would be having a better day tomorrow.

***

Carla tossed and turned all night. She woke up in a cold sweat from the nightmare she was having. In it, she was six years of age and there was a masked man who sat down next to her on her bed and began fondling her. Now, tears fell from her eyes as she looked around the room to make sure that she was safe. She was thankful that she woke up from her dream before the masked man began doing other things to her besides fondling. She got up and sat on the chaise lounge at the foot of the bed. Then she eased her body down on it.

Robert didn't sleep well at all after what Silvia had told him. He wanted to give Carla her space, but he also wanted to make sure that she was okay. He got up from the couch and headed to their bedroom. He walked into the dark room. The only light in it came from the moon.

"Are you asleep?" he asked.

She shook her. "No, Robert. I'm not," her tone low.

He walked in closer and saw the tears running down her face. He wiped them away. "What's wrong?"

She touched his hand that rested on her face and looked into his eyes. *I know a monster when I see one and my heart tells me that you are not one of them.* "I was just thinking," she said in a passive, childlike voice, almost as if she were reverting to her childhood.

"What are you thinking?"

She sniffled. "I think I want you to hold me."

He sat next to her and slowly stretched out behind her and held her close. "Is that better?"

She nodded. "I love you, Robert. I really do."

"I love you too.'' He kissed her cheek. "Very much,'' he added. He held her even tighter as she cried even more now. "You are safe with me, Carla.''

She nodded and held his arms that wrapped around her.

He held her until she fell asleep.

Chapter Eleven

Silvia yelled through the receiver, "Look, Carla! You need to leave Robert, and you need to leave him today."

"I don't believe you, Silvia. Robert would never touch our daughter. He loves her. I can't see him doing that to her," Carla cried. They had been on the phone for the past thirty minutes arguing about Silvia's accusation.

"If you don't leave your trifling husband, he's going to continue molesting your daughter and when she grows up, she is going to resent you for being a poor excuse for a mother!" Silvia yelled. "If you stay there and allow him to keep doing what he's doing, you don't deserve a daughter," her voice as cold as ice.

Carla sobbed on the other end. *Oh, my God. Could this be true? Has he really been touching our daughter?* Carla had become so confused and at the moment she became lethargic. She sat on the bed with her hand on her chest. She never thought of Robert as a child molester, especially not with him knowing what all she had been through.

Silvia knew her plan was working when she heard her sobbing on the other end. "Carla, listen to me. You have to protect your daughter, and the only way for you to protect her is if you leave him.''

Carla continued to cry. *If I don't leave him, I will be just like her.* She shook her head at her thoughts. *I have to protect my daughter.* "Silvia, let me call you back later." As soon as she hung up the phone, she began packing.

***

Robert walked into his house and looked at the mail that he pulled from the mailbox. He had bills from everywhere and he started opening them one by one. He saw credit card bills for thousands of dollars at a time. Then he went and examined his checking account records and became furious from the knowledge that their finances were getting out of control due to outrageous shopping sprees.

Robert made sure that the car notes, utilities and all other things were paid, but he allowed Carla to manage the accounts because it enabled her to feel useful since she wasn't working anymore. It was the agreement she and he made. And right now, he regretted that agreement. Even though they had enough money to throw away, he could not bear to waste it. Paying Silvia was an expense and he didn't consider that a waste. More like an investment.

He burst into the bedroom door. Furiously, he yelled, "What in the hell are all these purchases that you've been making? Macy's, Dillard's, Tiffany's, Saks and all this other crap!'' He threw each bill on the bed as he called them out. "What were you thinking, Carla? You are the greediest woman I know!''

She became angry with him having the audacity to call her greedy and it made her blurt out, "I'm greedy because I'm spending up all of your finances, but you can spend them on whatever or *whomever* you like!" she yelled. "How much are you paying her?"

"Paying who?"

"Silvia!"

He dropped his head and sighed deeply. "It's not even like that."

"How much?"

"It doesn't even matter because me paying her is not the problem. The problem is you," he said. Then he noticed her packed bags. "What is this about? Where are you going?" he asked, picking up one of her Louis Vuitton bags.

"Have you ever touched her?"

"Who? Silvia? I grabbed her arm once because she made an ignorant statement. Is that why you packed? Her?" He dropped the bag back onto the bed.

"You know what I'm talking about, Robert!" Carla began crying. "Have you ever touched our daughter? Have you ever touched our baby girl?" She cried even more.

Robert's heart immediately broke from the question she asked and he couldn't believe what he was hearing. "What? Wh-what did you say?" he stuttered.

"You heard me and you heard me loud and clear! Have you ever touched her, Robert?"

"I would never . . . You know me and you know that I love my daughter. Oh, my God! I can't believe you would even have the nerve to think that I would.'' Tears fell from his eyes.

Carla took her bags, went into Jazmin's room and grabbed her into her arms. Jazmin woke up and could sense that the environment was hostile and immediately began crying. Carla headed downstairs where the cab was already outside waiting.

Robert was right on her heels. "You are not taking my daughter anywhere! Carla, this is crazy!" he yelled and Jazmin continued to cry out for her father. "Give me my daughter, Carla!" he yelled again, while Jazmin continued to reach for him. She did not understand what was going on, but she saw the tears falling down her father's face. "Carla, please, just don't take her away from me. Y'all can stay here and I will leave. Just don't take her . . . Carla, she's my life!'' He cried.

Carla walked out and slammed the door behind her. She went to the cab without looking back. Robert couldn't contain himself.

He hit the door with his fist as he screamed from the heartache he felt. He couldn't believe the accusation that had been made, and it hurt him to his heart.

***

It was six o'clock in the evening and Robert sat at his kitchen counter with every light in the house off. He drank his third glass of vodka. Then the doorbell rang. He opened the door without even finding out who was there before he did, but at this point, he didn't even care.

Silvia stepped in, closing the door behind her. She walked into the thick darkness of his home and stumbled on a decorative floor item. She couldn't see a thing as she tried to feel her way around.

Robert walked away, grabbed his bottle of vodka and glass from the counter, then went into the living room.

Silvia got closer to the living room, and the light from the fireplace helped her to see a little better. "Robert, I wanted to ask you and Carla for a favor,'' she began. "My apartment is having some problems and they told me that I would have to move out for a while. I could really use a place to stay. I have no family here.'' She paused, and then asked, "Is Carla upstairs?'' She had talked to Carla earlier, and she already knew that she had left to go back home with her parents.

Robert sat in his chair, staring at the fireplace. He had his glass in one hand and his bottle of vodka in the other. He didn't say a word.

Silvia placed her hand on her hip. "Robert, can you answer me please?'' she asked impatiently.

"You can have the guestroom,'' he said, without another word.

"Thank you so much, Robert. I can't tell you how much I appreciate you . . . Is Carla upstairs? Do you want to make sure it's okay with her?'' she asked as though she knew nothing more.

"She's not here. She left . . . Just take your things to the guestroom.'' His tone was different from when they met at the meet and greet event. Once again, he sounded like the man from twelve years ago.

Silvia went to the car, got her things, and she took them to the guestroom. She found her way back downstairs to Robert. "Is everything okay?"

He didn't answer. The light from the fireplace shone upon his face, revealing the tears that were streaming down. He slouched in the black leather chair, continuing to drink.

Silvia looked down at the vodka bottle that was now empty sitting on the floor beside the chair. "Robert, what's wrong?" she asked as she kneeled down in front of him and looked up at him.

He sat silently, and the only sound in the house was the crackling of the fireplace.

She stared at him. "Robert?"

"She took my daughter." He shook his head. "She tried to say that I was touching my daughter." Tears continued to stream down his face. "Can you believe her?" He spoke as if he were trying to understand it all himself.

Silvia looked at the tears that ran from his eyes. "I'm so sorry, Robert," her tone now sorrowful. At that very moment, she almost felt remorse and regret for what she had caused in this man's life as she saw the tears of a loving father. The glow from the fireplace continued to shine on him as he now broke down in tears from the thought of Carla's accusation.

Silvia found him very attractive, and this time she wasn't going to resist her strong desire to be sexually intimate with him.

She kissed his tears and climbed on top of him. She licked his lips, and then kissed them softly.

Robert released the glass from his hand and it crashed to the floor. When he kissed her back, she could taste the strong liquor on his tongue. He gently ran his hand under her blouse. Touching her breast, he continued to kiss her intensely.

Her body responded to his gentle touch, and her desire for him intensified as she felt him become erect. She began unbuttoning his shirt as she continued to kiss him.

He picked her up, and she wrapped her legs around him as he carried her over to the couch. He laid her down and climbed on top of her, kissing her with intense passion.

She touched his manhood, then eagerly unzipped his pants as her passion continued to rise.

He then grabbed her hand, stopping her. "Wait, I can't do this," he whispered.

She whispered into his ear, "Yes, you can. You have done this before, Robert." She kissed him and gently pushed his pants down, now revealing him.

Robert thought about his first imagined encounter with her as he recalled the night that she hung out with him and Carla. He remembered her saying those exact words, *You have done this before, Robert.* He shook away his thoughts and kissed her once again. He started to wonder if this was his imagination again or if it was real. As soon as their bodies joined, she felt a surge of electricity and she gasped in his ear. He knew then that it was definitely real.

She moaned with each one of his long strokes as he pleased her. It was not at all painful as the first time, and she was enjoying the moment. She kissed his neck.

As he grabbed her hair, he became a little rougher.

Continuing to cover his neck with gentle kisses, she moved his shirt to kiss his chest. As soon as she moved his shirt away, she saw the tattoo of the scorpion, and her mind reverted to her past. She remembered ripping his shirt the night he raped her and seeing that same tattoo. Everything about that tattoo was embedded in her memory from then on.

He steadied his strokes, now looking into her eyes.

When she looked back into his green eyes, she snapped. "Get off of me!" she screamed and began hitting him and pushing him away. "Get away from me!" Tears flowed from her eyes. She hit and kicked him as the pain from her past rushed through her mind and body. "Don't you ever touch me again!"

Robert sobered up quickly and his eyes were wide with shock. He eased himself out of her. "Silvia, what's wrong?"

She got up and ran to the bathroom. Once she got in there, she slammed the door and locked it. Breathing heavily, she felt sick. She regurgitated everything she had eaten as she hung tightly to toilet. She continued to cry, and all of her pain struck her at once.

Robert stood at the door. He heard her throwing up and crying. "Silvia, are you okay?"

She continued to regurgitate.

"Just open the door, and let me help you. If I did something wrong, please, tell me." Robert had become very concerned. He knocked on the door again. "Just open the door, Silvia, and tell me what's wrong." When he heard the shower water running, he sighed, walked away and sat down in his chair.

Silvia hopped in the shower, and began scrubbing her body as if she had been raped all over again. She tried to shake her memory, but couldn't. She fell to the shower floor crying and shaking uncontrollably for another hour. She finally got out and grabbed a towel.

When Robert heard the door creak open, he got up from his chair. He quickly walked over to her and grabbed her arm. "Silvia, I'm sorry if I hurt you. I was drunk and I wasn't thinking." He paused and looked at her in the towel that wrapped around her. He desired to have her again, but he refrained. "Silvia?" He waited for her to respond. "Silvia, just say something!" he yelled at her.

Startled, she jumped at the bass in his voice.

He saw the fear that he caused her. He calmly stated, "I'm sorry." He let go of her arm and walked back to his chair and sat down with his elbows on his knees, head in hands. At this point, he was disappointed in himself.

Silvia went to the guestroom and lying on the bed, she cried uncontrollably, reliving moments from her past as she thought about Robert being on top of her once again. *I can't believe that I was willing to give myself to this man who took everything from me!* She cried herself to sleep from all the pain that struck her mind, body and spirit.

Chapter Twelve

Silvia woke up with a massive headache from all of the crying she had done. She got dressed and prepared herself for work. Hoping that Robert was still asleep, she walked briskly through the kitchen, heading to the front door. Then she heard him call her name. She looked up and saw him sitting in the living room.

He stood and walked over to her. "Look," he began, "I don't know what I was thinking last night and I don't know what I did to you, but I am so sorry if I hurt you. I had been drinking though I know that's no excuse for my behavior, but I don't handle my liquor well at all. That's why I try to stay away from it." He gently rested his hand on her shoulder. "I just wanted to tell you that I am sorry. I didn't mean to hurt you."

She looked at him and saw the sincerity in his eyes and felt the apology in his touch as he slid his hand down her arm and now held her hand. She couldn't help but notice that he looked as if he hadn't had a minute of sleep. She thought about his daughter before saying, "That's okay, Robert. Just forget about it." She pulled her hand away from his. She was embarrassed and upset that she allowed him to see her vulnerability last night.

"I left you a key on the counter. You can stay as long as you need to."

"Thanks." She turned around, grabbed the key from the counter and headed out the door.

When she got to her office, she sat down in her chair and reflected on everything. She began to feel sorry for Robert when it came to his daughter. She knew that he was a great father and loved his baby girl. At first it felt good, lying to Carla, but now she wished that she had left his daughter out of it, but it was too late. The damage was already done. The knock on the door pulled her away from her thoughts.

Michael stuck his head in her door. "Hi, Silvia. Do you have some of the floor plans ready for the Sterling building?" He walked in closer.

"Yes." She picked up the set of floor plans and handed them to him.

"Thanks . . . You okay?" he asked, as he saw the redness in her eyes.

"Michael, I thought we talked about keeping this professional."

"You are right." He nodded. "My apologies, but it just seems like something is bothering you, and has been bothering you for quite some time now." He paused. "Well, my door is always open if you would like to talk."

He was about to walk out of the door until he heard Silvia say, "Why do you care so much?"

He turned to face her. "Silvia, I can see that you are hurting and it's evident in every one of your actions. You have had man after man. Not once have you ever mentioned being in a relationship. I just want to see you happy and whole and right now, I can clearly see that you are not either one." He hesitated for a second. "Look, Silvia, I believe that the meetings we have on the weeknights at eight o'clock would be beneficial to you, but it is up to you to come. A lot of people have really shown great progress."

"Why haven't we ever gotten together, Michael?" she asked, disregarding everything else he said. "You talk about the men and my relationships. What is it about sex that you don't like, or are you just gay? Is that the real reason why I can't get the same reaction from you that I get from all the others?"

"You are a beautiful woman, and I am human. So I can't say that my flesh has not reacted to your advances. But I live by the spirit, not by my flesh. I'm not about all that foolishness. I'm at a different level in my life and I leave the *temptation* alone. I can't say that I never turned my back on God, because I have. I have had my days in college where you would have called me a dog, trying to prove that I was like all my boys, attempting to fit in. I have used many women, Silvia, but trust me, I paid for it. To every action, there is a consequence. I left my past behind when God called me out of that darkness."

Silvia looked at him with tears in her eyes.

He walked over to her and touched her hand. "I know that you have made many advances, Silvia, but I refuse to take advantage of you in any way; and to answer your question, I am not gay and I have nothing against sex. Sex is a beautiful gift created by God. He designed it for marriage and marriage alone. It is the world that has tried to pervert it and has abused it. It was created for husband and wife, and it's not for anything outside of that covenant.''

"I have respected the fact that you have not taken advantage of my advances.'' She choked on her next words. "I am thankful that you are different, Michael, and because of that, I have the utmost respect for you. The advances are done, I promise. I won't ever come at you like that again.'' She paused. "Thank you so much.'' She stood up and hugged him.

For the first time Michael felt as though she was making a turn, and he was thankful for a glimpse of it. "Come to the meeting tonight, eight o'clock. That's how you can thank me.'' He smiled.

She returned his smile. "I'll see what I can do.''

***

Silvia came in the door a little after five o'clock. As soon as she walked into the living room, she kicked off her Jessica Simpson stilettos and turned on the stereo. Keyshia Cole CD was already in and began to play *Heaven Sent.* She hit the Repeat button and began to dance. She just wanted to relax and no matter what was going on around her, dancing always helped her to do just that.

Robert heard the music playing while in his bedroom. He walked into the corridor and looked over the banister and saw her dancing downstairs. She captured his attention with every move she made. She threw some Latin dance and ballet in as her body flowed to the music with the words that Keyshia Cole sang through the speakers. He watched her and could see that she didn't have a care in the world as the music took over her body.

She danced as if no one was watching, and he couldn't take his eyes off of her. She was absolutely beautiful to him. The joy in her face as he watched her dance told him that dancing was something that she loved. He headed downstairs as he heard the music coming to an end. He walked up closely behind her as she continued to dance.

She pivoted, now facing him with her eyes closed. When she opened her eyes, she gasped at his presence as he stared back at her. Being that he parked his car in the garage, she had no idea that he had already made it there before her. The whole time she thought she was there alone. She continued to dance as she smiled at him.

"Wow, you are an excellent dancer," he said to her.

"Shhh!" She put her finger up to her lips as the music began playing again. She then took his hands into hers.

She moved her right foot forward and his left foot moved back as he began to dance with her. Their bodies flowing beautifully together as Keyshia Cole sang, "I want to be the one who you believe in your heart is sent from . . . Sent from Heaven…" through the speakers.

He took in her beautiful features and she took in his. They both felt connected. She took his mind away from his problems, and at this very moment, he appreciated her for that. She looked down at his waist and realized how beautifully they danced together. He then raised her head up and her eyes met his. When he saw the tears that were formed in her eyes, he couldn't resist kissing her lips softly. He wanted to heal that hurt he saw every time he looked into her eyes. She began kissing him back, now realizing that she was getting deeper than what she wanted to.

She pulled away from him. "I'm sorry. I have to go." She went and grabbed her stilettos.

"Silvia," he called to her.

She didn't even wait to put on her shoes. She grabbed her purse and walked out of the door without a response.

Robert sat down in his chair while the music continued to play. He didn't understand why he was feeling the way he felt about her, but his feelings were strong.

His cell phone rang and he answered it. "Robert?" Carla's voice trembled on the other end. "I miss you so much and Jazmin . . . Jazmin keeps crying for you. I'm so sorry I took her from you . . . We miss you . . . We miss you so much."

"I miss y'all too." He inhaled deeply. "Please, just let me come get you, Carla."

"No, Robert. I'm not ready for you to do that. I just need time to myself." She began crying. "I just want to spend time with Jazmin. Then you can come get her when I'm ready for you to come get her," she said. "I know that you would never have hurt her, Robert. I'm sorry that I even came to you with that. I don't know what I was thinking . . ."

Robert heard her pause. He could hear rambling in the background even though he could tell she tried to cover the phone. "Carla?" he called to her.

Breathing heavily, she whispered, "I'm here, Robert."

"What's going on?"

"You know I would never hurt her, Robert, that's why I took her. I wasn't sure, and then you know with the touching and all . . . I just didn't know what to do. You know what happened. You know that I couldn't do it. I couldn't let that happen to her. I know you didn't touch her. I know it. I just . . . I couldn't do it," she rambled.

"Carla, what's going on?" He was concerned by the noise in the background.

"Am I a good mother?"

"What?" he asked. Robert didn't understand any of this conversation.

"I just need to hear you say it, Robert. I need to hear it."

"Carla, you are not making any sense. You call and say how much you miss me. Then when I say that I want to come get you, you tell me no. I understand that you are just going through a rough time but, baby, just let me come get you and we can work through this together."

"No." She hesitated. "I want a divorce, Robert, but I want you to take Jazmin." She sobbed even more and sounded afraid. "She doesn't need to be here. She's safe with you and she needs you. I am not in a position to be a mother . . . or a wife . . . I just want you to be happy."

"And I am happy, baby." Tears fell from his eyes. "You make me happy."

"You haven't been happy for a long time, Robert. And neither have I. You know that."

He sighed. "Carla, let's not do this. Just let me come and get you and we can talk about this face-to-face."

She cried even more. "We are getting a divorce. I am just not fit to be a wife," she hesitated, "or mother."

"Carla, you are a great wife and mother." He attempted to calm her down with his words. "Please, don't do this, baby."

She exhaled. "Thank you . . . I needed to hear that."

"I love you."

"I have to go, but I will call you back later," she whispered as if someone was coming into the room with her. Robert could hear someone in the background, but he couldn't make out the voice. Carla's voice broke his concentration when she said, "Robert, I love you. Always remember that."

"I love you too. Carla, just please, baby. We can get through this. Just come back home . . ." He stopped talking when he heard the dial tone in his ear. He threw his phone across the room in anger and it hit the wall, shattering to pieces. His tears continued to fall as he thought about his daughter being in Chicago with Carla. He wanted her home with him, right now, where he knew she would be safe.

Chapter Thirteen

Silvia went over to Reesie's and spent time with her friend. After watching *Girlfriends* with her, she asked if she wanted to attend the meeting with her tonight. Reesie agreed and they headed for the Family Life Center. When they walked through the door, Michael and the group were in prayer together. Silvia and Reesie stood at the door and listened to his prayer as they waited for him to finish.

"Right now, Father God, in the name of Jesus; forgive us for our sins, Father, for we have fallen short of your glory. We know that you are the God of grace and mercy and your grace is sufficient. You have given us power, power to overcome our struggles and strength to get through the battle. You are God and God alone and right now we pray that our faith does not fail. Help us to continue to press toward your mark for you have called us with a high calling and you have called us out of darkness and into your marvelous light. Help us to make better choices and to be better people. Thank you for healing us, delivering us, and for setting us free. Give us a better mindset that we will begin to seek you daily, and give us a desire to please you, Father, and not ourselves. Thank you for being God in our lives and the God of our lives. Continue to carry our load,

Father, for you have made our burdens lighter. Thank you for the blood of Jesus . . .'' he continued to pray.

Tears streamed down Silvia's face as his prayer touched her heart.

Michael ended the prayer.

Silvia ran out of the door.

Michael turned after hearing the door of the building slam. He saw Reesie standing there with her eyes widened from shock. He knew then that it was Silvia who ran out once again. He asked the group to excuse him before leaving out to check on her. Reesie followed him outside, staying close by the door.

Once he got out into the parking lot, he called out to her, "Silvia!''

She kept walking to her car.

He caught up with her and grabbed her arm, turning her around to face him. "Silvia. You do this every time. You are always running. Just tell me. Why?''

Her tears continued to fall. "Michael, you can't save me so why . . .'' She paused to wipe away her tears. "So why do you keep trying?''

"You are right. I can't save you, Silvia, and I know that. I'm not trying to save you. I'm trying to lead you to the one who can.'' He hugged her. "Just come back in. Everything will be okay.''

Reesie stood and watched Silvia cry in his arms. She was saddened that her friend had been through so much, and deep down she could sense that Silvia partially blamed her for part of her hurt. She, too, blamed herself.

Silvia headed back into the building with Michael behind her and Reesie not far behind him. They all took their seats.

"Okay, everybody," Michael began. "Tonight we are going to discuss ways that we can redirect our focus whenever we are triggered. First of all, many of you are here because you have hit rock bottom, and you are ready for change. You don't want to be the same any more or do the same things anymore. You want to be better and I congratulate you on realizing that you are worth more. When we are dealing with addictions, we all have a rock bottom. My rock bottom is different from yours, but the point is we all have one. My desire is to be able to catch most people before they get to rock bottom, but unfortunately, it doesn't always happen that way. Life is all about choices and, with addiction, you can choose to recover and move forward in life, or you can choose to relapse and remain stuck in reverse. The choice is yours. Nobody has the power to make that choice but you." He looked over at Tasha. "Tasha, how's it going for you this week?"

"Actually, y'all, I have been doing so much better, and I haven't had a drink in five weeks. I must admit when I be going through, picking up a drink is tempting at times, but I've been doing better with overcoming the temptation," Tasha announced.

Everyone in the group clapped for her accomplishment.

Michael smiled. "That is excellent, Tasha, and the great thing about it is that you came acknowledging that you had a problem and that you desired to get help to overcome that problem. That is the first step. Now, you have been an example of the power of God and what He can do in our lives. With God all things are possible no matter how big the struggle. God will give us strength to overcome it. Nothing is too big or too hard for God. I know it may get hard for you at times, but don't fall into temptation. You've come too far to turn back now. You are doing great, Tasha, and I am so proud of you for not allowing temptation to get the best of you,'' he said.

Everyone clapped.

Michael looked around at each individual. "Would anyone else like to share?'' he asked.

"Well,'' Reesie began, "I've been coming to these meetings for a while now and I realize that you guys are so brave. These meetings have inspired me, and I want something better out of life.'' She looked around and hesitated when she became embarrassed. "I just want to say, keep up the great work.'' She wanted to tell them about her problem, but she decided to just keep coming and tell them at a later time.

Silvia's mouth dropped as she looked at Reesie. She was shocked that she had continued to come to the meetings without her, and that she didn't even tell her about it. This was only her second meeting.

"That is awesome, Reesie,'' Michael said. "Thank you so much for sharing with us and you do know that you can have something better out of life because God has something great in store for you, but it is up to you to get everything that He has for you. He has a great purpose and plan for your life, but you have to be willing to give Him your life and allow Him to work His plan." He looked around. "Anyone else?" he asked. He waited for a while, and then he continued, "Okay, well, would someone like to share their plan for when they are triggered? What do you redirect your focus on or to whenever you are triggered?"

"Well, I begin to journal. It helps me release a lot of emotions, and I feel much better after that. I also take those walks around the park," Tasha said.

"I call a friend and talk. Then, I also go walking and reflect on the good things that are happening in my life. Having my family there to support me in my recovery is also a great help," a former crack cocaine addict named Sharon shared.

"I work out. I take a five mile run," said a man named Gene, who was formally addicted to meth.

Ruby, a lady formally addicted to gambling and prescription pills chimed in, "I read and do gardening."

Michael nodded and said, "Okay those are all excellent things to do. What? We have journaling, talking to someone, taking a walk, working out, reading and gardening. Having your families' support is also awesome! Some other things that will be excellent is going into worship, praising God, praying and reading the Holy Bible. Get some Word in you so that you can speak it out when Satan comes at you trying to get you to revert. You have to speak the Word because that is your weapon in war. When the enemy comes in like a flood and tries to attack, you have to know where your help comes from."

"May I ask you something, sir?" a young lady named Jamie asked. She was new to the group and this was her first night. She has an addiction to meth and cocaine and was invited there by Gene who had been a friend of hers for six years. She sat with her hands in her lap, and her skin had sores all over it. She was extremely petite and you can tell that her weight loss came with her drug habit. Her face was pale and filled with sores as well.

"Yes, you may, Jamie," Michael replied.

She proceeded with her question. "Have you ever been addicted to drugs or alcohol?"

"No, I have never been addicted to drugs or alcohol."

Jamie folded her arms across her chest and rolled her neck. "Well, how can you possibly help anyone who is addicted to drugs and alcohol when you've never traveled this road? What qualifies you to help us?" she asked in hostility.

"Excellent question, Jamie. I will have to say that the Holy Spirit qualifies me to help along with my Masters in counseling, specializing in addictions, and my passion to help those who are addicts. I may not have ever been addicted to drugs and alcohol, but do I believe that an addiction is an addiction? Yes. Do I believe and understand that it can be a struggle? Yes. Do I believe that Jesus is a healer and deliverer? Yes. Do I believe that you can overcome addiction? Yes. Do I believe that you can have victory over the battle? Yes. Do I believe that I can help you if you want to be helped? Yes. Do I believe in you? Yes." He spoke with such confidence.

Jamie now unfolded her arms and smiled, waiting for him to continue.

Michael then said, "I've had to overcome many battles and I may not have been addicted to drugs and alcohol, but I've been addicted to something. Trust me when I say, I am more than qualified to help because I know where my help comes from. I have never been raped or abused, but can I help someone who has been? Yes. I am qualified to help others to redirect their focus no matter what their background history is. When I am helping someone, it's not about me. It's about that person. Counseling is about helping you to look at things from a new perspective. It's about facilitating personal growth and helping you to see yourself a little more clearly. I understand that addiction can be hard to overcome, but I also understand that God is powerful. He is more powerful and bigger than any addiction. God has called me to help substance abusers. He told me that I will help lead substance abusers to a different kind of substance and that substance is faith. Now faith is the *substance* of things hoped for, the *evidence* of things not seen. God will always bring evidence when we trust Him. I trust Him to help me redirect your focus to another substance . . . faith.''

Jamie's smile grew bigger. She was surprised, yet pleased with his answer.

Michael returned her smile and asked, "Did I answer your question, Jamie?''

She nodded with her smile still planted on her face. She felt comfortable in this environment, and she planned to continue attending the meetings. She felt as though she would get the help that she needed simply because of the valuable information she gained from Michael and the group tonight.

"Okay great!" Michael exclaimed. "Any more questions, comments or concerns?''

Sharon sat up straighter in her seat. "Michael, I just want to say something.'' She looked at Jamie. "When I first met

Michael, he had just started going back to school for counseling, but he was facilitating these meetings at the time and I must say; he was awesome even though he had not been fully educated in the area of counseling. That's when I realized that counseling was an art and that he was gifted in that area. At that time, just by facilitating the meetings, he made all the difference in my life. I haven't smoked crack in five years now, and he has helped me get to this point . . . Praise God!"

Everyone clapped their hands in celebration of her five years.

Sharon continued, "I can honestly say that even back then he was qualified, and now he's qualified through the world's system of things because he now has his degree and is licensed in that area. But he's been touching lives for years. Look at me. I have my marriage and family back. I have my life back. So believe me when I say, he's more than qualified."

Michael reached out his hand and grabbed hers. "Thank you so much, Sharon. God has given me the ability to help you all and I am thankful to know each of you. My purpose is to change the world and that's what I plan to do. I was created first of all to worship God and to submit to His will for my life. I am also here to touch lives and so are you all. Your story is a testimony to help someone else through and we all have a story." He smiled and looked around at each individual. "Would anyone else like to share?"

"Yes, Michael. I would like to share," Tasha said as she pulled out a piece of paper. "It is a poem that I wrote."

"We would love to hear it," Michael said to her.

She looked down at her paper, unfolded it and read:

Set Free

Addiction is something that will take your life away.

It breaks you down day by day.

You try to get back to that very first high, but it takes you, drags you.

Why, oh why?

You try to break free, but the habit won't leave.

It's powerful enough to tear down an entire family.

You think it will take away the hurt, but that hurt won't leave.

It can take your life just like a disease.

It's a sickness, and it wraps you up and takes you in.

It leaves you trapped in that cold dark sin.

It takes you fast like quick sand.

Sinking and sinking, you can't find level land.

It leaves you feeling alone, as if all hope is gone.

It is so deceitful and you know it's a lie.

But why, oh why, is it so hard to say goodbye?

You hope and hope for a brighter day.

If you take one more hit, it just might take your breath away.

It wasn't until I realized that I needed help

But when I did, I saw that there was nothing left.

It wasn't until I called out your name

I realized then that I would never be the same.

Jesus you are my light and my salvation.

You called me out of darkness, and I just want to say thank you.

If it had not been for your grace, where would I be?

Once blinded by my addiction, but by faith now I see.

Thank you for your mercy and for setting me free.

Thank you for healing and delivering me.

It wasn't until I felt your amazing touch,

You being who you are is why I love you so much.

For me, you laid down your life,

And now I choose to walk in your marvelous light.

You gave me power and strength to overcome.

You gave me a new life and a brand new song.

There's nothing that can keep me away from your love.

I'm like an eagle soaring to the Heavens above.

Thank you for your love and for saving me.

It is all because of your blood that I've been set free.

Tears of joy ran from Tasha's eyes. "I wrote this last night when I was in deep thought. I had wanted a drink, but God told me to write. So, I started writing and it took my mind to another place, and I enjoyed being in that place. There was peace there,'' Tasha explained with a smile.

"That is wonderful, Tasha, and that poem is absolutely beautiful. There is peace in being obedient," Michael said.

"Yes, there is and thank you so much, Michael. It is not until you know and understand where your help truly comes from, that you will be able to make a complete turn around in your life. God is so awesome and I am just thankful that He has gotten my life back on track. I am now in church. I have a job and a new place to stay. I am in school for my GED, and I've met so many new people. I also met this wonderful man who treats me so well, and he is so supportive of me.''

"I am so proud of you, Tasha,'' Michael said.

At that moment, everyone celebrated life.

Michael closed out the meeting with a prayer, after which he said, "Don't forget. Don't allow your past to hold you hostage. When the enemy comes to attack, remember where your help comes from. God will bring you through the attack every time when you trust Him. Be encouraged to take things one day at a time. Do not get overwhelmed with what life throws at you. Everybody inhale and count to five,'' he said.

Everyone inhaled and counted to five.

"Now exhale,'' he said.

Everyone exhaled.

"Now praise God in the midst of it all. The Word says, 'Let everything that hath breath, praise Him'." He looked around at everyone. "So, praise the Lord, everybody."

Everyone rejoiced as they walked out of the building.

"Y'all, be blessed and be a blessing!" he yelled to them in the parking lot. Finally he got into his car after locking up the building.

Chapter Fourteen

Emmanuel and Kim had been spending more and more time together. He spent much time with Trey, Jr., and Trey, Jr. loved him. Some of Emmanuel's friends tried to talk him out of being in a relationship when they found out Kim had AIDS, but they were not successful. He and Kim has been practicing celibacy and it gets hard at times, but they are determined to do things God's way, decent and in order. They had met each other's family and they loved each of them. Pastor Matthews and his wife had already known Kim for a long time and they were already in love with her before she and Emmanuel even met.

He and Kim were at dinner, enjoying their meals. Emmanuel stopped eating and stared at her. "Kim, you are so amazing, strong and beautiful. These past months that we have been spending together have truly been a gift from God." He leaned over the table and kissed her. "Everything about you is beautiful and I am so in love with who you are," he said as he looked her in her eyes.

Kim looked at him and hesitated. "Emmanuel. I don't know what to say," she said.

"I've seen your fear, Kim, and understand where it comes from. I am nothing like Trey. I would never hurt you and I promise you that. I feel like God has blessed me just because He allowed me to be in the presence of one of His greatest creations and I wouldn't do anything to mess that up. I love you, Kim. I really do and I want to spend the rest of my life showing you."

A violinist came over to the table and began playing KC and JoJo's *All My Life.*

Emmanuel got down on his knee and opened up a ring box and in it was a beautiful Neil Lane diamond ring. "Kimbrailee Kianue Whitmore, would you do me the honor of being my wife?"

Kim's mouth dropped as she looked at the ring. When she looked into his eyes, tears ran down her face. "Yes, Emmanuel! Yes!" She threw her arms around his neck. Then she pulled back and looked into his eyes. "Wait. I can't give you any children," she sadly stated. "Don't you want children?"

He looked at her and kissed her lips gently. "I already have a son. Trey, Jr., is more than enough for me. I love my lil' man, and I love you, woman." He kissed her again.

Kim's smile returned as she kissed him back.

***

Silvia came in after a long day of work. She kicked off her heels as soon as she came through the door. She went to the living room and sat on the floor. Max came to her side and she began petting him. She figured that Robert must have forgotten to let him out to the back yard before he left out this morning. During her time there, Robert helped her with her fear of dogs, and she began to really love Max. Being around him no longer bothered her. He began licking her face. Then she walked him to the back door and let him out to play.

She came back in, sat down on the floor, and laid her head back on the couch. *Why in the hell am I still in this man's house? I've already done enough damage.* She sighed as she thought about his daughter. Her plan was to seduce him and record them having sex, then send the video to his wife. But now she was having second thoughts about the whole thing. She had been talking to Carla on the phone almost every day, and Carla still had no idea that she was staying with her husband. Silvia nor Robert had mentioned it to her. But every time she talked to Carla, she realized more and more that she was suffering from depression.

She picked up the *Essence* magazine from the table and looked at President Barack Obama and First Lady Michelle on the cover. As she flipped through the pages, she saw the pictures of them holding hands, hugging and kissing one another. A tear slid down her cheek. She thought that they were one of the most beautiful couples she had ever seen, and the love and passion they showed towards one another in every picture made her think about the conversation that she and Michael had about relationships and marriage. It was the passionate way that Barack looked at Michelle that made Silvia desire to be looked upon that way by a man who truly loves her.

An article then caught her attention and she read Michelle's thoughts about her marriage and family and about Barack being a loving and caring husband, father and wonderful leader of our great country. Michelle spoke lovingly about her husband and as Silvia continued to read, more tears slid down her cheeks from the emptiness she felt. She quickly wiped her tears away when she heard Robert open the door. He immediately grabbed her attention and held it as she watched him walk in.

Robert headed straight for the kitchen. He threw some papers onto the counter and opened the cabinet. He pulled a glass and a bottle of Scotch from the cabinet. He stood there and held his head down for the longest. He then looked into the living room and right into Silvia's eyes.

"Oh, I'm sorry," he said. "I forgot. I didn't realize that you were here." He put the glass and the Scotch back in the cabinet and slammed it with a thud that made Silvia jump. She knew something was bothering him, and she knew that he wanted that drink bad.

She watched as he held his head down with his back leaned against the sink counter. He then picked up the papers from off of the counter and stared at them. Silvia could not take her eyes off of him. He looked so sexy to her with his tie loosened and his shirt half buttoned. He looked as if he had been working hard and his day was long. She was trying to fight her desire to have him, but it was strong.

He shook his head. "They served me my divorce papers today." He paused. "She says she can't do this anymore and she wants out of this marriage," he said out loud, not talking to any one in particular.

Silvia could hear the pain in his voice and she was sorry for what she had done to him and his family. She closed the magazine and placed it back on the table. Without saying a word she got up and walked over to him. She looked him in his teary eyes, then gently kissed his lips. She pulled back looking him in his eyes once again, she rubbed his wavy hair and kissed him again.

This time, he pulled back. "We can't do this,'' he said.

"Sì, se puede,'' she said. "This will be kept between us.'' She held the back of his head while looking deeply into his eyes.

He kissed her deeply and picked her up.

She wrapped her legs around him and he carried her to his bedroom.

Once he laid her on the bed, he kissed all over her and she enjoyed it as her body responded to his every kiss and his every touch. She sat up and unbuttoned the rest of his shirt and took it off, then pulled his undershirt over his head. Looking into his eyes, she ran her nails over his chest and gently kissed his tattoo. She then unbuckled his belt. She stopped for a minute as she took in his features, then kissed his navel. She took in his features once again.

This man was so sexy and beautiful to her and right now the only thing that was on her mind was having him. He reached over into his nightstand and pulled out a condom. She gently took it from his hand, opened it with her teeth, and slipped it on for him. He looked at her for a moment, then kissed her with passion.

Robert gently slid himself into her body, and he pleased her in every way imaginable with every gentle stroke. She grabbed the sheets as this man lit a fire in her that grew wild. She now wrapped her arms around his back, digging her nails into him. He looked at her with her eyes closed and saw the pleasure upon her face. He enjoyed every moment of gratifying her.

Silvia began moaning loudly as he released all of his stress and tension. She wrapped her legs tighter around his back as he continued to bring her pleasure. She began calling out, "Papi," and started whispering her beautiful language into his ear. No man had ever made her feel the way he was making her feel at this moment.

He gazed into her eyes and this time she was able to look back into his eyes without thinking about the past hurt he had caused her. Instead, when she looked into his eyes, she saw his tears and the hurt that she had now caused him. He felt her body tremble as his strokes got deeper. He wrapped her in his arms tighter. Feeling her release, he brought the moment to an end. They continued to look into each other's eyes. She has never been able to look any man into his eyes while having sex with them, and here she was staring back into the eyes of the man who hurt her many years ago.

Robert kissed her and eased himself out of her. He then lay down beside her and pulled her into his arms, something Silvia never allowed after sex. She always left immediately after and if they were at her place, she put them out immediately after. Cuddling was not an option. Attachment was not an option, but with this man, she started to feel attached.

He raised Silvia's head up and as her eyes met his, he kissed her. "This is something that I don't normally do," he began, "I haven't had sex with any woman other than my wife since I've been married, and I've been married for six years now." He paused and began thinking about his problems. "I can't believe it's about to end just like that. I just hope that this doesn't destroy Jazmin.'' He inhaled as he ran his hand up and down her arm. "I don't know what would have even made her think that I would touch her. I love my daughter and I wou . . .'' He choked on his words. "I would never in my life, do anything to hurt her . . . nothing. She's my daughter, my baby girl.'' Tears ran from his eyes. "I don't even know why she would have even thought that evil of me.''

"Lo siento, Robert.'' Silvia apologized and wiped his tears away. She was sorry for being responsible for this entire mess when it came to his family.

"It's not your fault. I'm okay with the divorce at this point because we have been having problems for a long time, especially after our last baby. I guess deep down I blamed her when we found out that the baby had died. She was full-term and we took for granted everything was going well. We were two weeks away from delivering. A week earlier she had stopped feeling the baby kicking and moving, so I took her to the doctor even though she refused to go. I mean, we argued about going for two days before she gave in. When we got there, they had checked for a heartbeat, but couldn't find it.'' His tears flowed even more. "Then, we found out that it was too late and she had to deliver her. The cord had wrapped around the baby's neck. It was devastating for both of us. Don't get me wrong, I love Carla with all my heart and I really don't want a divorce, but if it will make her happy, I will give it to her without a fight. My concern is for my daughter, and when she called and said that she was going to give her back to me, my heartbeat came back. I can't even see myself being away from her for too long... That little girl is my life, Silvia. I can't breathe without her. Now I'm concerned about having to move her back and forth between the two of us. I refuse to keep her away from Carla.''

"Maybe you should move back to where they are now," Silvia suggested. "At least you would be closer to her."

"No, I can't keep running back and forth . . . I have to believe that it's going to work out. Maybe even Carla will move back here. She just needs time and I will give her that. I know she may not be emotionally or mentally stable right now and that is apparent, but I refuse to take Jazmin away from her."

"What do you mean; keep running back and forth?" she asked, disregarding everything else he said.

"Well, I ran from here attempting to run away from my problems." He hesitated as tears ran from his eyes once again. "My parents were killed in a car accident about twelve years ago and it really messed me up. My dad had been drinking heavily at a party and decided to drive him and my mother home, but unfortunately they didn't make it there. He was an alcoholic and that's one reason why I try my best to stay away from drinking because I saw what it did to him. It gets pretty hard at times though. Sometimes I crave a drink, but I know that I don't handle them very well. I lose my mind when I'm drunk." He shook his head. "I'm an angry drunk, believe me. That's why that night when you first came to stay here, I didn't know what happened that made you react the way you did. I didn't know if I hurt you or something." He wiped his face with the back of his hand, and then looked her in her eyes. "So, do you mind telling me what happened that night?"

"Nothing happened."

He stared at her for a moment. For some reason, he wanted to know her. "What are your dreams and aspirations, Silvia?"

She looked at him. "What do you mean?"

"What is it that you love? What do you dream about?" He shrugged. "You know. What are your dreams?"

His question caught her off guard, and she thought for a minute before saying, "I love what I do. Architecture is my dream. Being able to create is something that I've always wanted to do." She paused, realizing that she was having pillow talk with this man.

"Are you sure that's all?"

She smiled and arched her back a little more before speaking. "I've always dreamed of being a dancer." She laughed softly.

At that moment he knew for sure that dancing was her dream. "When I saw you dancing the other day, you looked so happy and peaceful." He kissed her lips. "And I enjoyed watching you. You were amazing and beautiful. It was at that very moment I knew that dancing brought you joy."

"When I was younger, I wanted to open a school of dance. I wanted to help young girls work through their fears, their troubles, heartaches and disappointments, through dance. That was going to be their therapy." She sighed. "That *was* my dream."

"Why didn't you pursue that dream?"

Her eyes now saddened. "Because I became the girl with the fears, troubles, heartaches and disappointments."

He traced her lips with his fingertips. "Sometimes people, our situations, and even our circumstances may not make living our dreams easy, but that doesn't mean we can't live them. We just have to keep moving forward.''

Silvia inhaled deeply as she remembered Michael using those same words, *Keep moving forward.* She desperately wanted to move forward in her life.

Robert now touched her face and looked deeply into her tear-filled eyes. "I really think you should pursue *that* dream. You are amazing and even though you became *that* girl, you can be an example to the younger girls by allowing dance to be your therapy.''

She shook her head. "I don't think so, Robert.''

He became silent as he stared at her once again, taking in her beauty. His mind began to wonder and it made him ask, "Why hasn't some man snatched you up yet? I can't believe that you are single. Why is that?''

She waited a minute before saying, "Well, a long time ago, I was hurt badly. I had to bear the most unbearable pain at the hands of a man. So, now, I don't do well with relationships. I would rather keep it simple.''

As he continued to stare at her in admiration, it was as if he could feel the brick wall that she had up and he desperately wanted to help it fall. He asked, "Would you like to share with me what happened?''

You happened. "Guess what?'' she said, changing the subject. She refused to discuss it any further, especially with the man who had caused her that unbearable pain. She had never really shared her feelings about that night with anyone and she didn't plan on doing it now. "My apartment will be ready tomorrow, so I will be outta here.'' She forced a smile. He still had no idea that nothing was ever wrong with her apartment from the beginning.

"How about you just stay here with me?'' He paused when he saw the apprehension on her face. "Just for a little while,'' he added.

"I'm sorry, but I can't.''

He held her tighter, and looked into her eyes deeper. "Well, stay in here with me tonight.'' He kissed her, then reached into the nightstand and pulled out another condom. He put it on and once again, he pleased her.

What am I doing? This man is breaking every one of the rules, she thought to herself as she allowed him to wrap her in his strong arms. She didn't understand what was happening, but she felt a strong connection that was hard to break and it was something she wasn't use to. She ended up falling asleep in his arms. Something else she had never done with anyone.

Chapter Fifteen

Silvia woke up in a cold sweat from the nightmare that had her heart racing. Her eyes wandered to the unfamiliar place that she was in. Then she looked beside her and saw Robert still asleep. She quickly got up and fell to the floor as she tried to get away from him. "What in hell is happening to me?" she whispered to herself. Her nightmare was the reality of her past. With her past vivid in her mind, she quickly got up and ran downstairs to grab her purse. When she came back up, tears were streaming down her face. She stood in the corner as she watched the man who had caused her so much pain, her tears flowing steadily as she watched him inhale and exhale in his sleep.

Robert woke up and attempted to wrap his arm around her, rubbed the bed, and realized that she wasn't there. He looked at the clock on the nightstand: 5:05 a.m. He then heard Silvia breathing heavily and looked to the corner where she stood. He squinted his eyes to see a little clearer as he got up from where he lay.

He slowly began approaching her. "Silvia? Are you okay?" he asked. "What's wrong?"

She pulled up the gun.

He stopped in his tracks and frowned. Confused, he asked, "What are you doing?"

"Get away from me!" she yelled. "You will never, *ever*, hurt me again!"

"What are you talking about?" As he looked into her eyes, he saw pain and fear. He didn't understand what was happening. "Look, Silvia. Just give me the gun and talk to me. Tell me what's wrong." He began approaching her with caution and reached out his hand for her to give him the gun. "Just tell me what I did."

"What you did!" she yelled. "Okay!" She nodded. "You want to know what you did, Robert?" Her pain was uncovered as she spoke hastily. "You stole the little bit of innocence that I had left and didn't even think twice about it! I kicked . . . and I screamed . . . and I cried out for you to stop, and you didn't!" She cried even more.

Robert stood still with a puzzled look on his face, not having a clue as to what she was talking about.

"It hurt so badly!" She cried. "You treated me like I was nothing, like a whore!" she screamed. "I thought you were the most beautiful man that I had ever seen, but I quickly found out that you were the devil himself."

Robert looked at her and tilted his head as if trying to understand what all she was telling him. His expression changed as his memory from the past invaded his present.

When she saw the look on his face, she nodded, giving him confirmation. "I was the girl you raped in that room twelve years ago. I was the one whose virginity you had taken. I was

only eighteen. A virgin, Robert, and you took that from me!''
she screamed, now almost out of breath. "You left me for dead.
You took my life in that VIP room that night, and now, I'm
going to take yours,'' she coldly stated.

Robert closed his eyes as it all came back to him. "Oh,
my God, Silvia.'' He shook his head, wishing that he could
change things. "I'm so sorry. I promise, I was not in my right
mind that night.'' He walked up to her and the cold, steel barrel
of the gun touched his chest. "I'm so sorry. I didn't know.''
Tears now ran from his eyes. Right now at this point, he felt as
though he deserved what she was about to do to him, and he
didn't try to stop her.

Silvia pulled the trigger.

Click . . . Click . . . Click . . . Click . . . Click . . .

She dropped the gun and fell to the floor in tears. She
cried out from all of her pain.

Robert grabbed her and embraced her, and she continued
to cry in his arms. He held her tightly as tears flowed from his
eyes. He was remorseful for all of the pain that he had caused
her.

"Whhhyy?'' she screamed out, her body trembling.
"How could you do that to me?'' She tried to push him away.

He wrapped her in his arms tighter. "I'm so sorry. It's
okay, Silvia. You are okay now. I promise, I will never hurt you
again.''

"Get off of me!'' She began to fight him and he
loosened his embrace. "Stay away from me, you bastard!'' she

screamed, and ran out of the room. She ran out of the house and to her car.

Robert called out to her, but he refused to run behind her, knowing it wasn't anything that he could do to give her back what he had taken from her. He sat there in shock with his hands covering his mouth as his tears continued to flow. He saw the gun on the floor next to him and he picked it up. He opened the chamber and saw that it had one bullet in it, and if she had pulled the trigger once more, she might have taken his life.

Silvia drove around for hours. Her cell rang over and over again. Every single time it rang, Robert's name flashed on her caller ID. She pulled into Reesie's driveway, got out and banged on the door.

Brandon swung the door open. "What the hell is your problem?" he yelled at her.

Silvia pushed past him. "Where's Reesie?" She began looking around the house in a panic.

Brandon could see that something was seriously wrong with her. "She's gone to take Regina to work, and then to the grocery store." He watched her pace the floor. "What? You came to give me some?" He laughed.

She quickly walked up to him. "I hate you!" she screamed through her tears.

He grabbed her arm and pushed her up against the wall. He looked into her eyes. "Yeah, but I'm the one you love to hate."

He kissed her and she kissed him back. He picked her up and with her back up against the wall, she wrapped her legs around him. The wall helped to hold her up as he unzipped his pants. He began having sex with her. Silvia tried to get rid of everything, her nightmares, her past, her reality, her pain. Brandon was enjoying the moment that he had been waiting for ever since he met Silvia. He was rough with her, but she didn't care. She just wanted the pain from twelve years ago, to disappear. She grabbed Brandon's shirt and groaned loudly as he got rougher.

"Silvia!'' Reesie screamed out and dropped the bags of groceries after seeing her boyfriend with her best friend. "What are you doing?'' She could not believe her eyes and she was completely hurt by the two people that she loved the most.

Brandon heard the car when Reesie pulled into the driveway, but it was feeling too good to him and he wasn't willing to stop. Even when he heard the keys rattling at the door, he continued. And when he heard her call Silvia's name, he kept going until he was finished.

Silvia eased herself down.

Brandon stared Silvia in her eyes as he pulled up his pants. Then he looked at Reesie and walked past her. Almost out of breath, he said, "I have to make a run.'' He walked out of the door, slamming it behind him.

Tears streamed from Reesie's eyes as she stood there, shaking her head. "How could you, Silvia? You are supposed to be my friend,'' she scolded. "I am your friend, and you do me like this!''

"Really, Reesie . . . my friend . . . are you really? You were the one who introduced me to that god-awful lifestyle when you really wanted out of it yourself. If you were my friend, you would not have talked me into that foolishness, knowing what it would lead to. If you were my friend, you would have come to help me when you heard my screams in that VIP room." She walked over to her and looked her in her eyes. "You heard me that night. I know you did. I know you knew what was happening to me, and you didn't even get help. Instead of being my friend and helping me, you and Cato covered it up like I didn't matter. You let those guys walk away, but you are my friend? You call that a friend?" Her hands balled into fists at her sides. "I was raped, Reesie!"

In tears, "Silvia, get over it!" Reesie screamed. "You walk around here like you are the only one who has ever been raped, but you are not. At least you had a mother who cared about you. My mother had man after man after man and not once did she think about what those men did to her daughter. She only thought about herself and what she wanted. She was so selfish and she was never there. All she cared about was having a man and being able to have sex freely. She had a man for every bill and every bill they paid, they felt as though I was their return payment." She sobbed. "I was raped, Silvia! Every day of my teen years for six years, I was raped. You want to know who paid for me to go to college my first semester, my rapist. So don't you dare believe for one minute that you are the only one hurting because you are not! Everybody has a well-kept secret."

Silvia was shocked and didn't know how to respond to the secret that Reesie had just revealed to her. She walked out of the door and to her car without saying a word. She drove to her job, not intending to work. When she got there she headed straight past Regina at the receptionist desk and to Michael's office. She barged through his door.

Michael looked up and was shocked at her disheveled appearance. Her hair was all over her head, her eyes were red and swollen, and her clothes were not on her right. "Silvia? What is wrong?'' he asked, concerned. He got up and walked over to her.

"I think I've hit my rock bottom. I need help, Michael. I can't do this anymore!" She cried hysterically.

He pulled her into his arms. "Okay. Shhh, you are okay. Just breathe,'' he whispered in her ear and rubbed her hair as she continued to cry on his shoulder.

Chapter Sixteen

Kim was in worship while in the shower and she began praising God. "God, I just want to thank you for who you are and for all you have done in my life and the lives of everyone around me. Thank you for your son and for the death, burial, and resurrection. Thank you, God, for life and life more abundantly. Thank you for preserving my life. I know I deserved death, but you didn't see fit. Thank you for grace and mercy. Thank you for your blessings. Thank you for your love and thank you for the man who you sent to find me. I know that he is a gift from you because I see you in him. He treats me the way that you desire him to treat me and for that, I am thankful. He already loved me in sickness and in health. So I believe with all my heart that this will be until death do us part. My hope is in your Word and my faith is in you. God, I love you. I will keep you first in everything. My marriage will be your marriage. Keep it and preserve it. May it glorify you always. Thank you for being God.'' Kim remained in worship and cried tears of joy as she thought about God's greatness . . .

***

Robert continued to call Silvia ever since the morning she ran out on him and she continued to ignore every one of his calls.

She just wanted a break from everything, so she decided to take a trip back home to Dallas. She unlocked the door to her mother's house and walked in. Her arms were filled with gifts that she bought for everyone. She sat them down on the couch.

"Mami?" she called out to her mother as she looked around for her.

Her mother, Rita, walked around the kitchen corner. She looked at Silvia and was completely surprised. "Silvia, baby? What are you doing home?" She slowly walked over to her and hugged her so tight you would have thought that she was never going to let her go.

Silvia took a long look at her mother. "Mami, is everything okay?" Her mother didn't look well and she had lost a lot of weight since the last time Silvia had seen her. Her skin had rashes and blisters all over it. "What are these rashes all over you?" She examined her arm. "Did you have an allergic reaction to something?"

Rita ignored her question. "I'm so glad you are home, baby. God knows what He is doing," she said, looking up at the ceiling.

"What's going on?"

"Look, honey, you are going to have to take Angel . . ."

Shaking her head, she interrupted her, "No, Mami! I can't." She was hoping her mother didn't really mean that. "What do you mean, *take* her?"

Her mother put up her hand to stop Silvia's protest. "I can't take care of her right now. I've been diagnosed with

Lupus. My immune system is getting weaker and I'm losing weight. My hair is coming out everywhere. My skin is starting to look bad and I don't want Angel to be worried.'' She looked at her daughter. "It's progressing to another stage, Silvia, and it's beginning to attack my organs.''

Tears formed in Silvia's eyes. "Mami, why didn't you tell me that you were sick? How long have you known?''

"For six months now, but that's neither here, nor there. Carl has been helping me with Angel, but I can't put her off on him like that. He's picking her up from dance practice now.'' Her mother saw the fear in Silvia's eyes as tears fell from them. "Look, Silvia, before you say no, say *yes*. She needs you and I don't want her to see me like this. You only come home to visit once a year, and that is on Mother's Day. You never hardly come see her and every time you come, you bring her gifts like that's supposed to make it all right.'' She picked up a brochure off the table and handed it to her.

Silvia looked at the brochure, and then she looked at her mother. "What is this?"

Her mother answered, "It's a dance program. Angel was just talking to me about this yesterday, and she really wants to go. They are having a ballet class up there that she really wants to be a part of for the summer, so this is the perfect opportunity. She prayed about being a part of that program, and I believe by you coming here, God has answered her prayer . . . both of our prayers.'' She gave Silvia a second to take it all in. "When you leave here to go back to Baton Rouge, you are taking her with you,'' she firmly stated.

Silvia didn't have time to protest because Angel had come through the front door. "Silvia? Wow, it's not Mother's Day. What are you in town for?" she asked, then hugged her.

Without saying a word, Silvia went over to the couch and picked up one of the gifts that she brought for her. Avoiding eye contact, she handed it to her.

Angel opened it. "Wow!" Her eyes widened at the five books in her hand and she then looked up. "Thanks, Silvy! You got me the *Ballerina Diaries*!" She hugged her again.

Silvia laughed at the fact that Angel had given her that nick name when she was only two years old. She looked at how gorgeous Angel was with her long, beautiful, black hair, rosy cheeks and flawless skin. She was maturing so fast and Silvia had missed her entire life.

Her step-father, Carl, walked in the door and she hugged him, then handed him his gift.

"Silvia, you know that you don't have to come bearing gifts every time you come," he said

"Yes, she does!" Angel hollered out laughing. She walked to her room to put up her books.

"Yes, I do, Dad," Silvia replied to him. "You have been so great to me and to our family, and I love you so much."

Carl was Silvia's step-father, but he was the only father she ever knew. He came into her life when she was three years old and he has been there ever since. He was a hardworking, yet underpaid man, but he was going to do what he had to do to provide for his family.

She remembered the day that she was trying to get into college, but she found out that she didn't have enough. Carl brought her the last out of his savings which was only two-thousand dollars. It wasn't enough, but she didn't have the heart to tell them that it wasn't. That's when Reesie introduced the night life to her.

Silvia's mother didn't talk much about her biological father. All she knows is that he was some wealthy man who her mother later found out was married. Then he paid her mom to go away, and according to Silvia's mother, he never knew about her. She never told him that she was pregnant. After all, she was forty and she herself couldn't believe that she was pregnant, so she didn't expect him to believe her. Rita didn't want any part of him. So she raised Silvia using the money he paid her off with. She made sure Silvia went to the finest schools. She put her in all kinds of dance classes, gymnastics and different pageants. Then, when it was time for college, her mother was out of funds. Silvia was a spitting image of her mother whom she loved very much, so she tried to suppress the feeling of wanting to find her biological father. She just wanted to know who he was.

Silvia walked over and gave her mother her gift and kissed her cheek. She whispered into her ear, "Mother, I love you so much, but I can't take her with me. I have so much going on right now, and it's not the right time." She looked into her eyes. "Mami, please," she begged, attempting to get her to change her mind.

"I'm sorry, Silvia, but now *is* the time," she said as she looked in her daughter's eyes. She called Angel back into the room.

Angel walked in with one of the books that Silvia had just given her.

"Guess what, Angel?" Rita began. "Your big sister is going to take you to be with her for the summer. Remember the brochure we were looking at about that dance class in Baton Rouge? Well, your sister has agreed to let you stay with her for a while until you complete the program." She, Carl and Silvia gave looks between each other.

"Wow! Thanks, Silvy! The brochure makes it sound so nice, and at the end we have a recital." She turned to face Rita. "Will you be coming for that, Mami?" Angel asked.

"Of course!" Rita popped her on her butt. "Now, go pack," she said to Angel, but looked at Silvia whose arms were crossed in front of her chest. Her face showed her anger as tears filled her eyes.

Angel was so excited. She had never spent time with Silvia. She would only see her once a year and she only remembered those years after the age of five. She barely knew her so, her plan was not only to enjoy the dance class, but also to get to know her big sister over the summer and have tons of fun with her.

Silvia had never dealt with a child her whole life, so she didn't know what to expect. While Angel was packing, Rita sat in the living room and watched Silvia pace the floor. Carl walked over to her and put his hand on her shoulder. Silvia looked in his eyes.

"She is a really wonderful child, and you are going to be so great with her, Silvia. She's going to love being with you.

There's no need to worry,'' he told her, attempting to calm her fear.

She smiled at him and he hugged her.

Silvia was headed to the bathroom when she passed by Angel's bedroom. She heard her singing, "My God is awesome... awesome . . . awesome . . . awesome . . .'' and it compelled her to stop. She walked back to her door and watched her through the crack as she packed her bags. *Maybe this won't be so bad.* Angel sang like an angel, and Silvia didn't realize that she was so talented. She knocked on the door and walked in. "Are you almost ready, Angel?''

"Yes, almost!'' She continued packing. "This is going to be great! We get to spend time together and you will finally get to see me dance . . . We can talk about boys.'' She giggled shyly, and Silvia couldn't help but smile. "Mami hates it when I talk about boys. She told me that boys are bad and that I shouldn't like them, She said that they will get me in trouble. It will be cool having a big sister around. I know you will tell me the truth about boys.'' She walked over and hugged Silvia.

Silvia's heart melted. "So, are you ready?''

"I was born ready! Will we be going to church? If so, I need to make sure I have my Sunday shoes and dresses.''

"Church? You go to church?''

"Yes. I started going with Papi, and then I talked Mami into going. I really like it a lot and I know Jesus loves me,'' Angel told her with so much confidence.

Silvia did not realize that her mother was now going to church. Rita was raised Catholic but had never mentioned church during Silvia's childhood, so she was shocked by the information that Angel had given her.

"Okay. Well, go use the bathroom and let's hit the road," Silvia said.

"You didn't say if I needed my Sunday shoes and dresses."

"No, you don't need them. Now hurry."

When they left she was expecting Angel to fall asleep during the ride at some point, but she was up the whole time talking. She talked about everything. Silvia just nodded and laughed here and there at some of the statements she made. She made Silvia's road trip a lot more interesting, and her mind not one time reverted to what happened with her friend Reesie.

Chapter Seventeen

Silvia asked Angel did she need any help unpacking once they got home and Angel told her, "no."

Silvia only had a one bedroom apartment, so she gave Angel her room and she was going to take the couch. She ordered a pizza and rented some movies. Angel laughed so hard at the movie, *Enchanted* that she cried. Silvia watched her and began to play in her long beautiful hair that fell at her waistline.

"I really like this, Silvia. I'm glad you let me come to stay with you," Angel said to her, and then she stuffed a big piece of pizza into her mouth.

Silvia began to tear up and kissed the top of Angel's head. "Me too." She continued to play in her hair. "Okay, tomorrow we have to get you registered for this dance class. What else do we need to do?"

"After we register can I get some new dance shoes? I mean, if you have a lil' something extra. I could really use some new ones. I brought the ones Papi bought me about two months ago, but I'm really growing out of those and fast."

"Yes, I have more than enough to spare, and I would be more than happy to take you on a shopping spree."

Angel stared off into space and her face began to show the sadness that was in her heart. "Silvia, do you think Mami is going to die? Is that why she sent me here with you?"

Silvia inhaled. "No, not at all. Why would you ask that?"

"I know she is sick, Silvia. She hasn't told me, but I'm no dummy."

"No, you are definitely no dummy, but don't worry about that. Mami is going to be fine, and she's going to live a long time," she said out loud, but inside she wasn't so sure about that.

Angel talked and talked and Silvia realized what she had been missing all these years. She really was such a sweet child. They had called their mother to check on her and she was doing fine. Rita was so happy that Silvia and Angel seemed to be enjoying each other's company. She had been waiting for the moment that they would finally spend time together, real time. Angel had fallen asleep on the couch with Silvia and the movie watched them.

***

Silvia took Angel to breakfast, and then to register for her dance class. The instructor went into details about the program as she showed them around the school. When Silvia walked the dance floor it brought back so many happy memories of how she loved to dance, really dance.

She loved ballet and jazz, and she also loved gymnastics. Many of her past instructors told her that she could really go somewhere with her dancing and that her skills were rare and dynamic. They expected her to do great things when it came to her dancing. She never expected to be an exotic dancer. She had dreams, big dreams and being back in this kind of environment made her dream again.

They left the dance studio and headed for the mall. After they got there they went to every store. Silvia bought Angel a lot of different things, even stuff she didn't ask for. She really enjoyed being able to take Angel on a shopping spree and enjoyed that quality time with her. Her mind wasn't on a man or sex. Silvia held Angel's hand as they walked through the parking lot. She watched her long pony tail bounce up and down as she bounced. They were carrying so many bags and all of them belonged to Angel.

"Thank you so much, Silvia!'' Angel exclaimed.

Silvia looked at her and smiled. "You are more than welcome. Now, let's see, where do you want to go for din . . .'' Silvia stopped in midsentence when she heard her name called. Her heart began racing, and Angel immediately felt her tense up as she saw the person walking towards them.

"Silvia, I have been calling you. I'm so sorry, and I just want to ta . . .'' Robert, too, stopped in midsentence as he looked into the most gorgeous green eyes. His heart immediately answered the question that his mind was asking as he looked at this little girl.

Angel was frozen in place as she looked up at this six feet tall man and was amazed at how much he looked like her.

Silvia pulled her away from him and walked faster to the car.

Angel looked back at him, her mind beginning to wonder.

Robert caught up with them and grabbed Silvia's arm before she could go any farther. "Silvia?" He looked at her with question in his eyes.

She jerked her arm away.

"Silvia? We really need to talk," he said.

Silvia made it to the car and unlocked the door. "Get in the car now!" she yelled at Angel.

Angel stood, continuing to stare at Robert in amazement before getting in the car.

Silvia was about to close her door but Robert grabbed it before it could be shut. He looked at her. "Silvia?"

"She is my sister, Robert." She answered the question in his tone as she looked straight ahead, tears now running down her face.

He let her door go and it shut.

She sped off leaving him behind.

"Silvia, what's wrong? Who was that man?" Angel asked out of curiosity.

"No one . . . What do you want to eat, baby?" Silvia asked, changing the subject.

Her cell phone began ringing. She looked at the caller ID... *Robert Sterling.* She pressed Ignore, then put it on vibrate and threw it in the glove compartment.

Angel paid close attention to Silvia's actions. "Are you okay?"

"I'm fine, Angel! What do you want to eat?" she yelled out in frustration.

"May I ask you a question?"

Silvia sighed. "Yes, Angel, what is it?"

"Who was that man? Was he a boyfriend or something?" Her curiosity was strong.

"I told you, *he is no one!*" she yelled.

Angel did not say another word. She knew that Silvia was bothered by the man's presence. She continued to hear the phone buzz from the glove compartment, and Silvia paid no attention to it.

When they got to the restaurant, they were seated and the waitress took their orders. Silvia stared off into space as her mind wandered. She was trying to figure out what to do next. She had a strong feeling that Robert was not going to leave her alone until he talked to her. When their orders came, Angel reached for Silvia's hand and said grace. Silvia was surprised by her prayer. Just from that, she knew that Angel was a different kind of child.

"Silvia, I believe that God will heal Mami. Jesus is so awesome, and I've talked to him and I was led to scripture. You know the scripture about the stripes that were placed on his back and how he was bruised for our iniquities and wounded for our transgressions. I just hope that Mami believes it too. You know, believes that she was healed when the stripes were placed on his back?''

"What are you talking about, Angel?''

"I'm talking about Jesus. Do you believe in Jesus, Silvia?''

"Eat your food before it gets cold,'' Silvia responded, steering away from the subject.

Silvia had heard all these different people talk about their God and she has even heard people talking about Jesus before, but she had not accepted him as her Lord and personal Savior. Michael had talked to her about Jesus before and she's been listening to him in the meetings too, but to sit here and hear it come out of this child's mouth really touched her heart. Out of her mouth was perfected praise, and it caught Silvia's attention. She sat in deep thought as they continued eating their meals in silence.

***

Silvia had gone to another meeting at the Family Life Center, and this time Reesie hadn't shown up. She hadn't spoken with her since they had fallen out and was really hoping that she would see her tonight in the meeting.

Kim kept Angel with her as Silvia sat in the meeting and listened. Michael closed the meeting out in prayer and, by that time, Kim was bringing Angel back.

"Silvia, your sister is filled with so much wisdom. I really enjoyed talking to her," Kim told her.

Michael looked at Angel, and then Silvia. "It's amazing how you two look so much alike. She's so beautiful," he complimented.

"Thanks, Michael. We are a spitting image of our mother . . . Have you heard from Reesie?" she asked, quickly changing the subject.

"No," he answered. "I sure haven't. She had started coming regularly for a while, so it's not really like her to miss."

Silvia started getting a funny feeling in the pit of her stomach. "Yes, I guess I will pass that way before I go home . . . Angel, are you ready to go?"

"Yes, I'm ready." Angel looked at Kim. "I will see you at church Sunday, Ms. Kim," she told her.

They said their goodbyes and Silvia headed to see Reesie. She felt bad about what happened between them and she missed being able to talk to her friend. When she got there she told Angel to wait in the car. Silvia walked up to the door and was about to knock, but the door was already cracked.

Silvia walked in. "Rees? You here?" she yelled out as she looked around. The house was a mess and everything was thrown around. "Reesie?" she called out again.

No answer.

She walked to her bedroom and saw Reesie stretched across the bed with nothing on and blood was everywhere. "Oh, my God! Reesie?'' she called out to her. She saw that she was still breathing, but it was apparent that she had been beaten badly. She called 911 and once they arrived, she left for the hospital that they were taking her to.

They had Reesie in one of the rooms in emergency and Silvia and Angel sat and waited in the room with her. Silvia looked at her friend who had been severally beaten and she feared for her life. Her eyes were swollen and so were her lips.

Angel went over and touched Reesie's hand.

"No, Angel. Don't touch her,'' Silvia said to her.

Angel ignored her as she kept her hand on top of Reesie's. She began to pray. Silvia eyes widened with shock and her lips wouldn't move as she heard this young child pray. Reesie opened her eyes and looked at the young child. She didn't say a word as Angel's hand held hers.

Angel ended her prayer. She looked into Reesie's eyes and smiled. "They will never hurt you again.''

Reesie looked over at Silvia, her eyes barely able to open. "Who is this?'' she mumbled, her lips barely able to part.

"My little sister . . . Rees, are you okay?'' Silvia's tears were streaming down her face.

"They are looking for Brandon. I believe they are going to kill him. They came in there and stole everything. They were going to kill me. It was three of them. I was high when they kicked the door in, I don't even know what happened after they questioned me and knocked me out with that gun.''

"Reesie, you were raped by those guys!'' Silvia said. "They got DNA off of you."

"Well, I'm fine now,'' Reesie said through her tears.

"Are you serious? You say it like it's no big deal that these men raped and beat you. You could have died. Rees, they left you for dead!'' Silvia yelled at her. "They said if I wouldn't have found you that you would have been dead within twenty-four hours because of all the blood you lost. Those men raped you and tried to kill you.'' Tears fell from her eyes as she hugged Reesie.

"I'm fine, Silvia. I am not in pain or anything.''

Silvia was shocked that she wasn't in pain. She had been beaten badly until she was unconscious, and from the looks of her, she should have been in severe pain.

"Did they test me for any STDs?''

"Yes, they tested you, Reesie, but do you know who did this to you? They need to pay for what they did. You have to report them.'' The thought of them getting away with rape, angered Silvia.

"I don't know who they were,'' Reesie mumbled. "I just know they asked me questions about Brandon. This is what you don't understand, Silvia. Women get raped every day. Men will be men. We just have to deal with it . . . I'm okay.'' She looked at Silvia's tears and said, "It's okay.''

"What?'' she yelled out in anger. "It is not okay! They have no right to treat us the way that they do, Rees. I don't understand your way of thinking. You talk like this is normal.

Are you that use to being raped that it has become a norm for you?''

"What if I told you, yes? It has become a norm for me. You don't know me and you don't understand where I come from." A tear ran from her eye. "I was sexually abused and raped not just by one of my mother's boyfriends. Two!'' Reesie yelled through her teeth. "When I told my mother, she brushed it off and told me to deal with it. She said that 'men will be men', and I should have kept my legs closed if I didn't want them between them; and if they really did touch me, I better act as if they didn't . . . keep my mouth closed and to get out of her face. I've lived with that all these years, and I can live with this.''

"Why do we have to live in silence?'' Silvia asked in a hostile tone.

Ignoring her, Reesie looked over at Angel. "Silvia, she's so beautiful. I didn't know you had a little sister.'' She looked at Silvia. "You never told me about her.''

Silvia had forgotten that Angel was even in the room. "I have to go, Rees,'' she said as she grabbed Angel's hand and headed out of the emergency room.

Angel studied Silvia's actions as they got in the car.

"Angel, you wanted to know about boys? Well, I will tell you. They are some of the most evil creatures and no matter what, don't ever trust them. They will steal everything from you... your life . . . your joy . . . everything. Before you know it, you won't know who you are anymore.'' Silvia's tears flowed.

Angel looked at her and saw the pain in her face. "Silvia, I don't believe all boys are the same, and all of them are not evil. You have just been meeting the wrong ones.''

Silvia looked over at Angel and she wondered how this little girl became so wise, so young. Angel reached for her hand and held it until they made it home.

As she brushed Angel's hair, she thought about how she hadn't thought much about her past since Angel's been with her, and not once had she had sex with a man. She was now focused on Angel and to her that felt good.

Chapter Eighteen

Angel was getting ready for an audition for which she had only been able to practice a week. She was auditioning to be a dancer in one of the scenes of a big play that was coming to town. As soon as her dance instructor told her about the play, she began preparing for it. She did her own choreography and had been doing a really great job at practice. She and Silvia were running behind and rushing in order to make it there on time. It was starting at 5:00 p.m. and it was already 4:20 p.m.

When her cell phone rang, she quickly answered it and began to speak hurriedly. "I'm sorry, Mami. The call dropped. Sometimes I get bad reception here, but I was saying that I'm about to take her to Elegant Dance Studios so she can audition for that play I was telling you about. We are running a little bit behind. It starts at five, so we have to go, Mami; but I will call you to let you know how it goes. I love you! Kiss, kiss." She blew kisses through the phone and hung up immediately. "Angel, are you ready, baby?" Silvia yelled to her.

Once they arrived, Silvia waited with Angel back stage. Then the instructor told Angel that she was going to be up next. She was the last one on this list to audition.

Silvia could see the fear in her eyes, and she told her, "You are going to do great, Angel. No worries." She kissed her cheek. "I love you so much." She then took her seat in the audience.

The judges called Angel to the stage.

The music began playing Beyonce's *Halo*, and Angel began her audition. She danced beautifully and immediately captured the judge's attention.

Silvia watched her as she heard the music play. She listened to the lyrics as Beyonce sang, "Remember those walls I built? Well, baby they're tumbling down, and they didn't even put up a fight. They didn't even make up a sound. I found a way to let you in, but I never really had a doubt. Standing in the light of your halo, I've got my angel now. It's like I've been awakened. Every rule I had you breakin'. It's the risk that I'm takin'. I ain't never gonna shut you out. Everywhere I'm looking now, I'm surrounded by your embrace . . ."

Tears ran down Silvia's face as she watched Angel glide across the stage. She watched as she did her allégros, attitudes, brisés, glissades, royales, pirouettes and piqués. She danced effortlessly across the stage as she pivoted and glided as if she were floating on air. Most of her routine would have been difficult for a lot of people, but she made it look simple as she executed every detail precisely. Her presence was beautiful, and she was a true natural.

Robert stood in the back as he watched Angel's performance. She was truly beautiful to him as she glided across the stage. He knew exactly where her natural talent came from. There were very few people in the building, and he was able to spot Silvia from behind. He watched her for a minute, then returned his focus to Angel. As she finished her audition, tears formed in his eyes. He wanted to stay, but he wasn't sure if that was a good idea. Once the music stopped he was about to turn and walk out, but then he heard the judges say her name, which made him stop in his tracks.

"Little Miss Angel,'' the female judge began. "That was a beautiful performance, and you were a joy to watch. I'm almost speechless. Your name is every bit of what you looked like on that stage. It is my pleasure to tell you that you have the part,'' she said to her, and the other three nodded their approval.

Angel was overjoyed. She thanked the judges, then ran over to Silvia and hugged her.

Tears ran from Robert's eyes as he watched them. After Angel went over and thanked her instructor, she and Silvia started walking his way. He quickly wiped the tears from his eyes. He was trying to make his feet move to go back to the door unseen, but his heart wouldn't let him move.

As Silvia got closer, she realized who he was. She grabbed Angel's hand tightly and stood in front of her, shielding her. She cut her eyes at Robert. "What are you doing here?'' she hissed.

"Well, when I called you earlier, you told me about the audition.'' He stepped to the side and looked over at Angel. "I wouldn't have missed it for the world.''

Silvia clenched her teeth. "I haven't talked to you, and I haven't told you anything so . . .''

He cut Silvia's sentence off as he spoke to Angel, "You looked so beautiful up there." He tried to choke back his tears as he continued, "Angel." A single tear ran from his eye when he spoke her name. He then looked at the flowers that he held in his hand and held them out to her.

Angel just looked at him for a moment, then she reached for the flowers. "Gracious." She smiled. She didn't know who this man was, or why Silvia seemed to be so angry whenever he came around, but the feeling she pulled from him, was different.

"De nada," Robert replied, speaking her language back to her which made her smile even more.

Silvia thought about it, and she pulled out her cell phone and went through her calls list. She saw that it was him who had called right before they were about to leave out, not her mother. *I will never again answer my phone without looking at the caller ID.* "Why don't you just stay out of my life? You have done enough damage," she said to him. She grabbed Angel's hand even tighter before walking away.

Robert grabbed Silvia's arm and she turned to face him. "I'm sorry, Silvia. I swear to you. I never meant to hurt you," he whispered to her as he looked at the tears in her eyes.

His eyes told her that he meant every word he had just spoken. She turned and walked away. This time their ride home was silent as tears ran down her face. Angel watched her as she saw her pain flow from her eyes. When they got in the apartment, Silvia put Angel's flowers in a beautiful crystal vase. She smelled them and took them to the bedroom where she slept. When she came back out, Angel studied her.

"Silvia, are you ever going to tell me who that man is?"

"He's nobody, Angel."

***

Brandon walked into the Family Life Center after one of Michael's meetings. "Hey, I'm looking for a guy named Michael," he said.

"I'm, Michael. What can I do for you?" he asked, as he turned around to see who it was that he was talking to. He noticed that the young man looked distraught, and he stopped cleaning up in order to pay closer attention to him.

"My girl told me that she has been coming here, and it has been helping her," Brandon said to him.

"Who is the young lady that you are referring to?"

Brandon replied, "Reesie."

"Oh, yes. She has been coming here, but I haven't seen her lately. How is she?"

"She's fine. Look, I . . ." He shook his head. "I don't know what I came here for." He turned to walk away.

"Of course you know why you came here," Michael said, and it caught Brandon's attention. "You are the one Reesie has told me so much about." He walked over to him and looked him in his eyes. "You want out of the lifestyle, but you are scared to get out, and you are scared to stay in. You are on the fence." Reesie never told him that, but he could sense it from Brandon at the moment.

"What are you talking about, man? You don't know me," Brandon said angrily.

"I know your kind all too well. You got into the life style because it made you feel like you were a part of something. It made you feel as though you were somebody. The life style brought fast money, fast women and power. It made the hood afraid of you. They are so afraid of you that they won't even turn you in because of fear of retaliation. You have young men, *babies*, who look up to you and respect you because you have all the money, women and bad cars sitting on twenty-fours and they think that's what's up. See, you believe that you can't do anything else with money and women coming at you that fast. You feel stuck, but you know there's a way out and that's why you are here," Michael told him.

Brandon stood in shock at how Michael approached him.

"You are selling your own people death every time you serve them their drug of choice. Your type is what kills the hood when you are called to build it up, not tear it down. The big man sends y'all out to make the deal, while they sit behind the scene, hiding. But, *y'all*," he pointed at him, "the ones who work on the streets, are the ones that end up dead or in jail. Most of the money goes to the top people when y'all are the main ones who put yourselves at risk for deadly situations. They want y'all to kill and destroy each other and y'all don't even realize it. You are falling into their trap *every* day. They want you dead because if you are dead you can't do anything. You can't make a difference. But if you are alive, you can do the impossible and that's what puts fear in them. Brother, it is time to rise up and be the difference that we very much so need in our communities. When God has a plan for your life, Satan will try to take you out, but you need to stand still and see the salvation of the Lord. The enemy came to steal, kill and to destroy, but God sent His son so that *you* may have life and have it more abundantly.''

Tears formed in Brandon's eyes as Michael continued talking to him.

"You *can* get out of the lifestyle, Brandon. It has been holding you back way too long. I'm tired of seeing my brothers dying behind foolishness, behind nonsense. What profits a man to gain the whole world and lose his soul? Money is not everything and fast money will get you killed. Satan puts a lot of stuff out there, but he has nothing to offer. God has been trying to get your attention for a long time, and it's time for you to stop running because one day you will run out of time. You've been walking around all this time, sleeping. Well, now is the time for you to rise up.'' He walked up to him even closer. He looked deeply into Brandon's tear-filled eyes and boldly told him, "Wake up . . . Stop sleeping!''

It was as if reality was just hitting Brandon as tears now ran from his eyes.

"If Jesus returned right now, you would be left behind because you chose foolishness. But God has given you another chance to make the right choice, right here and now. You can get right, or get left. The choice is yours. God is the God of many chances, but what happens when you are all out of chances?'' He got even closer to him. "If your enemies take you out today, where would you spend eternity?''

Brandon's tears continued to flow. "I don't know.''

"Well, where you spend it is completely up to you. It is a choice.'' He pointed to him before saying, "*Your* choice. You can spend it with God, or you can spend it in hell, away from

Him. So, you tell me, Brandon. What do you want to do?''
Michael looked at him intensely.

Brandon looked Michael straight in his eyes and said, "I
want to spend it with God.''

"Well, there's only one way to the father, and that is
through the son.'' Michael paused and studied him. "The wages
of sin is death, but the gift of God is eternal life through His son,
Jesus Christ. For God so loved the world that He gave His only
begotten son that whosoever believeth in Him shall not perish
but have everlasting life. All you have to do, Brandon, is turn
away from your wicked ways and give your life to Jesus, the
only one who can save you. For if you confess with your mouth,
Jesus is Lord, and believe in your heart that God raised Him
from the dead, you shall be saved.''

Michael grabbed Brandon's hand, and the surge of
energy that he felt made him fall to his knees. He called out the
name of Jesus. Michael prayed with him and that night, Brandon
was led to salvation.

Chapter Nineteen

Silvia was in her office when her cell phone began ringing. She looked at the caller ID and answered it, "Hi, Mami, I had called you earlier about the party that I was going to throw Angel. All I know about her is the fact that she loves dance. Every gift that I have ever bought her has to do with dance. I want to do something different for her. Any suggestions?" she asked her mother.

"Why didn't you just ask her what kind of things she likes?"

"I don't know. I didn't want to just come out and ask her what she wants for her birthday."

"Well, Silvia, you don't have to come out and ask her what she wants for her birthday. Of course, you have learned something about her during the time that you have been with her, honey. Surely, you can think of something she would like."

Silvia sat and thought for a moment. "You are right." She twirled her pencil between her fingers. "You and Carl are coming here for the party, right?"

"Of course, Carl and I will be there."

"Great! I'm going to take her with me to pick out her outfit today. She's so excited."

"I'm so glad that you two are getting along so well. I knew all you needed was time, Silvia."

"Well, Mami, I will call you later. I have to get back to these floor plans." Silvia rushed her off the phone trying to avoid the next subject.

Silvia then called Kim to check on Angel. She was thankful that Kim was on vacation and offered to spend time with Angel while she was at work. The first day Kim met Angel she had invited her to the church. That following Sunday Angel had pulled out her Sunday shoes and dresses that Silvia told her she didn't need to pack and she began getting ready to go to church. She had asked Silvia to come with her, but she refused. She just dropped her off and after church, Kim brought her back home.

Kim answered the phone on the third ring and Silvia let her know that she was about to be on her way to pick Angel up. She started packing up her things to leave the office.

Silvia pulled up in Kim's driveway and sat in the car for a minute. She remembered back to when she had sex with Kim's late-husband, Treyvionne Whitmore. Silvia was sick when she found out that he was HIV positive, and she immediately got tested. She was thankful that she tested negative and she was also thankful that even though Kim caught her cheating with her husband, she forgave her. Even though Kim forgave her, she didn't like to face her because every time she did, she thought about all the hurt she caused her. She blew her horn, and Angel walked outside and got in the car. Kim waved to them.

They headed for South Park's Shopping Center, and Angel picked out a beautiful outfit for her birthday party on Saturday. Silvia had sent out invites to all the girls in her dance class. When they were walking by the pet shop Angel saw a puppy in the window.

"Oh, Silvy!" Angel exclaimed. "Look at the puppies! Let's go see!" She pulled Silvia by the hand.

Silvia watched her fall in love with a Maltese puppy as she sat on the floor and played with it.

"Silvy, this is what I want for my birthday. Please!"

"You are not getting a dog, Angel. Mami would have a fit."

"That's why I am not asking her. I'm asking you."

"We are not getting a dog. Simple as that."

Angel smiled as she looked past Silvia, and at the person who stood behind her. "Hi!" she said.

Silvia slowly turned around and was surprised to see who stood there. "Robert? Are you following us or something?" she asked, disturbed by his presence.

He held up the bag of dog food that he had just purchased. "No, I had to get Max some food, but it is funny that we keep running into each other," he said to Silvia, but he looked at Angel. "She's a pretty one, isn't she?" He now leaned over and petted the Maltese with her.

Angel nodded as the dog continued to lick her face, then Robert's hand.

"I was looking at this one when I first came in," he said. He watched her as she continued playing with the Maltese. "I see that you like her a lot, huh?"

Angel poked out her lip. "Yes, but Silvia won't let me have a dog. I asked her to get me her, for my birthday."

"Wow!" Robert exclaimed. "A birthday? How old are you going to be?"

"I will be twelve on Saturday and we are having my party at Benjamin Park. I say it's too hot for a party at the park, but Silvy says that by the time we get there at five o'clock, it won't be so hot, but I don't know." She looked at Silvia and smiled before adding, "But if she gets me this puppy I won't even care about how hot it is outside as long as I can play with her."

"Wow, did you say twelve?" he asked Angel while looking in Silvia's eyes.

"Angel, let's go," Silvia said as she pulled her up by her arm.

Then Robert grabbed Silvia by hers.

She turned and looked him in his eyes. "Look, I want you stay away from me and my sister. You and I are done, Robert. We no longer have a deal together anymore so just leave... me . . . alone."

He fixed his eyes on hers. "You are right. We no longer have a deal together, but tell me, Silvia." He leaned in closer and whispered into her ear, "What do we have together?" He then looked at Angel and said to her, "Bye, sweetie."

Angel smiled. "Bye!"

Silvia snatched her arm from his grasp and walked away with Angel.

***

Silvia dropped Angel off at play practice. She had been attending play rehearsal ever since she got the part to dance in the play. Silvia decided to stop by Reesie's house to check on her. She visited her while she was in the hospital but since she's been home, she hasn't seen her. She had only been communicating with her over the phone.

When she arrived there, she knocked on the door, and Brandon answered it. She hesitated and drew in a deep breath. She stepped inside. "Hey. Is Reesie here?" she asked dryly. She felt a little awkward being around him since she hadn't seen him since they had been together.

"Naw, she went to spend time with Regina at her house. She called and said that she was on her way if you wanted to wait for her." He walked away from the door and took his seat on the couch.

"No, just tell her I came by." She got ready to walk out.

Brandon could sense her discomfort which made him say, "Look, Silvia, you can wait here. I'm not going to bother you or anything like that. She really needs you, and she's been hoping that you were going to stop by. She would hate it if she missed you.''

Silvia studied him for a second. Then she closed the door behind her and went and sat in the chair.

Brandon watched her as she bit her nails. "I'm sorry for the way I treated you and for the things I said to you in the past. I was wrong,'' he admitted.

His words shocked her and she stopped biting her nails. She looked up at him. "That's fine, Brandon. Your apology is accepted.'' He looked different to her, but she didn't understand exactly what it was that was different about him.

He looked at her for a minute longer, and then excused himself to his room to lie down.

Reesie came through the door and saw Silvia sitting in the chair. "Silvia!'' she exclaimed and hugged her. It was as if she hadn't seen Silvia in years. "I feel so much better and guess what?'' She paused. "Brandon is getting out of the game, and we are moving out the hood so that he won't fall into the trap anymore. We are thinking about moving in the apartment complex that you live in.'' Her smile grew bigger. "He wants to marry me, Silvia!'' She held up her hand, showing her the ring that Brandon got for her.

Silvia looked at the ring, and then looked back up at her. "That's great, Reesie,'' she said. "But do you trust him?''

"He is trying to be a better person. I started to leave him, Silvia, especially after I caught you two together, but I forgave him just like I forgave you.'' She looked into Silvia's eyes. "Trust me. I can see that he is trying to do better. He wants to be a better man and guess what?'' She paused. "He is saved now. We both want something better. I am recovering from my cocaine addiction and Brandon left the weed alone. We really want to do better, Silvia. Mr. Michael's pastor is going to marry us before we move, but he said we would have to come to premarital counseling every Saturday for seven weeks before he marries us.'' She grabbed Silvia's hand. "I want you to be there with me when we say our, 'I do's.' I want you to be my maid of honor.''

Silvia nodded and hugged her friend.

Chapter Twenty

Angel and her new found friends were having a great time at her party. Rita, Carl and Silvia sat at the picnic table as they watched her have her fun. Silvia paid close attention to her mother. She looked weaker and her skin had gotten worse. "Mami, how are you doing?"

Rita smiled. "I'm doing fine, honey. Do not worry about me. Carl has been taking really great care of me." She looked longingly at Carl, and then kissed him.

Silvia watched as her mother leaned back in Carl's arms. Then she thought about Reesie getting married. Kim had also told her that she was getting married, and Silvia started feeling as though something was missing in her life as the people around her seemed to find true love. She hadn't had a relationship since college and had never felt as though she had loved any man in a romantic way. Carl was the only man she ever told she loved.

Silvia's attention was taken away from her mother and Carl when she saw Robert with Angel. Her eyes were wide with shock as she saw Angel holding the puppy they saw in the pet shop. *Oh, my God. What is this man thinking?*

Her mother looked at Robert from a distance. "Who is that man Angel's talking to?" She squint her eyes even more. "Is that a puppy?"

Silvia stood with her mouth wide open as Angel ran over to them with the dog on her leash.

"Silvia, look at what Mr. Robert got me for my birthday!" she exclaimed as she bent down and picked up the Maltese. "I decided to name her Chloe." She walked over to Rita. "Can I bring her back home with me when I leave, please, Mami?" she begged.

Rita looked at the handsome stranger as he walked over to where they were sitting, and then she looked back at Angel with the dog. "I guess that would be okay, honey."

"Oh, I brought something else for you," Robert said as he reached in his pocket. He pulled out a small gift wrapped box and handed it to her.

Angel un-wrapped it and opened the small box. It was a beautiful necklace with a pair of diamond ballet shoes as the pendant. "This is beautiful! Thank you so much!" She hugged him.

Robert took the necklace out of the box and put it on for her.

Rita studied Robert closely and covered her mouth as she looked first at him, then Angel. She watched Silvia's behavior change within seconds.

"Angel, how about you go play with Chloe," Silvia said.

"Okay!" Angel looked at Robert. "Thank you so much again, Mr. Robert!"

He replied, "You are so welcome, sweetie."

Angel ran over to her friends with Chloe and enjoyed the rest of her party.

Silvia looked at Robert with hurt in her eyes. She shook her head at him and began pacing back and forth, biting her nails.

Rita continued to watch her daughter's behavior with concern.

Robert watched Silvia for a second before walking over to Rita and Carl. "I'm sorry. How rude of me. I'm Robert Sterling," he said and shook both of their hands.

Rita looked in his gorgeous green eyes. "I'm Rita," she said, and pointed to Carl. "And this is my husband, Carl. Very nice to meet you, Robert. How do you know Silvia?" She paused and looked at Silvia. "And Angel?" she asked, curious to know his answer.

Robert began, "Well . . ."

"Mami, just let me handle this," Silvia said before Robert could even answer.

"Nice to meet you, ma'am," Robert quickly said.

Silvia walked around the corner and Robert followed her. "What are you doing here?" she hissed angrily. "Stop playing this little game you are playing. We are done, Robert. So, please, just stop."

"I am not into games, Silvia, but I can clearly see that you are. We need to have a serious talk and I think you know that."

"Talk about what? We have nothing further to talk about," she shot back at him.

"Oh, but I think we do." He walked up closer to her and looked her straight in her eyes. "When are you going to tell her?" He referred to Angel.

"Tell her what?"

"That you are her mother."

Tears immediately ran from Silvia's eyes. "I don't know what you are talking about." She turned to walk away.

He grabbed her and pulled her back around to face him. "She deserves to know that much, Silvia. I'm sorry. I can't change the past and I am truly sorry for what I did to you, but that little girl deserves to know the truth."

"What truth, Robert? That you raped me? You want her to know *that* truth?" she yelled at him, as the tears continued to flow from her eyes.

She was so loud that her mother and Carl heard her. Rita looked at Carl with tears in her eyes. She wanted to go console her daughter, but she didn't want her to know that they were able to hear her. She knew that it would just embarrass her.

Now tears fell from Robert's eyes. "I made a mistake and I'm so sorry. You have to believe me when I say that. I'm *not* that same man. I can't change what I did to you, but in the midst of the wrong that I committed against you, that beautiful little girl was conceived.'' He brushed her hair away from her face. "No matter how you feel about me, Silvia, that little girl is my daughter and you can't deny that.'' He now touched her face. "She deserves to know *that* truth.'' He rubbed the back of his pointer finger against her tear, kissed her forehead, then walked away.

***

Silvia paced her kitchen floor while Angel played outside with Chloe.

"Silvia, stop pacing the floor. What is going on with you?'' Rita asked. She knew that anytime Silvia was nervous or scared, she would wear out the floor with her pacing.

"Mami, you and Carl can have my bed. I already changed the sheets for you and Angel can have the couch. I'll sleep on the floor,'' Silvia said, changing the subject.

"Silvia, sit down,'' her mother said firmly.

Silvia took her seat on the bar stool at the kitchen counter next to her.

Rita touched her daughter's hand. "Who was the man at the park?''

Silvia just shook her head. She pulled away her hand and began biting her nails.

Rita grabbed her face. "You are acting really strange, baby.'' She pulled down Silvia's hand and held it in hers. "Was he the one who raped you when you were in college?'' she asked, knowing that her mind was still on Robert since leaving the park.

After Silvia was raped, Rita and Carl came down and stayed with her while she was in the hospital. They knew about the rape and after she had gotten out of the hospital, she went to stay back home as she recovered. She returned to school a year later.

Tears ran down Silvia's face as her mother questioned her.

"Carl, bring me my purse, honey!" Rita yelled into the living room where Carl was watching TV.

He brought her the purse, then stood beside Silvia.

Rita pulled an envelope from out of her purse and handed it to Silvia.

She stared at the envelope, and then opened it. Her eyes were wide with confusion as she studied what was in her hand. "Mami, what is this?" she asked her as she continued to look at the birth certificate.

"It is time for you to take her, Silvia. Looking at that young man today was confirmation that it is time for the truth. We can't keep living this lie. It isn't fair to her. She is a very bright young girl and sooner or later, she will figure this out." She looked at Silvia for the longest. "The young man at the park, Robert . . . she looks just like him, and those green eyes would stop any doubt." She rubbed Silvia's hair. "Baby, Angel needs to know."

"I need to know what, Mami?'' Angel asked Rita after coming in the door on the end of her sentence.

Silvia stood up and looked at her mother as she shook her head.

Angel looked at Rita, Carl, and then Silvia. "I need to know what?'' she repeated.

Rita looked at Angel. "Baby, we need to tell you something,'' she began. She inhaled deeply before continuing, "Silvia is not your sister . . . and I'm not your mother.'' She paused and looked at Silvia as she continued to shake her head with tears streaming from her eyes as her eyes begged her mother to stop there. Rita grabbed Angel's hand. "Silvia is your mother, Angel.''

Silvia's knees buckled and she almost fell to the floor with her mother's declaration, but Carl caught her. She cried hysterically as she looked at Angel.

Tears immediately ran down Angel's face. "Is that true?'' she asked, looking at Silvia.

Silvia slowly nodded.

"And Mr. Robert . . . my father?''

Silvia didn't say a word as she continued to cry.

Angel walked over to her and looked her in her eyes. "Is he my father, Silvia?'' she yelled.

Again, Silvia slowly nodded.

"You told me that he was no one!" Angel yelled. "You are *not* my mother! You are a liar! All this time you've been lying to me! How could you?"

Silvia stood still, not able to utter a word as Angel's words hurt her.

In tears, Angel backed away from Silvia and ran down the hall.

"Angel!" Rita called to her, but Angel ran to the bedroom.

Silvia looked at her mother angrily, grabbed her keys and headed for the door. She drove around until she got to her destination. She rang the bell over and over again.

Robert came to the door. "Silvia, what is wrong with you? Where's the key that I gave you?" he asked.

"Why couldn't you have just stayed away from us?" she yelled at him as the tears ran down her face.

"What?"

"She knows, Robert!"

"Who? Knows what?"

She began pacing the floor. "Angel!" she yelled. "She knows everything. She knows that I'm her mother and that . . ." she hesitated with her next statement as she stopped, and looked him in his eyes, "you're her father."

Robert pulled her into his arms. Hearing her admit that to him made his heart skip a beat. "It's okay, Silvia. Everything will be okay.''

"I can't do this. I never asked for any of this. I didn't ask to be a mother.'' She shook her head. "I can't be her mother. I can't explain to her why. I can't tell her what happened to me. I can't even look at her the same.'' She became overwhelmed with her reality.

Robert just held her without saying a word.

She kissed his lips. "I need you tonight. I have to make this go away.'' She didn't even realize what she was saying. She touched his manhood and he grabbed her hand.

"What do you mean? Make what go away? You can't make this go away, Silvia.'' He looked at her confused. "You think us having sex is going to make this go away?''

She desperately looked into his eyes. "It will for now . . . At least it will for me.''

"Well, I don't think sex is the answer. It will only confuse and complicate things for us right now.''

She kissed him again. "I haven't had sex in almost two months, Robert, and it's driving me crazy. I just need you right now. Please. We can forget about all of this.'' She touched his face before adding, "At least for now.''

"What do you mean? Right now you are not making any sense, Silvia,'' he said, still confused. "We just need to talk about this.''

"Talk?" she yelled. "Well, I don't want to talk! Right now, I just want sex! Forget all this other stuff, Robert! Everything else is irrelevant right now!''

Robert did not understand her behavior and he didn't know how to respond to her at the moment. He walked away from her and went to the living room. He sat down and thought about Angel and what all of this meant for him.

Silvia came up behind him and massaged his shoulders, hoping that would get him to do what she wanted him to do. She bent over the back of the chair and kissed his neck.

He pulled her around the chair and she now faced him. She bent over him and he gently kissed her lips. "I want to do this, Silvia, but I'm not,'' he said as he looked into her eyes.

Silvia stood straight up and looked down at him. "Really, Robert, you can't give it to me when I want it, but you can take it when you want it? Is that the way the game goes?''

He got up from his chair. "That's the thing . . . This is not some game. A long time ago . . .'' He hesitated not wanting to state this fact, "I raped you, Silvia, and knowing that fact bothers me.'' He shook his head as if he was trying to forget again. "Do you know how much I've tried to get rid of that thought? I had pushed that night so far back in my mind that it became unreal. It no longer existed to me.'' He thought back to that very night and said, "I was so drunk that night. I had just buried my mother and father, and my Frat brothers invited me out to take my mind off of them. My mind was so far gone that night, and I was so angry. I was angry at everybody and I felt so lost, empty, and alone. I was in so much pain, and I wanted somebody . . . anybody to feel my pain. I know that was no excuse for my behavior and I'm sorry. I had buried that night so far in the back of my mind, but as soon as you brought it up, it all came back to me at once.'' He looked into her eyes as tears fell from his. "I didn't know that you were a virgin until it was too late, and I'm so sorry that I took that from you.''

"The other five men that you left me in that room with, raped me and one of them beat me so bad, I ended up in the hospital for three weeks!'' she yelled.

Robert covered his mouth as it dropped. He stood in complete shock by what she had revealed and he couldn't even speak.

"Did you know that they did that to me?''

He shook his head. "I swear to you, Silvia, I knew nothing about that. I have not spoken to any of them. I moved away that same week and lost all contacts.'' He took a deep breath. He had no idea that she was raped by his Frat brothers and he now felt even guiltier for leaving her there alone with them.

"When that pregnancy test came back positive, I was so scared. Believe it or not, out of all of those men who raped me that night, I knew whose baby I was carrying. I just had a feeling. Then when she was born and I looked into those green eyes; that was confirmation. She was your spitting image and I hated that fact because every time I looked at her, I saw you. I couldn't remember any of the other men's faces, but I clearly remembered yours. I couldn't keep her because she reminded me of you and the pain I felt from that night, but I couldn't give her away because I was already in love with her. That's when my mother came up with a plan.''

"I'm so sorry, Silvia. I was wrong for what I did to you. Will you please forgive me?"

Silvia's stare was piercing as she remained silent. She wanted to say that she forgives him, but her mouth wouldn't move.

"Just say that you forgive me . . . Please? I swear to you I never meant to hurt you."

Silvia felt like her heart was being pulled by his words and she didn't like that feeling. "You know what, coming here was a mistake." She turned and headed for the door.

He pulled her back around to face him. "Just say it, Silvia. Just tell me that you forgive me." He waited for her to say something . . . anything, but she said nothing. His cell phone rang and he answered it.

Silvia listened to his side of the conversation.

"What happened? When? How's she doing? Okay, I will take the first flight out," he said and quickly hung up the phone.

Silvia could tell by his tone that something was seriously wrong.

"I have to go catch a flight out to Chicago." He headed up the stairs.

Silvia was right behind him. "What's going on, Robert?"

He pulled out a suitcase from his closet and replied, "Carla tried to kill herself and slipped into a comma."

Silvia covered her mouth and gasped. "What?" She had been keeping in touch with Carla since she left, but she just realized that she hadn't spoken with her in weeks.

"God, everything is happening all at once!" Robert yelled angrily as tears ran down his face.

She walked over and hugged him. "I'm sure she's going to be fine. She'll wake up and come out of this brand new, Robert. Everything will be okay." She attempted to comfort him.

She was hoping that she was right. When Robert first offered her the deal with Carla, her intentions towards her weren't good at all, but after really getting to know her, those intentions had changed. She even thought about talking her into coming back home with Robert, but the only thing that was stopping her from doing that, were her feelings for him.

Chapter Twenty-One

Robert went to the hospital, and his mother-in-law, Catherin, met him at the desk. She showed him to the room. He went in and saw Carla lying still with all the machines hooked up to her, and he tried his best to think positively.

He turned to his mother-in-law. "Where's Jazmin?" he asked.

"She's with Cravis."

"I'm going to get her. Where are they?" he asked angrily.

"Calm down, Robert," she said. "They just went to get a soda out of the machine. We haven't brought her in here to see her. We don't think that's a good idea, so he and I have been taking turns walking around the hospital with her."

Robert walked over to the bed. He leaned over and kissed Carla's lips. Tears shed as he listened to the beeping of the machine. He looked up at Catherin and asked, "What happened?"

"Well, Robert. You know she was majorly depressed and I guess she got tired. She sat around the house all day and cried, cried, and cried some more. I took off work a lot just to be there with her. She was in no condition to keep Jazmin alone." She walked over and touched his hand. "This had nothing to do with you. She told me what happened and the reason she left. Believe me. She knows that you love Jazmin and that you would never hurt her. That's why she called you to come pick Jazmin up . . . Carla was in a battle all by herself, baby. You couldn't have saved her if you wanted to."

Robert felt overwhelmed and sat down in the chair next to the bed as he held his wife's hand. He whispered into her ear, "I'm so sorry, baby. I love you so much and when you wake up from this, we are going to do this together. Our marriage is going to be better. You are going to get better. I'm going to fight for you, baby. You will not have to fight this battle alone. Just wake up for me. Please." He kissed her cheek and his tears continued to flow as he watched the machine help his wife to inhale and exhale. He laid his head on her hand and was hoping that she would wake up for him, for their daughter, and for their marriage.

He heard the machine flat line and he jumped up from where he sat. Her mother stood in the corner, shaking her head, crying. The nurses and doctor rushed in and one of the nurses asked Robert and his mother-in-law to leave the room. After six minutes of trying to revive her, they pronounced her dead. The doctor came out of the room and gave them the news.

Robert hollered out from all of the pain he felt. He fell against the wall and slid down to the floor. Then he heard, "Daddy!" Jazmin ran over to him as happy as can be, and he cried even more as he hugged her tightly.

His father-in-law, Cravis, looked first at his wife, then at Robert; and he knew from the looks on their faces, that his daughter had passed away.

***

Silvia was spending time with Reesie at her house while Angel was at practice. Angel hadn't really been speaking to her since she found out the truth and it hurt Silvia's feelings. She didn't know what to say or how to explain the situation to Angel. She knew that Angel wouldn't understand. Carl had taken a vacation, so he and Rita were still staying at her apartment. He was planning to stay for the rest of his vacation, but Rita planned to stay for the rest of the summer, just to take some pressure off of Silvia.

Reesie watched her as Silvia stared off into space. "What's going on with you, girl?"

"I just have a lot on my mind . . . I have something to tell you. Angel is not my sister . . ."

"She's your daughter." Reesie finished her sentence for her.

Silvia's eyes grew wide. "How did you know?"

Reesie looked Silvia in her eyes. "The day she came to the hospital with you, I knew. It's not hard to figure some things out . . . After you were raped and left school for a while, when you came back you still had a little baby weight on you. I figured that you probably had a baby, but I thought you may have given it up for adoption or something. I didn't ask because I knew it would have been a touchy subject, but you could have told me." She now whispered, "Is green eyes her father?"

Silvia nodded. "I don't know what to do. She's not talking to me right now and it really hurts. Then I tried to destroy Robert for what he did to me by destroying his family and now his wife is in the hospital. The other night I was over there and someone called and told him that she tried to kill herself."

Reesie gasped.

Silvia shook her head. "I hope she's okay. I really messed up, Rees. I told her that he was touching their daughter. I can't believe I lied about him touching his daughter. How could I have been so evil?" She shook her head again and a tear ran down her face as she thought about Jazmin. "I wish I would have left her out of it."

"Do you think his wife tried to kill herself because of that?"

"Possibly, but I don't know . . . I hope not."

Reesie turned off the TV, and then looked at Silvia. "Listen, Silvia. I know you blame me for your rape and I'm so sorry. I promise I didn't know that you were being raped that night. I was in another VIP room and I had no idea. After we closed up, I looked for you and that's when I walked in the room and found you. Mr. Cato drove us to the hospital, but he told me to leave you in there. I didn't know what else to do. I couldn't be questioned. I was so high and full of liquor. Then you know we were under twenty-one. Mr. Cato would have been in big trouble along with me. I gave the nurse your parent's information and I disappeared." She cried. "Silvia, I didn't want to leave you, but I had no choice. I've felt guilty for a long time for leaving you like that and I'm sorry."

"Reesie, let's not talk about this. Please. I have enough on my mind."

They were interrupted when they heard a car pull into the driveway and they knew that it was Brandon because they could hear the song, *Breaking Down* playing extremely loud again, which seemed to be one of his favorite songs. They heard the car doors slam and suddenly they heard heavy gunfire. Reesie and Silvia dropped to the floor.

Brandon and four of his friends had gotten back from the store and were headed in the house when three guys drove by and began firing weapons at them. The front passenger shot Brandon in the neck and he fell to the ground. The passenger in the back of the car pulled out a chopper and shot Brandon's friend, Austin, in the chest. Brandon's friends, Ronnie and Dameon, immediately pulled out their guns and fired back. Dameon was shot in his leg, but he continued firing.

As they continue to shoot, Brandon's friend, Sheldon, pulled out his gun and ran up behind the car as they tried to speed away. He shot out the back tire, ran a little closer and shot the front passenger, then the back seat passenger, and then the driver, each one of them shot in the head. He ran back over to the house and saw their friend, Austin, who had been shot in the chest, lying on the grass in a puddle of blood. His death-stare let him know that he was already dead. He ran over to Brandon, took off his shirt and added pressure to Brandon's wound. "Hold on, man. You'll be all right. Just keep breathing,'' he told him.

Brandon looked up at his friend as he held him up. He fought for his life as he struggled to keep breathing.

Ronnie had already called 911 and help was on the way.

Dameon limped as blood ran from his leg. He went to check out the people who had been shooting at them. He wanted to make sure that they were dead because if they weren't, he was going to make sure that they would be.

Reesie ran out of the house and screamed when she saw Brandon on the ground covered in blood. She cried hysterically.

"Reesie, go back in the house!" Sheldon yelled, not wanting her to cause a panic.

Reesie got down on the ground next to Brandon and held his hand.

Sheldon began praying for him as he continued adding pressure to his wound.

Silvia stood in the doorway and couldn't believe her eyes as she looked down and saw Austin with a big hole in his chest and Brandon with blood everywhere.

"Keep breathing, Brandon," Sheldon encouraged. "Everything is going to be okay. Keep fighting. You gon' make it. You gon' survive this," he kept telling him over and over again.

Sheldon and Brandon had grown up together and had been great friends their entire lives. After high school, Sheldon went off to the military and did some great things while in the Marine Corps. He had been trained to shoot and he was one of their top sharp shooters. He was never into the street game, but Brandon was his friend; and when Brandon told him he wanted out, he was going to help him get out by any means necessary.

Chapter Twenty-Two

Silvia paced the waiting room floor as she waited to hear what the doctor had to say about Brandon. Reesie was outside getting some fresh air with Ronnie at her side and Dameon was in the emergency room getting treated.

Sheldon walked up and touched Silvia's shoulder. "You okay?" he asked her. He knew that what she had witnessed earlier affected her greatly.

"I'm okay," she said as she bit her nails. She looked up at him. "Do you think he's going to be okay?"

"I believe he's going to be fine. He's going to make it through this. I know Brandon and he's a fighter."

Silvia's attention was taken away as she saw Michael walking toward them. "What are you doing here?" she asked him.

"Reesie called me and told me what happened. How's Brandon?" he asked.

She answered, "They haven't said anything yet, so we don't know." Tears now ran down her face.

Michael walked over and hugged her. "He will pull through this," he assured her.

Reesie and Ronnie came back in and Michael asked everyone to come together and pray. They all joined hands and Michael began to pray . . .

The doctor and a room full of nurses were all working to save Brandon. The doctor was performing surgery on him when the machine flat lined. "We are losing him!" he yelled as they worked hard to try and save him. They used the defibrillator, but it failed to revive him. After minutes of trying, the doctor said, "We lost him," to the nurses that desperately tried to save him. He looked at the clock, "Time of death 4:57 p.m."

Two of the nurses stood on each side of Brandon and covered his face with the sheet.

At the time they were working on Brandon, he had drifted away . . .

Brandon sat on a rock surrounded by green pastures, and it was absolutely the most beautiful scenery he had ever seen in his life. Then, out of nowhere, a man appeared in the middle of the field, and Brandon watched as the man walked over to him.

"Brandon, I could have allowed you to be taken out today, but I am willing to give you another chance. But the choice is yours. What do you want to do?" the man asked.

Brandon boldly said, "I want to live!"

The man who asked him the question, vanished, and suddenly he heard Michael's voice saying the words he said when he first met him. "You've been walking around all this time, sleeping. Well, now is the time for you to rise up . . . Wake up . . . Stop sleeping!" . . .

Brandon gasped for air and the doctor and nurses heard him. They uncovered his face and looked into his eyes as he stared back at them. The doctor looked at the clock which read: 5:00 p.m. . . .

Right after Michael ended the prayer, the doctor came out.

He asked, "Who is Brandon's family?"

"We are," they all said unanimously.

"I'm Dr. Barnett." He shook everyone's hand and continued. "Brandon has pulled through, but I must tell you, during surgery, we lost him. He was pronounced dead at 4:57 p.m., but at 5:00 p.m., he gasped for air," he informed them.

"Praise God!" Michael exclaimed.

"We were able to remove the bullet, but as of now we don't know if he will be able to walk. We will know something after the swelling goes down. Only then, will we know if he will have some feeling. We are hoping for the best outcome, but the good news is that he is alive," Dr. Barnett said.

"Yes, that's great news," Sheldon said. "Thank you so much, doctor." He shook his hand.

"Right now he is resting, but he is allowed two visitors at a time during visiting hours."

"Well, is it okay if I just go in and see him for a minute?" Reesie asked as tears fell from her eyes. "I'm his fiancé."

"Okay, yes. But just for a minute. He may not respond right now, but just know that he is okay."

Reesie nodded and Dr. Barnett led her into the room to see Brandon.

***

Robert sat in the living room of his in-laws and held Jazmin as she slept in his arms. He wanted to cry, but he had to stay strong for his baby girl. He got up, took her upstairs and laid her down in the bed. When he came back downstairs, he sat on the couch and stared off into space.

Catherin walked over to him and handed him a drink. "After we cremate Carla, you can go back home and take some time to yourself. We will keep Jazmin for as long as you need us to. I know you need time to grieve, and being a single father won't be easy for you," she told him.

He sat the drink on the table. "Cremate her? Is that what she wanted?"

"Well, baby, we have decided to cremate her tomorrow. It would be best. We are not going to cause a lot of attention to our family."

"Is that what this is about? She embarrassed your family by killing herself?" He looked at her intensely. "Is this what she would have wanted, Catherin, or is it what you want?"

He shook his head. "Your family held all kinds of secrets only for them to later kill her."

"What are you talking about, Robert? You know nothing about this family," she said angrily.

"I know that your husband touched her when she was a child, and he tried to make it all right by buying her everything she wanted in life. You were the reason for her depression. You tried to cover everything up when the whole time, you knew. You killed your daughter and money can't buy you out of that fact," he said coldly.

"Robert, you are way out of line. I loved my daughter and . . ."

"No, you loved money and you raised her to be just as greedy as you were," he said interrupting her. "Money can't buy anyone happiness, and it sure can't buy love."

"Shut up . . . Just shut up, Robert!" She pointed her finger at him. "You don't know what you are talking about!" Tears ran down her face. "I'm going to take it as though you are hurting and you are speaking from that place." She stood, poised. "I loved my daughter, and I love you as though you are my son. I know that you are hurt right now and you are speaking out of anger." Her tears continued to flow as she now touched his hand.

He pushed it away. "She told me everything, Catherin. She told me about the touching and how you knew about it and tried to cover it up." He paused. "It is because of what she's been through that made her not know how to love me. Do you know there were many times when she wouldn't want me touch her because it made her feel dirty? Those were her words, not mine! I had to beg her for sex because it made her feel uncomfortable!''

Catherin covered her mouth. "I'm so sorry.'' She shook her head. "I didn't know that it would affect her like this,'' she confessed. She cried hysterically behind what she had allowed to happen to her daughter.

"Well, it had a major effect on her life and our marriage. She could barely function.'' He looked at her. "I'm leaving tonight and I'm taking Jazmin with me. Her Godparents want to keep her for a while, and I'm taking her there with them. I would not dare leave her here with you and Cravis.''

"I would not let anything happen to Jazmin!'' she yelled angrily through her tears.

"Well, you shouldn't have let anything happen to your daughter. You should have protected her.''

"You don't understand . . .''

"I don't understand what? That you wanted to cover up what was happening to your daughter? That you wanted to keep your family's name intact? You don't understand that her silence killed her.'' His forehead creased as he looked at her and slightly shook his head. "You must understand that.''

Catherin grabbed her chest and fell into the chair, sobbing.

Robert continued, "She was so embarrassed and she thought it was her fault. She needed help, but she suffered because of you. You wouldn't allow her to get counseling as a child because you were afraid that she would tell that your husband, her father, was molesting her!'' he yelled. "You even talked her out of continuing counseling after we lost our baby.'' He spoke with such disgust. "You are sick! You allowed him to do that to her. At times, she wouldn't even let me put Jazmin to bed, afraid that I would touch her. She never said it, but I knew, and that hurt me as a man and as a father. Then, she accused me for the first time, and it broke my heart.''

Sobbing uncontrollably, "I'm so sorry.''

He stood. "It's a little too late to be sorry, don't you think? Your daughter's dead.'' He walked away, leaving Catherin to grieve.

When he got upstairs, he packed Jazmin's bags, and then began packing some of his wife's things to take back with him. Carla's journal on the nightstand caught his attention. He picked it up and ran his fingers over the cover. He wanted to open it, but feared what he might find written on the pages. He carefully placed the journal in the suitcase with the rest of her things.

Overwhelmed, he sat down on the bed beside Jazmin and cried at the thought of going back home alone with her. He couldn't stand the thought of being a single father and Jazmin growing up without her mother. He prepared to take her to her Godparents for a while until he could sort things out. He knew he needed time and being a single father was going to be a challenge. Right now he didn't know where to start.

Chapter Twenty-Three

Angel was outside playing with Chloe and Silvia sat on the couch as she drank her Moscato. She had been drinking more and more lately as she attempted to drown all of her troubles. She continued to go to the meetings with Michael and they were helping her in some areas, but as she attempted to stop having sex, her drinking began to get out of control.

She hadn't been able to get the images out of her mind of the day that Brandon was shot. She kept picturing Austin as he lay lifeless on the ground. That day played over and over in her mind. She deprived herself of sleep many nights because of the past that she seemed to relive every night in her nightmares for over twelve years, and now because of the images she saw that day at Reesie's place. Carl had left to go back to work, and Silvia spent nights laying in the bed next to her mother while Angel slept on the sofa.

Rita walked into the living room and sat on the couch next to her. "Silvia, I'm getting concerned about your drinking. You really need to slow down, baby,'' she warned.

Silvia put her drink on the table and lay her head on her mother's lap.

Rita began to rub her hair as she did when Silvia lay in her lap as a child. "You need to be an example for your daughter. Her seeing you drunk all the time is not good for her, and it's not healthy for you." She continued rubbing her daughter's hair and it brought Silvia comfort. She hesitated before her next statement, "I'm going to be leaving soon, Silvia, and Angel will be staying here with you. I will help you find a good school for her here."

Silvia sat up and looked at her mother. "Mami, she can't stay here with me. She hates me and I don't know what to do. She hasn't really talked to me since she found out the truth, and I don't even know what to say to her. What do I tell her, that I was working in a strip club and that I was raped by her father?"

Rita's eyes showed her surprised. "What did you just say?" She was never told that Silvia was raped in a strip club, let alone worked there. "What do you mean, *worked in a strip club*?"

Silvia realized that she had revealed her secret and was lost for words.

Her mother was appalled. "I thought you were raped at a friend's house. Are you telling me that you stripped while you were in college?" Rita asked with disappointment in her tone.

"I'm sorry, Mami. I only did it to pay my way through school."

"To pay your way through school? Oh, well, that makes stripping okay," Rita said sarcastically. She shook her head. "I am so disappointed in you. I raised you better than that. How could you not tell me that you needed more money for school?"

"You and Carl were already struggling and I didn't want to burden you. You couldn't afford to send me to school."

Rita sighed. "Silvia! I would have broken my back to put you through school. All you had to do was tell us the truth. You should have told us that you needed money." She stopped the conversation when she heard Angel come through the door with Chloe. Rita got up and went to the bedroom.

Angel looked at Silvia as she sat on the couch with her head in her hands. She saw the glass of Moscato on the table. Angel knew that she had been drinking once again and she was tired of seeing her like that. "When are you going to stop drinking?" she asked angrily.

Silvia looked at Angel for the longest as she thought to herself, *I am depriving myself of sex for you, and now you want me to stop drinking.* She continued to stare at Angel in silence.

"Are you going to answer me?"

"I'm going to stop drinking, Angel. I promise."

"I don't need you to make me any promises. I just want you to do it. I have been seeing you drunk quite often and I'm tired of it." Angel cried. "I want to go home!"

"What is it that you want from me, Angel?" Silvia yelled in tears.

"If you are supposed to be my mother, why won't you act like it?" she yelled and ran in the room with Rita.

That was the first time Angel really acknowledged what was revealed to her. Silvia's tears ran from her eyes as she lay on the couch. She was ready for her life to be different.

***

Silvia sat in her office and thought about everything that had taken place over the past few months. Michael knocked on her door and came in. "You want to come to lunch with me, Silvia?" he asked.

"Okay, Michael. That's fine. Just give me a minute," she said, as she began packing up her stuff. She decided to ask him for the rest of the day off.

Once they got to Raymond's, they were seated and the waitress took their orders. They sat in silence for a while as Michael studied her. He could clearly see that she was bothered about something. As they sat quietly the waitress brought them their orders, and Michael said grace before they began eating. He watched as Silvia barely ate her food.

"I know that we agreed to keep it strictly professional and to keep your personal life out of this, but is something bothering you, Silvia?" he asked.

"I'm fine. I'm just a little tired today and would like the rest of the day off, if that's okay with you."

"Yes, that would be fine. Whatever you need is fine with me. Were you able to finish up the Sterling floor plans for the new building? If not, that's okay. He's putting a halt on it right now anyway. Unfortunately, his wife passed away.''

"What? So, she died?'' She was shocked by the news considering she had not heard from Robert.

"Yes, she did.'' He took a sip of his water. "You knew her?''

Tears formed in her eyes. "Yes, we met at the meet and greet, and Robert had asked me to hang out with her since she was new in town.''

"Well, yeah, he said that she had been going through some things. It's unfortunate that it had to end the way it did.''

The tears ran down Silvia's face.

He saw that she was really bothered by the news which made him ask, "So you and Carla were pretty close, huh?''

"Yes, you can say that.'' She hesitated, then blurted out, "Robert is Angel's father.''

Michael studied her for a minute before saying, "And you are her mother?''

She nodded.

"She doesn't know that, does she?''

Silvia looked down at her food and sighed. "I was working my way through college,'' she began. "I worked at a Gentlemen's Club and one night I was raped by six men, Robert being one of those men. Then, I found out that I was pregnant.'' Tears fell from her eyes as she shook her head. "I couldn't keep her. I couldn't be a mother. I wasn't ready. So my mother took her in as her very own and she became a sister to me. So, yes, I hid that from her.'' She looked up at him. "But now she knows.''

Michael sat quietly and nodded. He thought about how he never picked up that vibe from Robert, and the news was a real surprise to him. His silence encouraged her to continue.

"I worked as an exotic dancer, Michael, and this was all my fault. I should have been more careful. I should not have let it go that far.'' She then whispered, "You know what one of the guys told me after he raped me? He grabbed my face and told me to look at him. Then he said that it was my fault and that I deserved to be treated like the whore that I was. Then, he beat me unconscious. The next thing I remembered is waking up in the hospital and barely being able to move. I was in so much pain.'' She cried hysterically.

"This was not your fault. Rape is about power and control, Silvia. It was not even about sex for these guys, and it doesn't matter what kind of work you use to do or what you were wearing or not wearing. No one has the right to rape you. No one deserves that.'' He lifted her head and their eyes met. "It was not your fault, Silvia,'' he repeated, hoping that she would understand that. "So you have to stop beating yourself up.'' He now touched her hand. Now he knew the story behind her pain. "Have you forgiven Robert for what he did to you?'' He now placed his hands underneath his chin as he awaited her answer.

She shook her head. "I don't know how to. When I saw him for the first time after twelve years since it happened, I snapped,'' she admitted. "I tried to destroy his family and his wife is dead because of me.''

"What are you talking about? Her death had nothing to do with you. You don't have that kind of power. According to Robert, she had problems for a long time. Stop blaming yourself for everything. I know it may be hard, Silvia, but you have to let that go. You have to forgive him for what he did in order for you to move forward in life. Your unforgiveness only hinders *you*. Your past has held you back for too long and you have a future . . . I'm not at all condoning what these men did to you, but I'm telling you that forgiveness is vital in order for you to recover from what they did." He took a sip of his water. "You have to forgive yourself as well. Stop using your body to try to punish men. The Lord said that vengeance is His, not yours."

Silvia couldn't believe her ears. "Why do you think that I'm using my body to punish men?"

"Because I can see it in your eyes every time you look at a man," he said. "You think that you gain power over them through that, but you are not. You are not hurting them; you are only hurting yourself. You need to open up your heart and forgive the men who did wrong by you."

"I don't know if I really can. They ruined my life." She looked down at her shaking hands. "*He* ruined my life."

"Is Robert the *he* that you are referring to?"

She nodded slowly.

"He didn't ruin your life. Only you have the power to ruin your own life with the choices you make. You choose what path you take, and you are the one who allowed your past to lead you down a path of destruction. I'm sorry that you were raped, but you have to find a way to move forward in your life. Rape can cause a lot of damage, but you have the power to stop the damage and not let it control you. People react to rape in many ways. Some women withdraw from men and refrain from sex. Then you have those who become promiscuous . . . You can be one of those who overcomes it. You are a survivor, Silvia. I can see your pain and I am telling you that you can move past your hurt and live,'' he said with gentleness. "Looking back to the day we first met. You have grown a lot. I see your growth, but I can also see that you are now at a standstill. Your feet are planted in this place of pain. But Silvia, let me tell you this. We all go through pain before we get to promise. Think about how Jesus went through his pain as he was beaten badly before going to the cross. That cross represents promise. You have to go through pain to get to promise.'' He now looked at her with much compassion. "You have to move past your pain to get to your promise,'' he spoke with loving-kindness.

Silvia nodded as tears fell from her eyes.

Michael continued, "You need help to move past that pain and get to your promise. It's time to heal, Silvia. I know this great counselor.'' He pulled out his wallet and pulled a business card from it. "You need help through this, and it would be good for you to see a counselor.'' He handed her the card. "I know a lot of people, especially people in the church who may have their opinions about counselors, psychologists, and therapists; but the truth is God has placed people here to help others. He has given us all types of tools to help each other in this life. I believe that counseling is one of those great tools. There is nothing wrong with you getting help considering all you've been through.'' He pointed to the card he handed her. "This woman is Christian and she is a great counselor. She has helped many victims of rape and domestic violence. They are now victors and their stories are amazing testimonies of God's grace."

Silvia looked at the card in her hand and nodded.

"Stop trying to take vengeance into your own hands. You need to stand still, so that you don't get hurt. Allow God to deal with your situations and circumstances."

Silvia gasped at his words. "The day that I saw Robert in the grocery store, I dropped your grape juice on the floor and glass was everywhere. One of the employees told me to be still, so that I don't get hurt and it kept playing over and over in my mind and I didn't understand why. But I think I understand now."

"What do you understand?"

"It was as if I was being warned. I just needed to be still and not try to get revenge because in the end, I hurt myself as well others. Now Jazmin is motherless." She cried.

"You need to be honest with Robert. And most of all, you need to be honest with yourself. You need help, Silvia."

She nodded as she continued to cry. "I know. It's just that I feel so broken and lost; and I don't know if someone like me can be helped."

"You can be helped, Silvia, but *you* have to make a conscience decision that you need and want to be helped. I can imagine that you feel broken but the Word tells us that we are hard pressed on every side, yet not crushed; we are perplexed, but not in despair; persecuted, but not forsaken; struck down, but not destroyed. No matter what those men did to you, you were not destroyed, you were not crushed. Even though they tried to kill you; you are still here. You still have life. You have a brand new day to become better. God desires to help you. He will not leave or forsake you but guess what; *you* must trust Him to heal and deliver you. It's time to get to your promise.'' He reached over the table and took her hand into his. "You have a story inside of you and it's time for it to be told. It's time to heal, Silvia. Break the silence.''

Chapter Twenty-Four

Robert walked into his dark and empty house, still grieved by the death of his wife. Jazmin was still staying with her Godparents until he was able to figure everything out. He was lost without Carla. Of course, he was the main one taking care of Jazmin even when Carla was alive, but he knew that her death left him unable to really function at the moment. He went into the kitchen to fix himself a drink.

He was on his second drink when he decided to lie down on the couch so that he could just pass out and forget about life.

The doorbell rang.

He lazily got up from the couch and answered the door.

Silvia walked in with her eyes locked on his the whole time.

"Is something wrong?" he asked concerned by the tears he saw in her eyes.

"I came to check on you. I heard about Carla. Are you okay?"

He sighed. "I hope that I will be." He paused. "It's like a bad dream that I can't wake up from." He headed back over to the couch to lie down.

Silvia closed the door behind her and followed him.

He was lying supine as he stared at the ceiling.

She kneeled down beside him and rubbed his wavy hair. "I'm so sorry this happened," she said, as she watched the tears fall from his eyes that were extremely red.

He now looked into her eyes, searching them for the hope he needed.

She gently kissed his lips and allowed his hands to explore her body. She unzipped his pants, revealing his manhood. She began pleasing him, and doing so became her number one priority at the moment. One minute turned into twenty. He moaned loudly as his fingers intertwined in her hair. Before he could climax, she stopped and climbed on top of him. She kissed his stomach, his chest, and then his neck. She sat down on him and she moaned as their bodies connected. Silvia enjoyed every minute of pleasing him as she moved her hips around. Her aim was to take away his pain, the pain she had caused him.

He noticed as she began gaining control of him. Switching positions, he grabbed her around her waist, picked her up, and got on top of her. He became rough now as he pulled in her hair. His lips touched her ear as he breathed heavily.

It had been a while since Silvia had been sexually intimate with someone and she was enjoying every minute of this even though it was a little painful as he became rougher with her.

After bringing the moment to an end, he laid on top of her for a while, catching his breath. She ran her fingers gingerly down his spine. As he looked deeply into her eyes, he began to sober up. He kissed her lips.

She stared into his eyes for a moment before tears formed in hers. Her feelings became overwhelming. "I don't know what I'm doing anymore," she uttered.

He kissed her lips again and gazed into her eyes. "What do you mean?"

She pushed him off of her, got up, and fixed her clothes. "This is not supposed to be happening!" she yelled as she began to freak out from her feelings. She paced back and forth.

He got up from the couch. "Silvia, calm down and talk to me. What are you talking about? What's going on?"

"This is crazy. How is it that I have feelings for someone who did this to me?" She referred back to him raping her. "How is that even possible? I don't understand any of this!"

He walked over to her and gently grabbed her shoulders so that she would stop pacing. He looked into her eyes, studying them for a moment. "You have feelings for me?"

She nodded and the tears fell from her eyes.

He wiped them away, pulled her into his arms, and held her tight.

Silvia was feeling so many different things at once. Her feelings had grown for Robert and she couldn't begin to understand why. She felt torn. She cared for him a lot, and deep down she didn't like that feeling because of all the pain that he had caused her. She also felt sad and guilty about Carla's death. She wanted to tell Robert about everything. She wanted to tell him about the allegation that she made to Carla and how that was the reason why she killed herself. She felt as if this was all her fault and couldn't change it. Carla was dead.

She felt as though her guilt was eating her alive. She wanted to reveal everything to him, but she was fearful of him not wanting to be around anymore. She had become attached, something she had never felt before, and it scared her.

***

Silvia walked into her living room and saw Angel lying on the living room floor watching the TV show *One on One*, with Chloe by her side. She laughed at different parts of the show. Silvia sat on the couch and watched her. As the show went off she looked over at Silvia long and hard before asking curiously, "What is Mr. Robert like?"

Silvia looked at her daughter and studied her for a moment. "What do you mean?"

"What is he like? Was he a good man?" She now sat up, eager for answers. "It seem as though you didn't like him very much and didn't want him around. Was he a bad boyfriend or something?"

Silvia swallowed hard. Changing the subject, she asked, "What would you like to eat tonight?"

"I would like to get to know my biological father, Silvia. Will I be able to spend time with him?"

"We will see, Angel. Go upstairs with Mami and clean up for dinner. I have to run to the store."

Silvia headed for the door without waiting for Angel's response. Angel's questions disturbed her. She drove back to Robert's house, and this time she used her key that he never took back.

"Robert!" she called out to him, but there was no answer. She called his name again as she began to panic.

Robert briskly walked down the stairs. "What's wrong?" he asked with genuine concern.

"She has started asking me questions about you. What am I supposed to tell her? She has become curious," she said, as she paced back and forth.

"Calm down. It's okay. What exactly did she ask?"

"She asked me were you a good man, and were you a good boyfriend. Then I panicked. What am I supposed to say to that?"

He shook his head. "The truth."

"I can't tell her that truth. I can't have her looking at me the way you did."

"And how did I look at you, Silvia?"

Tears ran from her eyes. "Like I was some whore that you could have your way with."

"No, not at all. I thought you were one of the most beautiful women that I had ever seen. I just made a mistake by the way I did things." He pulled her head up and her eyes met his. "If I would have gone about things the right way, I would have cherished you, Silvia." He wiped away her tears.

"She wants to get to know you and she asked about spending time with you," she blurted out.

He was relieved by her words. He was hoping that would be something that Angel would want, but he wasn't sure if it would be. So he was going to leave it up to her, and he was happy that she wanted that because he wanted it just as much. He now smiled. "I would love that," he said without hesitation. "I can pick her up for lunch tomorrow. I want to spend as much time as I can with her before school starts."

Silvia smiled at his words and appreciated the fact that he wanted to spend time with Angel. She knew that he wanted to be a father to her. "Okay, you can come by to get her tomorrow, but please watch what you say to her. Don't tell her about anything from the past." She paused and thought for a moment. She then continued, "Let's come up with a story now. Let's just tell her that we didn't work out because we were on two separate pages and leave it at that. Don't explain anything further."

"I don't think lying to her is the answer. That wouldn't be a good idea . . . How about we just cross that bridge when we get there?" He embraced her.

She looked up at him and kissed him.

He took her hand and led her upstairs where they were sexually intimate once again.

As they now lay in bed together, she chuckled.

"What is so funny?" he asked, as he played in her hair.

"She wants to get to know you, yet I don't even know you myself."

"Get to know me then, Silvia, and let me get to know you," he said with all seriousness.

She shook her head. "I don't think that's a good idea."

"Why not?" He brushed her hair away from her face and kissed her forehead.

She looked in his eyes and began to get butterflies in her stomach. "I have to go." She attempted to get up, but he grabbed her arm.

"Answer me, Silvia. Why isn't it a good idea?"

"Let's just let it go. Our past is too difficult."

"Well, let's get beyond our past." He paused, then added, "Together."

She looked in his eyes for a long while, searching them. *This man is serious.* "I don't like this," she said.

"You don't like what, being with me?"

"This feeling!" she yelled out in frustration. Now calming herself, she inhaled deeply. "I don't like this feeling. Even when I'm not with you . . ." She looked deeper into his eyes before saying, "I still feel you."

"I feel the same way, but I can't say that I don't like what I'm feeling. I care for you, Silvia, very much; and I like that feeling."

He saw the tears form in her eyes. "I have to go, Robert."

He let go of her arm.

She got dressed and left without saying any further words.

Chapter Twenty-Five

Silvia sat on the couch at Reesie's as she watched her feed Brandon his breakfast. "How have you been?" she asked him.

"I'm taking it one day at a time. What about you?"

"I've been doing okay. You look well."

"I'm in a wheelchair, Silvia, and I'm not able to do anything for myself so you don't need to lie to me. I am thankful to God for life though." He smiled. "I don't look well, but I feel well. I am determined to walk again. God's will is not for me to live the rest of my life like this. Plus, I am determined to be standing at the end of that aisle, waiting for my woman to meet me there." His smile grew bigger.

Reesie leaned over and kissed his cheek as tears ran from her eyes.

Silvia was surprised that Brandon was in such good spirits. She watched as Reesie took care of him and at that moment she realized how much Reesie really cared for him. She was so tender and gentle with him. She finished feeding him and they began watching a movie. They laughed and laughed.

Brandon didn't seem a bit bothered by his situation, and it made Silvia look at him in a whole different light.

***

Robert pulled up in Silvia's driveway and turned off his engine. He sat there for a minute as anxiety crept in. He was excited about spending time with Angel, but it also made him a little nervous, hoping that they would hit it off. He got out of his candy-apple colored, GLK-Class Mercedes-Benz SUV and walked up to the door. He rang the bell.

Silvia came to the door and opened it. Standing there, Robert captured her full attention. He had on some blue jeans that he wore well and a red Polo shirt. She couldn't resist looking him from his head to his toes. She took in the scent of his Giorgio Armani cologne as he walked an inch past her. He turned to face her.

"I haven't told Angel that you were coming. I wanted to surprise her," she said to him.

He kissed her lips. "I hope she takes to me well."

Rita walked in right before he kissed Silvia. She was a bit confused as she watched this man kiss her daughter, so she cleared her throat, interrupting them.

He looked over at Rita. "Oh, I'm sorry. How are you, ma'am?" he asked.

"I'm fine." She looked at Silvia. "What is going on?"

"He stopped by to pick up Angel for lunch," Silvia informed her.

"Okay, well, she's in the bedroom. I'll get her," she said. After looking at Robert one last time, she left the room to get Angel.

Angel came out and looked right at Robert who now sat in the living room on the couch next to Silvia.

He stood up as soon as his eyes met hers.

Angel's mouth dropped as she saw the tears form in his eyes. She ran over to him and hugged him, and he embraced her. She didn't understand what made her hug him, but she felt as if she had finally found something that she had been missing her whole life. Carl was a great father, but deep down she knew he was not her biological father, though she never asked any questions. Now, she had found the missing piece to her puzzle.

Silvia stood and tears ran down her face as she watched Angel with Robert.

Robert chuckled at how tightly Angel embraced him. "I came to take you to lunch if that's okay with you," he said to her.

Still embraced, she nodded.

As they headed out the door, he looked back at Silvia and mouthed, "Thank you" to her.

Rita watched as Silvia stood with her tears running down her face. "You did the right thing, honey. Acknowledging that he's her father and letting her spend time with him is a big step. I'm so proud of you." She hugged her and Silvia broke down even more. "But I need to ask you something," she continued. "What was that kiss about?"

Silvia wiped away her tears. "What are you talking about?"

"When he first came in, he kissed you. What is going on with you two?"

"I can't believe you are asking me this? Nothing is going on," she spoke aggressively.

Silvia's tone let her mother know that there was definitely something going on between them that she didn't want her to know about. "Silvia, the man kissed you and you kissed him back. Are you working on being together or something? I'm not trying to be in your business, but I want to make sure that you know what you are doing?" She rubbed her hair. "You are my daughter and I love you. I don't want to see you hurt again. I'm not saying that people can't change, but you have to be careful. I don't know him, but I love you and I'm looking out for you. He already hurt you once, and I don't want to see that happen again. Seeing you lying in that hospital almost killed me."

"I know, Mami, but we are not trying to get together or anything like that."

"Are you two sexually intimate?"

Silvia sighed and lowered her eyes to the floor. Embarrassed, she answered, "Yes, we have been." She now looked into her mother's eyes. "But it's not like that."

"Well, tell me what it's like, Silvia, because I see a man who raped and beat my daughter almost to the point of death . . . Don't you dare give yourself to this man! I don't want him touching you ever again!"

"He raped me, Mami, but he wasn't the one who beat me like that.''

"What? You are really beginning to confuse me.''

"There were six of them,'' she slowly began. "He was the first one to rape me, and when he left the room, I was raped by the other five and beaten by one of them.'' She cried hysterically. "I'm sorry I never told you that.''

Her mother embraced her. "Oh, my God, Silvia.'' She wrapped her in her arms tightly as if protecting her. "How come you never told me about this? You've left me in the dark about so much. Six men? You didn't even report six men. Why?'' Tears escaped her eyes.

"I was so ashamed. I didn't know how to tell you everything,'' she confessed.

"Tell me. What do you plan to do about this man?'' She raised Silvia's head up. "What are you going to do about what he did to you? Can you go to the police?''

"It's been over twelve years and right now, I really just want him to be a father to Angel at this point. He has a three year old daughter as well. I can't lie, Mami. When I saw him for the first time after twelve years, I wanted him dead. And you should have seen him when he first saw Angel, when they first saw each other.'' She wiped the tears from her eyes. "Now, Angel's heart is involved. Did you see the look on her face when she saw him today? I don't want to take that away from her.''

"Is your heart involved?''

Her mother's words struck a nerve, and she just stared at her without speaking.

"It seems as though your heart is now involved as well. I'm not saying people can't change, and I'm not saying don't forgive this man, but I am asking you to be careful. I love you, Silvia, and I don't want to see you hurt ever again." She embraced her.

***

Robert watched as Angel finished her meal. He couldn't believe that he was just finding out about her. He was disappointed at the thought of missing out on most of her life. When she looked up at him, he smiled. "You are so beautiful," he said to her.

"Thank you." She giggled. "I look just like you, Mr. Robert."

"Yes, you do." He chuckled and looked at her closely. "You don't have to call me Mr. Robert. Whatever you want to call me is fine with me." He was hoping that she would soon be comfortable with calling him Dad.

Her smile slowly faded. "How come you never tried to come see me?"

"I'm sorry, Angel, but I didn't know about you. If I did, I promise I would have been there," he assured her. He couldn't stand the fact of not having been there for her as a father even though he had known nothing about her existence.

"How did you meet Silvia?" She asked the question that he wasn't really prepared to answer.

He took a deep breath. "Well, I met her at her job, a long, long time ago."

"How long were you together?"

"Well, we weren't exactly together. I made some mistakes, Angel, but your mother was a good woman."

"Did you love her?"

"I love you and I fell in love with you the first day I saw you. When I looked into those beautiful green eyes that day I saw you with Silvia, that was one of the best days of my life," he said to her, and tears formed in his eyes as he watched them fall from hers.

"Do I have any brothers and sisters?"

"As a matter of fact, yes, you do. You have a three-year old sister named Jazmin," he informed her. "And I had a little girl who didn't make it and I named her . . ." He hesitated as tears now ran down his face. "Angel."

Angel's eyes lit up. "Are you serious?"

He nodded. "When I went to your audition that day and heard the judges call you Angel, I was in awe. My last baby girl actually had some of your features, believe it or not. Even Jazmin looks like you." He smiled. "I can't wait for you to meet her. She's going to be thrilled with having a big sister around."

Angel smiled at the thought of having a little sister. "So is her mother your wife or girlfriend?"

Robert took a deep breath. "Yes, her mother was my wife." His demeanor now changed and his eyes saddened. "But she passed away."

She looked down at her empty plate. "I'm sorry to hear that."

"It's okay. I know she's in a better place, so I can live with knowing that."

"So, she was saved?"

Her question caught him by surprise. "Huh?"

"You said that she was in a better place."

Robert thought about her question and felt as though he knew the answer.

He sat silently until he heard her say, "Mr. Robert." She paused and looked him in his eyes. "Are you saved?"

"Wow, that's a big question for such a young girl." He took a sip of his Sprite, trying to figure out what to say to her.

She saw the look on his face, so she said, "I was just asking have you accepted Jesus as your personal savior. That's all." She waited for his response, but he still said nothing, so she asked again, "So, have you, Mr. Robert?"

"Well," he began . . . His phone rang and he was relieved. "Excuse me, sweetie, let me take this call." He answered it and Silvia's voice was on the other end. She was concerned about Angel being out with him so long. He could tell she was disturbed, but he couldn't figure out why. Confused, he wrapped up their conversation, hung up the phone and told

Angel that he was about to take her home. He informed her that he would like to spend as much time with her as possible and that made her smile.

When he brought Angel back home, he walked her into the apartment and Silvia was pacing the floor. Angel just looked at her strangely as the look on her face made it seem as though she was filled with fear. Silvia stopped pacing and studied Angel. She grabbed her and asked, "Are you okay, Angel?"

Angel frowned. "Yeah, I'm okay."

"You sure?"

"Yes, Silvia. I'm sure."

Relieved, she said, "Okay . . . Okay, good. Go to the room." She continued to pace.

Confused, Angel walked away.

Robert watched Silvia and he too, was confused by her behavior. Once he saw Angel leave the room, he asked, "Silvia, what is wrong with you?"

"I don't want you harming her, Robert." She shook her head. "I can't live with that."

"What? Harm her how?"

"I don't want you touching her. I don't want what happened to me, to happen to her!" she whispered loudly.

Hurt by her words, tears formed in his eyes as he stared at her. "What? I would never . . . What would make you say something like that?"

"What did you tell her, Robert?'' she asked, ignoring his question.

"I didn't tell her anything about what happened. We just enjoyed getting to know each other.'' He took slow steps towards her. "I would never hurt her, Silvia. *Never,* and I need you to understand that.''

She shook her head. "I think that this was a bad idea.''

"She's my daughter and I want a relationship with her, and she wants the same with me. You shouldn't try to stop that because of your own insecurities.''

"I'm so scared,'' she confessed.

He pulled her into her arms. "Scared of what?''

"I don't know . . . everything . . . you,'' she finally admitted and never had she been afraid of any man, but this man made her feel different from any other man. He made her feel vulnerable.

He continued holding her. "You don't have to be afraid anymore. I will never hurt you again, I promise. And I will never do anything to hurt our daughter.''

They had no idea that Angel stood in the hallway and heard their entire conversation. Tears ran from her eyes as she tried to put the pieces together.

Chapter Twenty-Six

Reesie sat in her living room and watched TV while Brandon was asleep in the bedroom. Someone knocked on the front door. She got up and opened it, and to her surprise Dameon stood there. She invited him in.

"Hey, what's up, Rees? Where's Brandon?'' he asked.

"He's asleep. What's up?''

"I just came by to hang out with him. It's been a minute since we were able to do that, but since he sleep, I'll just chill with you.'' He went and sat on the couch and she followed him.

She sat down on the couch next to him and put up her feet. "That's cool. I'm just kicking back, relaxing, and watching a movie on my day off. Trying to stay out of trouble.'' She was trying to stay in the house and away from the streets where the drugs were easy to come by.

Dameon rubbed her leg. "I know that you have been goin' through a lot with Brandon bein' down and all. Now you have to take care of the household and be the provider. You know?'' He squeezed her thigh. "I know that's not easy, and I know you hate that waitressin' job that you had to get." He looked in her eyes. "I can take care of you, baby girl. I will pay all of the bills here, and Brandon doesn't have to know anything. All I ask is that you give it to me on the regular. I been wantin' you, Rees, and you know that. I know Brandon can't satisfy you now. He can't even get it up." He chuckled. "Let me be that man you need."

Reesie looked at him, and then looked around as if Brandon could walk in the room and hear them. "Dameon! I can't do that to Brandon. We are getting married," she whispered.

"Look, I got somethin' for you." He held up a bag of cocaine. "Brandon doesn't have to know a thing."

Reesie looked at the bag of cocaine long and hard. After seeing that bag in his hand, she instantly craved it. "What if he finds out?"

"What can he do?" He chuckled. "Not a thing. Trust me." He set the bag of cocaine on the table for her.

Reesie wanted that cocaine badly as she gawked at it sitting on the table before her. She had been clean for a while now, since going to the meetings that Michael facilitated. "Dameon, I can't do that," she said. Her eyes were still on the bag of cocaine.

"Yes, you can. He won't even know. I'm not goin' to say anything. Are you?" He kissed her lips. "I can take away your financial troubles and give you what you want." He kissed her again.

She gently pushed him away.

He picked up the small mirror from one of the end tables. Then he got up and went into the kitchen to get a straw. He came back and grabbed the bag of cocaine off the table and prepared it for her. He snorted it, and then looked at her. "Here Rees," he said, reaching it toward her, then pulled it back when she reached for it. "The only way you can have it is if you give me what I want. I scratch your back, you scratch mine." He smiled and handed it to her.

Reesie took the straw and sniffed the cocaine into her system and she immediately got a high. She sniffed it again and her nose began to bleed a little. She wiped it with the back of her hand and sniffed it again.

"Slow down, baby," Dameon said to her, as he took it and put it on the table.

He kissed her lips and she kissed him back. He unzipped his pants and she already knew what he wanted, and she gave it to him without hesitation. As he moaned, a tear escaped her eye. She has never cheated on Brandon since they have been together even though she knew that he had cheated on her several times with several women, including her best friend Silvia. Now, here she was cheating on him with one of his best friends. Dameon stopped her, he then asked her to get on top of him. Minutes later, he climaxed. Reesie looked at him.

He moved her off of him, got up and pulled up his pants. "I've been waitin' for a long time to do that," he said with a big smile on his face. "So, do we have a deal, Rees, cuz I ain't gon' lie, I'm gon' want it again and again and again. As long as you give me what I want, I'll give you what you need, money to pay your bills and that white stuff you love to keep your nose happy." He laughed, and then looked at her intensely. "Since

Brandon been down, I been runnin' these streets and I will take care of you and Brandon, Rees.''

She nodded.

He threw another small bag of cocaine on the table.

She picked it up and held it to her chest.

He walked over and kissed her lips. "I'll get with you later,'' he said, and headed for the door.

When he left out, she went in the bedroom and got into bed next to Brandon. She held him, and then kissed his shoulder. He didn't even wake up because he couldn't feel it. She cried at the fact of knowing that. He would never be able to touch her or have sex with her again, and that bothered her. She had been so stressed lately as she now had to take care of him both physically and financially, and that was a bit much for her.

There were many times that she thought about going out and scoring some cocaine, but here it was. Satan brought it to her door step with a deal she didn't want to turn down. She knew that at this point, she had relapsed, and she was about to have a real struggle.

***

It was five minutes after twelve o'clock in the morning, and Silvia couldn't sleep because of the stormy weather. She hated it whenever it would storm. It was bad enough that she had never been able to sleep well after that night in the club. Waking up in cold sweats from her nightmares was tiring. She tossed and turned all night on the couch.

Since Angel was asleep in the room with Rita, Silvia decided to grab her purse and her keys and headed for the door. She drove around until she figured out her destination. She hadn't been dealing with any men except for one since Angel had come to stay with her, so he was the only one in her system right now, and she needed him to give her what she felt she needed.

She used her key and walked into Robert's house, and it was completely dark inside. She found her way up the stairs and to his bedroom. She walked over to his bed and pulled back the covers, then got into bed with him. She kissed the back of his neck.

He stirred, waking up out of his sleep. "What . . ."

Silvia interrupted him as she put her finger over his lips. "Shhh! Make love to me, Robert," she whispered, kissing his lips softly.

He kissed her deeply, as he ran his fingers up the small of her back, then brought them around her side, up her stomach, then caressed her breast. He got on top of her and kissed her lips, breast, stomach, and then he began kissing her in her most intimate place and pleased her in ways that most men couldn't. As she received him, she kissed his neck. He gave her the pleasure she wanted and she gave him pleasure right back. She moaned even louder as she begged him not to stop. He was in the middle of climaxing as she spoke her beautiful language into his ear.

Then they heard a small voice, "Daddy?"

Robert's thrust stopped abruptly and he slid himself out of her. "Oh, my God, I forgot," he said aloud. He immediately fixed his pajama pants. He could only see by the moonlight shining through the window as he got up and went over to his daughter. He picked her up into his arms as she attempted to rub the sleep from her eyes. "It's okay, baby girl," he said. He walked to her bedroom.

Silvia was so embarrassed and she covered herself up. She had no idea that he had gone to pick up Jazmin from her Godparents. She assumed he was still there all alone.

Robert lay in bed with Jazmin for a while, attempting to wait for her to fall asleep.

"Daddy, what was that noise?" she asked after lying there for a minute.

"Nothing, baby. You must have been dreaming. Go back to sleep."

"Is mommy back home?"

After Carla died, he tried to explain to Jazmin that her mother was not coming back, but she never did understand him when he said, "Your mommy went to a better place, and we won't see her again until we go to that special place with her." A tear ran down his face as he thought about the question she asked. He knew that she had seen Silvia in his bed. "No, baby, mommy's . . ." He covered his mouth to try to stop the sound of his cry. "Mommy's not coming back."

"Well, who was that going night night with you?"

"Go to sleep, baby. It's late." He gently rubbed her back. She played with his ear until she dozed off. He waited a minute before kissing her cheek and leaving the room. He walked back into his bedroom and closed the door.

Silvia watched him carefully. Even in the moonlight, she could see the sadness that filled his face. "I'm so sorry, Robert," she said. "I didn't know she was here."

"What was this all about anyway, Silvia?"

"I couldn't sleep, so I came over. I wouldn't have come if I would have known . . . Do you think she heard us?"

"Yes, I believe she did." He sat on the side of the bed, massaging his temples, attempting to relieve his pressure. "This is so hard."

"What is?"

"Being in the position I'm in, being a single father. How do I raise a little girl on my own? A little girl needs her mother." He shook his head. "I love that little girl with all my heart and I would give her anything in the world, but I can't give her back her mother. How do I explain that to *my* little girl?" Tears ran from his eyes.

Silvia sat up and put her legs on each side of him. She rubbed his back, then gently kissed it. "I'm so sorry this happened to your family." She tightly wrapped her arms around him as he broke down into tears.

Chapter Twenty-Seven

Silvia walked into her front door at 7:10 a.m., and her mother was up waiting. "Where have you been? You know this is Angel's first day of school," Rita scolded.

"I'm sorry, Mami. Where is she?" Silvia couldn't stand to tell her mother that she spent the night comforting the man who raped her.

"In the bathroom getting prepared for school. You should have been here with her this morning to help her. This is not simple for her. You know this is a new school and a new city. She's not use to moving around, Silvia. Now, where have you been?" Rita placed her hand on her hip as she waited for Silvia to answer her.

Silvia just looked at her mother, not knowing what to say. She hated lying to her. She had done enough of that about her past.

"Were you with him?" Rita asked, referring to Robert.

At that time, Angel had walked in and heard the end of their conversation.

Silvia quickly walked over to her disregarding her mother's last question. "Wow, you look so beautiful. Are you ready to go?'' she asked her.

Angel nodded and went over to kiss Rita goodbye. She walked out the door to Silvia's car and waited for her to unlock it.

She watched Silvia walk towards the car and rolled her eyes at her.

"What is up with the attitude this morning?'' Silvia asked after seeing the look on Angel's face. She unlocked the car and they both got in.

Angel buckled her seatbelt, and then folded her arms across her chest. "Are you sleeping with my father?''

Silvia was shocked by her words. "That is none of your business,'' she snapped. "What is up with you?''

"I don't want you to mess this up for me,'' she said, as she thought back to the conversation that she heard between them.

"Mess up what?''

"Me having a relationship with him. I want to get to know my father, Silvia.''

"And I'm not going to stop you from getting to know him, sweetie.'' She grabbed her hand.

Angel snatched her hand away. "Well, what was that about the other day?'' she inquired. "The conversation between you and him.''

"What did you hear?" Silvia asked in an angry tone.

"I know that, for some reason, you think he would hurt me, and I know he hurt you in the past."

"From now on when I tell you to go to your room, that means go to your room. You are not to eavesdrop ever again. Do you hear me?" she yelled. The last thing she wanted Angel to know was that the man who is her father raped her and that she was conceived as a result of that.

Angel jumped at her tone. "I'm sorry, but I was scared that you were going to send him away and tell him to never come back. Silvia," she turned to look in her eye, "I don't care what happened between you two. I want him in my life. I need him. I need my father."

Silvia nodded. "I know and I wouldn't do anything to jeopardize your relationship with him," she said, meaning every word.

"Silvia," Angel began in almost a whisper. "Why did you lie to me? Why did you have me believing that you were my sister this whole time? I don't understand." Tears fell from her eyes.

Silvia sighed, attempting to hold back her tears. "It's complicated, Angel, and right now you wouldn't understand."

"I want to know the truth, Silvia."

"I'll explain everything to you at a later time, Angel. Just, please, not right now." Silvia didn't have the heart to tell her the truth and she was hoping that with time, she could skip over this subject. She pulled into the school's parking lot. "Here we are. I believe you are going to like it here. It's a really good school.''

She and Rita had gotten Angel accepted into the school a few weeks ago, and the plan was for her mother to go back home after Angel's first week. Silvia had been looking for a two bedroom townhouse so that they would have more space and their own rooms. Angel wasn't thrilled about her move, but she was thrilled about getting to know her father, and that's what kept her happy about being in what she called, "this foreign land.''

Angel nodded and she dried her tears. "Okay.''

Silvia grabbed her hand when she motioned to get out of the car.

Angel turned to face her.

Tears came to Silvia's eyes. "I love you, Angel.''

"I love you too.'' She hugged her and got out of the car.

Silvia sat and watched Angel walk through the doors of the school and her tears poured from her eyes. She was overwhelmed with knowing that she was about to take on the responsibilities of being a mother.

She went and filled out an application for a townhouse that she had her eyes on for a while. She was riding down the street when her cell phone rang. She smiled when she heard Robert's voice on the other end.

"Hey, you, what are you doing?'' he asked.

"I just got through filling out an application for a new place. I'm trying to find something bigger for me and Angel. I dropped her off to school this morning." She sighed. "I can't believe that I'm doing this."

"Doing what?"

"Attempting to be a mother."

"Look, Silvia. Do you mind meeting me for brunch right now? We need to talk."

Her stomach started fluttering. "Sure. What's wrong?" she asked, concerned.

"I just want to have brunch, that's all."

They agreed on the location and Silvia headed that way, wondering what it was that Robert wanted to discuss. She rode around and tried to figure out what he wanted to talk about. *Oh, my God, what if he wants to take Angel from me?*

She walked into the restaurant and was seated immediately. She saw Robert when he walked in.

He walked over to the table and sat down across from her.

The waitress came over and took their orders, then left them alone.

Robert sat in silence and stared at Silvia for a moment.

"What is it, Robert?" she asked eagerly.

"I've been thinking . . ." he began.

"You are not taking her from me," she said before he could even finish his statement.

"What?" He looked puzzled. "I'm not trying to take her from you." He reached over and took her hand into his. "I was going to say that I know you were looking for a place for you and Angel, but how about y'all come stay with me and Jazmin?" He put up his hand before Silvia could protest. "You don't have to pay anything and you can save up your money. It would be nice."

Silvia lowered her eyes and gently shook her head.

He saw the apprehension on her face. "Look, Silvia, I'm not asking you for sex or anything. We will all have separate rooms, bathrooms, phone lines, everything . . . You wouldn't have to worry about anything when it comes to finances. Everything will be paid for."

She looked up at him and snatched her hand out of his grasp. "What is this? Ever since you came back into my life, you have been trying to buy me. First, you pay me to spend time with your wife. Then you ask me to come stay with you and tell me how I won't have to pay anything because everything will be paid for." She started whispering loudly, "I remember when we were in that VIP room. That night you kept touching me and when I told you no touching, you had the nerve to tell me you're buying. Is that what this is about? You think you can buy me?"

"No, I don't think that I can buy you and that's not what I'm trying to do." He sighed heavily. "I just thought that it would be a good idea and a nice experience. I thought it would be great for me and Angel to spend time together. Then she and Jazmin can spend time together, getting to know each other as well. I have more than enough room in that house and I can't lie.'' He paused and gently took her hand again. "I need you, Silvia. I really need your company.''

When she saw the seriousness in his face and heard the sincerity in his tone, she told him, "Let me think about it.''

The waitress brought them their food and they ate in silence, both of them in deep thought.

Chapter Twenty-Eight

Silvia had dropped her mother to the airport after taking Angel to school. She didn't know what to expect now that her mother had left. She had been a big support with Angel so her leaving left Silvia in fear, fear of failing at being a mother.

She sat on her couch in deep thought about the offer Robert made to her almost a week ago. She wasn't sure if moving in with him would be a good idea or not. He was right. He had more than enough room and she liked the idea of not having to pay bills. The doorbell startled her. She opened the door and there Reesie stood.

Reesie waltzed her way through the door. "Hey girl, how's it going?'' she sang.

Silvia went back over to the couch and lay down. "I'm good. Are you off today?''

Reesie threw her purse on the couch and sat down next to Silvia's feet. "I quit. What about you? You off today?''

"You quit?'' Silvia asked, disregarding her question.

"Yes, I will find something else. I hated that job, Silvia. You know I was never use to working a regular job. I always liked my money fast. Then I met Brandon and he liked his money the same way. Ugh, a regular job? I hate living like this. Brandon's nurse thinks I'm at work though, but I'm going to use this day to look for something different. I guess I will look into retail or something." She rolled her eyes at the thought. "Why aren't you at work?"

"I called in sick. I'm not feeling well at all, it's probably the flu. I also had to take Mami to the airport earlier today."

"How do you think it's going to be with just you and Angel?"

Silvia got up from the couch and ran to the bathroom. She began throwing up into the toilet.

Reesie walked in behind her. "What's going on with you?" she asked, as she covered her ears, trying not to hear her regurgitate.

Silvia continued to throw up into the toilet. "I don't know. I guess nerves."

"I know you, Silvia, and your nerves have always been bad, but throwing up was never a sign of that." She folded her arms across her chest. "I think you pregnant."

"No, I'm not, Rees."

"What makes you so sure?"

"Because I'm on the pill," Silvia said with an attitude. "Now let's drop it." She stood up and went to the sink. She began washing her mouth out, and then ran back to the toilet to throw up some more.

"That's it! I'm going to the store and I am going to get you a test."

Silvia replied angrily, "I don't need a test so stop saying that."

"Well, let me run up here to the corner store and get you a test, then we'll see about that." Reesie watched her hang over the toilet. "Stop being so stubborn and let me get you the test." After Silvia didn't say anything, she left out to go get that test. She had become concerned about her friend and she had a feeling that there was a strong possibility that she was pregnant.

Silvia finally finished up in the bathroom and lay back down on the couch. Chloe jumped on the couch and licked her face. She had grown to love dogs since Robert helped her with her fear. She lay there and petted her as she continued licking her face.

After fifteen minutes, Reesie rushed back through the door with the test in her hand. "Silvia, I got it for you. Do you want me to stay with you while you take it?" she asked, throwing her purse on the couch.

"You can take that test back with you, Rees, cuz I'm not taking it. I'm not pregnant!" she yelled.

"Okay." Reesie placed the test on the counter. "Well, it's on the counter. I'm going to leave now. I have to go look for this job," she lied.

When she was on her way to the corner store, Dameon had called her and asked her to meet him at a nearby hotel for some money to pay some of her monthly bills, for some dope and of course for what he wanted from her.

Reesie headed out of the door.

As soon as she left, Silvia ran back to the bathroom to throw up. She was not feeling or looking well at all. She started to feel worse as time passed.

She walked back from the bathroom and the test on the counter caught her attention. She picked it up and looked at it for a minute, then headed back to the bathroom. She took the test and stood and waited. Once it got its reading, she held it for a while as she stared at the results with tears in her eyes. Then the doorbell rang, startling her once again. She dropped the test in the trash and hurried to the door thinking that it was Reesie coming back for something.

She opened the door. "Robert? What are you doing here?" she asked surprised.

"Well, you told me to come here to pick up Angel when she gets out of school so that she could meet Jazmin today and spend some time with us, remember? I'm a little early, but I didn't think you would mind." He looked at her intensely. "Are you okay today?" he asked. He wasn't use to seeing her with her hair all over her head, in pajamas, and her skin flushed.

"I'm okay. I just forgot. That's all." She went and sat on the couch.

He walked over to the couch, moved her blanket and sat down next to her. "Have you been like this all day?" He felt her forehead. "You don't feel like you have a fever, but you don't look like you feel well either. You sure you okay?"

Slightly raising her voice, she responded, "I'm fine, Robert."

He sensed that she had an attitude so he didn't want to say anything further that would upset her. "Okay, well, I need to use your bathroom. Is that okay?"

"Yes, you know where it's at," she said, attempting to fight the urge to throw up again.

He got up and went to the bathroom. As he stood there using the toilet he looked down and what he saw in the trash caught his attention. He flushed the toilet and pulled the pregnancy test from the trash with his thumb and pointer finger. He stared at it as he took in the results. *Oh, my God! She's pregnant!* He dropped it back into the trash and washed his hands. He stood there for a minute in deep thought about what this meant.

As soon as he opened the bathroom door, Silvia ran in, pushing past him as she went for the toilet.

"Are you okay?" he asked, concerned as he watched her.

"I'm fine. I probably have the flu or something," she said after she finished depositing into the toilet. She got up, washed out her mouth, and then rinsed her face with cold water.

"Are you sure about that?" he asked, wanting her to tell him about the results of the test without him having to ask her about it.

"I'm sure!" she yelled, and the tears fell from her eyes. She pulled down the lid on the toilet and sat down. "It's just nerves, nothing to be worried about." She attempted to lower her voice.

"What are you nervous about?"

"Everything. I'm about to have to take on the responsibility of being a mother now that my mother has left Angel to me."

"You'll be a great mother, Silvia. I wouldn't worry about that if I were you." He ran his fingers through her hair. "How do you feel about more children?" he asked, trying to fish.

Irritated by his question, she pushed his hand away from her hair. "I don't feel. I'm not having any more children."

"Hmmm . . . That's funny considering that the test in that trash, reads positive."

"You went in my trash! Who does that!" she yelled, her tone revealing to him every bit of her frustration.

"I saw it and it caught my attention." He looked at her intensely. "So, were you going to tell me?"

"Tell you what? I am not pregnant! My friend Reesie was over here earlier and that was her test, not mine!" she yelled her lie to him. "Maybe you should mind your own business, Robert, and stop being so nosey, snooping through people's trash."

"Okay, I'm sorry. I just got concerned. That's all." He leaned over to kiss her cheek.

The doorbell rang.

"Would you like me to get that for you?" he asked, as she remained seated on the toilet.

She nodded and he went and opened the door.

"Hey," Reesie said dryly. She looked at him with his green eyes and she knew exactly who he was. "What are you doing here?" she asked, wondering if he had done something to her friend.

He reached out his hand to her. "I'm Silvia's friend Robert, and you are?"

She looked at his hand, then back up at him. "Reesie . . . Where's Silvia?"

He ignored her question. "Reesie? Wow, congratulations!"

Confused, she glared at him. "Congratulations for what?"

"On your pregnancy. You are having a baby, right?"

She now looked at him like he was crazy. "What are you talking about? I'm not pregnant."

"I thought not . . . Silvia is in the bathroom." He went over to the couch and sat down.

Reesie walked in the bathroom, and Silvia was still sitting on the toilet. "What is he doing here? Isn't he the one..."

"Yes," Silvia said, cutting off her question. "He's here waiting for Angel to get home. She's going to spend time with him and his little girl today."

"Well, I left my purse here . . . Oh, did you take the test?" she asked, not even thinking about the conversation she just had with Robert.

"Yes, it was negative," she lied. "I told you it is probably just the flu or something."

"Okay, cool. I know that was a relief for you." She touched her hand. "I just wanted you to be sure," she said. "So, you and green eyes are getting along, I see." She smiled as her eyes lit up. "He's so handsome. If I were you, I would definitely be tapping that." She giggled. When she saw Silvia's demeanor change, she knew. "Oh, my God, you are!"

"Reesie, let's not talk about it right now."

"Okay, that's fine, but, Silvia, you know I want to know the details later." She hugged her. "I mean, *every* detail." She winked at her.

"Yeah . . . Sure thing," she replied dryly.

Reesie walked into the living room and saw Robert sitting on the couch with his head in his hands. She reached beside him to grab her purse.

When he felt her, he looked up.

She smiled at him. "Nice to meet you." *Sexy!*

He sat his back on the couch and smiled. "Nice meeting you as well, Reesie."

She left out.

Silvia came out of the bathroom and sat on the couch beside him.

He just looked at her and hoped that she would tell him the truth about her pregnancy. With her lying to him, he wondered if her plan was to abort the baby. His head was pounding at the thought as he waited for his daughter to come home from school. Right now, he didn't have any words for Silvia and she could feel his tension.

Chapter Twenty-Nine

Robert's attention was on Jazmin and Angel as they got out the car. Jazmin had taken to Angel really well, which brought him great joy.

She was holding Jazmin in her arms as she walked to Robert's door. "This house is huge!'' she exclaimed.

He smiled and opened the door.

She walked in and put Jazmin down as she looked around in amazement.

Max ran up to her and sniffed her.

She reached down to pet him. "What's his name?'' she asked.

"Max,'' he told her. He watched as Max licked her face, and it made him laugh.

Angel asked for a tour of the house, and Robert showed her around as she now held Jazmin in her arms once again. He saw that she had fallen asleep on her shoulder so he took her from Angel, and he went to lay her down in her bed.

He finished showing Angel around and she loved the house and how much at home she felt. "Look, Angel," he began. "I know that you and Silvia were looking for a bigger place and, of course, I already talked to her about this; but how would you feel about you two staying here?"

Angel's eyes lit up. She smiled and nodded. "I would really like that!" Her smile quickly faded when she thought about Silvia. "But what did Silvia say?"

"She hasn't gotten back with me yet. I was thinking that maybe you could talk her into it."

"Well, I know she went looking for a place on yesterday, so I don't know if she is planning to take you up on that."

"That's why I said maybe you can talk to her about your thoughts on it. How do you like it here in Baton Rouge, anyway?"

"I like it okay."

"And how is school going for you so far? Have you met a lot of new friends?"

She smiled. "I've met a few. There's a boy who really likes me."

"What makes you think he likes you?"

"He asks to carry my books to class every day."

"Well, don't get caught up in that, okay? You are such a beautiful young girl and, of course, boys are going to like you; but I want you to focus on school. Don't worry about these knuckle heads that mean you no good." He made a mental note:

I'm going to have to get a gun to keep these little boys away from my daughter.

Angel thought that it was a good opportunity to ask, "Did you mean Silvia any good?"

His eyes slanted as his head tilted. "What do you mean?"

"I heard you guys when you brought me back from lunch the first time we spent time together. I know that some kind of way, you hurt her and because of that, she thinks that you are going to hurt me."

"I did hurt her, but that was a long time ago, Angel. I would never hurt you, and I will never hurt her again. I promise you that."

She nodded and smiled. "Okay, I will talk to her about us staying here then."

***

Silvia stood in the bathroom as she looked at the results of her third pregnancy test which also read the same as the other two… *positive.* She had not planned to be pregnant. She didn't feel ready for any more children. Besides, she didn't feel ready to be Angel's mother. The news upset her and she cried all over again. She knew that the baby she carried was none other than Robert's.

She had stopped having sex with all these random men and the only person she had been with over the past few months was Robert, and it was now on a regular basis. She released a sigh. "Why do I always end up pregnant for this man?" She spoke out loud to no one but herself. She didn't understand it because she had been on birth control for years, and she may have forgotten to take a pill here and there, but she didn't expect to get pregnant. Her first thought was to get rid of the baby, but she had a problem with abortion. She couldn't see herself ever going through with that. She shook her head. *What am I going to do?* She tried to think of a plan.

She went and lay on the couch as she continued crying. She heard the key in the door. Then she watched as Angel walked in, Robert right behind her with Jazmin in his arms. She quickly wiped her tears away as they each came in.

"Are you still not feeling well?" Angel asked.

"No, not really," she said as she sat up. Her eyes were bloodshot from crying so much.

Angel walked over to her and observed her closely. "Have you been crying?" her voice soft.

Robert spoke before Silvia could respond, "Angel, why don't you take Jazmin to the bedroom and play with her for a little while." Even though he spoke to Angel, his eyes remained on Silvia.

Angel looked up at him, and then back at Silvia as she took Jazmin's hand and took her to the bedroom.

Robert stared at Silvia for a moment before asking, "What's going on?"

"I'm just really tired," she replied. She got up and went into the kitchen. She opened the cabinet and pulled out a glass. She slowly set the glass down on the counter and opened the refrigerator, pulling out a bottle of Chardonnay. She began pouring herself a drink.

Robert grabbed her arm. "What are you doing?" he asked firmly.

"I'm pouring me a little Chardonnay. Would you like some?" She continued pouring it into her glass.

He looked at her intensely. "If you are sick, you don't need to be drinking." He tried to keep his cool.

She turned around and smiled at him. She placed the wine glass up to her lips and he hit it out of her hand.

Wine went everywhere and the glass hit the floor, shattering.

Silvia gasped.

"What the hell are you trying to do?" he spoke furiously. He stood so close to her he could see the fear in her eyes as she saw the anger in his.

Angel ran in after hearing the glass shatter and saw Silvia's back up against the refrigerator with Robert standing closely to her. "What are you doing to her?" she screamed.

He took a deep breath, trying to calm himself before saying, "I'm sorry, sweetie. She just dropped her glass to the floor." He now saw the fear in Angel's eyes as well. He spoke calmly. "We were just talking, Angel, and she accidently dropped her glass." He now looked at Silvia as if warning her to fix her face so that she wouldn't scare their daughter. "Go back to your room, sweetie. Everything is fine,'' he said to Angel, attempting to settle her fears.

Angel looked at Silvia a while longer before saying, "Silvia?''

"I'm fine, Angel,'' her voice shaky. "Go back to the room with Jazmin.'' Her eyes stayed on Robert's.

After looking at her for a minute longer with much concern on her face, Angel left the room, hoping that everything would be fine.

Robert continued looking at Silvia intensely. He grabbed her arm again. "When are you going to tell me that you are carrying my child?'' he whispered to her, his tone angry.

"What are you talking about? I told you. I'm not pregnant.''

His grip tightened around her arm. "I don't know what kind of game you are playing, but you will not harm this child in any shape, form or fashion.''

His eyes told her that he meant every word. "Let go of me. You are hurting me and for the last time, I am not pregnant. Nobody is carrying your child, Robert.''

"Just be honest with me, Silvia.'' He got closer to her. "What are your plans? Are you planning to have an abortion? That's something I need to know.''

Tears ran down her face and she stood in silence. She had no idea what her plans were, but keeping this baby was not a part of it.

He waited for her to speak, but she didn't say a word. The look in her eyes told him everything, and his tone and demeanor changed. "Please, Silvia, I beg you. Do not abort our baby. Whatever you need, I will be here for you. I will be here for our children. I can promise you that. Just don't do this.'' He stared into her eyes. "Please,'' he begged.

She just looked at him and nodded as tears continued to run down her face.

He pulled her into his arms and hugged her as she sobbed loudly.

Chapter Thirty

Reesie was outside in the car pleasing Dameon. He moaned and grabbed her hair as he climaxed. She sat up in the seat and cleaned the corners of her mouth with her pointer finger and thumb. He looked at her as he handed her a roll of twenties and a small bag of cocaine.

A smile spread across his face. "Reesie, I know that we been doin' our thang, but how do you feel about steppin' out the box?"

Reesie looked at him as if he confused her with his question. "What do you mean by that?"

"I know a lot of men who would pay for stuff as good as yours. You down?"

"What?" She shook her head. "You know I don't get down like that, Dameon." Her New Orleans accent started coming out a little more.

"I was just sayin' it will give you a lil' extra money in your pocket and a lil' extra dope if you feel me."

"So, what you tryin' to be, Dameon, my pimp?"

"No, but I will protect you from the wrong ones. Rees, I'm just sayin'. I know you ain't use to that minimum wage crap. It's no point in workin' them dead end jobs, you feel me? I can take you places and you know you a bad woman.'' He wrapped his hand around her thigh, then ran it up her skirt, touching her in her most personal place.

She closed her eyes and moaned.

He continued, "Your body most definitely can take you places.''

She moaned more.

He smiled. "With a body as bad as yours and a face as pretty, you with your Creole self can make thousands in one night.'' He removed his hand, now licking his finger. "Hell, yeah, we can make this happen.''

She now looked at him. "But what about Brandon?''

He frowned, and then shrugged. "What about him?''

"Dameon, our deal was for it to be me and you, not all these outside men.''

"I know, baby, but you too good at what you do for you not to use it to your advantage. Brandon will never know. Then again, who cares? When he was out here in these streets he did you dirty anyway. So what do you care?''

"I thought you were his friend.''

He sighed. "And I am. I'm lookin' out for my boy. I'm makin' sure y'all house gon' be provided for. Hell, he can't work, so everything falls on you and me, boo.''

In deep thought, she dropped her head and sighed.

He lifted her head so that her eyes would meet his. "I got you, baby. I won't let nothin' happen to you." He kissed her lips. "Trust me."

"I'll have to think about it, Dameon . . . I have to go." She opened the door to get out of his car.

He reached over and grabbed her shirt tail, pulling her back in. He kissed her lips again. "You do that."

She got out and went in the house.

When she opened the door Brandon was sitting in his chair, watching TV. "It took you long enough out there. You found what you were looking for?" he asked.

She had lied to him earlier, saying that she had to look for something in the car. "No, I didn't, but I'm not going to worry about it. Are you hungry, baby? I can fix you something to eat."

"No, I'm good," he said. "I want to thank you for still being here for me. I know this is not easy and I really appreciate you for everything. I understand why you put our marriage on hold and I will understand if you don't want to marry me." He waited for a minute before yelling out in anger, "I can't move my legs!" And the tears ran down his face.

Reesie got up and wiped them away.

"I'm sorry for the life I led, I really am. It did me no good. All the fast women, money and cars were not worth this," he admitted. Then he added, "God, whhhyyy?" He screamed out in anger. His tears continued to flow as if he were just realizing everything that was taking place and it caused a meltdown.

Ever since Brandon had gotten shot, he was in good spirits. He was happy to be alive, but it was something different about today. He began getting angry as he thought about the possibility of him being in this situation for the rest of his life. Right after he was shot, he and Reesie had stopped going to their meetings with Michael. It was a lot of trouble for them to try to go, with Reesie having to dress him and get herself ready as well. The circumstances discouraged them both, and they decided not to worry about going anymore.

Reesie had put a hold on their wedding because she had to work, so he thought, and they were never able to make it to pre-marital counseling with Pastor Matthews. But for Reesie, that was just an excuse. She had been taking him to rehab, but it didn't seem to be helping and that's what angered him most. His hope started slipping away from him. He still wasn't able to move any parts of his body on his own and it scared them both. She was no longer sure if she would be able to take care of him for the rest of his life and that bothered her. That was too much of a commitment for her, and the thought stressed her out.

Reesie hugged him, attempting to comfort him. She kissed him, and then headed for the bathroom. She could barely take seeing him like that, plus she felt guilty for getting with his friend. As soon as she closed the bathroom door, she covered her mouth as she cried. She reached in her pocket and pulled out the bag of cocaine she got from Dameon. She put it up to her nose and inhaled deeply. She craved it. She quickly opened the bathroom drawer and rambled through it as her tears fell into drawer. She pulled out her little mirror and straw and prepared it.   She sniffed the cocaine into her system.   *I can't do this anymore.*   She kept sniffing and sniffing until she passed out on the bathroom floor.

***

Robert was parked at the school, waiting for Angel to come out. He was going to take her to get something to eat before taking her home.

When she got in his SUV, she slammed the door and didn't say a word to him.

He stayed parked as he looked at her. "What's wrong, Angel?" he asked.

"What was that about yesterday? I thought you said that you would never hurt her. She cried all night, Mr. Robert."

He sighed deeply. "I told you that you don't have to call me that." He didn't like the fact that his daughter called him by his name. "And I didn't hurt her. She's just going through some things right now, and I am going to do everything in my power to be there for her. You don't have to worry about me hurting her, Angel. That, I won't do."

"She seems to be really sad a lot lately, and I don't like seeing her like that."

"I understand and I don't like seeing her like that either. You have my word that I will do my best to make her happy."

"Promise?"

"Yes, I promise."

She heard the song that played on the radio, *You Are*, by Kirk Franklin and she turned up the volume. "This is the song that I will be praise dancing to!" she exclaimed. "We haven't set a date yet, but it will be on a Sunday during church . . . When I find out when, will you be there?" she asked him. She had made Holy Temple Ministries her church home and accompanied Kim and Trey, Jr. there every Sunday. She became a part of the youth department's choir and praise dance team.

Robert nodded in response to her question.

She sat quietly as she listened to the words of the song. Her mind was far from everything else as she meditated on the goodness of God.

Robert sat and listened to the words pouring through the speakers, "Jesus, you are my joy within. You are the shelter from the wind. You are the forgiver of my sins. Jesus you are, yes. Where can I go? Who can I call? Who's there to catch me when I fall? Your hands they hold me through it all. Everything I need, you are . . ." Tears ran from his eyes as the words ministered to him. He felt a void and desired for that void to be filled. He knew that he needed something different in his life. It was time for change.

Chapter Thirty-One

Silvia had just come back from the doctor's office and Robert was waiting in the parking lot of her apartment complex. When she saw him, she sighed knowing that he was about to question her about her appointment. She had told him that she didn't need him to come with her even though he wanted to.

When she got out of the car, he got out of his.

Not making eye contact, "Robert, please," she said, holding up her hand as he approached her. "I don't need to be interrogated about the appointment. Everything was fine. The baby is fine. I am fine!" she yelled. The tears ran down her face as she struggled to unlock her door.

Robert touched her shaky hand as he helped her to unlock it. He twisted the knob and pushed the door open for her, watching her carefully.

She walked in, hoping that he wouldn't follow.

He walked in behind her and grabbed her arm. "Okay. Well, what's wrong, Silvia?" By the way she was acting, he wondered if her appointment had anything to do with an abortion.

Silvia was silent as her tears continued to flow.

"Answer me!" he yelled.

She jumped at his tone.

He saw that he scared her and he calmed down. He let go of her arm. "I'm sorry I yelled. I'm just concerned."

She walked away from him and went into the kitchen.

He followed.

"Well, the baby is fine. I'm five weeks pregnant," she said. She pulled a knife from the drawer, and then pulled out the rest of the stuff she needed to make a sandwich. She started fixing herself a sandwich, spreading the Miracle Whip over her bread slowly. She really wanted a drink, but she tried to fight the urge.

Robert continued to watch her actions carefully.

She put down her knife and turned to face him. She then kissed his lips gently and he passionately kissed hers back. She jumped up and wrapped her legs around him and he held her in his arms as he continued to kiss her. He sat her on the counter and she unzipped his pants. He looked into her eyes, and then softly kissed her lips. He unbuttoned her top, then he touched her breast and it immediately responded to his touch. When their bodies connected, her body responded to each one of his long strokes.

He was about to stop when he heard the keys rattling at the door.

"Keep going, Robert," she whispered into his ear. "Please, don't stop."

He knew that he needed to stop, but he didn't want to. He tried to pull away from her, but she grabbed him tighter which made him keep going as she whispered her beautiful language into his ear.

The door opened and he quickly helped her down from the counter. He turned his back to the door as he pulled up his pants.

Silvia folded her arms across her chest, holding her blouse together.

Angel looked at them in total shock. She didn't say a word as she left to go to the bedroom.

Robert was so embarrassed and Silvia began to cry even more from the thought of Angel seeing them. He kissed her cheek and hugged her. "This was my fault," he said.

Silvia shook her head. "No, this is my fault. Just like everything else . . . I should have stopped this before it got started."

Confused, he squint his eyes. "You should have stopped what? What exactly are you talking about?"

"Us. I should not have let it go this far."

"I'll go talk to her," he said, changing the subject back to Angel.

"No!" Silvia grabbed his shirt when he tried to walk away. "What do you plan to tell her, that we were having sex?" She shook her head vigorously. "She doesn't need to know that." She cried. "I don't want her to know that."

He held her in his arms. "I am just going to go see how her day went. I just want to make sure she's okay. That's all, Silvia."

She let him go and he headed to the bedroom.

He knocked on the door where Angel was and walked in. "Hey, sweetie. How was your day?"

She lay on her bed, reading her book. "It was fine." She rolled over so that she wouldn't have to look at him.

He knew for sure by her reaction that she had seen him and Silvia and was now embarrassed by what she saw. "Is everything okay?"

"Yes."

"Do you have anything that you want to talk about?"

"No."

Robert really didn't know what else to say. He could hear the disappointment in her voice and he knew that she was upset. "Okay. Well, if you ever want to talk." He paused. "About anything, I'm here for you, Angel." He rubbed her hair.

She moved her head away from his touch. "Okay."

Tears formed in his eyes at the fact of knowing that he hurt her. He got up and left the room. When he went back into the living room, he saw Silvia on the couch and joined her there. He touched her stomach. "Can I ask you a question?"

"What is it, Robert?"

"What made you name her Angel?"

She sat silently before speaking, "I named her Angel because I knew the night that she was conceived, angels had surrounded me and protected me from death." Tears escaped her eyes. "I stayed in the hospital for three weeks. The doctor said that I was beaten so badly it was a miracle that I survived . . . It's a miracle that Angel is even here."

"When you brought that night back to my memory, you made me realize how much I hurt you and I would have given anything to go back to that night and make it disappear . . . but when I saw that little girl." He choked on his tears. "I hate what I did to you, Silvia. I really do. But that little girl in there, I love her with all my heart and I wouldn't change her being here for nothing in the world." He leaned over and gently kissed her lips. He gazed into her eyes. "Have you thought about what I said about you and Angel moving in with me and Jazmin?"

"I don't know, Robert. I think we should stop here."

"Stop here? What do you mean, stop here?"

"Stop this."

"We have children together. There is no stopping here."

"No, we have a child together, not children."

He leaned back and studied her. "What do you mean by that?"

"I mean that we have Angel together. The baby that I'm carrying is not yours,'' she said.

"You are lying, Silvia, and I know it,'' he said with absolute.

"Go home, Robert,'' she said, as the tears ran down her face.

He sat still and stared at her for a moment. He then got up and headed for the door.

As soon as he left out, she broke down in tears.

Robert sat in his SUV and thought about what Silvia had just told him. He knew that she was lying and that the baby she carried was most definitely his. He knew that she just needed space and time, and he was willing to give her that.

***

Silvia and Reesie sat at one of the tables at Raymond's as they ate their meals. Reesie was mostly silent as she tried to figure out what had happened to her the other day. The only thing she remembered was waking up on the bathroom floor. She couldn't remember anything else and it scared her. She only knew that her habit was way out of hand, and she didn't know how to control something that was controlling her all over again.

She looked up and stared at Silvia. "What's wrong with you?'' she asked. "You have been real silent lately.''

"Nothing,'' Silvia replied.

Reesie smiled, trying to make it seem as if everything was okay. "Sooo, you told me that you were going to give me the details about green eyes.'' She waved her hands in the air. "So, tell me girl. I want to know. Is he as good as he looks?''

Silvia pushed her hair behind her ear; her eyes stared at the table. "I think I'm falling for this man, Rees.''

Reesie's mouth was wide open. "That good, huh?'' She smiled. "I knew it. I knew it! He had that swagga' when I saw him walk.''

"Reesie, it's not about the sex!'' she yelled. "I mean, don't get me wrong. This man takes me to a different level and the sex is mind-blowing.'' She paused for a second as she thought about the many times they had been together. "Okay, yes; the sex is good. It's really good, but like I said, it's not about that. I've never felt this way before and I don't know what the hell it is. It's like I feel this connection with him, a bond of some sort." Tears ran from her eyes and she laughed. "Sorry, Rees,'' she said, wiping the tears from her eyes. "I have been so emotional lately. It's like I'm on an emotional rollercoaster or something.''

Reesie reached for her hand and squeezed it tightly. "Silvia, this man was your first. Then you have a child with him. Maybe that's the bond you feel.''

Silvia snatched her hand away from Reesie and covered her mouth. She quickly got up from the table and hurried to the restroom without saying another word to Reesie. She was trying to make it there before she threw up all over the restaurant floor.

After she finished throwing up into the toilet, she went over to the sink to rinse out her mouth and rinse her face with cold water, hoping to feel better.

Reesie came into the restroom and watched her carefully. "Are you okay?"

Irritated, she yelled, "I don't know when this morning sickness will end!"

Reesie's mouth dropped.

When Silvia saw her friend's expression, she said, "Yes, Rees, I'm pregnant and I don't know what to do." She dried her face with a paper towel and shook her head. "I can't possibly keep this baby."

Reesie covered her mouth. "For who?" she asked, disregarding the other part of her statement. "Green eyes?"

"Can you stop calling him that, Rees!"

"Well, is it his?"

"Yes, but I lied to him. I told him that it isn't his." She began crying. "I feel like I don't know what I am doing anymore. God!" she yelled. "He wants me and Angel to move in with him until we are able to find another place . . . but I'm so scared."

"What are you scared of?"

"I hated this man so much, Reesie, and I wanted him dead." She cried. "But I messed up."

"Messed up how?"

"I realize that this man whom I considered to be a monster actually has a heart." She hesitated because she didn't want to reveal something she felt, but she did anyway. "And now mine is involved." She began getting angry with herself for having feelings for him.

"So, again, I ask you. What are you scared of?"

"I don't want to be attached to him." She banged her hand on the counter. "The man raped me!" she yelled. "How do I explain falling for a man who stole everything from me? He's the reason why I'm so messed up."

"Maybe he has changed, Silvia. He seemed really nice at your apartment the day I met him," she stated. "Just see how it works out. He's just asking for you and Angel to stay with him for a while, not for you to marry him."

"I don't know if I can handle that . . . or this baby."

Reesie helped her stand up straight. "Silvia, you can handle anything. When we were back in school, you became tough. You stood strong after those men came in and raped you. You didn't allow that to destroy you. It made you a woman."

She pushed Reesie's hands away from her and looked at her as if she didn't understand her words. "Who filled your head up with that crap?" she yelled.

"What is your problem?"

"I'm sooo tired of you talking about rape like it is something of the norm! Like it's just something that people do and we should just get over it!" She rubbed her stomach as she caught a pain. She calmed herself before speaking again. "Since I got raped, I hadn't been the same and you sit here and talk about it like it is completely normal, like it made me better or something. Well, Rees, it didn't. That night, a part of me died in that room and I haven't been able to live ever since.'' Upset, she walked out of the restroom and out of the restaurant doors without paying for her meal.

Reesie pulled out her cell phone and called Dameon. She wanted him to give her what she felt she needed, but there was no answer. She called again . . . no answer . . . and again... no answer.

***

Dameon looked at his cell phone and pressed Ignore each time he saw Reesie's number pop up on his caller ID. He was busy at the table with Ronnie and Ricky, at what he called the, "trap house,'' weighing and bagging dope. This was a little shack he paid for in full for what he called, "business purposes.''

Sheldon was sitting on the couch. While the other guys did their thing, he watched the game. He didn't really like being in the environment but was there because Ronnie called him over there to talk even though Dameon was the one doing all the talking, as usual. He talked way too much noise and now that Brandon was out of the game, he thought he was running the show on the streets.

The football game caught their attention as they watched Drew Brees throw that ball across the field to the hands of a running back who touched down.

"Whooooa! Did y'all see my boy?'' Ronnie said as he stood up and slapped hands with Ricky.

"Hell, yeah! My boy bad. Saints all tha way, ya' heard me? They got this game locked fa sho','' Ricky said.

Sheldon slapped hands with Ronnie and said, "Yeah, man! Them Saints off tha hook. Brees make this here look like a breeze on that playing field. It's nothing for him to make a miracle happen on that field because he knows what it's all about." He now slapped hands with Ricky.

Dameon added his two cents. "Y'all know my Cowboys gon' come back on that . . ."

"Naw, man. Them Saints got this. I'm tryin' to tell ya, my boy," Ricky said, cutting Dameon's statement off.

"Okay, okay. Forget about all that nonsense. You know what I been thinkin' about?" Dameon asked with a smirk on his face. He looked at Ronnie, Ricky, and then Sheldon. "I'm goin' to start runnin' women." He laughed a devilish laugh. "That's the business to be in, right? Think about it, sell dope and women... Can anybody say, mo' money!" he yelled out as he laughed again. "I'm already workin' on one of 'em now. All I gotta do is keep dope in her nose and she good. She lives for that mess."

Sheldon shook his head. "Man, I didn't realize how ignorant you were until now. You been trippin' hard lately." He looked at him long and hard. "That money and dope got your mind warped."

"What you talkin' 'bout Sheldon? I need to hip you to the game. I know you'll have our backs real good considerin' you sharp shooter and all." He laughed a haughty laughed.

Ronnie looked at Dameon like he had lost his mind.

Dameon sucked his teeth. "Man, you worked them boys over real good that day they did that drive by."

Sheldon tried to keep his composure. "That was self-defense. I'm not down with the foolishness, never was and after seeing Austin laying lifeless on that ground and Brandon in a wheelchair, I can't believe y'all still down with it. At some point in life you have to wake up, or you just may end up dead before you ever had the chance to really live. I know you having to look over your shoulder, is not the life you want to live."

Ronnie looked at Sheldon while he talked, and then looked back down at what he was doing. Sheldon made so much sense to him and it had been on his heart to get out of the dope game. He looked up again and his eyes met Sheldon's. He quickly looked back down hoping that he couldn't see his eyes water.

Dameon sat back on his seat. He pulled off his latex gloves and threw them on the table. "You think just because you went off to the military, you can talk down on us? When your daddy died, Brandon took care of your momma with this *drug* money. He made sure she had everything she needed when *you* were out of the country."

"I know what Brandon did and he knew I wasn't down with his lifestyle. *I* sent my momma money every week." His octave went up a level. "She didn't need that *drug* money. Brandon was the one who wanted her to save the money that I was sending and to use the money he gave her. He wanted to feel as though he was there for her, helping her, by doing that. That was his way of being a friend."

"Well, now you out of money, ain't it? Can't you use some money, and fast?" Dameon asked, laughing.

Ronnie looked up to see Sheldon's reaction.

Sheldon got up from where he was seated and headed straight for Dameon. "You know what, man? I am well-taken care of and so is my family." He pointed his finger at him. "You got some major issues."

Dameon stood up and Sheldon walked closer to him. Now they stood chest-to-chest, eye-to-eye, toe-to-toe, mano a mano.

Sheldon didn't break his stare and stood, unmoving. "I don't know what's up with you, but you better get your mind right, home *boy*," he said to him and walked out of the door.

Chapter Thirty-Two

Brandon's sitter, Ashley, opened the door for Sheldon who spoke and walked in. He sat down on the couch across from where Brandon sat in his wheelchair.

"What's been up, man?'' he asked, but his attention was on Brandon's sitter whom he watched walk to the back.

She was a beautiful petite girl who looked no older than eighteen. She had curves in all the right places and her brown-skin, flawless. She had captured Sheldon's attention even with the way she moved.

Brandon laughed, knowing where Sheldon's attention was. "I'm good, man . . . She's beautiful, isn't she? One of the most beautiful women I've ever seen,'' he said with all seriousness.

"Yes, I agree. When did you get her as your nurse? What happened to that other girl?''

"Oh, yeah, she got fired from the company. They say she was stealing from the clients or something like that, but this one, she's God-sent. She's an angel, man, so sweet.'' He chuckled at the next statement he was about to make. "Christian. Can you believe she be in here studying the Bible with me and praying with me?" He said it like he was still shocked at how strong this young woman's faith is. "Then, she invited me to go to church with her this coming Sunday." He paused, seeing Sheldon's reaction.

Sheldon showed that he was impressed as he nodded.

"Yes, like I said, God-sent," Brandon continued. "He knows who to send in our lives at the right time because I needed that Word in my life, but who was I gonna get to read to me and all that other stuff. And to think, she did it without me even asking. I need that in my life. When I first went to that center and talked to Michael, he led me to Christ. I started going to his meetings with Reesie, but I hadn't been to a church service. Right before I got shot, I had planned to go to church that following Sunday." He sighed. "Never made it. Then Reesie stopped going to the meetings and, I mean, she was doing so well when she was going, but now it seems like something's different with her." He stared off into space. "I don't want to believe that she's using again, but I feel it." His face saddened.

Sheldon looked at his friend and wanted to be honest with him. "Are you and Reesie still supposed to be working something out together? In other words, are y'all just living together? Is she just like helping you out here, or is it something more serious?" he asked. He had seen Reesie a few times with Dameon and felt as though they had something going on, but since he wasn't really sure, he didn't want to bring it up to Brandon.

"I don't really know what we are doing. At one point she used to get off work and come here to take care of me, but then that stopped. I will say this, Ashley has been working overtime and not even getting paid for it, but Reesie is never here anymore.'' He began whispering, "Can you believe Ashley has spent many nights here on the couch due to Reesie not coming home?'' He saw Sheldon's reaction. "I can't stay here by myself. I don't know what Reesie be thinkin'.''

"Well, sounds like Ashley is a great girl,'' Sheldon replied. He wanted to stay away from the conversation about Reesie to keep Brandon's focus on something good.

Ashley came back into the room. "I changed your sheets, Brandon. You need anything else right now?''

"Naw, I'm good, Ashley.'' Brandon realized that he hadn't introduced Sheldon and Ashley, so he took this opportunity to do so. "Ashley, this is my boy, Sheldon. Sheldon, this is Ashley, the best nurse ever.''

Ashley reached her hand out to Sheldon.

He took her hand. "Yeah, I'm,'' he almost forgot his name, "Sheldon. Nice to meet you.''

"Nice to meet you, Sheldon.'' She took her seat on the chair and began reading *Still I Rise* by Maya Angelou.

"So, how old are you?'' Sheldon asked. "You look so young to be a nurse.''

"I'm twenty-four and I'm not a nurse. I don't know why Brandon keeps calling me that.'' She laughed. "I work for a sitting company, but I'm in school for nursing,'' she said. Then she remembered she forgot to brush Brandon's hair. "Oh, I forgot. Let me go get the brush.'' She placed the book on the end table and left the room, then returned with the brush. She gently brushed his hair.

Brandon closed his eyes as she hummed her own tune.

Sheldon watched as she stroked Brandon's hair. It appeared as though she really cared. The look on her face as she took care of his friend told him that she did. When Brandon told him how she feeds him spiritually, Sheldon knew then that she cared about him.

"Okay, I'm all done." She turned her attention to Sheldon. "Were you going to be here for a minute? I just need to run to the grocery store to get a few things for him to snack on."

"Of course, I will be here. You go ahead."

She looked at Brandon to make sure that he was okay with that. Then she grabbed her purse and headed for the door.

"Brandon, you were right. She's a great girl," Sheldon said. He didn't want to say the next statement considering that he wasn't sure what his plans were with Reesie, but he decided to say it anyway. "It seems as though Ashley is kinda feelin' you."

Brandon chuckled. "Naw, man. She's just a caring person. I bet she's like that with all of her clients."

Sheldon smiled, knowing that with what he just saw, she was not like that with all of her clients. He looked at Brandon for a minute and said, "You know your boy been trippin' ever since you been out the game."

"Who? Dameon?"

Sheldon nodded.

"Yeah.   Ronnie been telling me about that. He say he been trippin'."

"Yeah, he has. He been talking about running women or whatever now," he said, shaking his head. He had a feeling that Reesie was going to be one of those women if she wasn't already. "I ain't with all that foolishness. I don't know how you got hooked up with that fool."

"I don't know. I made a lot of bad choices. To be honest with you, that fast life is hard to shake. The day that I was shot, that morning, I was contemplating getting back in the game. That night, I was supposed to be meeting up with Royce so I could sell again. I realize now, God definitely don't want me to be a part of that street life. Michael tried to tell me, and there I was about to be disobedient. Look where it got me . . . in this chair."

"Yeah, sometimes we need to stand still and know who God is. If we don't yield to Him, He has a way of getting our attention; and for those who won't listen to Him and yield to His instructions, He can allow them to be taken out at any time. Thank God for grace and mercy, but does grace run out? Obedience is better than sacrifice. Don't sacrifice being obedient to Him because of your own selfish desires for the things of the world."

"You right, Shel. Every day I thank Him for sparing my life. By the way, thank you."

"For what?"

"You took care of them boys that did this to me and Austin."

"No, B. Don't thank me for that. I hate that I took those boys' lives." He shook his head. "I reacted."

"If you wouldn't have, somebody would have. Come to find out, they were the ones who broke in here looking for me. They were the ones who raped Reesie. It was bound that they were gon' get what was coming to 'em. What goes around comes around. Real talk. Somebody was gon' take them boys out."

"Yeah, maybe, but I hate that they were taken out by me. Now I'm living with that over my head."

Ashley walked through the door and grabbed their attention.

Sheldon got up and helped her with the groceries.

She smiled. "Thank you so much. You are such a gentleman."

"You are welcome. Where should I put them?"

She pointed. "You can put them on the counter and I will put them up." She touched his hand. "Thank you for staying with him."

"Not a problem."

"Has Reesie called or anything?" she asked. She started putting away the groceries.

"Naw, you may have to stay here tonight. If you can't, I'll stay with him."

She stopped and looked at him. "No, I don't mind, but do you think she's not coming?"

He shrugged. "I don't know."

"Okay, that's fine." She pulled out some fruit to prepare for Brandon. "I guess I need to feed my friend. I'm sure he can use a snack."

He smiled and whispered. "You really care about him, don't you?"

"Yes, very much so. I enjoy being here with Brandon, so I don't mind this at all. He may think that I keep him company, but believe it or not, he keeps me company." She smiled.

"What y'all in there doing?" Brandon yelled to them.

"I'm just helping Ashley with the groceries," Sheldon said, winking at her. He took her hand. "It was a pleasure meeting you, Ms. Ashley. I guess I better go ahead and get out of here."

She shook his hand. "Okay. It was a pleasure meeting you as well."

"Take care of my boy."

She smiled. "Will do."

Sheldon walked back into the living room. "Hey, B., I'm about to head out," he said to Brandon.

"All right, man, I appreciate you coming by."

"Keep your head up."

"I can't help but to."

Sheldon left out of the door.

Ashley brought the fruit over to Brandon and began feeding it to him. After he finished chewing, he just looked at her and smiled.

Her forehead creased. "What?"

"You know what Sheldon told me?" He chuckled. "That he believed you were feelin' me." He laughed loudly now.

"What's so funny about that?"

"Cuz it's crazy."

"So, what if I was? You know . . . *feelin'* you?"

He looked at her long and hard now. She kissed his cheek and it confused him. "I'm in a wheelchair," he told her, as if she didn't know.

"So, there's a rule about feeling people in wheelchairs?" She smiled at him. "Look, I do like you, Brandon. You are smart, charming, funny and extremely handsome in, or out of that wheelchair."

Brandon was shocked with her words while she continued feeding him his fruit. He was happy that she told him this because ever since she became his caregiver she brought so much joy to his life. He had never enjoyed a woman's company as much as he enjoyed hers.

When it came to being around women, if it wasn't sex-related, then he had never been interested in having them around. But sex didn't compare to the way Ashley made him feel. She made him feel like he was somebody worth taking care of, and that made him feel good.

Chapter Thirty-Three

Kim was so excited. Today was her day. She was in the pastor's study, praying, when her father came in on her.

He stood and watched her.

She looked up and saw her father standing there. It brought tears to her eyes.

"I'm so proud of you," he told her. "And this young man is really something special. I didn't like that Trey and I guess I had good reasons." He shook his head and balled his fists up together. "If I would have known about all that he put you through, I would have killed . . ."

"Daddy, no!" she exclaimed, interrupting him. "Let's not bring him up. Let's not bring up the past. This is going to be a happy day for all of us. Emmanuel loves me in a way that I thought no man would. He's wonderful, Daddy." She smiled from ear-to-ear. "I'm happy, Daddy." She grabbed his hand and looked him in his eyes. "I'm truly happy."

He hugged her tightly. Then he let her go. He looked at her for a long time. "You look beautiful, Kimbrailee.'' A tear fell from his eye.

She'd never seen him cry and it made her eyes swell with tears once again.

He shook his head as if telling her not to cry, and then he said, "Well, hurry up and let me give you away to this wonderful man.''

They both laughed and walked to the doors that were about to open for the bride to enter.

The doors opened and the words of Stevie Wonder filled the room, "You are so beautiful to me.''

Her father escorted her down the aisle and when she got halfway, she saw tears falling from Emmanuel's eyes as they were fixed on hers. He mouthed the words along with the song, "You are so beautiful to me.''

She looked down and saw Trey, Jr., holding the ring pillow and she smiled at how his attention was on it. She looked back up and into the man's eyes of whom she loved and her tears began to fall. She finally made it to the front and her dad gave her away.

Emmanuel now took her hand and looked at her in amazement. He mouthed the words, "I love you so much.''

They prepared to recite their vows and Emmanuel went first.

"Kimbrailee Kianue Whitmore, I have never loved a woman as much as I love you. This is the day that I pledge my love to you. You are my joy, my air, my sunshine. When I first saw you, I immediately knew that you were the one that God created for me. Your spirit spoke out to me." He paused as he choked on his words. "Kimbrailee, I love you with all my heart and I promise to love and cherish you from this day forward. I promise to be with you in sickness and in health, for richer and for poorer, for better and for worse until death do us part. I promise to love you and to be faithful, forsaking all others. I will always be here for you. You are the better part of me." He reached up and wiped her tears away.

Taylor Davenport, who was Kim's maid of honor, had her eyes on Michael, who was the best man. A tear ran from her eyes and he smiled at her.

Michael winked and mouthed to her, "I love you."

She smiled like a little school girl and mouthed to him, "I love you."

It was now Kim's turn to make her vows. Amidst happy tears, she took a deep breath and began, "Emmanuel Silas Matthews, you are the man that I've always dreamed of. You have shown me what true love really is. You, too, are my air. You help me to be better." She cried even more and he wiped away her tears. "I love you so much. You showed me that I can live and love again. You showed me that I had reasons to smile and be happy. All that I have been through, I know that there's a God who loves me greatly, and I am thankful that He gave me you as one of His most precious gifts." She paused as more tears flowed. "Emmanuel, I promise to love you and respect you, honor you and adore you in sickness and in health, for richer or for poorer, for better and for worse, until death do us part.'' She exhaled. "I love you so much.''

They went through another song and the rest of the wedding, and Pastor Matthews was elated to announce his son and new daughter-in-law, husband and wife.

They began the reception, and Kim and Emmanuel danced their first dance as husband and wife. They laughed together as the crowd cheered them on.

He whispered into her ear, "I can't wait to make love to my wife.'' Then he looked into her eyes and she stared back into his. They smiled and continued their dance.

The man on the mic opened the floor for everyone to dance.

Michael went over to his fiancé, Taylor. He reached out his hand to her and asked, "May I have this dance, beautiful lady?''

She took his hand. "Of course, you may, my handsome man.''

They joined Emmanuel and Kim on the dance floor. Many others joined them as well.

"I can't wait to make you Mrs. Michael Bradberry,'' he said, and she smiled at his words with her head resting on his chest. "You look so beautiful, Taylor.'' He took a step back to look at her some more and he added, "Amazing.''

"You look quite handsome yourself, and I can't wait until I'm Mrs. Michael Bradberry," she said with a confidence she didn't have. She laid her head back on his chest.

"Well, we don't have long at all until we say our, 'I Do's'," he said. He smiled at the thought of making her his wife.

Her eyes watered as she thought about Keith, her late-husband. She loved and cared for Michael with all her heart, but a part of her missed Keith greatly. She felt that he was taken from her way too soon. After he passed away, she tried to fill that void she felt by spending as much time as possible with Michael. She didn't even take time to grieve. She wasn't ready to think about Keith being gone away from her and their children forever. She wasn't willing to accept that.

Michael gently lifted her head and saw the tears in her eyes. "What's wrong?"

She shook her head. "Nothing, I'm so happy that Kim found her true love."

Michael softly kissed her lips. "And I found mine," he said. He held her tighter in his arms as they continued to dance.

Chapter Thirty-Four

Silvia did not want to go to this doctor's appointment alone, so she had asked Robert to accompany her since she couldn't get in touch with Reesie. All of her STD tests had come back negative, and she was a bit surprised by the results. She had had unprotected sex with quite a few men in her past; and she just knew that something was going to come back positive, but she was thankful that she was wrong.

"I'm glad you called me," Robert said, breaking her away from her thoughts. He was thankful that she had come to her senses and was honest with him about the baby she carried, being his. He gently took her hand into his.

She squeezed his hand and smiled. "Me too."

The nurse called her back to a room and asked her to undress in the little closed off section of the room. While Silvia undressed, the nurse prepared everything for the doctor and Robert took that time to look around at the different charts on the wall about the stages of pregnancy.

Silvia came out wrapped in a gown and got comfortable on the table. The nurse asked her different questions and she wrote Silvia's answers down in the chart. She left the room to her and Robert, and they waited for the doctor.

He stood beside her and smiled. "So you have been feeling okay lately, not throwing up as much which is great," he said to her. He knew that she felt awkward, so he attempted to make conversation with her. He looked at how much her stomach had grown which wasn't very much. He was happy to know that she was going through with having the baby. He was about to touch her stomach, but he stopped, knowing it would make her uncomfortable.

She felt the baby move for the first time and the flutter made her laugh. She then gently grabbed his hand and placed it on her stomach. She looked at him and smiled.

He felt the flutter against his hand and he, too, smiled.

For the first time, Silvia smiled at the fact of her being pregnant and Robert enjoyed seeing that. He leaned over and kissed her stomach. Then their eyes met and he kissed her lips. He pulled away when the doctor came into the room.

The doctor smiled. "I love to see two love birds," she said. "Don't stop on the account of me." She looked between the two. "Are you ready for your ultrasound?"

They both nodded, but their minds were on the statement she had just made about them being, "Love birds."

"Let's get this started," the doctor said with cheer in her tone.

They listened to the baby's heartbeat, and Silvia looked into Robert's eyes as they continued listening.

"Sounds great! Strong, healthy heart beat so that's good. Now, let's have a look at the baby." The doctor turned the screen so that they could both see. "That's the head. That is a foot. Oh, and this right here." She now pointed with her finger and drew a circle around the segment. "Makes it a boy!" she exclaimed.

Tears immediately fell from Robert's eyes. The thought of his first son made him smile. Silvia looked at him and immediately knew what he was thinking. He leaned over and kissed her lips.

The doctor smiled and looked at Robert. "Well, we have us a healthy looking baby boy." Now she looked at Silvia. "And a healthy mother. Any questions?"

They both shook their heads. They couldn't think of anything at the moment, nothing but the joy they both felt.

When she saw they had no questions, she said, "Okay, you can get dressed. If you think of anything, feel free to call me. You can stop by the front desk before you leave and set up an appointment. I would like to see you back in a week. Okay?"

Silvia nodded, but her eyes stayed on Robert's.

The doctor left the room.

Silvia got dressed, and Robert got caught up with watching her. She was about to grab her shoe, but he reached down and got it for her. He was about to give it to her, but he kissed her lips instead, and she kissed him back. He dropped the shoe to the floor, picked her up and put her up on the table. She began unbuckling his belt as their tongues danced to their own tune.

A nurse opened the door, catching them. "Oh, I'm so sorry. I thought the room was empty." She glanced at Robert, then at Silvia, and she hurried back out of the room.

They looked at each other and laughed.

He fixed his belt, then picked up her shoes and put them on for her. "Let's get out of here," he said. He picked her up off the table and gently placed her on the floor.

When they left out of the room, the nurse who had come in on them, was in the hall with another nurse. Robert and Silvia were sure that she was gossiping about what she just saw. The nurses looked Robert up and down and realized why Silvia couldn't keep her hands off of him. They giggled to each other at the thought.

Silvia made her appointment at the front desk and they left. They rode in silence as Robert took her to his house.

He pulled into his driveway and thought to himself for a minute before saying, "I'm sorry. I should have asked you did you want to come here, or did you want me to take you home." He looked at her. "So, do I need to take you home, or are you okay with being here?"

"I've thought about it, Robert," she said to him.

"Thought about what?"

"I'll do it."

"Do what?"

"Angel and I . . ." She looked at him. "We'll move in with you." She paused and added, "On one condition."

"What's the condition?"

"We stop acting as though this is a relationship."

Her words taking him aback, he replied, "I'm sorry. I know that we aren't in a relationship, but sometimes I just feel like something is missing and whenever you are around, I feel as though you fill that void." He gently lifted her chin. "I didn't mean to make you feel uncomfortable."

She raised her voice a little when she said, "I know, but all of this just confuses me."

"Confuses you how?"

"You make me think that you actually care."

He sighed. "And I do care. Look, I know that I have hurt you in the past, and I don't want you to hold our history against me. I have really grown to care a lot about you." He looked into her eyes to make sure she understood and, he repeated, "A lot."

A tear fell from her eye and he wiped it away.

"I would never do anything to hurt you again." He touched her stomach. "Or our children."

"You keep saying that, Robert, but . . ."

"Yes, and I mean it." He interrupted her as if he knew what she was going to say. "I will keep repeating it until you understand it." He leaned over and hugged her. He then touched her stomach and asked, "What are we going to name our son?"

She placed her hand on top of his and smiled. "I'll leave that assignment to you."

"What about Daniel?"

"I think that's an excellent choice." She now kissed his lips.

He got out of the car and walked around to open her door. He reached out his hand to her and she took it as she got out. They walked up to his door and after they walked in, Silvia stopped and kissed him. He pulled away from her and took her hand. "Let me show you the different rooms and you can choose one."

"That sounds great." She walked upstairs with him.

He pushed open one of the bedroom doors and said, "This is the room that Angel chose. I had a decorator come over and decorate it."

Silvia looked at the room and was amazed at how beautiful it was. She walked inside and looked at the exquisite art that surrounded the walls. She walked over to the canopy bed and ran her hand across the soft covers. She looked back at him. "Robert, you've talked to Angel about staying here?"

"Yes, we've talked about it."

"How come I didn't know that you had spoken with her about it?"

"Well, she was supposed to talk to you about it and I thought that she had."

"It's like you are trying to form an alliance with her or something, like you are trying to get in good with her and eliminate me."

"What? No, that's not at all what I'm doing. I wanted Angel to talk to you about us all living together. That is all. I'm not trying to turn her against you or anything like that." He rubbed her hair. "Silvia, listen to me; I would never try to take Angel away from you, or turn her against you."

She exhaled. "I'm sorry. It must be my hormones tripping." She laughed, trying to make light of what she just accused him of.

He hugged her and took her hand into his once again. "Let me show you a few more rooms and you can decide what you would like to do with your room after you choose one."

He led her to a room that looked like a master bedroom. She walked in. "Oh, my God, Robert! This room is huge."

He chuckled. "So, are you saying that you want this one?" He pointed at the door. "Because there is an even bigger room down the hall."

"Well, I will take that one for me and the baby, but can I do something with this one." She started picturing a beautiful scene in this amazing bedroom, and she wanted to make that vision come to life. The things that she had in mind, she wanted them to be a surprise to Robert. She just knew that he would love the end result.

"Actually, I have another room that can be for the baby, and it is right next to yours." He saw the look on her face as she continued to look around the room. "What exactly do you have in mind for this room?"

"It'll be a surprise. Just let me get some of my workers in here to change it up a bit." She wrapped her arms around his neck and kissed his lips. "You'll love it!"

"Okay. I trust you, Ms. Architect." He tried his best to refrain from touching her too much, remembering their conversation in the car. "Let's go take a look at your room."

They walked down the hallway and around the corner. She noticed the bedroom that they were about to walk into, was right next to his. She walked into the room and was ecstatic. It was huge, and she loved how it was decorated. She didn't plan to make any changes to it. She was amazed at all of the beautiful rooms in this house that she had never gone into while she was there spending time with him and Carla. She looked around the room, and then turned around to face Robert. Without a word, she slowly sat down on the bed.

Robert watched her and by the look in her eyes, he knew what was on her mind.

She scooted back and allowed her legs to open, revealing her beautiful thighs.

Robert put his hands in his pockets, trying to refrain from walking over to her and touching her. "So, you like it?" He asked, attempting to get her attention back on the bedroom.

She bit her bottom lip and stared at him for the longest. She put her finger up to her lip. "I was thinking," she purred. "Maybe we could christen this room. You know, just to have a memory of you while I sleep in this bed."

He saw the come-hither look in her eyes, and they drew him in. He walked over to her and gently pushed her back down onto the bed. He then carefully grabbed her ankle and pulled her to the edge of the bed without thinking twice about it. She smiled and pressed her red-bottom Louis Vuitton heel into his chest. He smiled back at her as he grabbed her ankle and gingerly kissed it. He then ran his finger-tips up her thigh and stopped. He looked longingly into her eyes. "Silvia, I don't want to make this out to be about . . ."

Silvia sat up and kissed him, shutting him up. "Shhh! Let's not ruin this moment, Robert."

He kissed her lips tenderly and fulfilled her desire.

Chapter Thirty-Five

Ashley helped Brandon get into bed. She covered him up and prayed with him. Once she was done doing that, she sat on the edge of the bed next to him. "Well, if Reesie isn't home soon, I will just lay on the couch until she gets in," she said.

"Or you can just lay in here and talk to me."

She smiled at him. "Brandon, that's so sweet, but it would be inappropriate of me."

"Who's going to tell?" He moved his hand to touch hers which was next to his side.

She looked at him with her eyes squinted. "Brandon, you touched me!" she exclaimed.

After being shot, he had been paralyzed from the neck down and never once had he been able to move since then.

He shocked himself as he looked at his hand touching hers. He attempted to move more than just his hand, but nothing else would move. He tried to move his hand again, but only his fingers rubbed up against her hand.

She saw the look on his face when he couldn't move his hand again. "Brandon, don't get discouraged. This is a start," she said. "Soon you will be walking and moving along just fine." She smiled. "Praise God!"

Brandon looked at her and a tear ran down his face.

She wiped it away.

"You give me so much hope and confidence in myself, and not only that, in the Word." He inhaled as if it were his first time. "You are a breath of fresh air."

When he said that, a tear ran from her eyes. She lay down beside him and they talked each other to sleep.

Ashley woke up in the middle of the night and forgot where she was. She saw Brandon asleep next to her and smiled. She got up and headed to the kitchen to get a glass of water.

She walked up the hall and when she looked into the living room she saw Reesie on top of Dameon while on the couch. As she pleased him, he moaned lightly. Ashley looked on the table and saw the bag of cocaine and had remembered Brandon talking about her past drug habit.

Reesie looked up into her eyes and she quickly got off of Dameon. She grabbed her top from beside him and covered herself. "What are you doing here?" she whispered loudly. When she first came home, her mind was not on Ashley being there.

Ashley stood in total shock and thought to herself. *Maybe if you two weren't so high, you would have noticed my car in the driveway. And how could you not know that I was here? You know your boyfriend can't be left alone.*

Reesie snapped her fingers, snapping Ashley away from her thoughts. "Hellloooo. I'm talking to you," she said.

"I'm sorry. I was coming up here to get some water. I was, um, here waiting for you to get off work and fell asleep."

"Fell asleep where? You normally be on the couch when I get off late," Reesie snapped.

And I will never sleep on that couch again. She thought about what had just taken place on the couch. "I'm sorry, um, I'll leave now."

Dameon looked at Ashley and licked his lips, wishing that she was the one who was on top of him.

Ashley quickly went to the back and grabbed her things. Without waking Brandon, she left.

She could not believe what she had just seen happening between Brandon's girlfriend and one of his best friends. All she could do was pray. She didn't plan on revealing that information to Brandon. She knew that he would be hurt. "What am I thinking? He deserves to know that she is no good for him," she said out loud to herself. "But I don't want to be the one to tell him, so, Lord, you reveal it to him."

Reesie looked at Dameon. "Do you think she's going to talk?" she asked.

"No, and if you think that she will, I will make sure she won't."

"What do you mean?" Reesie covered her mouth as she gasped. "Are talking about killing her, Dameon?"

"Don't worry," he said. "I'll take care of her." In his mind, he only had one way to take care of her, and it had nothing to do with killing her.

***

Regina walked Robert down the hall of Bradberry and Co. and she made sure that she swayed her hips from side-to-side, hoping that they caught his attention. She remembered sending him to Silvia's office the first time he came in and she figured since Silvia reacted the way that she did, she must not have been interested, but she was and she was about to take advantage of this moment. She turned to face him. "So, what are we going to be doing for you today, Mr. Sterling?"

Robert replied, "Well, I just wanted to discuss some business with Michael about a new building."

"Good! Very good! You are a real business man and I'm sure that you could use a real woman on your arm." She ran her hand down his arm in a very seductive manner.

He chuckled lightly as he shook his head. "You know that I could have made my way to Michael's office myself. I've been here many times."

"And that I know. You are one of my favorite people who walk through that door. You are easy on the eyes and . . ."

"Let me cut you off there," he quickly interrupted. "I'm seeing someone."

"Ha! Your wife. I know that you are married and that doesn't bother me at all."

Robert stopped walking and looked at her in disgust. "My wife passed away, but you know it's sad that a man being married doesn't keep you from wanting to be involved with him. That is what you are telling me, right? You are telling me that you would have no respect for my marriage? Correct me if I'm wrong."

Regina stood up straight and ran her hand over her clothes as if she was trying to make them more presentable. "No, that's not what I was saying. I just . . . You know what? Forget it, um, Mr. Michael's office is right down the hall." She pointed him in the direction. Embarrassed, she made her way back to the front desk.

Robert tapped on Michael's door and walked in.

Michael looked up from his work. "Hey, Robert. What can I do for you? Are you ready to move forward on your building?"

"Actually, um, I have something new to present to you. I want to have a new building designed as well as move forward with the other one."

Michael smiled. "Okay, great." He pointed to the chair in front of his desk. "Have a seat . . . What is the new building going to be for and give me your vision."

Robert took his seat. "The new building will be for a studio."

Michael frowned. "What type of studio?"

"A dance studio."

Michael squinted. "A dance studio? Is this studio for someone you know, or are you planning to sell it and make a profit?"

"It is for a good friend of mine."

"Really? Okay, well, let me get some information from you and I will pass it to Silvia to get started with the floor plans."

"Is there someone else who can do the floor plans?"

"Yes, but everything goes through Silvia because she's head of that department . . . Is something wrong?"

"The dance studio is actually a surprise for her."

"Wow. I had no idea." Michael remembered his and Silvia's conversation about Robert. "Why are you doing this for her?" He was curious to know Robert's motives behind this studio.

"I just want to do something special for her. I want to make her dream a reality." He looked at Michael. "I know you may not understand this, but to be honest, Silvia and I have history and I'd rather not discuss it."

"I understand. Well, let's discuss your vision so we can make it happen." He smiled.

Robert was so glad that Michael didn't pry any further. He began telling him the vision, and Michael wrote it down.

Chapter Thirty-Six

Reesie woke up on the couch with a headache. The night before, she and Dameon had done so much cocaine that she passed out. She saw Ashley at the stove cooking breakfast with her earplugs in her ears. She didn't even realize she had come in.

She got up and looked in the refrigerator and the cabinet. Both of them were packed with food. "Where did all this food come from?" she shouted, as she slammed the cabinet door.

Ashley was startled when she heard her voice and the sound of the cabinet. She thought that Reesie was still asleep. She pulled the earplugs from her ears. "Well, I went to the store the other day and brought some things back."

"Is that part of your job, to buy groceries for *my* boyfriend?"

"Oh, your boyfriend? I see . . . Was he your boyfriend last night, or did you forget about that?"

Reesie's tone changed. "Look, please do not tell him."

"How could you do that to him, Reesie? He doesn't deserve that."

"You don't know what the hell you are talking about. You know nothing about the way he treated me in our relationship before he was shot, and you think he don't deserve this. You don't know him; you just think you do," she whispered to her. "What? Are you falling for the charm? Well, that charm is fleeting." She looked deeply into her eyes. "Believe me."

Ashley was shocked by her words. "I'm sorry you feel that way." She got closer to her. "And I'm not falling. I'm just doing my job, honey." She lied because she went beyond her job and, yes, she was falling.

Dameon walked in the door and scared the both of them.

Ashley looked at Dameon, and then back at Reesie. "Wow, he has a key," she said to her, being sarcastic.

"So do you," Reesie shot back at her. "I will be ready in a minute, Dameon. I need to take a shower right quick!" she yelled to him, but she looked at Ashley. She then headed to the bathroom.

Ashley continued cooking and Dameon walked up behind her without her even realizing it. She turned around and he was extremely close to her. "Oh, my God, you scared me!" she said as she put her hand over her chest.

His eyes shot her the most evil look. "Sorry," he said. He grabbed her uniform pants and pulled her to him. "Why are you so nervous?" He chuckled. He could see fear all over her. He could even feel it. He put his nose in the nape of her neck and took in her scent as if he could smell it. He now looked into her eyes. "I won't bite. I mean, I want to, but I won't, unless you do something to make me bite." His nose flared as his lips turned up.

Her voice trembled. "Could you please get away from me?"

The tremble in her voice let him know that he had her right where he wanted her. "You look beautiful by the way," he said, ignoring her. He pulled at her uniform pants a little more. "I bet your body is just as beautiful." He pulled her closer to him. "If you don't want me to find out how beautiful it is, I suggest you keep your mouth closed about what you saw last night." He kissed her lips. "You understand?"

Tears swelled in her eyes. She nodded.

He let her go and walked away when he heard the bathroom door open.

Reesie walked in completely naked. "Hey, what you doing?" she asked him.

Ashley looked at her nakedness in pure shock, then looked away. *This girl must not have it all.*

After nobody answered her, she reached around Ashley and grabbed a glass to fix herself a drink. "I decided to take a quick bath and have a lil' wine before I leave out. Just give me a minute," she said to Dameon. After fixing her glass of wine, she headed back to the bathroom.

Dameon saw Ashley's reaction to Reesie's nakedness. He looked at her and shrugged. "She use to strip. She has no problem with showing off her body. Maybe you should think about that.'' He laughed out loud. His laugh was cold and disturbing to her.

Ashley cut the stove off and went to go wake up Brandon. She was waking him up a little bit earlier today due to the fact that she didn't want to be alone with Dameon.

"Brandon,'' she called his name once she got in the room.

He didn't wake up.

She sat on the bed beside him. "Brandon,'' she whispered into his ear.

He still didn't hear her. He was deep off in his sleep, but when she touched his chest, he felt her. His eyes opened. When he looked in her face, he smiled. "Good morning. Did you stay the night?'' he asked.

"No, I didn't.'' She raised him up so that he could lean against the headboard. "Reesie came home and I left.''

He looked at the tears in her eyes. "What's wrong, Ash?''

Dameon walked into the room before Ashley could respond. "What's up, my boy?'' he asked as if he were excited to see him.

"Hey what's up? I haven't seen you in a good minute. What's going on? I would shake your hand, but you know.'' Brandon chuckled.

"Yeah, man, I know," he said to him, but looked at Ashley who was now standing. "You have you a wonderful nurse."

"Yes, she is awesome, I must admit," he said looking at Ashley. He then looked at Dameon. "What's up with cha? What you doing over this way?"

"Oh, I been takin' Rees to work. You didn't know?"

"Naw, she didn't tell me, but thanks for looking out."

"Yeah, I been takin' really good care of her for you," he said with his eyes fixed on Ashley. "You know you my boy, and anything I can do to help, I got cha." He now looked at Brandon. "What's mine is yours, right?"

"Yeah, man, and like I always told you, what's mine is yours."

"Ta sho'."

When Brandon was heavy off in the drug game, he did take care of Dameon and he always told him, "What's mine, is yours." Brandon was always loyal to his boys when it came to money and helping them out. It was the women that he was never loyal to and now he held much regret. At one point he was messing with Dameon's ex-girlfriend, but it was his girlfriend at the time. When Dameon found out about it, he acted as though he didn't care. Deep down it bothered him, but he had planned to play his role as his friend and he knew that one day, he would get revenge. Since Brandon couldn't move around and take care of business, he was using this opportunity to get back at him through Reesie.

Reesie came out the bathroom and she walked in the room wrapped in her towel. She looked confused and a bit of fear set in. The room became silent. She looked around at everybody. "What's going on?" she asked nervously, thinking that Ashley had told Brandon what she had seen last night.

"Nothing, Rees. Everything's good." Dameon said to her, knowing exactly what she was thinking.

"What's up, babe? Come give me a kiss before you leave. I barely see you anymore," Brandon said.

She walked over and kissed his lips. Then she looked at Ashley. *You . . .*

Brandon interrupted her thoughts. "You didn't tell me that Dameon was taking you to work, I thought Silvia was."

"She is . . . I mean, she does . . . well, sometimes . . . but Dameon . . . now will take me today," she rambled and made no sense at all.

Brandon was so confused by what she just said, and now he just looked at her with suspicion.

"Yeah, man, we gotta go," Dameon said and he looked at Reesie like she was stupid. "Rees, you gon' be late."

She went through the dresser drawers and grabbed some clothes. She left out of the room behind Dameon and didn't say anything further.

Brandon watched them leave the room and was now in deep thought. He started getting a feeling that something wasn't right with this picture and tried to shake his gut feeling. He always looked at Dameon as a friend, but little did he know he was his enemy.

When Dameon and Reesie got in the living room, he quickly turned, facing her. "You so stupid. What the hell, Rees?" he whispered loudly.

She looked at him dumbfounded.

"Just put your clothes on."

She put them on. "Does he know anything?"

"Hell, do you? Now I see why Brandon always called your butt slow. The only thing you good for is for giving away that stuff between your legs and oh, using that mouth of yours."

His words hurt her feelings. "Is that what you think of me?"

"That's all I can think of you." He reached in his pocket and pulled her out a bag of cocaine. "Here. Take this and stop your whining." He kissed her lips. "It ain't cute."

Chapter Thirty-Seven

The ushers of Holy Temple Ministries opened the doors, and Robert and Silvia walked in together, along with Reesie. Silvia tried to slip into the back row after Reesie, but Robert tightly grabbed her hand, letting her know that she wasn't going to sit on that row. She looked at him with confusion. Then he nodded towards the rows up front and led her to the seventh row. Five minutes later, Ashley wheeled Brandon in and sat on the end of the fifth row next to Brandon in the aisle. Kim and Emmanuel sat on the first row together alongside Taylor and Michael. They waited for the service to get started as they listened to the pianist play.

Kim and Ashley got up and went to the back so that they could prepare the praise dancers.

The youth pastor got up and did "Call to Worship." The praise dancers came out and stood in their places. The music began playing and they danced beautifully together. Angel was in the lead, and she had Robert's and Silvia's full attention as the words played through the speakers. Robert realized that they were the same words that played on the radio the day he picked her up from school.

The words of Kirk Franklin filled the building. The second verse now played, "Jesus you are my cornerstone. You are my friend when I'm alone. You're the convictor when I'm wrong. Jesus you are, yes. You're the peace within my storm. You are the shelter from all harm. I love it when you hold me in your arms. Everything I need, you are . . .''

Just like in the SUV, Robert's tears began to fall.

Silvia stirred in her seat as she listened to the words of the song and watched her daughter dance. The baby leaped in her womb. It was as if he could hear the words and felt the music and it made Silvia smile. She touched her stomach, then looked over at Robert and saw the tears that fell from his eyes. She wiped them away and he looked at her. She grabbed his hand and placed it on her stomach. He felt every flutter of their unborn child and smiled at her. Then their attention went back to their daughter as she praise danced.

The praise dance ended and Angel went to change so that she could come back and sit with her parents and hear the Word.

Pastor Matthews got up from his seat in the pulpit and prayed before he got ready to deliver a Word from the Lord.

Silvia thought back and remembered that she was in this same place over three years ago and how she ran from the building like she had stolen something.

"Praise the Lord, everybody!'' Pastor Matthews exclaimed from the pulpit, grabbing her attention.

The congregation began to sing praises to the Lord.

"I want you all to do me a favor. Inhale."

Everyone in the congregation inhaled.

"Now exhale." They all exhaled and Pastor Matthews continued. "Now, the Word tells us plainly. Let everything that hath breath praise the Lord."

Everyone shouted for joy.

"I want you to go with me in your Bibles to II Corinthians 10:4-6." He waited for everyone to turn in their Bibles, and once they got there, they stood for the reciting of the Word. Robert and Silvia looked on with Angel. Of course, they knew nothing about finding that scripture. They didn't even bring a Bible.

Pastor Matthews continued. "Read with me. I'm coming from the New King James version, but we all know that the different versions are all saying the same thing. Jesus is the way, the truth and the life."

Everyone recited the Word together. "4. For the weapons of our warfare are not carnal but mighty in God for pulling down strongholds, 5. casting down arguments and every high thing that exalts itself against the knowledge of God, bringing every thought into captivity to the obedience of Christ, 6. And being ready to punish all disobedience when your obedience is fulfilled." The congregation took their seats.

The pastor joyfully said, "What a word. How many of you know that we go through warfare?"

Most of the people shouted out.

"When we are going through, we mustn't fight with weapons of the world or fleshly weapons, but we must fight with the Word of God. The Word of God is mighty in pulling down our strongholds, and if we be honest with ourselves, it's a lot of us in here who have strongholds. We have situations and circumstances in our lives, and some of us are dealing with strongholds."

Many shouted out their "Amens".

"Let me share with you how to deal with strongholds. Study the Word of God. Get it into your spirit and into your hearts. When Satan comes in like a flood, you spit the Word at him. The Word is your sword and shield. With your sword, you could win any war. But you can't just speak the Word, yet doubt. You have to have hope in that Word and have faith that God will perform His Word. You already have the victory, so why do you act as though you are defeated. There's power in the name of Jesus! God can loose you from those strongholds! Be encouraged to live free! We sometimes allow our past to hold us hostage when Jesus took our past, present and future to the cross; and how many of you know that whom the Son sets free, is free indeed? You must trust Him that He has already set you free. Get out of that bondage because God has given you the power to do so! You can walk in liberty because of the blood of Jesus. You are the victor not the victim. There is victory in Jesus! If you are in him, you have victory! Somebody needs to praise Him up in this place right now! Your victory is in your praise!"

Almost everyone in the building shouted out praises.

"So many of you are suffering from past hurt, pain and disappointments, and you won't let go of it. That's a stronghold. Some of you are suffering from addiction. That's a stronghold."

Silvia stirred in her seat and Robert felt her tense up.

"Some of you are dealing with unforgiveness, hate, fear, depression, anger, greed, gossip, adultery, gluttony, fornication, envy, lust. Those are strongholds! Some of you have ungodly soul ties that need to be torn. Those are strongholds. A stronghold is anything that has you bound and tries to keep you from getting closer to God, our Father!"

Tears fell from Silvia's eyes. Robert saw the look on her face and it saddened him. It was a look of guilt, hurt, shame, pain and even remorse.

He grabbed her hand and squeezed it, attempting to comfort her.

Still in tears, she looked at him.

His thumb gently rubbing the back of her hand, he smiled and focused his attention back to the pastor's message.

"God will pull down those strongholds, but you have to give them to Him. Let go! We serve a strong and mighty God! Allow Him to pull down those strongholds and when you give them to Him completely, then He will loose you and set you free from every one of them that has tried to bind you. That word, *completely*; that's an important word. You can't give Him half of it or little bit of it and you steady try to hold on to the rest of it. Give it to Him completely and totally. Don't hold on to any of it. Just let it go! People struggle with it because we struggle with ourselves. God can break the chains that have had you bound, and He can tear down walls that have tried to block you from living in peace and with joy. God is a deliverer, He is a healer; and He is well able to set the captives free. He can loose you from any addiction and set back that you have had in this life. He can deliver you from you. We needed deliverance from ourselves. That's why we needed a savior. He can loose you from any stronghold, no matter what it is!'' He took a sip of water. "Nothing is too big or too hard for God.''

Reesie sat in the back and knew that she was one of the ones he was speaking to throughout the message. She got up from her seat. "I'm sorry. Excuse me,'' she whispered to each person she had to cross over to get to where she wanted to go. She left out of the building and waited for Silvia outside.

Pastor Matthews continued, "If you are in need of Salvation, you can come to the altar today. If you are in need of prayer, come to the altar. If you need healing . . . deliverance. Come to the altar. God can take care of it all when you trust Him. The praise dancers have already ministered to somebody today. Jesus, you are. How many of us know that Jesus, you are.'' He hit the podium. "He is whatever you need Him to be. He can be a comforter, a friend, a brother, a father, a mother, a provider, shelter from the storm, but most of all, a Savior. He can save you from yourselves. You been traveling a dark road, and you have some things that you've done in life that you regret; but right here, right now, you can make it right. God requires more of you. Will your heart and soul say yes? He desires more of you. Will your heart and soul say yes? Somebody has been struggling. Right now, let it go. He's ready to loose you and set you free. All you have to do is say yes.''

Robert's spirit began to stir and he felt chill bumps. He felt as though this man of God was talking directly to him as a tear ran down his face.

"He's calling you out of darkness right now. All you have to do is say yes. Will your heart and soul say yes? I can feel some spirits stirring in this place and I can hear you saying yes. If your spirit is saying yes, harden not your heart, and come to the altar. There is peace for you here! There is love for you here! There is joy for you here! There is grace for you here! There is more for you here! In Jesus you will find more! In Him you will find greatness.'' He paused as he looked around the congregation. Then he looked back at the choir and said, "Choir,'' and they began to sing *Yes* by Shekinah Glory.

Robert listened to the words of the song as it ministered to him, and tears flowed from his eyes. He stood up and Silvia looked at him strangely as she let go of his hand. He headed to the altar.

She felt a burning in her heart to go to that altar, but her feet wouldn't move. Her tears flowed as she bent over in her seat crying. Angel rubbed her back as Silvia called out to God to help her move from her place of pain, to promise. When she called out the name of Jesus, her feet were released from their place that they were once stuck in. She got up and made her way to the altar.

Many others continued to come down to the altar. Brandon was about to ask Ashley to wheel him down, but he saw her head bowed as she worshiped God.

I can do this with your help, God. I know I can. He moved his arms to the side of his chair and tears ran down his face. He put his hands on the wheels, and then he wheeled himself to the altar.

Many came for prayer and few came down and were led to salvation. The building seemed as though it shook from the people worshipping and praising God. The Word had gone forth.

Chapter Thirty-Eight

Michael saw Silvia, Robert, Angel, Reesie and Brandon, and he invited them all to lunch after church along with Taylor, Emmanuel, and Kim. He even invited Ashley since Brandon was her guest.

The hostess walked them to a table for ten.

They all took their places and looked over their menus. After they each found what they were going to order, they sat and waited for the server to come over. Everyone was silent which shocked Michael considering that they had such a big group at the table.

"Sooo," Michael began. "It amazes me how the world is so small and a lot of us connect in so many ways," he said, as he looked around the table. Then his eyes stopped on Brandon. "Brandon, how's everything going with you?"

"Everything is great. That Word was what I really needed," he said and he looked at Ashley. "Thanks for inviting me and taking time out to bring me with you. I know that's not easy for you."

Ashley smiled. "You are very welcome, and it was my pleasure." Tears came to her eyes. "When I looked up, and you were gone from my side and down at the altar, I thought someone had wheeled you down there. When you told me you wheeled yourself, I couldn't do anything, but give God the glory. God is so awesome. He's going to bring you out of this completely." She squeezed his hand and he was able to squeeze hers back.

Michael and Taylor said, "Amen," together.

Reesie looked at Brandon and how happy he looked. She had spent all night out with Dameon, and she got him to drop her to Silvia's just before dawn. She only went to church because Silvia and Angel were going. Silvia let her borrow a dress from her considering she didn't bring any clothes with her. She didn't even know that Brandon was going to be there; and now, sitting next to him, she felt guilty that she didn't even come home to help him get ready. She began really falling off with taking care of him ever since she relapsed.

Michael looked at Reesie. "Well, Reesie, how have you been? I haven't seen you lately. Everything okay?" he asked.

"Yes, Mr. Michael, it is . . . everything is going good... I mean, as good as it can get . . . I don't know . . . better most days, I guess." Her voice trembled as she tried to find the right words.

Michael looked at Brandon, then back at Reesie.

Everybody else's eyes stayed on her.

"Are you sure you are okay?" Michael asked her.

Reesie nodded. "Excuse me for a moment." She got up to go to the restroom.

When Ashley watched Reesie walk away, she knew that she had to have been troubled and it saddened her to know that.

After a few minutes passed, Silvia excused herself to go check on her friend. As she walked away from the table, Robert's eyes were fixed on her. He then excused himself to make a call to Naomi to check on Jazmin. She had caught a little cold, so he asked Naomi to keep her so that he could keep his promise to Angel. He did not want to miss her praise dance and he was thankful for the worship experience.

Silvia walked into the restroom and saw Reesie just standing, looking in the mirror. "What's wrong, Rees?"

Reesie shook her head as she continued to stare in the mirror.

"Why did you come over to my place in the middle of the night?" She looked at her and added, "With Dameon." She walked over closer to her. "What are you doing with him, Rees? You know he bad people." She waited for her to speak, but she didn't. "Forget it, I need to pee right quick and when I'm finish, you need to come back out of here with me before these people think you crazy, girl," she joked.

Reesie stood in place, still staring into the mirror.

Silvia went into the stall and looked in the toilet. She quickly came back out. "Rees, you didn't flush!" she whispered loudly. "What are you doing? I thought you were done with that crap." She referred to the plastic bag that once had cocaine in it, but now floated in the toilet. "Talk to me, Rees."

Reesie continued to stare, her eyes as wide as golf balls. "Take me home. I want to go home." A tear rolled from her eyes.

Silvia went back in the stall, flushed the toilet and got her some tissue. She handed it to her. "You know that we rode with Robert this morning. Do you want me to just go out there and make him leave now?" she asked, upset at her friend.

Reesie stared at her and nodded. She was like a zombie. When Silvia saw that she wasn't using the tissue she gave her, she took it from her and wiped her tears for her.

It hurt Silvia to her heart to see her friend like that. "Okay, I will ask him for the keys, and I'll take you home."

She walked out and Reesie was right behind her.

Silvia tapped Robert on his shoulder. "Robert, can I get your keys so I can drive Reesie home?"

He looked at Reesie, and then back at Siliva. He finally replied, "I don't mind taking her home. That way you can stay and eat with your friends."

Brandon's eyes stayed on Reesie. "What's wrong, Rees?"

His question was met with her silence.

"Look, I will take her home," Ashley said. "All of you can enjoy your meals." She looked at Brandon. "And Brandon, I will come back to pick you up in a few."

Brandon ignored Ashley's statement. His only concern at the moment was Reesie. "Rees?" he called to her.

Reesie just looked at him without saying a word, her eyes filled with sorrow.

Silvia interrupted, "No, everyone, I will take her if someone will just let me borrow their car." She now turned to Robert. "Or SUV," she said to him with attitude.

"What's wrong with her, Silvia?" Brandon asked her since Reesie wouldn't respond to him. He felt in his heart what was wrong, but he just needed to hear her say it. He knew what he saw and he knew the signs.

Silvia looked Brandon in his eyes and shook her head, letting him know that he didn't want her to say it in front of everyone, so she said, "It's okay, Brandon."

Michael paid close attention to Reesie, recognizing the signs of someone who has relapsed. "Let me take her home," he said. He figured that it would be an opportunity to talk and pray with her, maybe encourage her to come back to the meetings.

When he offered to take her home, Taylor grabbed his arm that rested under the table. He looked at her and she looked him in his eyes and shook her head discreetly.

He kissed her, and then stood, disappointing her.

"Everyone, just stop!" Silvia yelled. "I will take her home. It's not that big of a deal."

Robert then handed her the keys without protest.

Michael sat back down in his seat.

"Silvia," Angel began. "Let me go with you." She stood up.

Robert grabbed her arm. "You can stay with me and Silvia will be right back. Okay, Angel?"

She looked at Robert and sat back down in her seat, shocked at how tightly he grabbed her arm.

Silvia looked at him and was bothered by his forcefulness with their daughter, but she shook it off because her friend needed to get out of there as soon as possible.

"Come on, Rees. Let's go," she said angrily.

Reesie looked at Brandon one final time before following her friend.

Chapter Thirty-Nine

Emmanuel walked up behind Kim as she was putting on her lotion. He picked her up.

She screamed and hit him. "You scared me!"

He kissed her lips. "Well, can I make it up to you?"

"Where . . . is . . . Trey . . . Jr.?" she asked in between his kisses.

"I wore him out at the park today. He is knocked out, baby." He kissed her neck and she moaned at his gentleness.

After they had gotten married, they sent Trey, Jr., to spend a few nights with Taylor and the twins; and they had christened every room in the house. He enjoyed making love to Kim and she had never felt what she felt with him, with her first husband, Trey. Emmanuel made love to her when Trey only had sex with her.

He picked her up, kissed her and carried her over to the bed. Their tongues danced to a beautiful rhythm. "I love you so much, baby."

"I love you too," she said to him.

He kissed her again. "I believe I love you more." He laid her on the bed and kissed her again, then grabbed a condom and put it on.

She watched him as he did it.

She lay back on the bed and he lay on top of her and stared in her eyes. He kissed her nose, then her cheeks, her forehead, then her lips. He began making love to his wife, kissing her lips passionately. As the tempo of his pelvis got a little faster, she bit his lip. "I'm sorry," she whispered.

It didn't even faze him. He kept his strokes long and steady. "Did I tell you how much I love you?" he said as he looked her in her eyes.

"Yes, you did, but you can tell me again . . . and again... and again." Her "agains" were said with each one of his strokes.

He kissed her as he ceased the moment. He lay on top of her for a while as he looked in her eyes. "I love you," he said, catching his breath.

"I love you too."

He slid himself out of her and sat on the edge of the bed. He was about to take off the condom until he saw a tear in it. He looked back at Kim who was looking at him. She touched his arm as she continued to lie down. Breathing heavily, she smiled at him. Her smile faded when she saw the look on his face. It concerned her.

"I have to go to the bathroom." He smiled at her, kissed her, and headed for the bathroom.

Kim got up and followed him. She opened the door without knocking and she saw him standing over the toilet as he pulled off his condom.

Unfamiliar with his behavior, she asked, "What's wrong, Emmanuel?"

He shrugged. "The condom broke," he said as he put it in the toilet and flushed it.

Tears immediately swelled in her eyes and she covered her mouth. "Are you serious?"

"Yes, babe, but it's okay. No need to flip out." He pulled her hands from over her mouth.

"Are you sure that it tore? Was it a big tear?"

"Kim, I'm fine. Don't worry about it." He walked over to the sink and washed his hands, then looked in the mirror at the cut on his lip from when she bit him. "You got my lip bleeding, baby." He chuckled.

Kim just stood there with no more words to say. Fear had taken over her tongue and her body.

He walked over and kissed her lips. "Let's take a shower together." He waited for her to respond, but she didn't. "Look, Kim, I'm fine."

"What if . . ."

"Kim!" he yelled her name so loudly that she jumped. "I'm sorry." He looked at her. "I'm sorry. I didn't mean to yell." He lifted her chin. "I'm fine, baby and so are you." He kissed her lips. "Now relax and shower with me." He kissed her, then grabbed her hand.

He turned on the water and they got in together.

***

After Silvia dropped Angel off to school, she decided to go have a talk with Robert. She used her key to get into his house. She was so angry with him that she hadn't been answering his calls since the Sunday that they attended church together. When she opened the door, he was on his way out to go to work, and she was glad that she caught him.

"Is something wrong?" he asked.

"What was that about Sunday?" she asked angrily.

"What?"

"You grabbing Angel's arm like that?"

"What?" Now he was a little more agitated by her question. "Is that why you haven't been answering my calls?"

"You bet' not ever touch her." Her voice was shaky as if she wanted to cry.

He took off his suit jacket, walked over and laid it on the arm of the couch. Then he looked back at her, his eyes squinted. "You can't be serious. I told you that I would never hurt her or you."

"When you grabbed her . . ." She stopped in mid-sentence.

He stood straight up and faced her. "When I grabbed her... What?"

"It reminded me of when you grabbed me," she blurted out. "And I know it scared her."

He rubbed his forehead as if she was making it hurt. He sat on the arm of the couch. "I'm sorry, Silvia. It won't happen again." He grabbed her hand and pulled her to him. He kissed her and held her in his arms for a minute.

Silvia climbed on top of him and they both fell over onto the couch. They laughed as she kissed him.

"What a way to start my morning," he said, as he ran his hands over her ample behind.

"Mmmm-hmmm, papi. We may as well start it off right." She kissed him and allowed his tongue to meet hers. Her cell phone rang and she stopped to answer it. "Hello? Yes, I'm, Ms. Martinez . . . Oh, my God . . . What happened to her?"

Robert could only hear her side of the conversation and it concerned him. He knew something was wrong as he watched her begin pacing the floor as the person on the other end explained to her what happened. He looked at the worry lines that creased her forehead as the person on the other end spoke to her. He wondered if it was someone from Angel's school. He grabbed her arm to stop her from pacing.

"Okay. Well, I'm on my way!" She hung up and headed for the door.

Robert grabbed her hand, stopping her. "What's wrong?"

"They said Angel took ill." She covered her mouth as if the news was just making sense to her. "They had to rush her to the hospital. I have to go."

"*We* have to go," he said, as if reminding her that Angel was a part of him too. "I'll drive."

On the way at the hospital he called his neighbor, Naomi and asked her if she would pick up Jazmin from day care later on and if she would mind keeping her overnight. After Carla's death he allowed Jazmin to stay with her Godparents for a while; and after he picked her up to come back home, there were many nights that he asked Naomi to keep her due to him not being able to handle the pressure.

Once they arrived to the hospital, Silvia and Robert went to the front desk. "Yes, I'm here for Angel Martinez," she told the nurse behind the desk.

The nurse directed them to Angel's room in ICU. Silvia and Robert walked into the room together and when she saw Angel with her eyes closed and the machines hooked up to her, she buried her face in Robert's chest and immediately began sobbing.

Robert embraced her as he shed tears of his own.

She didn't even notice that the doctor was in the room, but Robert saw him standing next to Angel with her chart in his hand.

"Sir, what happened to her and what's going on?" Robert asked him, without moving. Silvia's face was still buried in his chest.

"Hi, I'm Dr. Walsh, and who are you to the patient?" he asked.

"I'm, Robert Sterling and this is Silvia Martinez. We're Angel's parents."

He walked over to Robert and extended his hand.

Robert shook it.

"We are running some tests to find out. We were told that she passed out at the school. Her teacher said she had complained of a really bad headache and sensitivity to light. When they got her here, her heart rate and blood pressure had dropped drastically. So right now, we have her hooked up to a heart monitor and we have some fluids going into her system. As soon as we get the tests results back, we will let you know what's going on."

"Thank you. Thank you so much," Robert said to him.

Robert walked Silvia over to the bed, and she leaned over and kissed Angel's forehead. She looked back up at Robert. "Do you think she's going to be okay?"

"Yes, I believe she's going to be fine."

"I don't understand what could be wrong. She seemed fine this morning." She cried so loudly that one of the nurses came to close the door. "I don't understand. Am I being punished for all the wrong that I've done?"

"No, Silvia. It has nothing to do with you. She's going to be okay. I remember Naomi telling me just last Sunday that everyone goes through trials and tribulations in life. It doesn't matter what you've done or didn't do. No one is exempt from the troubles that will arise in life, but it is up to us how we choose to handle them." He raised her head up. "Angel will be okay and we will get through this together. Trust that God will bring her through." He looked deeply into her eyes before adding, "Us through."

She was surprised by his words and nodded. His presence there; brought her comfort.

At that very moment, the machine flat lined, and Silvia's eyes were wide with disbelief as she gasped.

She covered her mouth as the doctor and two nurses rushed in. This was all surreal to her. Everything was happening so fast.

Robert immediately felt as if it were a déjà vu moment as he thought back to the moment in the hospital with Carla.

The nurses directed them out of the room and they stood in the hall.

Silvia burst into tears and Robert held her tight in his arms as he silently prayed, *God, I may not know how to pray, but I know we need you right now. That little girl needs you. We need you. Please, God, save my daughter.*

Five minutes later the doctor came out and informed them that they stabilized Angel and that she was okay. He told them that they could go in for a minute, but when Silvia asked if she could stay the night, he informed her that no one could stay overnight with intensive care patients. He let her know that they were going to take really good care of Angel. He told them that they are welcome to stay in the waiting area, or they could come back in the morning for visiting hours.

They went back in for a few minutes, said their goodbyes to Angel, and left. Silvia got in the SUV with Robert. He sat and waited a few minutes before he started the engine.

Silvia stared straight ahead and said, "I don't want to be alone tonight." A tear ran down her cheek.

"I understand. Do you want me to take you to get some of your things?"

She nodded; her eyes still straight ahead.

Robert saw the worry in her face and it saddened him. "Everything is going to be okay, Silvia."

"What if she doesn't make it through the night?"

"Don't think that way . . . She will."

Silvia now looked into his eyes. "Promise?"

"I promise," he said, hoping that he was right.

He put the car in gear and took her to get some of her things, and then to his place.

Robert sat in the living room, craving a drink, but he refused to get one.

Silvia paced his living room floor as she bit her nails. Little did he know; she craved a drink too.

"Silvia, why don't you come and take a seat with me." He patted the couch next to him.

She ignored him and kept pacing.

He got up and pulled her into his arms. "She's going to be fine."

Silvia's cell phone rang and she jumped. She covered her mouth as if she knew it was a bad call.

Robert went over to her purse, pulled it out and answered it for her. The person on the other end asked for her and he gave her the phone.

Silvia took it and placed it to her ear, afraid to say hello. "Hello," her voice was shaky. She listened as the other person talked. She said, "Oh, my God . . . When?" she asked. "Okay, I will try to get there as soon as I can." She hung up the phone.

"What's wrong?" Robert asked. He was very concerned as he watched Silvia with both hands over her mouth, her eyes wide and filled with tears.

"My mother is in the hospital. Carl said she's not doing well and that I need to come see her. He said the doctor told him to call in her family because she doesn't have long."

Robert pulled her into his arms and hugged her tight.

"It seems like everything is going wrong in my life all at the same time. Now I have to figure out how I'm going to be with my mother and with Angel. Now I have to choose between the two." She cried as he continued to hold her.

"You go be with your mother, and I will stay with Angel." He raised her head up with his finger. "We can go be with Angel in the morning. Then you can go take a flight out to be with your mother later tomorrow, or you can wait until Monday, whichever day you want. Whatever you need, I'm here.''

She kissed his lips. "I need you,'' she said, and kissed him again. "Let's just go to your room, and we can forget about this for a while. I really need this right now, Robert.''

He gently pushed her away. "Silvia, you do this every time. Sex is not the answer. It's not going to make things better.''

"It will for me.''

"Trust me. It won't. What you need right now is rest.'' He took her hand and led her to the bedroom that was set up for her.

She lay on top of the covers and he lay with her as she cried in his arms. She looked at him and thought about him losing his wife. She felt like she was being punished for what she did to his family. "I'm so sorry about Carla.'' She cried.

He looked at her strangely. "It's okay, Silvia.'' He wondered what made her bring up his late-wife at a time like this.

"I'm sorry she accused you of touching Jazmin. I'm so sorry,'' she shrieked.

He squeezed her in his arms, attempting to calm her down. "It's okay. It was normal for someone like her to be skeptical about things like that. After I thought about it, I began to understand her position more and more.'' He swallowed hard because he didn't want to tell Carla's secret, but he decided to share it with someone he now trusted and that person was Silvia. "Carla's father molested her when she was a child.''

Silvia covered her mouth and gasped. That was one secret that Carla never mentioned to her. *Oh, my God. I triggered her. I know I am the reason she killed herself.* She felt so much guilt and she wanted to tell Robert, but she couldn't stand the thought of him being angry with her. Not right now, she needed him. She didn't speak another word as she broke down from the weight she carried.

Robert held her in his arms until she cried herself to sleep; and once she did, he fell asleep. After an hour passed, she began to stir in her sleep.

She woke up and looked over at Robert who was asleep with his cell phone in one hand and hers in the other. The cordless phone was next to his head on the pillow just in case the hospital called. They made sure that they left the nurse with all three numbers.

Silvia got up and went downstairs. She walked into the living room and reached into her purse, pulling out her wallet. She opened it up and pulled out the business card that Michael had given to her. She then dropped the wallet back into her purse and walked into the kitchen. She stood at the counter and stared at the counselor's name on card. She wanted to call Michael badly, but she realized that he and Taylor were out of town, and she refused to bother him. Desperately needing someone to talk to, she covered her mouth, attempting to muffle her cries. She put down the card and opened up the cabinet and pulled out a glass. She pulled out the bottle of vodka that Robert kept there. She stood in deep thought for a minute, and then she poured a little into her glass.

She thought to herself. *I'll just taste it. A little taste won't hurt. It'll just take off a little pressure and ease my mind so I can relax.*

"What are you doing?" Robert asked, and she jumped at the bass in his voice.

"I can't do this, and you won't give me what I need, Robert. I just need something to help me relax. I have to have something to take my mind away from this. I'm not as strong as you!" she screamed through her tears. "I'm so scared. Can you imagine what I'm going through right now? She's my daughter!"

"She's my daughter too, Silvia, and you don't need sex or a drink to get through this." He touched her stomach. "Think about our son that you are carrying," he said, as tears ran from his eyes. "It's not about you any more, Silvia." He grabbed the glass from her hand and set it down on the counter. He took her into his arms and she sobbed uncontrollably. They both eased themselves to the floor and she cried in his arms. "I promise we will get through this." He kissed the top of her head and rubbed her hair as he tried to calm her down.

Chapter Forty

Robert was up early and had prepared himself for church service. He sat on the side of the bed for a minute and watched Silvia as she slept. Even though he knew that her sleep wasn't peaceful, she still looked beautiful to him. He gently stroked her cheek, waking her up. "I'm about to head to church. Would you like to go with me?" he asked her.

Silvia was shocked to see him up and ready for church. Right now Silvia's mind was stayed on Angel and her mother. Angel had just taken ill, and she couldn't believe that Robert was talking about going to church instead of going to visit their daughter.

Silvia received a call from Carl saying that her mother's vital signs were better even though she was not yet responding, so she decided to wait and fly out Monday to be with her. Right now, her concern was for Angel. She and Robert spent all day with her on yesterday during visiting hours, but the doctors still hadn't found the cause of her illness. She was responding better and that made her feel hopeful.

Silvia shook her head. "You weren't going to the hospital today?"

"Yes, I am going to head that way after church."

"Well, I want to be with Angel."

"And so do I, but I am going to church first. Then I will make it out of service just in time for visiting hours. It makes no sense to sit in the waiting room and worry ourselves crazy. In order for me not to lose my mind, I need to be in church."

Robert was never one who went to church, but he enjoyed the worship service so much the other Sunday that he decided that it was the place to be if he wanted to get a Word that would help him in this journey called life. He knew that he needed to be in a place of worship, especially with everything that he was going through right now. He knew that he would find hope there as Pastor Matthews delivers the Word.

Silvia sat and thought for a minute before she agreed to go with him. She got up and prepared for worship service. Right now, she needed a word of encouragement to get through this battle.

Robert and Silvia walked into the church doors of Holy Temple Ministries, and the smiling faces of the ushers greeted them. One of the ushers led them to the eighth row and they sat together as they waited for the service to start.

One of the associate Ministers did "Call to Worship" and opened up with prayer, "Father God, we stand before you today acknowledging that we are not worthy of your love, but we thank you for your grace and your mercy that has kept us. Thank you for being who you are and for your loving-kindness in spite of ourselves. Forgive us for every one of our sins and cleanse us from all unrighteousness. Thank you for the blood of Jesus. Lord, we need you to cover us, Father. Protect us. We pray

right now that you show up in this place. We are in need of you,
Father, and we need to hear a word from you. We pray that you
give Pastor Matthews a word that is in season and that it will
encourage and build up your people. May it pierce the hearts of
those who don't know you, and may they be led to your saving
grace on this day. In Jesus name we pray . . . Amen.''

Silvia was almost in tears from his prayer.

The congregation praised God as the choir sang Zion
songs.

Pastor Matthews got up from his seat. "Make a joyful
noise unto the Lord for He is worthy of all the glory, honor, and
praise. Praise the Lord everybody for Jesus is Lord.''

People stood up and began praising God for who He is
and for all that He has brought them through.

Pastor Matthews continued, "You may not understand
my praise, but He knows what He has brought me through and
there's a story behind my praise. He understands why I praise
Him the way that I praise Him . . . Whatever mess you are in,
He can bring you out. Whatever you are going through, He can
bring you through it. Praise your way through right now in this
place. He's going to bring someone out today. I haven't always
lived right, but God . . . Somebody should have shouted right
there, because we all have some but God moments in our lives.
God's grace is sufficient and His mercies endureth to all
generations.''

People rejoiced all over the building.

He continued, "I'm a living witness and I am a
testimony of His grace and mercy. He can heal the sick, raise

the dead, deliver and set the captives free. That's the kind of God we serve . . . He's worthy of my worship!''

People shouted out "Hallelujahs'' and "Amens" all over the place.

"Turn with me in your Bibles to Romans 12:17. We will recite verses seventeen through nineteen. Then we will go down to twenty.'' He paused as everyone in the congregation stood.

Everyone recited with him, "Repay no one evil for evil. Have regard for good things in the sight of men. If it is possible, as much as depends on you, live peaceably with men. Beloved, do not avenge yourselves, but rather give place to wrath; for it is written, 'Vengeance is Mine, I will repay,' says the Lord.''

He paused and said, "Now verse twenty.''

Everyone now recited verse twenty together. "Do not be overcome by evil, but overcome evil with good.'' Everyone took their seats.

Pastor Matthews took a sip of water and continued, "Evil intentions. I know I'm not the only one who has ever had evil intentions towards someone. I'm not the only one in here who has had ulterior motives. I know I'm not the only one in here who has ever harbored unforgiveness and tried to take vengeance towards my enemies into my own hands. But how many of you know that nobody can handle your enemies better than God can. The Lord said vengeance is His. I can assure you that taking vengeance into your own hands is never worth it in the end. Christ overcame evil and because of what he did on that cross, we, too, can overcome. Unforgiveness is a sickness and it will eat you alive. It can and will kill you. People are hurting in this place. I say to you, let it go and let God have it because He knows how to handle it. You can't overcome evil with evil. Good overcomes evil. Do good to those who try to persecute you. God will deal with them. He tells us plainly in His Word that He will make your enemies your foot stool. This means that He will use your enemies to elevate you. He wants you to live in peace. No matter how someone has wronged you, God wants you to do good unto them and live peaceably among them. Do not give place to wrath. Let it go and forgive them. You must forgive your enemies because it is commanded of you. We are also commanded to love. Love covers a multitude of sins. Love your neighbor as you love yourself. You, too, must love your enemies and I know that's a hard thing to do, but it is the right thing to do. There's a blessing in our obedience and we are commanded to love and forgive. Love and forgiveness are vital to your health and spiritual growth. Unforgiveness only hinders you. Forgive those who have tried to tear you down. Some of us bring trials and tribulations to ourselves when we allow unforgiveness and hate to fill our hearts. But through every trial and tribulation, God will see you through each one of them when you have faith. When the enemy tries to take you out, God will sustain you. Stop harboring all these past issues. Stop harboring all this unforgiveness. Let it go. I'm talking to somebody up in here!'' he shouted across the pulpit.

Silvia squirmed in her seat, knowing that she was one of the ones he was talking to. She let go of Robert's hand considering that hers had begun to sweat.

Pastor Matthews took another sip of water and continued, "You see, God knows the heart of every man. You may fool man, but you are a fool if you think you can fool God. There is nothing that you can hide from Him. You can't even hide yourself from Him. Many of us walk around here with all these hidden issues when all we have to do is give our issues to Him. We punish ourselves when we hold grudges against people who have wronged us. God desires you to be whole, but you can't be whole if you are trying to carry your burdens. They will weigh you down until you won't even feel like living. Let it go. It's far too heavy to carry that load alone. Give it to Jesus . . . The doors of the church are open. God desires to heal somebody today. He desires to deliver someone today. Bring everything to Him. Come on down to the altar. He desires to make you whole today.''

People began crying out all over the building.

Silvia broke down and Robert held her as he tried to comfort her, but she couldn't find comfort in him. She got up and went down to the altar.

Her tears continued to flow as Pastor Matthews whispered in her ear and began prophesying over her, "Someone has hurt you so bad and you felt as though you had no reason to live. You could have died that night, but God didn't see fit. He has great things in store for you. You have to walk in purpose, for your destiny is great. He brought you out of that thing for a reason. It's time to let it go and rise up. Jesus died so that you can have life and have it more abundantly. He's calling you out of darkness, but it's up to you to walk in His marvelous light. You have been giving yourself away to man after man, but Jesus is saying that it is time for you to give yourself to Him. He loves you. He cares for you. He desires to heal your broken heart.''

Chill bumps rose up on Silvia's skin as his words spoke to her.

Pastor Matthews continued, "You've been hurt by so many men in your life, but it's time to let it go. You can't keep harboring that unforgiveness. It has tried to kill you. Satan has tried to bury you, but God! You tried to seek revenge, but it backfired. You must go to the one you have wronged and ask for forgiveness and you, too, must forgive. Trials and tribulations have risen up in your life, but God will see you through; just trust Him. You've been fearful of attachment, but God is saying, attach yourself to Him for He will never leave you nor forsake you. You have to trust Him. You have to stop battling this demon. You've been battling it for too long. God desires to heal and deliver you, but you have to trust Him. He wants to loose you from that thing, but you have to give it to Him. You have to make the choice to let it go.''

Silvia fell to the floor and cried.

Pastor Matthews began to pray over her.

***

Robert and Silvia rode home in silence. He looked back and forth between her and the road. He knew that there was something that was bothering her, but he decided to keep silent. He pulled up in his driveway and they got out of the car. He opened the door and Silvia walked in. She placed her purse on the couch. He watched her for a minute as she paced the living room floor. He learned that whenever she did that, something was really bothering her.

"What's wrong, Silvia?'' he asked.

You tried to seek revenge, but it backfired. You must go to the one you have wronged and ask for forgiveness and you, too, must forgive. Tears fell from her eyes as she kept thinking about the words of Pastor Matthews. "I'm so sorry, Robert," she said sincerely.

Puzzled, he stood up straight and studied her. "Sorry for what?"

"That day when I saw you in that grocery store, it took me back to the night that I've been trying to forget. And that day you walked into my office and back into my life, I wanted revenge. I wanted to hurt you the same way you did me." She sobbed. "I hated you, Robert!" she yelled. "And I wanted you to pay for what you did to me!"

Robert walked over to her and he wiped away her tears. "I understand, Silvia."

"No, you don't!" she yelled. "I messed up. When I saw you in that grocery store that day, I knew exactly who you were and when you came to me about a deal, I was more than ready for revenge. At least I thought I was. I took that opportunity to try to destroy your family and to ruin your life," she confessed.

Robert now squinted his eyes. "What do you mean?"

"Carla left you because of me." She tried to wipe away her tears that seemed to not go away. "This was all my fault."

"What are you talking about? What was your fault?"

"I lied to her, Robert. I told her that you were touching Jazmin. That's why she left you." She hesitated with her next statement. "I'm the reason she killed herself."

"What?" He couldn't believe his ears. "You lied to my wife about me touching my daughter? What were you thinking,

Silvia?'' he yelled. "I can't believe that you were so vindictive and would do that to my family!''

"I'm sorry. I didn't mean for any of this to happen.'' She wiped away her tears that flowed like a river. "You have to believe me.''

"You didn't mean for what to happen?'' he yelled. "You didn't mean to hurt my wife and daughter? You didn't mean to hurt me? You didn't mean to destroy my family? Tell me! What exactly didn't you mean?''

"I'm sorry, Robert. Will you just please forgive me?'' She attempted to hug him.

He pushed her hands away from him and turned his back to her as his tears began to flow. He tried to gain control of himself before he turned back around to face her. "How could you do that, Silvia? Did you even think about how that would have affected my daughter if it would have gone any further? That could have damaged her! Your lies almost ripped everything a part! God,'' he said in disgust. "I can't believe that you would do something like that!''

"You don't understand. I . . . I . . .'' Silvia tried to search for her next words.

Frustrated, he yelled, "You what?'' He waited for her to respond but she still couldn't find her words. "You know what, Silvia? Right now, I just need you to leave. I need some time to think,'' his tone a little more calm.

Silvia looked at him for a minute. She walked closer to him and touched his face. She attempted to kiss his lips, but he pulled away. She turned around, grabbed her purse, and left out of the front door. She sat in her car and thought about all the hurt that she caused Robert's family. Her tears escaped her eyes once again. She rubbed her stomach as she felt her son moving inside of her. She broke down into more tears. Her heart was so heavy and she didn't know what to do.

She slipped her gear into reverse and heavily placed her foot on the accelerator without even thinking. Her tears blurred her vision and before she knew it, she was out of the driveway and into the street. Her mouth dropped as she looked directly into the headlights of a speeding truck and the last thing she heard was rubber burning, tires screeching.

Robert was sitting on the sofa with his head in his hands when he heard the loud sound of heavy metal destroying metal. The sound was so close, his heart instantly skipped beats from the vibration. He slowly looked up. "Oh, my God," he said, hoping the feeling that he had wasn't real. He got up and ran to the door. He took a deep breath before twisting the knob. When he opened the door, the sight that he saw left him completely devastated.

A Note from the Author

It is my prayer that you enjoyed the storyline and that it touched you in a positive and powerful way. Thank you so much for taking time to read this novel. My readers and supporters mean so much to me and I love me some you. I enjoyed writing this story and it was definitely heartfelt. I write with purpose and that purpose is to encourage, empower, and inspire. Whatever visions that God gives to me; I will give birth to those visions and bless someone in the process. That is my intention as well as my desire with every storyline that I share with you.

This storyline was difficult to get through because I know that there are so many people hurting in this world from so many different things, and within this storyline, there were many issues. We hear about all types of violence; rape, abuse and the misuse of so many people all around the world and it grieves my spirit to know that people are hurting because they live in silence. We live in a sick and sinful world, but we can be the difference. Let's not be so quick to judge one another, but get to know each other's story and encourage one another to be better. Everyone has a story that needs to be told. People hurt when they live in silence and are entrapped by fear. It takes courage to speak out. There is hope.

It is my belief that no one has the right to rape, abuse or misuse you in any shape, form or fashion. Sexual abuse is NEVER okay. God does not intend for you to be hurting at the hands of others. If you have ever been raped or abused in any way, report it. Do not be scared or fearful of what others may think or say. Do not live in silence because silence can kill you. You don't have to suffer in silence and you are not alone. There is help and there is hope. So many people suffer from living in silence and God's desire is for you to have life and have it more abundantly. That is why He sent His son, Jesus Christ, and all you have to do is accept Him into your heart. He wants you to live free and whom the Son sets free is free indeed. You don't have to live in fear and you don't have to live in silence. God is with you through it all. By sharing your story, you can help someone else through their story and help them to face many of life's challenges. We all have a purpose. We were created to worship God, commune with Him and to please Him by being obedient to His Word. We as Christians are called to help others, to build up others and encourage them. We are called to minister to the brokenhearted. Read and study Isaiah 61:1-2. We all have a call and a purpose in life.

If you are struggling with strongholds, there's a God who is strong enough to tear them down. We serve a God who is strong and mighty. He is able to handle all of your situations and circumstances. You don't have to struggle. Let go and get help. God is your strength and your refuge. There is no need to fear. God loves you so much and He cares about everything that goes on with you, whatever it may be. Do not take vengeance into your own hands because you will only be hurting yourself and others that you didn't even intend to hurt in the process. Allow God to handle your battles for you. God can shelter you from your storm. Stand still and see the salvation of the Lord and be still and know that God is God. He cares for you and He loves you no matter what you've done. We have all these hidden issues but one thing about it, we can't hide them from God. We can't even hide ourselves from Him. So give your issues to Him. He can take you and clean you up, but the choice is yours. There is hope.

If you struggle with a worldly lifestyle, you have a way out. All you have to do is call out to God and ask Him to help you walk away from that lifestyle and help you to live according to His will. God has called each of us with a higher calling, but it is always up to us to answer that call. It does not profit a man to gain the whole world and lose his soul. God has called us out of darkness and he desires us to walk in His marvelous light. He gives us a way out of every ungodly lifestyle. Seek Him and continue to pray without ceasing. Jesus is the way, the truth and the life. He can help you out of any lifestyle and help you to live a better one, but you have to desire that. There is hope.

If you struggle with addiction, it is my strong belief that God is stronger and bigger than any addiction. He can and will get you past your addictions, your struggle and your battles but you must trust Him. Even if someone says there is no cure for something, I can assure you that there's a cure for everything and that cure is Jesus. The stripes were placed on His back for that very purpose and the Holy Spirit was sent to comfort you and help you with every struggle. Whatever sickness and/or disease that has tried to kill you, Jesus can cure you. Your battle that has tried to tear you down and take you out, God can raise you up. When life tries to knock you down, God will help you to stand. We serve a powerful God, but the key is to trust Him to be our power source and in Him is where our strength is. The battle is not yours. There is hope.

If you are suffering from depression or dealing with any kind of mental illness, God is able to see you through. He is able to heal and deliver you. Seek help. God has placed many counselors and therapists here on earth to help you. Do not suffer in silence. Talk to someone. There is nothing wrong with seeking help. That takes courage, and I commend those of you who make use of the tools that God has placed here on earth. If you ever feel suicidal, go to your nearest hospital and get help. Nothing that you are going through is worth taking your life over. Your life is valuable and precious.

No matter what you are going through at the time, it will not last always. Be encouraged. Things will get better. Trust God that He has everything under control no matter what your situation looks like. Keep moving forward, and do not give up. Continue to pray without ceasing. God will see you through when you trust Him. There is hope for you no matter what your situation or circumstances may be. You are significant, and God cares for you greatly. He loves you beyond measure, and He is your help in times of trouble. There is hope. Seek Him.

I remember one day I was traveling on the interstate and all of a sudden it started pouring down rain and I could not see my way through it. I started to just pull over until it settled, but then I heard the voice of God saying, "No. Do not pull over. Do not stop. Keep going." I was obedient and I kept driving through the storm while I prayed. All of a sudden the sun shined so brightly as if it had never been a storm. I was in awe to see the sun shining so bright after a terrible storm like that. That's the kind of God I serve. While we are in our storm, we sometimes feel as though we will never get through it . . . But God! He is able to bring us through every time, but we have to have faith. I said all of that to say this, do not give up in the midst of your storm, because your breakthrough is near. It may be raining in your life right now, but the sun will shine again. Keep praying and keep believing. God will see you through.

You are in my heart and prayers. Always remember to stand still and know that God is God no matter what your situations and circumstances are. Remain in worship and pray without ceasing. God loves to commune with you and no one can break that communion between you and Him, except you. He loves you greatly. If you feel as though no one else understands, He does. Take everything to Him in prayer. May God bless you in all that you do and remember, pray, praise and prosper. God has great things in store for you. Choose life and be blessed. To God be the glory.

Miracles and Blessings,

Terri T. Thrash

Imagine. Innovate. Inspire.

Be Creative. Be Unique. Be You.

"I write to Encourage. Empower. Inspire."

Reader's Group Guide:

Reader's R.A.P. (Reality and Purpose) Session

1. When Silvia reverted to her past in chapter one, how did the scene make you feel? How did you think she would take her vengeance out against Robert?
2. Michael showed great patience with Silvia. Why do you think that he was so patient with her? Do you think that you would have been as patient with someone like Silvia? Why or why not?
3. "Everybody has a story." Do you believe that people who "act out" have a story behind their reasons for acting out? Do you think someone's past, most often, dictates their future choices?
4. What did you think of Michael's counseling techniques throughout the storyline? How do you view counseling? Do you believe that it is a helpful tool? Why or why not?
5. When Silvia ran into Robert at the meet and greet, how did you feel about Silvia's reaction?
6. How did you feel about Robert's proposition to Silvia?
7. What did you think about Carla throughout her appearances in the book? How did you feel about her story?
8. Do you think Silvia hid her hostility towards Robert well?
9. What was your first impression of Carla and Robert's marriage and why?
10. Michael asked Silvia a question about her sex life because he felt as though she had a problem in that area. Do you believe that Silvia struggled with a sex addiction?
11. What were your thoughts about Brandon and Reesie and their relationship?

12. What did you think of Emmanuel Matthews? What did you think about his response when Kimbrailee told him that she had AIDS? Do you think that someone who has HIV/AIDS is treated differently when it comes to having relationships?

13. Have you ever taken revenge into your own hands against someone and found out that it wasn't as sweet as you thought it would be? Would you like to share your story?

14. Why do you think Silvia had such a strong dislike for "church people"? How do you view "church people" and why?

15. Reesie said, "Everybody has a well-kept secret". Do you believe that her statement is true?

16. Did you see a changing point in Silvia and, if so, at what point did you see that change?

17. How did you feel about Silvia's plan of revenge towards Robert in regards to his family?

18. Do you think people who have been abused and live in silence, suffer? How do you feel about rape/sexual abuse? Do you think that a situation like Silvia's and Carla's can affect someone's relationship/marriage?

19. Was/were there a/any character(s) that you related to in the storyline? Why do you think that you could relate to that/those character(s)?

20. What was the strongest message that you received from *Ulterior Motives*? Is it a message that you could apply in your everyday life?

The Evidence Journey continues…

Temptation

Coming Soon

A Taste of Temptation... Enjoy!

Taylor sat at the conference table in the conference room of Johnson, Jordan and Davenport Law Firm, the law firm that her late-husband, Keith Davenport, made partner with long before he passed away. She was in deep thought as she waited for the meeting to start. She had just remarried to her childhood friend, Michael Bradberry, less than two weeks ago, yet she was still missing her beloved, Keith. She couldn't understand why she seemed to be missing him more and more lately. He was in every one of her thoughts, and she couldn't shake her memories of him which always seemed to bring her to tears.

Kimbrailee Whitmore-Matthews, head of the paralegal division sat to Taylor's right and Tom Banks, head of the investigations division sat to her left. There were a few other attorneys gathered at the table with her as they waited for the meeting to begin.

Richard Johnson, one of the senior partners, walked in. He said, "Well, I called this meeting because we have someone new joining our team." He stood with his back straight and his hands crossed in front of him. His white hair neatly combed towards the back of his head. His skin was pale and wrinkly, looking as if he would soon retire from life here on earth.

Taylor's eyes watered as she looked past him and at the man who stood behind him. "This is Kenneth Dupont, a world renowned attorney from Los Angeles, California, and his credentials prove that he will be a great asset to our law firm. So, if you will, please join me in welcoming him to the team."

Everyone clapped.

Kenneth nodded, greeting everyone. He thanked them for their warm welcome. He took his seat in front of Taylor and his eyes lingered on her for a while. Then his attention went back to Mr. Johnson.

"Now to the next order of business," Mr. Johnson continued. "Taylor, how's the Tommy case coming along?"

Her attention was still on Kenneth.

Kenneth was tall, handsome, shoulders broad and his complexion was honey, the same as Keith's. He reminded her so much of him that he had her in a complete trance as she daydreamed about her past.

"Taylor?" Mr. Johnson called to her again. "Are you okay?"

Taylor came back to reality when she heard her name. "Sir?" her voice trembled.

"I asked about the Tommy case. How's it going?"

"I'm sorry, sir, could you please excuse me." Taylor got up and walked towards the door.

Kenneth's eyes were on her until she left out of the conference room.

When she walked into the hallway, she inhaled deeply, then exhaled as the tears ran from her eyes. She went to the water fountain to get some water, and then headed to her office.

After the meeting ended, Kenneth tapped on her door.

She wiped away her tears, cleared her throat and said, "Come in."

When she watched him come in, it almost overwhelmed her. She tried to control her breathing.

"Are you okay?" he asked.

She took a deep breath and thought to herself, *Oh, my God, he even sounds like him*, then she answered, "Yes, I am okay. Thanks for your concern."

"Okay, I just wanted to make sure that you were okay and I wanted to personally meet you since we will be working on that Tommy case together." He smiled and extended his hand.

Hesitantly, she shook his hand.

He held onto her hand for a while before she finally pulled away from his grasp.

"Nice to meet you," she finally said. "But what do you mean, working on the Tommy case with me?"

"Well," Kenneth began, "that was one of the things we discussed in the meeting. Mr. Johnson wanted someone to work with you on the case and I told him that I would." He paused when he saw her demeanor change. "You don't mind, do you?"

"No… No, that's fine. I could use the help," she told him, then she thought to herself, *This can't be happening. I can't possibly work with this man.* Her eyes slowly traced every inch of his body.

"I hear that you graduated law school about what, five years ago? Mr. Johnson told me that since you came to this firm, you've proven to be one of the best and for some reason, I can believe that," he said as he looked her in her eyes. "You are probably the best at other things as well, I'm sure."

"Thank you, I try my best." With the last part of his statement now registering to her, she said, "Wait. What?"

He waved his hands in the air. "Never mind about all that . . . Anyway, they were just telling me that your husband, as young as he was, made partner a while ago, and he was one of the greatest."

"Yes, he was." Her tears caught in her throat. She looked down, then continued, "but he passed away."

Kenneth walked closer to her and touched her hand. His touch even reminded her of Keith. "I'm sorry," he said. "I heard and I didn't mean to…"

"No, that's okay," she interrupted. "I just remarried about a week ago," she informed him.

His hand still touching hers, he looked longingly into her teary eyes, "Happily married?"

Kim knocked on her door and, relieved, Taylor quickly said, "Come in."

Kenneth quickly removed his hand from hers, but his eyes remained locked on her eyes.

Kim looked at Taylor, then at Kenneth. "I'm sorry. I didn't know you had someone else in here," she said. "I'll come back." She pivoted.

"No, Kim, you can stay," Taylor quickly said.

Kim stopped and turned back around after hearing the urgency in Taylor's voice.

Taylor continued, "I need to see you anyway." She now looked at Kenneth, trying to get him to leave her office.

"Okay... Okay," Kenneth said, his hands in the air, surrendering. "I get it." He looked at her. "I'll be back to get with you on the Tommy case." He stared deeply into her eyes before adding, "Partner." He shook her hand once more, then headed towards the door.

Taylor watched him walk away and even his walk reminded her of Keith.

When he turned to close the door, his eyes met hers and locked once again. He smiled and slowly closed the door.

She exhaled when she heard the door close. She was truly amazed at how much this man reminded her of Keith in every way to the point of it being eerie to her. She shuddered at her thoughts.

Kim watched her for a minute. "Are you okay, Taylor?" she asked.

"I think so."

Kim looked at Taylor as she turned and looked at the picture of Keith that sat on the bookshelf behind her. She knew

Taylor's thoughts. Kenneth reminded her of Keith just as much as he reminded Taylor of him.

She broke into her thoughts when she asked, "Taylor how was the honeymoon?" She attempted to take her mind off Keith and redirect it to her current husband, Michael.

Taylor swirled her chair back around to face her. "It was wonderful, until Michael received a call about Silvia being in some accident. He cut our trip short to go check on her," she said, her tone sarcastic. "He had to go be with her. Can you believe that?" she asked, trying to grasp the concept of it. "Silvia tried to ruin my marriage with Keith and now look, she has somehow managed to show up in *this* marriage." She let out a forced chuckle.

Kim didn't know how to respond to her, so she remained quiet and let her continue to voice her feelings.

Taylor continued, "First it was Keith, who was all about work and now, it's Michael, who is all about people. What ever happened to the kind of men who cherish their wives?"

"Michael does cherish you, and so did Keith. You are newlyweds just give it some time."

"Yeah, maybe you are right," she said as she swirled back around and looked at the picture of Keith and her thoughts went to Kenneth as she longed for her beloved. Temptation had already set in as she thought about how handsome Kenneth was and how she already felt connected to him somehow. For some reason, she couldn't wait to work closely with this man, but she knew in her heart that she didn't need to work closely with him. It was a certain feeling that he gave her. Temptation was already setting a fire that she wasn't so sure she could handle. She released a long sigh. *God, please give me the strength to work with this man.*

After Kim left her office, Kenneth knocked on the door and walked in. "Hey, I'm eager to get started working with you." He walked over to her desk and placed three files in front of her. He took off his suit jacket and laid it on the chair in front of her desk.

Taylor watched him as he rolled up his sleeves. The black buttoned-down Hugo Boss shirt made him look extra sexy. *And, God, his cologne . . .* Taylor thought as she took in the scent of his Issey Miyake.

Pulling her away from her thoughts, he asked, "You think we can start doing some things tonight?" He shook his head. "I mean today." He smiled wickedly.

Taylor choked on her words for a minute. "Today? I don't think today would be good."

"Well, why not?" He grabbed her hand that rested on the desk. "I thought we could get close today." That wicked smile appeared once again. "I mean, work closely together today since we are going to be *partners* and all . . ." He continued to talk but Taylor couldn't hear another word he spoke.

Her eyes looked at the veins in his hand that traveled up his arm, and she loved his smooth honey-colored skin. His fingers began to deeply massage her hand. She closed her eyes as she thought, *God, this feels so good. His touch even feels like his. This is crazy.*

"Taylor, are you paying attention to me?" he asked, as he continued to massage her hand.

Yes, I'm paying way too much attention to you. "What did you say?" She now slid her hand away from his tender touch.

"I wanted to get started working on some things today... with you."

Taylor's eyes traveled up his strong arm to his neck, lips, and then his eyes. "You were saying?"

"I was saying that you are so beautiful, and I'm going to try to keep this strictly professional for as long as I can." He licked his lips. "But looking at you," he now looked down at his pants, then back up at her and continued, "is making this very hard."

Taylor tried her best to gain control over her thoughts. "I suggest, strictly professional." She got up from her seat and walked over to the file cabinet.

Her legs captured Kenneth's full attention as she bent over looking for the Tommy file so that they could get started on it. "Mmmm. I love that dress on you . . . I'm sorry. I mean, you look really nice."

Surprised, Taylor turned around and looked at him. She then looked down at the brown and tan Jones Wear dress that she was wearing and smiled. "Thank you. Now about this Tommy case," she said, changing the subject. She turned around, digging into the file cabinet.

Kenneth got up and walked up closely behind her. He placed his hand on her shoulder and she turned around and gasped at how closely he stood to her.

"What are you doing?" she asked.

"I just thought that I would help you find that file."

She looked longingly into his eyes as memories of Keith forced their way to the forefront of her mind. Her eyes filled with tears. She cleared her throat and pointed to the seat that he filled minutes before. "Could you sit over there for me please?" As he walked away, her eyes stayed on his muscular frame until he sat down. She turned around and began looking for the file once again.

Kenneth's eyes traced her legs once again, and then they looked longingly upon her apple bottom. He smirked at the thoughts that filled his mind with pleasure. *It will be my pleasure to work with this woman.* That thought alone made his smile grow bigger, along with the bulge in his pants.

Behind the Imagination:

The Heart and Mind of Terri T. Thrash

What made you want to start writing? I've always enjoyed writing. When I was younger, I wrote poetry, short stories, and I even started a horror story when I was in middle school, but I never completed it. When I was a little girl, my father use to always tell me that I was living in a fantasy land, but little did he know that I would one day grow up and use my imagination writing books. The imagination is powerful and it is a gift that I refuse to take for granted. I may write fiction, but there is a real purpose behind my writing. As long as I touch lives through my writing, I know part of my purpose is being fulfilled, and that brings me great joy. Writing and creating is just a part of who I am, and it's what I love to do. God made this all possible when He gave me the gift of creativity and I am thankful for that gift.

Where do you find the time? It's all about making time to do what you love. I have a love for writing, and I make sure that I take time out to do it. When you really want to do something, you will make time for it, and that's what I do.

Have you ever thought about ghost writing? I have never thought about ghost writing until someone mentioned it to me one day. I'm not sure whether or not I would ever ghostwrite in my future, but I can say that it's not a part of the plan as of now.

What are your future plans when it comes to your writing, and where do you see it going? My future plans when it comes to writing are to write, write, and write some more. I believe writing is a part of my purpose, and it is what I love to do to inspire others . . . I see my visions going very far, to the big stage and even to the big screens one day. I see a life-long beautiful career in writing.

How often do you plan to release your works? I will release the works of my hands as often as God tells me to. Whenever He gives me a vision, I will give birth to it, but in His timing. His timing is always perfect.

What made you write "Evidence", and what made you title it that? God had given me this vision a long time ago and one night in June 2011, He told me, get up, go to the computer, and start writing. I made the choice to be obedient and I began to write down the vision that He had given me. Once I began writing, the vision unfolded. There's a blessing in our obedience and I believe that people's lives have been touched through "Evidence" . . . When I first started writing "Evidence"; I didn't know what I would title it, but when I prayed about the title, it was given to me shortly thereafter. God showed me that evidence would be all throughout this novel. There was evidence of infidelity in this novel, evidence in the justice arena, evidence of secrets, lies, and deception from the characters in the storyline, evidence of faith, and most of all, in reality, the evidence of God that surrounds us daily.

Will your life story ever be written in one of your novels? A part of me will be found in each one of my stories, but a whole novel based on my life, I'm not quite sure about. At this point I don't think so, but sometimes we don't see the whole picture. If God tells me to write it, I will.

How was the writing process? Was it difficult? The writing process was great and I really enjoyed it. Being able to give birth to characters and create scenes is truly an amazing gift that I am grateful for. I love being able to create and having the vision to do so. There is definitely beauty in that . . . The writing process wasn't difficult, but it took determination and perseverance. Going back through the manuscripts over and over again and editing is where the work came in, but it was well-worth it. I loved every minute of the writing process. It was definitely a learning experience and, of course, I am still learning.

How can aspiring writers get started writing? How did you start? Just start writing and see where it takes you. I just started writing and when I did, it took flight. There are different ways of writing and different styles of writing. Find your craft, learn it, and master it. When you get prepared to publish, carefully do your research on the publishing companies. Make sure you pay attention to every detail when researching publishing companies and choose wisely. If you are an aspiring writer, seek out workshops, books, and other tools on writing to better understand your craft. A few things that you need to do right now are to: GET STARTED, be CONSISTENT, and be encouraged to COMPLETE your works. You only fail if you don't try.

What would you like to say to aspiring writers? If your dream is to be a writer, then write with your whole heart. Do it with purpose, and do it with meaning. Be steadfast and keep going no matter what the road looks like ahead. There will be some challenges, just be prepared. When God places an assignment in front of you; work diligently on what is presented to you. Seek God in all that you do and allow Him to direct your path and direct you in your writing. Pray without ceasing. There will be many challenges on your literary journey, but I guarantee you that it will be worth it. Even when the road gets rough, keep moving forward. Do not give up on God and the talents that He has so graciously blessed you with. Do not give up on yourself. Writing takes work, but it will all be worth it when lives are touched and mindsets are changed through your writing. Learn your craft, master it and boldly present to the world. Write daily. The more you write, the more skilled you will become. Read, read and read. Be willing to learn, and never stop learning. Be

YOUnique and embrace who God has created you to be. Don't allow anyone to kill your dreams or your visions. Take things one moment at a time and enjoy the journey. Remember; Giving birth is rarely easy, but it is always worth it. Be encouraged. Blessings to each of you on your journey!

Each and every one of you, are very important to me and I would love to connect with you.

Find Terri:

www.facebook.com/Terri T. Thrash

www.twitter.com/@MsTerriTThrash

www.instagram.com/@divinely_inspired_writer

email:divinelyinspired28@yahoo.com

For exclusives, up and coming literary works, events and more, please visit Terri at www.TerriTThrash.com

Thank you for your love and support!

I love me some you!!!

www.ingramcontent.com/pod-product-compliance
Lightning Source LLC
Chambersburg PA
CBHW051544250626
47157CB00001B/178